Seventh

Lewis Hastings

Orbis 2014

Published by Orbis 2014

First published in 2017.

ISBN 978-0-473-39789-0

Typeset in Garamond 11/14pt

Cover image *Ghost In The Machine* by Jacob Sutton. London.
Credit: 'Seventh' numeric logo design by Russell Budden.

Also available from Lewis Hastings

Actually, The World Is Enough

For my dear father Peter – it was during the last few golden days and hours we spent together that you insisted I wrote this and the subsequent series of Jack Cade novels. Your support, passion and pride was endless. I so wish you could have been here to enjoy them – I hope they have a library in heaven, and you are able to get this story out on loan, as I know you would never have paid for it...

This is for you – in loving memory.

1934-2014

"Step forward now, policeman,
You've borne your burdens well.
Come walk a beat on Heaven's streets,
You've done your time in hell.'

Anon.

"We will that all men know we blame not all the lords, nor all those that are about the king's person, nor all gentlemen nor yeomen, nor all men of law...but all such as may be found guilty by just and true inquiry and by the law."

Jack Cade
Rebel Leader
England
1450

Prologue

Craiova, Romania – February 2002

She was stood at the double height window, staring onto the street below. Her breath, fast but measured, was steaming up the glass and creating a spectral haze as she exhaled. Seconds later the glass cleared offering a view back out onto the almost deserted road.

The streets were quieter than normal; there was a threat of snow in the air, a few random solitary flakes fluttered from the sky and into the amber glow emitted from the street lamps. The chilled nocturnal air created a halo around the lamps which stood guarding the approach to the magnificent historic building in which she found herself, trapped.

She forced herself not to shed a tear.

Part of her wished he had slapped her forcibly across the face, at least that way she would be visibly afraid, rather than the current sense of hidden nauseating terror that absorbed her.

Then, the extreme cold of the deep winter night would soon enhance the bitter sting that would have formed upon her left cheekbone, but she would recover, within an hour it would have dissipated, leaving only another psychological scar.

It always ended like this.

He had pushed her to the edge once more, teasing, playing with her; not dissimilar to a mocking, darting Mongoose. A small yet skilful animal, daring, almost challenging the cobra to strike, until slowly he had lured her in, closer, more intensely until she could close her eyes once more and relax, feel his breath upon her face and then his alcohol-soaked tongue licking the side of her neck.

She would once more give way, give in and want him.

This was when the punch would come; literally. This time it was delivered powerfully, up and under her left ribcage with enough force to take her breath away and probably crack the lowest bone, a bone that defied the attackers' attempt to rupture her spleen.

It was what he did best, combining intense pleasure with cruel and endless punishment and yet she clung onto the relationship – as so many women do. It had been years now.

She had met him in 1987, almost stereotypically, in a crowded bar. The bar in question was called *Byzantin* and was located in the medical district of Bucharest which was *the* place to see and be seen during the late Eighties.

He was sinister yet captivating, like the proverbial moth to the flame she was drawn to the light, ignoring the growing sense of heat and palpable danger.

Having left home in Sofia a few days before, she had crossed into Romania, travelling across the Danube Bridge at Giurgiu without interruption and once across the border had hitchhiked her way nonchalantly to the Romanian capital.

Her father Yosif forbid it, telling her at great length that it would lead her into the lion's den. He told her, he pleaded with her, explained at great length how a similar journey had destroyed his life once already.

The repeated threats achieved only a sustained resistance and an enhanced desire to experience everything he had warned her against.

Despite the warnings and in spite of everything Petrov left home, fare welling a potentially stellar role in the Bureau of Statistics and a Motherland which many believed offered a higher degree of safety than her intended destination.

In reality both nations were emerging from many years of Communism, like inquisitive bear cubs finding their respective feet after hibernating through a long and arduous winter.

He shook his head solemnly. She was just like her bloody mother.

Her mother was called Simona Petrov and she had died in 2001, the result of post-surgery complications. She was an exquisitely beautiful woman, five foot ten with piercing green eyes and equally dramatic red hair. Her death was neither marked with sorrow nor recognition.

She was an extremely rare commodity in a part of the world that celebrated striking women. It was a pity her husband was as mundane, both in his professional life as a senior Government employee, as he was in his personal life.

He gave her everything she could possibly require in an emerging Communist state yet failed to reward her ceaseless quest for affection and so wholly unannounced she walked away from him one spring afternoon.

She was unable to confide in anyone about the fact that she had fallen hopelessly in love with a handsome but low-ranking Pharmacist, three years her junior but wiser in so many ways. They had spent the summer months schooling each other in the art of seduction and lovemaking – when and wherever they were able to.

It was the thrill of being caught that drove them to seek out new locations, the more daring the better, at a time when even covert love affairs were heavily frowned upon by society and importantly, the state.

Time would prove that the risks were taken without consideration of the consequences. The local authorities were alerted by a conscientious dog walker who had interrupted them one Sunday afternoon in the Park Borisova Gradina.

The autumn leaves had generally acted as a natural alarm system, warning the couple of approaching walkers, but this day their passion had overwhelmed them as they sank into the bronze carpet of decaying foliage, laying in the shadows of their magnificent benefactors and giving no thought to the consequence of being caught. They were deep in woodland yet in the heart of a major city.

It was thrilling beyond belief.

Somehow she had escaped, running through the maze of trees, semi-naked and seeking refuge even deeper in the Beech forest. She waited until eleven, emerged under a moon-less sky and blended fully-clothed with the foot traffic before heading home and quietly getting into bed.

The next morning she maintained a state of normality. Her husband kissed her frigidly on the cheek and left for work, oblivious or possibly aware and either unwilling to confront her or more importantly unwilling to contend with the price of failure.

She was frantic; unable to enquire about her lover who was now incarcerated, stripped of his position within the Faculty of Chemistry and facing at least a five year sentence for an act against public decency.

Petrov's family had learned of the betrayal three days later and forced her husband to cast her out into the world without a support network.

He had no choice, though desperately in love he had to sever all ties with her, as his Secretary General had calculatingly reminded him, his career and reputation depended upon it.

The twenty four year old now estranged wife of an older and well respected Government official decided that her future lay in bordering Romania – it was not without risk, but she spoke the language and she had nothing left to lose.

She had been told stories of hope and of compassion after gathering some possessions she attempted to say goodbye to her own family. They too rejected her and so the next evening she headed north in the back of an asthmatic van loaded precariously with farm supplies.

She wasn't alone; a new life was growing rapidly inside her. Contrary to everyone's preconceived ideas the child was not the result of one of her many clandestine meetings in a woodland glade but rather the consequence of a brief Sunday morning interlude with her husband, still drunk from the night before and vulnerable to her advances.

Quite what a life her unborn child would have was as unknown as the timing of her next meal, or for that matter the next compassionate act.

She drew her coat up around her neck, tucked her knees into the foetal position and eventually slipped into a disturbed sleep as the driver continued north on the two hundred kilometre journey. The roads were remote and poorly maintained; as a result the journey took six hours.

The driver was in his sixties, for a brief glimpse of her naked breasts and twenty five Lev's he was prepared to take her to a safe location where a friend had a boat.

She obliged. It was a currency she was prepared to exchange.

He was more than happy; he hadn't seen such an exquisite body in forty years and the image of her in the back of his van, her blouse unbuttoned and revealing had entertained him enough. Thankfully he wanted no more and ironically appeared to be a man of morals.

At dawn the next day the van stopped. She heard voices outside and strained to hear the conversation. She shivered involuntarily; either the cool morning or fear, or probably both had caused this.

As agreed the driver banged on the panel that separated them, it was the signal for her to leave. He asked that she didn't look at him when she departed, perhaps he was ashamed?

She left a small amount of money on top of a box of carrots. It was the least she could do. She would need more for the next journey and she was cautious about revealing just how much she had. It was money that she had secreted from her husband and until she could find a new source of income it was all she had to her name.

The van turned around and headed back towards Montana.

She stood alone at the side of the Danube in a northern provincial town called Kozloduy. In half an hour she would be met by a local fisherman who had agreed to take her across the Danube and along the Jiu River towards Craiova, the largest city in the region and the sixth largest in Romania.

A sum of money changed hands. The fisherman was evidently unaware of the previous 'business arrangement' as he didn't once look at her with licentious eyes. He spoke briefly, offered her bread and wrapped a blanket around her shoulders.

The small boat navigated across the Danube and then began the long journey, threading its way across the Romanian countryside.

Simona Petrov was eventually and somewhat unexpectedly the recipient of good fortune. Craiova provided her with an opportunity. She met a Bulgarian man whilst buying rudimentary foodstuffs, their eyes locked, a little longer than comfortable and yet they both knew that there was a degree of chemistry, a raw sense of something primitive that neither could explain.

He was a man who would succeed in making her content. In exchange for the inevitable physical relationship that would follow her childbirth, he supported her, providing her with food and warmth and importantly the love she craved so heavily.

She could ask for no more. And she didn't. She had at last found happiness with a man who accepted her and incredibly, her unborn child.

They would start to create a life in a country which was bucking the trend of Eastern European nations and one which was forging its own links outside of the Iron Curtain, links with Western Europe and a brighter future.

In 1970 she gave birth to a very healthy daughter, at nearly nine pounds she was quite the heaviest child any female in her family had delivered, but she was tall and slender and her green eyes were like opals, glistening in a sandstone vault. She had a healthy head of hair; chestnut, tinged in places with streaks of natural red.

She would name her after the man who had become her saviour, who had offered her shelter and the base necessities of life; her redeemer was called Niko and his adopted daughter would be known as Nikolina.

Her mother promised herself she would not expose her daughters' origins unless pressed; choosing instead to pursue the status quo and portray a background entwined around Romanian genealogy.

Nikolina spent her formative years in Romania, learning the language and maintaining her own Mother tongue, she learned Russian too, and English and Serbian. She was a bright girl who soon created a reputation as a bold and rather extrovert young lady.

In 1985 and much to her mother's shock Nikolina enquired about her family history. Having studied the nation, its people and its culture at school she finally asked the decisive question of her mother; would she allow her the opportunity to return to Bulgaria?

At the age of fifteen and against her mother's better judgement she travelled back to Sofia and met with her father. Despite the sense of betrayal, on both sides of the equation, Nikolina and her natural father became close. He soon found that through her he could recount the happier days with her mother after all, she looked incredibly like her.

He explained how much he regretted not pursuing their marriage and how, despite common opinion, he still deeply loved her. He also found his daughter's company to be especially fulfilling.

They sat for hours, talking back and forth in differing languages, interchanging to try to outwit one another and laughing at the schoolboy mistakes that her father made when transitioning from Bulgarian to Russian.

As a challenge and for no other reason they both learned rudimentary Turkish too. He played chess with her relentlessly, until one day she finally allowed him to draw with her.

She was gifted and growing exponentially more beautiful. He was looking at her one day; she was deep in thought, pondering whether to move knight or rook.

He smiled. If or when the time came he would protect her with his own life.

He met his supervisor one Thursday morning, brushing the sheets of rain from his overcoat and shaking off the cold. After three cups of strong Turkish coffee his manager agreed that when the time came Nikolina Petrov would join them at the Bureau of Statistics.

In the spring of 1987 she joined her father at the Bureau and in six short months, by working long hours and studying at home became a rising star, translating information received from their 'Statisticians' who were domiciled in neighbouring countries.

She was indeed brilliant, so much so that she had soon learned that the data she was translating and analysing was in fact raw intelligence. Quite how much she would be allowed to learn about the Bureau was subject to weekly meetings; for now the risks far outweighed the consequences. She was worth ten of any of the male staff in the unit. They would nurture her, protect her and train her.

She was now an asset and a deployable one, they could send her almost anywhere in Eastern Europe; with her looks, which belied her age, her training and her linguistic skills she was quite simply a sensation in the chilled, shadowy and staid halls and meeting rooms of the 1st Main Directorate.

Her father was immensely proud of her but now saw how quickly the government had wrapped its tentacles around her. She was no longer his.

They were teaching her more advanced linguistics, drilling down to local dialects; they taught her how to drive and how to use rudimentary weapons. She learned the art of close quarter combat – how to utilise her slender build to act as a lever upon her opponents. She grew to adore the sessions by day and by night studied, and if very fortunate would find herself deployed on surveillance operations.

She started to travel. Initially this consisted of domestic and regional journeys, they were often arduous as the transport systems were in places archaic, but with government and offshore investments beginning to flourish they could only improve. With each trip she learned more, remembered much more and grew steadily more confident.

Meanwhile her father stole secrets from under the nose of his employers and sold them to Russia.

Gorbachev's superpower state was calling upon its satellites to implement Glasnost – freedom of speech – but despite this it still craved secrets from its bordering nations and was highly suspicious of Bulgaria's drive towards westernisation. It had to be stopped before it created a wave of enthusiasm among lesser Eastern Bloc states.

Yosif Petrov had become a spy. Somehow, at some point he needed to be taught a lesson, or two.

An opportunity arose. The Directorate required a female to head into Romania to collect intelligence on a rising star in the world of organised crime, he was hurting his own people, but damaging the Bulgarian economy, furthermore he was bribing officials and that was simply unacceptable.

Her father was called into the Meeting Room.

"Yosif, Yosif, my friend, my brother. Your daughter is a fine young woman, she is ready, you should be proud. She will go to Romania tomorrow and carry out a set of orders. If she is successful then the world will be truly at her feet."

Yosif Petrov knew that a reply was neither expected nor warranted; he nodded curtly and walked back to his own frigid office. He closed the door and picked up the telephone.

His daughter answered.

"It is me; they want you to go to Bucharest tomorrow. Please, for me, say no, it will be dangerous, risky; I do not want you to go. You are far too young…" He paused but the answer was not what he wanted to hear.

He had used a straightforward set of words that conversely excited her rather than dissuaded her.

She travelled the very next morning; a simple kiss on her father's cheek proclaimed her departure. She was like a schoolgirl heading away on a summer camp, except this diminutive female was capable of killing any predator.

Two men spoke quietly in a corridor of the 1ˢᵗ Directorate.

"So, she has left to carry out her duty?" enquired the first.

"She has sir. At best she will find him and kill him. At worst she will gather information which we will use to kill him," replied a younger male, clearly subordinate.

"Good. It will be her swan song, her final effort, a grand gesture to the glory of our homeland, in memory of her father, a great man. He will be proud. The Durzhavna Sigurnost will be proud. Deal with him as we dealt with Markov in London. Then when, or if she returns we must ensure she too is eradicated, she is young and quite disarmingly pretty and we have trained her well – however, in time she will not be missed."

The junior member of staff nodded politely and allowed the elder to walk away. His task was simple, eloquent and ruthless. Deploy, retract and erase all evidence. Such a pity, for his superior was right; she was attractive and so exceptionally gifted.

She walked alone along the Bulevardul Ion Mihalache on a brutally cold December night in 1987 and despite her head screaming 'No' she walked, confidently, almost arrogantly off the street and into *Byzantin*.

On the other side of its imposing twelve foot high polished teak doors she found herself drawn to the Western music, the alluring smell of alcohol and cigarettes and the sense and sound of hedonistic pleasure.

He had been exquisitely clever in the way he had manipulated her from Day One. To her mind it was Day One, an event in her life that would act as a catalyst for a series of further occurrences.

She had been equally astute in how she had manipulated him too.

He observed her entering the crowded space and was immediately captivated by her. Either way, he would have her. He could have any woman in the city, none of them resisted – those that did were more of a challenge; he was wealthy, powerful, corrupt and evil. All the traits a father loathes and all the characteristics a daughter is drawn to.

Moth: flame.

Her first drink arrived with a comment from the barman. She pushed it away and shook her head. The barman looked over his shoulder. A male looked back at him. He had cold, hooded and black eyes, olive, pock-marked skin, a strong, straight nose and thick black hair that shone with blue-grey hues.

He wore a plain white, short-sleeved, open-necked shirt which revealed a few dark chest hairs, nestled among them was a simple but expensive platinum necklace.

The shirt masked a slim but muscular frame which was only evident in his forearms, which bulged with veins and a network of scars. On his left wrist he wore a Patek Philippe wristwatch, elegantly adorned with phases of the moon and three subsidiary dials, it was also platinum and was signed by the maker, highly expensive, but again, quite discreet.

On the inside of his right wrist a tattoo of a wave jostled for attention among his thick, black, short hairs. Unlike similar marks his tattoo was black.

The male gestured to the girl to take the drink. She felt alone, isolated and on the edge of a significant decision; powerless, yet vaguely in control. Aroused, scared and perversely, excited. The skin crawled across her shoulders. Someone had just walked slowly across her grave.

She took the drink and smiled at the male.

She was his.

He was hers.

What was she thinking?

Her training had shaped her into a highly accomplished and yet somewhat inexperienced agent. Never had the Bulgarian government seen such a rise to readiness. They had filled her head with knowledge and confidence. All she had to do was draw him in and take the opportunity to carry out her instructions.

Kill the man called Alex; retreat, remain alert, stay under cover, return and live a life as a heroine of the Bulgarian people.

The Intelligence Division had briefed her thoroughly.

Alexandru Stefanescu was a career criminal. Starting with low-hanging fruit he burgled his neighbours, stole old cars and progressed to more sophisticated burglaries.

It was at this time he crossed the border into Bulgaria and really began to shine as a criminal. He was always one step ahead of what he considered to be the enemy, but he knew that one day they would be waiting for him.

Having learned his tradecraft whilst in Sofia, Bobov Dol and Stara Zagora Prisons, he soon gained a reputation as a formidable fighter with a ruthless streak that preceded him. His physical size was at best average. He was far from a powerful man – but his strength came from within. His forte was an ability to see deep within the mind of his enemy and use his, or her own power as a self-destructing weapon.

What his mentor saw was an evil – inexplicable – to inflict pain on his fellow human that even he, with a career of harm found distasteful.

He repaid his mentor in kind and after three years had risen through the ranks of organised criminality, creating fear, notoriety and a growing band of brothers from his homeland who melded with occasional converts from other Soviet states, all eager to experience the trappings of wealth that they had been sheltered from for so long.

He had become an underground rock star, feeding off his own reputation, stronger by the day, stronger still by night. His thoughts were always of betrayal, retribution and reward. He led as he expected to be followed; loyalty first, nothing else mattered.

The emergent group needed a name to which to fasten their loyalty. Alexandru christened them *Primul Val* – The First Wave. It was a name that suited the group, and the birth of a menace – but he always intended for the name to be short-lived. He had another, and in time that would follow.

By the late Eighties he was responsible for the movement of stolen goods out of Romania and Bulgaria and into Western Europe in exchange for high value vehicles, prostitutes and drugs.

He would consume the women, drive the cars but never go near the drugs. He despised their ability to destroy a strong man, or his family. But the lucrative aspect to their sale was addictive enough for him to overlook the issue of morals.

He was also the only man to break into the Headquarters of the Durzhavna Sigurnost; turning a photograph of the Director upside down, just to prove a point. He left it so perfectly square that a spirit level would have failed to find fault.

He was arrogant beyond belief, a burgeoning icon with a selected band of followers baying for more.

He was walking back to his palatial flat a few days after his most daring feat when a group of specialist police stopped him at gunpoint, cable-tied him and took him away in an unmarked, anonymous blue van. Those that saw the event soon forgot. It was better for everyone that they did.

By the time the team had arrived at Pazardzhik Prison, an institution with an infamous reputation, he was bruised beyond recognition.

What privileges he had were removed and four days later after attempting to stab a hospital orderly with a makeshift knife he was beaten senseless once more by the very nursing staff charged with caring for him.

Arriving back on the wing he was attacked, proselytised and tortured, forced to shower in freezing cold water, to lie in his own faeces whilst strapped to what loosely constituted a bed and kept awake for days on end.

They would break him.

But in spite of the endless abuse he never gave in. He was Roma and that meant loyalty to his beliefs and his people; a race who had lived through hatred, prejudice and genocide.

Did these people really think they could break his will?

His subsequent and unexpected escape caused frustration, embarrassment and anger and his captors were duly punished; the Prison Governor soon found himself in Stefanescu's cell, enduring the same treatment, strapped to his still-putrid bed for twenty two hours a day until he gave in, unable to take the mental torture a day longer. Better to die at his own hand than theirs.

Arriving back in Bucharest Stefanescu gathered his people around him; he would gain a sense of retribution and take every opportunity to crush those that had left him with his mental and physical scars.

He continued to grow wealthier, exploiting collapsing European borders, infiltrating government units and seeking out officials who were prepared to be corrupted. And there were plenty of them it seemed.

He had an eye for beautiful cars, boats, watches and women. Women of a size and type that he found alluring were retained for special occasions, the rest were abused and wholly taken for granted.

He had a sixth sense for business which in another place, at another time he could have exploited – arguably the next Trump, Jobs or Branson he quickly recognised a commodity and where and how to gain a return. His many private hours in prison were devoured by thoughts, unable to even gain access to books he wrote his own internal business plan – and God himself would need to step in and deal with anyone who chose to get in his way.

With an eye on the future he had also noted a sense of change in Europe which he considered fortuitous. His people, long the bane of many a politician were ready to move, to travel as they had for centuries. This time the travel involved heading north, deeper into the European Union, however this could only happen when what many saw as the most powerful alliance on the globe allowed it to happen. Opening the door, even slightly might allow a flood of immigrants into already over-populated countries such as France and Germany and Great Britain.

Alex knew that somewhere in the halls of power, the very existence of his people, his nation and those that were geographically aligned to it was currently under discussion. It had to be, Europe was expanding rapidly and with the dissolution of the Soviet Union it was just a matter of time before trade talks and the political benefits of immigration were discussed.

Like a limited number of similarly-minded people he was ready to exploit the situation for all it was worth. Dishonesty, deceit, treachery, call it what you like, they were all by-words for success, wealth and status. To gain the latter he was willing, and very content to do whatever it might take.

Stefanescu and the girl drank together, watching, alert to a sign of weakness. To the awe of his cohorts he buckled first.

"So, tell me, what is your name my pretty Bulgarian friend?"

"My name is Nikolina, and yours?"

He laughed a cackling laugh that haunted her. But she knew she had to stand her ground.

"You have some courage coming into my world and asking me my name Miss Nikolina, what, are you a spy?" He regarded her through his granite eyes, never once leaving her own stare.

He liked her, a lot.

"What kind of spy would walk into the lion's den, alone, at the age of twenty one and try to seduce the number one criminal in town?"

He laughed again, clapped his hands warmly and ordered more drinks, he owned the club so they were free, he owned everyone in it too, and the six adjoining buildings either side.

"Come here woman; let me get to know you better."

She sat on the leather sofa and slid slowly towards him.

"Your summation of my success was a little insulting Nikolina. I am the 'Number One Criminal' – full stop."

Without shame or warning he pushed his hand up her dress and stroked the inside of her thigh, probing with his fingers until she gasped. It was a genuine response. Apart from the pathetic boys at college who craved her and were rewarded with a kiss, this was, despite all of her training and exposure to danger, the closest she had come to a true sexual encounter.

"You feel more like a sixteen year old to me, and if you ask my friends I much prefer them to twenty one year olds. Now, I will give you one opportunity to be honest with me, how old are you?"

She told the truth, causing him to smile a broad smile and involuntarily rub his hands together, steepling his fingers, a non-verbal sign that he was in control.

She had been confident that she had the upper hand but started to have an over-bearing sense of fear that she was perhaps too isolated, too vulnerable and too foolish.

He pirouetted around her, imbibing her with drink but she seemed able to avoid its effects. He was captivated by her looks and her youth, but above all her incredible confidence.

This one would be most enjoyable.

"Another drink?" he enquired.

"Just water thank you…I'm sorry, I want to call you something and I still don't know your name…"

"My, you are persistent my pretty young thing, most persistent indeed. I can only hope you are this willing later. Well? Will you join me?"

It was time. She took her bag which contained her purse, a supply of forged identity documents, some low level narcotics and make-up, lots of make-up.

She also had a small collapsible umbrella. Her hands brushed against it, giving her confidence and courage, in truth she was now scared and rather naïve, and yet somehow she was still energised by the whole experience.

She was seventeen going on thirty, skilled, devious, quick-witted but seventeen, female and acting on her own.

She could only hope her short but highly intensive regime of exercise, defence and psychological strengthening would support her.

He dismissed his entourage and led her to his apartment where she saw for the first time the opulent trappings of his success.

A sorrowful Polar Bear skin lay next to an enormous Gothic fireplace which was roaring, its fresh pine logs spitting against the fine metal guard. A tattered Romanian flag hung defiantly from the ceiling and works of art, no doubt stolen, adorned the walls. There was more gold than she had ever seen.

On a table, placed perfectly on a silver tray were two crystal glasses containing mineral water. He beckoned towards them.

"Your water Nikolina…"

She hesitated, fractionally but enough for him to detect.

"By the way, forgive me, my name is Alexandru Stefanescu. It is my pleasure to meet you. Don't worry child, all that talk downstairs? It was just that, I am not the monster many think I am; I am a tiger but a toothless one. Some call me The Jackdaw but you can call me Alex."

"Hello Alex." She replied, sensing a slight thaw, a chance to strike.

"You know you can take either of those glasses my dear. I place an inordinate amount of value on honesty. Feel free to go back downstairs and ask my people."

He winked, putting her at ease long enough that she drank the water. To her surprise it tasted of water, clean, clear and able to moisten her throat which dried to a level that she was almost unable to speak.

An hour later, perhaps longer she became aware of him on top of her, she was unable to push him away, when she tried she realised she was tied down. He finished his athletic performance, gaining praise from the other three members of his clan who were all naked and watching, their flaccid state an indicator that there were either recovering from the same activity or waiting for more.

She turned her head to the left upon hearing a noise, it was another female. Two other men were busy abusing her but she seemed unable to even speak, her drug-induced state much worse than her own.

Meanwhile the video cameras whirred away behind her, capturing her face but not those of her abductors.

She felt physically sick. How could she have been so gullible? Now, she was truly afraid. How did she miss the opportunity to kill him whilst she was alone with him? All that was required was a deft jab with the umbrella, the tip of which was loaded with Castor Oil seed from which the chemist's had extracted Ricin. He would have been dead within twenty four hours, with no trace of the toxin. Her job, her singular task, done.

But instead she lay immobile, naked and broken.

He walked up to her, crowing like the bird that gave him his nickname, strutting almost, more powerful than ever, another young woman to count towards his sickening tally and there was no doubt she would not be the last.

For the first time she saw pure evil and every ounce of training ebbed from her body.

He had taken away her liberty, her dignity and most likely was about to bring her limited life to a close too.

He clenched her cheeks with his thumb and forefinger and squeezed, gently at first until he found the trigger point.

"You were amazing; we did things I did not know were possible! My friends, they found you incredible too. As a reward I will give you all the riches I have, you can choose anything, that golden necklace by the bedside, it is yours. Do you know why?"

She shook her head rapidly.

"Because I like you, I find your spirit most uplifting, your fight, your courage. Are you sure you are not from gypsy stock?"

Again, she turned her head from side to side.

"And you Nikolina now have a decision to make."

He released the grip allowing her to speak.

"I am sorry, whatever I said to upset you I am truly sorry, just let me go and I promise I won't tell a soul."

He looked hurt, at least that is the face he portrayed. "Nikolina, Nikolina, I am so very hurt, I thought we were friends? You don't remember the game we played? How you made a choice? How you agreed that we would become lovers? How I made you so powerful?"

She didn't.

He turned the camera towards her and held her head so she could endure the imagery. The footage left little to the imagination, every possible angle had been filmed, quite skilfully, certainly well enough to release onto a willing and voracious marketplace. Towards the end of the film the males backed away leaving just her and the other female alone on the enormous bed.

Stefanescu made them kiss each other; touch each other and then unexpectedly, fight.

He told them that the winner would be judged by him and him only, and that the victor would make a choice that would affect both of their lives.

The other girl, poor thing, stood no chance whatsoever. At first she was like a wildcat, scratching, writhing and bucking, fending off and striking out, but quickly Nikolina worked out her weakness and used her attackers' own strength against her, repeatedly, until she was able to get on top of her and suppress her energy, slowly choking her to the point of unconsciousness.

Her training had returned. Initially she had been drowning in genuine fear but her secondary response had been kick-started by a flood of adrenalin and a primal desire not to be second.

Stefanescu had never been so aroused. It was visible, tangible almost.

He saw in her a level of training and willingness and pure, raw combat that he had never experienced in a woman before.

He held Nikolina's hand aloft and shouted "The winner!"

Somehow she managed to take a breath, a chance to recover, for she didn't know if there would be a round two. She would be ready, in fact with adrenalin fuelling her she felt that she could easily fight two of the men in the room, and at that moment, they were incredibly vulnerable; it was a target-rich environment.

But she knew that she needed to wait for the chance to get him alone, to entice him and then strike. Despite the atrocities committed against her she felt strong; her instructors had told her that she would be able to rise above any such treatment. But then they were male, they would, wouldn't they?

He had placed a restore point in her mind – one she could return to at any moment, awake or subconsciously, and in doing so he had signed his own death warrant. Her original mission, her primary goal was to find him and kill him – prevent him from becoming any more of an embarrassment to the region, but now she found that she wanted to wait, if it took the rest of her life.

She was willing to wait until the ideal moment arose when she could drive her thumbs into his voice box, jarring it from side to side, crushing it and depriving him of his primary life source. A rapid set of kicks could follow, or a punch, driven into his solar plexus, then two in quick succession to the temples. Then, and only then she could really start to enjoy a sense of personal recovery and blind revenge. Forget allegiance to her state – Alexander Stefanescu was her prize and she would claim him. One day.

"So my pretty Nikolina, now, as the winner you get to make the choice. Should you die or should your opponent?"

His words were colder than the local lakes that were adjacent to his palace of ill-gotten gains; frozen, dark and forbidding.

"Come now, the choice is easy no? Who is it to be? You?" He cast his eyes sideways without compassion, "Or her?"

He pulled a mocking sad face and held the anonymous females' head up by her pony tail; her eyes were lifeless, she had made the decision that for her the hell was about to end. She pitied the poor cow that had won, for her the journey was only just starting.

Nikolina cleared her throat, knowing that this was no longer a game of cat and mouse; she was the mouse and even as she spoke the metal bar was heading towards her fragile neck, soon she would lay lifeless; so close to the cheese, and yet, so far away.

She had missed the prize and the only way to try again was to act as judge, jury and executioner.

She nodded to the younger girl. She hoped it would be swift.

"Good choice, then you get the first prize my love, and that of course, is me. For we are now as good as man and wife. It is our tradition. Come, we must celebrate."

A lookout checked the street for the authorities – most of whom were in his boss's back pocket anyway – all was clear.

They exited the back of the building in a blue Mercedes van. Both girls were in the back, Nikolina was now dressed but her opponent was still naked. Her heroin-affected eyes, dark, lifeless and wretched looked back at Nikolina, but there appeared to be no hatred. There appeared to be no life at all.

The van travelled for about fifteen minutes until it reached a car park alongside the Lacul Floreasca.

Stefanescu exited along with his closest allies. He nodded to the rear of the Mercedes. They opened the rear cargo doors and removed the girl, her mouth was taped but she probably had insufficient energy to scream.

They walked to the edge of the lake where another employee was stood with a spade.

Stefanescu looked at his new bride once more.

"So, my lover. I just want to make sure that you are happy with this. Last chance, you or her? How strong are you my little lioness?"

"Her." She could say no more, knowing that she was condemning her sparring partner to death.

"Good girl, you have passed the test. Now, come and enjoy some sport."

They walked her to the lake edge. All that needed to happen was for the larger of the two males to strike her across the head and at least, for her, the nightmare would be over. She made an assumption that one or both would dig a grave in the permafrost and cover her, allowing nature to play her part in the conspiracy.

The moon appeared from behind a dark curtain and threw a shaft of light onto the lake, it increased the risk of being detected but these were professional people, they always had a Plan B.

Stefanescu looked to his employees.

"Why are you waiting, my little Niko has made her decision. Do it and remember I have twenty on three minutes!"

His words were beyond sinister, he was enjoying this.

The spade struck the shallow ice once, then again before it broke through to the water beneath. Another six blows had created a hole about two feet in circumference.

They removed the tape from her mouth, grabbed her by the arms and pushed her head first into the hole, kicking her legs down, deeper into the water until she was submerged. A gentle current took her.

Stefanescu pulled Nikolina to the lake edge. She knew she was next.

"Watch my pretty, you have twenty on her only lasting a minute, remember, winner takes all! Now watch, enjoy and don't forget to breathe!"

She did. It was the most grotesque thing she had ever seen. The girl without a name, who had earlier put up such a valiant fight now drifted under the moonlit ice; for a few pitiful seconds her fingers had frantically scratched against the translucent tomb, trying to regain her bearings, trying to fight. She was lost in so many ways.

Her eyes became wider by the second, her lips taut and her hands now pathetically pounding on the ice, desperate to escape.

"One minute boss!" shouted the younger of the two helpers.

"She has guts I give her that. Pity she lost Niko! But now, you are my girlfriend, the world is yours. Take what you want, it is free. Everything is free. For a price!"

At one and a half minutes she started to gulp for air, a large flat bubble rose from her lips and slowly dispersed, her skin rapidly greying and her hair lifeless. Her naked form drifted under the lake, being carried on the gentle current towards the centre. It was ironically a beautiful moment, a scene of such raw exquisiteness, perhaps the subject matter of one of the great classically-trained artist's.

The moon departed behind another darkened cape as the spectacle came to an end. By the morning, the entry hole, the beginning of her demise, would be gone, frozen over and complete once more. They might find her the following spring.

The next morning Nikolina got a message through to her superiors. 'I am in the Lion's Den. All is well. I need time. But the operation will be successful.'

She promptly vomited. When she had composed herself she vowed to rid the earth of this evil being – in a way befitting his own malicious thoughts and deeds. Whether she would be present at his death hardly mattered, someone, somewhere would carry out her will. However it happened, it needed to happen slowly.

The mission would take a little longer than she or her organisation had hoped, but they had complete faith in her. It would be a successful assignment - No more Jackdaw, one less traitor and vitally, no loose ends.

No-one could quite anticipate that Nikolina knew that she was the loose end. She was, after all, in the words of the people who had trained her, an extraordinary girl and she was two steps ahead of them.

She would remain in the Den for another four months until one day her boyfriend announced, quite unexpectedly and with little fanfare that they were heading to Spain. A chance had arisen, an opportunity to work with a contact from within the Spanish Roma community and a chance to exploit the capitalists that ruled Europe.

They had never met and neither man knew much about the other.

He was being offered an opportunity to steal countless high-end vehicles, rebirth them and ship them around Europe, into the Arab nations and possibly the Far East, and she would play a large part in enticing the co-leader, before consuming him like a female praying mantis feeds upon its lover.

Actually the 'steal' part would have little or nothing to do with him. His role was almost entirely detached from the tarnished world of car theft – he was the logistics man, the strategist, using his own people to facilitate what would be one of the largest auto-related inquiries the European police, and in particular Interpol would initiate.

He needed to meet the leader of Fratia – The Brotherhood – there were three brothers, one in Spain, one in Bucharest, the last in London. His need was simple. He chose the weakest first for although he was financially astute, unlike his brothers he had a reputation for comparative gentleness; once he was gone the dominoes would fall.

The strangest fact of all was that Nikolina was beginning to enjoy the hedonistic lifestyle of a modern underworld criminals' whore. As long as she gave him what he wanted she could live a life beyond the grasp of any girl her age: As long as she had an exit plan.

Of all the women he had tortured, destroyed, belittled and abused she was without a doubt his favourite. He almost felt a sense of compassion when he thought of her. Slowly, unpredictably he began to fall for her and it made him happy. He was becoming soft in his old age, God alone help the next person that betrayed him for he would need to unleash years of pent up energy carrying out his varied levels of punishment.

A few weeks of negotiations, posturing and bribery would result in Stefanescu gaining a foothold on the illegal car market. Despite his detestation for the stuff he even managed to negotiate some good quality heroin and transport it into Romania, the best cocaine too and some of the finest escorts he had ever laid eyes or hands upon.

The deal was done, the final handshake came and Stefanescu walked away, his signature laughter ringing inside the leather-clad Audi 8, itself stolen, reborn and now, his. It was, he thought, payment in kind for what Fratia – or least its leaders had planned for him.

Their intentions, far from honourable were simple. Convince Stefanescu and his weak brother, and his band of inbreds to do the hard work, to carry out the burglary, theft and handling of countless European vehicles, skilfully give them a new identity and then store them on old Second World War bases around France before distributing them under the banner of a legitimate company. Why not use new software to alter the digital odometers too? And probably launder some of their excess cash?

What The Brotherhood had failed to account for was in Alexander Stefanescu's eyes a fundamental error. They had overlooked the fact that even at their lofty heights they needed to know *every* one of their team. Arrogance had allowed them to proceed with a business plan, involving rapid expansion and audacious profit margins, they even had a fictitious website to attract new, foolish and wealthy buyers looking to save a few thousand Euro's. They were a class act.

But they did not look inwards – and that cost them dearly, with their lives.

Andrei Dalca, only twenty eight years old but already enviably wealthy had, as far as Alex was concerned betrayed both him and their people. Steal from someone else if you have to feed your family, but never from your own. It was…it was just not allowed.

Niko had done a quite simply spellbinding job of luring him. Despite Dalca's wealth, taste for hedonism and unusually a penchant for Russian fine art he had rarely been successful with women. His brother Cezar had willingly accepted the striking genes of his father, leaving Andrei to live in his shadow, with a crooked smile and a slight affectation of blinking almost repeatedly. He detested the brightness of the sun, yet lived in a country renowned for its endless summer days.

When he had met Niko in the nearby town he had literally walked into her, he was exiting his blue Maserati, parking it in plain sight of the police in a restricted area. She had timed her moment, it was faultless.

Their collision was so skilfully crafted that not even his bodyguard reacted. Dalca brushed him away quickly when he realised that he was about to manhandle the girl.

"No it is OK. It was my fault. Entirely."

He smiled at her and she repaid with a hypnotic look. He held her for a second, feeling her slim body beneath the hip-hugging navy shift dress. He ran his hand up her back, feeling only skin and then let her go.

"Sorry. Miss?"

"Natalia."

"Miss Natalia I am so very sorry. What must you think of me, barging into you in this way?"

"I am thinking that it is how you normally pick up girls…"

She feigned an annoyed look which only added to her allure.

Again timing was everything. She ran her hands through her hair and then clasped them together and giggled. "I am joking. It was my fault. It is OK. Now, if you would allow me to get going, I must get to the beauticians."

"Tell me why a girl as pretty as you needs to go to a beauticians? Over a drink, at my bar. Tell me and I will pay for your drink, your meal and your beauty treatment. It is the least a gentleman can do."

She paused, her training was reaping rewards – for her abusive lover if not her country, but she saw it all as a chance to build her reputation – and she knew that success here would mould Alex even further.

"OK. One drink and no meal. But I will let you give me the cash for my eyebrow treatment!"

"You are so rude. But I love your attitude. Do you have any idea who I am?"

She shook her head. "A man who picks up girls in a cheap Ferrari?"

She had him eating from her palm, a tamed lion and one who ironically did not expect to sleep with her on their first, and last ever date.

After the drink, a local version of Sangria, she posed Dalca a question.

"If you are as important as you say you are, then yes I will meet you again. But will you meet with my brother Alex? He is also a businessman from our beloved homeland. I think you would like him. He is looking for work. Please."

She locked her eyes onto his and for the first time in years he did not blink.

Dalca was besotted. "Yes. I can do this. Get him to ring me on this number." He handed her a white card with his number embossed upon it.

They had drunk a toast or five to their new-found venture. As the lesser members of Fratia had left the superbly decorated clifftop home in Sa Riera and were ferried back into the nearby town to continue their celebrations they did not think for a second that Dalca would be vulnerable. He had earned his reputation as a ruthless businessman, sitting high above the town on the steepest of cliffs with roads that spiralled up the precipices towards his gated status symbol.

The term ruthless was perhaps erroneous. Where finances were concerned he was indeed merciless but he did not possess any elements of cruelty. He had once rescued a fly from its web-based death such was his compassion.

Dalca leaned forward to clash his small green glass containing Tuica, a spirit derived from plums and at least sixty percent proof. His smile was warm and genuine. It was also brimming with confidence.

'Look at this man before me, on his knees in my home – the great Alexander – The Jackdaw – actually he is nothing, I have scraped worse from the bottom of my shoe. Despite what you think I know all about you. I am one, or two steps ahead of you."

He tilted his head backward exposing his throat – it was all The Jackdaw needed to set the record straight.

A simple cut throat razor had brought an unexpected end to his new associates' life. Fool. He should have known better.

He actually enjoyed the feeling and the sound of the blade slicing through his windpipe. He pushed himself back to avoid the pressurised blood and stood over him, grabbing a handful of his silky black hair he spoke.

"I would say that this sends a message to your people Andrei – such a shame that you cannot deliver it in person."

Dalca was unable to answer as he drowned rapidly, his words replaced by a pathetic sound, a mixture of effervescing blood, escaping air and panic.

"I also feel it important for you to understand that your dear brother's will not miss you, for their fate is also sealed. As I stand here and watch you fight for your life they are doing the same in London and our beautiful city of Bucharest. It is only right that I mark the occasion with a toast."

He tipped Dalca's head back further and poured the colourless liquid, straight from the bottle into his mouth until it spilled out, down his neck and mixed with his oxygenated blood.

"Come now, surely you will join me in a toast?"

He paced now seeking another opportunity to carry out a malicious act, whilst Dalca was still alive. He only had seconds.

He opened the razor once more and in two decisive, clinical swipes had carved a cross over his face. A mark of betrayal. He had instructed the two teams in London and Romania to do the same.

"I pity you. You are a little boy still and now you won't get to see and enjoy the obscene symbols of your own success. I shall have to add them to my own collection. For example…"

He continued to talk, even though he knew that the younger male had barely a moment left to live.

"…This fine Faberge piece here. If I am not mistaken is an Imperial Easter Egg, given by Nicholas the Second to the Dowager Empress Maria. It is delightful. But it does not go with your décor. So revolting." He tossed it onto the stone floor causing it to shatter, then walked over to it and stamped on it repeatedly, each time a more aggressive action until it was almost certainly irreparable.

"But this, this is most exquisite my friend. May I? Thank you, a truly wonderful gift and one that I accept most humbly."

He picked the walking cane up and admired it, another Faberge piece it was no doubt worth millions. Where it had come from he simply didn't care, the fact that its purple amethyst handle captivated him was what was important, that and the fact that he now considered it his own.

He ran his hand over the white enamel, rose and yellow gold detail, and his fingers selecting and feeling the string of white pearls until he had counted every one. When he had finished he knew that Dalca was dead.

He walked over to him and placed the razor into his lap having washed it in the remnants of the Tuica before dropping the bottle at his side. It smashed and allowed the last remains to seep into a broad crack on the stoneware floor.

"Do not ever forget this night Andrei. I know I won't."

He whistled theatrically as he strutted from the living area swirling the cane in his hand and laughing as he turned off the lights with the tip of the cane and pulling the main door shut behind him.

He walked to his awaiting car, got in, lovingly placed the cane on the rear parcel shelf and grabbed Niko's face and open mouth kissed her, licking her neck, his tongue darting into her eyes, his hands holding her cheekbones, wiping his former business partners' metallic, fresh blood onto her face as he did so.

He had her in the back of the car whilst his driver watched discreetly in his rear view mirror, wiping his blood stained hands over her semi-naked torso.

Even his driver, who was now used to such behaviour thought that his boss was becoming a little unstable, narcissistic and dangerous. He wouldn't mention it, he had a family and bills to pay, and besides the Bulgarian girl was very attractive.

They remained in Spain, but now, with the additional wealth that his growing business empire attracted they could travel anywhere. He took her to far-flung places and showered her with gifts, everything, the best. Weeks seemed like months as they tried valiantly to dent his ever-growing bank balance.

He even told her in a moment of apparent weakness that he loved her. But still he abused her. It was as if she were his highest paid escort – competing for attention among all the others he entertained when she was asleep or deliberately oblivious.

She had long lost contact with her Controllers but she had made a pact, and one day she would carry it out. However with each day, with each month the desire lessened.

At some point in February 1988 and with a significant amount of anxiety she announced that she was pregnant. She had been hesitant, knowing that he would probably beat the child out of her or at best ensure its early termination. However contrary to her thoughts, and certainly those of everyone who knew The Jackdaw, he mellowed, altered and became suspiciously paternal.

"She will want for nothing. She will have the best of everything. She will be protected, taught how to survive and never have to look over her shoulder like I have done all these years. She will be proud of her Roma ancestry. She will have your temperament but my striking looks!"

He laughed at himself, "Listen to me, the Expectant Father, Alexandru Stefanescu, a father, who would have thought it possible, eh, my little Nikolina, who?"

All she could think of in reply was "Yes, Alex, she will be very resourceful."

She became less attractive to him but he nurtured her every waking moment – that was when he wasn't nurturing two or three hookers from various parts of the world; he had introduced themed months to which he invited his closest friends, it was July so this was 'Africa' and he found himself entwined in a hot tub with two young girls who said they were from Nigeria.

His reputation continued to worsen, or, through his conceited eyes to improve. He had even gained a place in the Interpol ranks of the despised, infamous and wanted.

Thumbing his nose at them he travelled back and forth to Romania, conducting deals, enforcing his reputation and revelling in his own magnificence.

She gave birth on the 5th November 1988, a girl. Slender like her mother used to be, with flaming red hair, vivid green eyes and the appearance of a gypsy dancer. He was infatuated.

He held her up and looked into her jade eyes, "We must call her after my Mother; her name will be Elena Stefanescu."

For fourteen years Nikolina had endured his subtle beatings, hiding the wounds and psychological harm from her growing daughter.

Elena was everything her father said she would be; beautiful, multi-lingual, bright, witty and resourceful. Against everything he stood for he insisted she became educated and that she was never to be exposed to obvious criminality, and never, upon his life, ever to commit a crime.

It was, he said, what he had worked for. If anyone should ever harm his little girl he would tear their eyes out with his bare hands.

She had changed him, weakened him, scraping the mortar away from the brickwork of his life, softening the foundations of his empire.

Because she was so bright and perceptive she also saw the subtleties of a hideous domestic situation. Her mother was on one hand an apparently capable person, confident, possibly even trained by the military, articulate and gifted in linguistics and yet desperately, desperately sad.

Each time she saw her mother flinch she knew another punishment had taken place, she never once saw physical proof but she knew and as each day progressed she grew to hate her father, little by little until the hatred became a driving force.

Unlike her mother she was realistic and knew she couldn't act alone, but in a quiet and rare moment alone they formed an alliance that went far beyond that of a mother and her daughter.

"Why do you choose to live this way mother?" she had asked.

"Because I do Elena, because when this started I had a mission, a purpose, but the longer I remained with him the more I forgot the reason. I once even thought that I loved him."

"And now?"

"And now, I know that it is too late to change anything, but for you the future is clearer, do not be like me, a star that was never allowed to shine."

It was agreed that at some point, sooner or later one of them would seek retribution for his cowardly, callous acts and they would do this alone, together or with an unforeseen ally.

He was oblivious to his daughter's plans and blinded by love, which was now so genuine he could only see her for what she was; his most successful venture to date.

Seizing the opportunity to enhance her education and knowledge Stefanescu sent her to a private school in Montpellier, France where she would learn the local language and be schooled in the finer things in life too. Money, he said, was no object.

Later she would travel to another similar institution in Bulgaria – he wanted her to know about her past. He would miss her terribly and he told her so. He gave her a trust fund to live off, more than most of the students would see in a lifetime.

Sadly, she would never know of her grandfather, who had died during the harsh winter of 1990, found alone and frozen in his sterile apartment complex. The reports were thorough; he had died of pneumonia, a complication of influenza. The information, along with his history was cross-shredded, steam pulped and then burned.

Within a week the Directorate had contacted her. She was walking along a side street, back towards college when a kindly looking male approached her and enquired about her mother. He knew all about her, her father too and her grandfather. Clearly he was to be trusted.

After only three more meetings she had been unwittingly or deliberately converted.

The day arrived. Nikolina took the chance, he was drunk on power, arrogant beyond belief, rising to the status of Interpol's most sought-after organised crime leader and heading for even greater infamy.

She withdrew the aging umbrella from her bag and fired the mechanism into his leg.

He flinched and slapped at his limb, apologising for startling her. He was in seventh heaven and not even a pesky bee could upset his day. He had scored another huge financial success. He was being warm, even, some might say, loving towards her.

It was most surreal. Had she done the right thing?

Yes.

If the chemist's had done their job he would be dead within a day, less, hopefully. She would wait long enough to see the initial impact then leave. She knew her exit plan intimately for she had lived it for the last few months.

So what if she never returned to the Motherland? Yes she would miss her dear father, yes the Bureau would certainly be lost without her, but she knew what their ultimate plans were; her Papa had told her.

Sadly she also knew that his days were numbered. They had said their goodbyes, agreeing that one day they would meet in heaven, where, with any luck he would finally take her Queen and be able to rest – the game won.

Alex Stefanescu slept well that night, however his partner of fifteen long years hoped he would never wake up.

She left quietly at four the next morning. With minimal luggage and a pile of Euros she was able to move quickly. She walked into a part of town where she was unlikely to be recognised and got into a taxi outside a nightclub, still busy disgorging its patrons.

"Airport."

Her instructions were simple. The driver nodded, switched on his meter and pulled away from the rank.

She checked in at Malaga Airport, placed an envelope into the nearby post box, trusting that the recipient would deliver the message and then continued with her journey, passing through Spanish border control and into the gate lounge.

She feigned a smile at the pretty cabin crew girls as she boarded the 737 to East Midlands Airport. Other than a region in England she had no idea where the East Midlands was and didn't care. She had money, she had skills and she needed to get away whilst she could.

Hopefully by now that evil bastard was dead.

For the immediate future she had a different challenge and had to put her beloved Elena into a private compartment deep within her mind. She would be safer there. She made a promise to watch over her.

Her father, despicable though he was had provided for her.

Even that cold, calculated tyrant of a man wouldn't harm her; he was wrapped around her finger, which had come as a shock, even to him. He had once told her earnestly that he would protect her with his life – or end hers rather than allow someone the pleasure. Despite apparently mellowing he still held a streak so ruthless that at times he even feared himself.

Nikolina had always wanted to visit London and London was where her final challenge lay, albeit she wouldn't exactly be a conventional tourist. All she needed was a friend, someone to trust, to deliver a message to and then hopefully gain asylum.

The message was simple, yet complex, at a level even she, with her myriad departments and layers of security could not fathom. She had a message, not a note, or a report or a higher-level communique, just a plain and unequivocal statement to deliver to the British Foreign Office. It was a story, of sorts, told to her by a man she had grown to know very well, she hated him and loved him in equal amounts. But she knew deep within her soul that to retain the information would be damaging to both her, her country and her intended new sanctuary.

Once delivered she had hoped to plan her own future. It was relatively straightforward for someone who had grown up in a country as divorced from simplicity as it possibly could be.

Her next task and possibly her last was to reunite with her daughter. For now, yes, she was safe. For now, perversely, her father would never harm her. Wherever she was, she was safe. She took some comfort from that. But he had told someone, deliberately she suspected, in her hearing that he would kill his offspring if he had no choice. As a mother it was abhorrent.

However long it took, months, years, it mattered not; they would reunite. She would receive the letter – God willing, and when she was old enough to read it herself she might be able to form an opinion.

She had arranged to meet a man who could ensure her immigration into the United Kingdom would be anonymous, painless and whilst expensive, permanent.

She walked head-down along the aisle until she reached row 29, placed a small bag in the overhead storage compartment, sat down and put her seatbelt on. A large male was sat next to her; he was very casually dressed and reeked of cheap antiperspirant.

He smiled and said hello; it was all she could do to reply, smile back and turn her head away before she laid her blonde hair on the headrest and slipped into a welcome and long overdue sleep.

Survival was in her female genes, her mother had seen to it and she had made a pact to pass them on to her own daughter.

She was pure, defiant and compelled and no one would prevent her from achieving her goals. If she kept uttering these words they would come true. She had failed her first goal, now she needed fate to play its part, she certainly couldn't achieve the rest on her own.

Part One

Summer 2014

Seventh

Chapter One

Coromandel Peninsula, New Zealand.

The sun radiated in a consistently azure-blue sky and at just a few minutes after five thirty in the morning it had the makings of another good-looking day. The air was crisp and provided a refreshing start after what had been a warm, sultry, almost uncomfortable night. The crickets had serenaded the neighbourhood until the early hours and now their raucous, day-time, hissing, clicking, ever-present counterparts had commenced their own day-long appeal for a mate.

He tolerated the cicada, but much preferred the melodic, peaceful and vaguely tropical song of the cricket. He had also endured the relentless humidity of a February night in the Southern Hemisphere, somehow considering it more than worth the exchange when he finally climbed out of his bed and prepared to run to the nearby beach.

A creature of habit he would normally make the bed before leaving, a legacy of his disciplined past. Conventionally he would crease the Egyptian cotton sheets and place them methodically in situ before arranging the pillows, just so.

Exactly four minutes after leaving his home his overtly-coloured Asic Gel Kayano running shoes left the sterile concrete surface of the pavement as he leapt onto a wooden walkway that took him swiftly into the heart of a pine forest.

The air was incredibly fresh and almost instantly his nasal passages filled with the heady scent of crushed conifer needles as he ran along the natural, quiet carpet. It was one of his 'special moments' and something which he always looked forward to.

He set himself a pace and began to breathe deeply as he zigzagged through the trees, each one towering above him, their boughs allowing shafts of sunlight to penetrate through the canopy and onto the forest floor.

Strands of light cascaded through the vegetation, illuminating fern fronds and revealing a curtain of dust particles. The path stretched for almost a mile and today he was the only occupant. As he started to feel the resistance of a gentle incline he acknowledged his senses isolating themselves once more. His nose was now alive with the scent of the forest, his eyes squinting to avoid the piercing rays and his ears embracing the ever-changing sounds, the most notable of which was the distant pounding of waves upon a shore.

Moments later and at the top of a larger mound he reached his favourite part of the run. Exiting the forest he found himself once more on an incredibly beautiful beach. It was one of his favourites, in a country quite literally full of dramatic, superlative-rich, pristine shores.

He breathed in the ozone-laden air, as salt particles hit his face and occasional specks of seawater cooled his already burning skin. Looking out to sea he observed an ever-present, distant, hazy chain of small islands and nodded his approval to no one in particular before continuing his run. He felt at peace. He always did when he reached this place.

As the surface changed again, the miniscule grains of silica bit into the rubber surface of his shoes and now all that he could hear was the sound of his feet hitting the ground, his breathing, the powerful swoosh of the inbound waves, that and the distant call of a flock of Variable Oystercatchers, busy foraging for food on the immediate shoreline, scampering back and forth to avoid the waves.

He turned right and began to head towards a curve in the bay where a small area of cliffs met the sea.

Cursing himself for not placing them in beforehand, he fumbled in his red short pockets and removed a pair of Sennheiser earphones. Preferring not to stop he continued to run, placing the smooth rubber pieces into his ears and switching on the device strapped to his left arm. His pace had slowed, ever so slightly, but enough to annoy him; his overt anger would have probably been amusing to onlookers as he chastised himself.

Not even the Oystercatchers were interested.

It was one of the myriad reasons he chose to live here.

He soon found his speed increasing as a random musical track burst into his head, filling his ears with sound, drowning out nature's own symphony and alerting the senses, importantly increasing his desire to run as fast as he could.

"Rebel Yell" had always been one of his 'power tracks' and this morning was no different. He was sprinting now, as fast as he possibly could. As he rounded the curve in the shoreline he noticed another inhabitant; he was not alone.

About two hundred metres in front of him stood a darker-skinned male, taller than him and very powerfully built.

His physical activity had created a film of sweat on his body which only sought to emphasise his impressive physique. The right side of his body was clearly marked with a striking tattoo that ran from his right shoulder, beyond his hip and onto his calf. It was a tribal tattoo, borne out of the South Pacific and etched onto his body the old-fashioned, exquisitely painful way with a hammer and a piece of tusk. It had taken many months of commitment and recovery until it took up pride of place, a mixture of cultural and personal design.

In his hand was a rake and at his feet a number of canvass sacks. His activities were no more sinister than collecting the overnight bounty that nature had provided – sea weed. The male was harvesting the plant material, probably for his garden, but possibly to eat, to feed his family or even to sell. Who knew?

As he reached the male he slowed slightly, inhaling vast lungful's of air but not stopping, he raised his right hand up and was met by the stronger palm of the harvester. Their palms clashed in a classic high five and in seconds they were both alone again; The Harvester and The Runner, the only occupants on a beach many miles long.

The only other visitor to its familiar abrasive surface had been a few resident seabirds and the insistent pounding of the Pacific Ocean.

It was a genuinely great day to be alive and to breathe in the ozone, stand, close ones eyes and listen to the brutal, persistence of the ocean.

He reached the end of the beach. Stopping, he dropped his head and shoulders and started his post-run regime. Stretching his arms high above his head he gulped in huge amounts of fresh air then shook out his limbs. Exhausted but filled with endorphins he pulled his T shirt over his head, revealing what for him was considered a reasonable body, a figure that showed evidence of regular exposure to the sun.

He stopped, took another deep breath, flipped off his beloved running shoes and music player and then ran full-on into the surf.

The immediate sensation changed. Now he was really alive; highly-oxygenated air bubbles fought for superiority around and above his head as wave after wave pounded over the top of him. Sounds were suppressed now but he was still incredibly aware of his surroundings. He surfaced after a few minutes, like a Cormorant hunting its prey.

He looked around and saw a much larger wave. Its deep blue core was full of raw power, the tops were arctic white and disintegrating in the wind, their ever-present, rumbling noise was immense. He took a deep breath and plunged head-first into the foaming arc.

Being alone in an ocean so potent and yet serenely beautiful had its own allure. He could easily get into difficulty and no one, anywhere would be able to save him.

Bursting through the wave he launched himself shorewards on the next, skilfully surfing into the beach where he lay for a few moments, each subsequent wave battering him, surrounding him and eagerly tugging him back into the sea. His face lay on the sand, somehow allowing his eyes to macro-focus onto the microscopic composition of the beach. Once again he realised why he did this every morning.

He'd battled his ocean nemesis and won, once more.

Legend had it that the Seventh Wave was always the most powerful. As long as he acknowledged this he would always be safe.

Having replaced his shoes and put his T shirt and music player back on, he began a slow jog back to his home. Traffic had started to increase as local folk commenced their short and enviable commute to work. A few drivers waved as he ran, he didn't know them but this was a beach community so everyone waved, it was how it was, apparently.

On the last phase of his return run he began to think about the girl he had spent the last week with; the last night with.

It was a long story but in essence and all too heavily clichéd he had picked her up at a bar. Historically this was completely out of character and yet it seemed right. Clearly she saw something in him – not just that on the face of it he was reasonably well off and lived in a great waterfront home.

At forty, even if he said it himself he was in great shape, both physically and mentally. Tanned, but not overly so, his five foot eleven frame was lean and muscular in the right places, it was often said that his legs were somewhat out of proportion to his upper body but impressive nonetheless.

He had thinning mousy brown hair, his temples were greying now, or as he liked to refer to them – tinted with titanium. The colour combination of tanned skin and greying hair allowed his most natural feature to shine – he had fiercely blue eyes; eyes it seemed that captured many a girls' heart. It was often said that just blinking as he spoke added a certain, something.

He had a strong sense of right and wrong and a wicked sense of humour – but above all he had a past and in many ways it controlled and haunted him. His only way to suppress the voices was to live a life that combined relaxation with work – he'd finally added the word Consultant onto his Linkedin profile and to date it had done him no harm; none whatsoever. Worst case it had allowed him to live on the Pacific Coast of New Zealand where he would spend all summer, only occasionally leaving for Europe in the Southern Hemisphere winter and then, only if he felt like it.

He arrived back on the driveway of *Spindrift* – his summer home. Whilst it only had two bedrooms it was more than comfortable with a timber construction, Birchwood interior walls and ceilings, a log burner, a kitchen with stainless steel appliances and bench tops, two bathrooms and his favourite acquisition, an outdoor shower.

The gardens were minimal, planted with palms and succulents and Kikuyu grass. If nothing else it meant his garden maintenance bill was also minimal. A large black sail fluttered in the breeze, attached to the front wall of the property and then onto two wooden pillars. It provided much-needed shade from the fiercely hot New Zealand sun.

At the back of the property lay another small garden and his piece de resistance, a boat mooring. The mooring was a necessary, if not expensive extra when he bought the home a few years before. His was the only vacant one, the rest of the adjoining properties all having impressive ocean-going yachts and motor cruisers tied up in the modern canal complex.

He vowed that one day he would fill the vacant area with a sleek black powerboat - although, truth be told he wasn't quite sure why or when he would ever use it and more importantly what it might be called. He pondered for an hour once as he sat on his own private jetty and tossed pebbles into the water captivated by the symmetry of the ripples.

Parked on his driveway was his actual vice. An equally sleek, equally black vehicle; it wasn't his first choice, that would have been a Porsche 911 or perhaps the new Cayman – against the advice of his more hirsute male friends he had ended up buying a 2010 model Obsidian Black Audi TT - the 3.2 V6 quattro version. Much to the delight of those same friends - the few that he had - who all referred to it as 'The Hairdresser's Car'.

As was always the case, once they were placed firmly in the heated passenger seats and exposed to the 280bhp that the four wheel drive system managed to deliver seamlessly to the road, their minds changed. As the exhaust system wailed off the cliff edges with the car darting and weaving through the Kamai Ranges most passengers conceded that it was indeed a very agreeable car.

And he enjoyed it, he enjoyed it immensely, and besides it put the fingers firmly up at 'her' which made it somehow even more bittersweet.

And so it was the car that attracted the girl – the girl who came into his life that Thursday evening in the eastern coastal town of Whitianga.

Whether she made a habit of it or not didn't really matter, she had spotted his car when it pulled up outside the bar.

He parked, plipped the alarm and walked into The Oceanside. He wore a striking blue shirt that did nothing to hide the equally blue eyes that discreetly and professionally scanned the room. She was immediately besotted.

Quite how she found herself in this Pacific venue was a mystery to many but not to her. She knew exactly why she was there.

Many months before – before she had commenced her intricately-planned journey from Europe, across South East Asia and into the South Pacific, she had read the letter once more, for the last time in fact, before burning it and disposing of the ashes on a long walk through the city. She had contemplated burning the ashes too. In a country that trained people to be suspicious it was an almost laughably-normal activity and as far removed from paranoia as chalk, from cheese.

The letter was simple, not that of a loving relative. It lacked any form of code and was written in plain 'English' but at best, ambiguous.

Do this, recover this item, go to this place, find this man. Do not trust anyone else. Do not ask questions. Use your instinct. If that fails you – walk away, burn the papers and head for a new country, seek asylum. You can never return.

Having left home two years earlier she had travelled across Europe and into Asia, as planned, all the better to create a time-stamped journey, one that could later be easily verified, stopping as many other travellers did to take in the usual singles sites such as Phuket and Bali.

She'd met plenty of people en route to the Antipodes – even slept with a few men, she was single, so why not? She'd avoided the perilous pitfalls of modern travel – drugs, smuggling and alcohol-fuelled sex. And now here she was in a bar on a Thursday evening and thinking of a way to approach the male without appearing too – forward.

What little information she had received, and raw instinct had put her here, near to this place, with an item, safely secreted and now, she hoped before her was the man. Somehow via a process of varying degrees and skill and luck she had arrived.

But something changed the moment she looked at him.

Figuring that you only live once she walked up to him as he sat on a bar stool. He'd just had a remarkably boring tonic water and lime delivered. He became aware of her approaching, glancing at her via the bar mirror. She was almost perfect; taller than average, slim, lightly tanned, green eyes; she wore a simple summer dress, but she wore it elegantly and most importantly, she was a redhead.

'My God she is beautiful' he found himself thinking in the time it took her to transition from her sofa to the bar.

"And she's coming towards the bar. She's alone; this can only mean one thing."

She stopped at his side, tried hard not to look and then turned towards him.

He turned to meet her gaze.

"Look love, I'm flattered but I probably can't afford you, so thanks, but no thanks."

Her look was instantaneous and the slap that she delivered to his face was even swifter. Christ it hurt.

"How dare you? How could you? Why did you?"

He quickly slipped into professional mode.

"OK, so three questions, which would Madame like answering first?"

"Forget it, you are too old for me anyway and as you say I am too much girl for you, plenty more fish in the ocean." Her head bowed before she made a move toward the door.

At that exact moment something triggered in his mind, her voice, importantly her accent told him that she wasn't from the area, the country or even the region. He had three seconds to analyse everything: Late twenties, incredibly attractive, slim, confident, probably Eastern European. No, definitely Eastern Euro and most likely Russian – or Bulgarian. But why now? Why here? Why him?

He smiled, having just asked himself three questions too. She looked around as she opened the door and headed along the street. In her mind she had never been so insulted.

He watched her strut along the quiet road, her hair tussled by a sea breeze and her dress, simple, white and yet very attractive, soon clinging to her very female form.

"Shit, what a mistake. Go and find her, at least apologise," offered Big Stan the Bar Manager, "She's stunning bro, I will if you won't!"

He knew in that moment that she was far too good for Stanley Foster, the muscular and egotistical weekend rugby warrior that he was, so he realigned his glass with an existing condensation mark on the bar, winked at the barman and walked outside.

She was gone.

A moment later the indicators flashed on the Audi and he was inside starting it up. The V6 came to life and the red and white dials on the dashboard indicated that all was well. Engaging Sport he pushed the accelerator, all four Bridgestone tyres bit into the road surface and launched the coupe down the street.

She had to be somewhere.

Turning down the first road he found it to be empty. Gunning the throttle he reached the intersection, looked left and then right. In his past life he always took right if in doubt so did just that. The car whipped through the six-speed gearbox and in a licence-threatening moment he was well over the local speed limit. Turning right again he found himself on the waterfront where one of the local fishing boats was returning from a few days at sea, surrounded by desperate gulls, the promise of a free meal proving to be too tempting to ignore.

He flew by the boat ramp and just as he indicated to turn right he spotted her, sat on a bench, staring across the river mouth. He pulled over, abandoned the car and began to walk towards her.

His internal dialogue was a confused mish-mash of words and feelings, but like her he felt that you only live once, so decided to exorcise a few demons and in doing so apologise and hopefully allow her to have some dignity.

He walked quietly towards her, sat on the right hand side of the bench and placed his hand out in a gesture that indicated that he wished to shake hers. She lifted her head and he noticed that her green eyes were now even more opaline, surrounded by myriad reddened blood vessels.

For reasons unknown to her she took the hand. He squeezed, ever so gently and she returned the same pressure. He smiled, again she reciprocated.

"I'm not entirely sure where to start, so my mother always told me that apologising is a good place. I'm sorry. I was out of order back there. I have lived a life that has made me somewhat cynical and therefore…", he blew air through his teeth, "therefore the chances of a woman quite as attractive as you approaching a man like me in a bar and only wanting to be sociable seemed about as likely as you winning the Bulgarian lottery."

He paused expecting her to interject but she just nodded, clearly waiting for him to finish.

"Again, I'm sorry. I fully appreciate that you may wish to tell me to 'Q hodi se ebi, be!' and should you choose that course I will do the gentlemanly thing and retire."

She tried to control it but her laughter came quickly.

"Where you learn Bulgarian?"

"Now that's a long story but it started around the early two thousands – if you allow me to buy you a meal I can explain and then perhaps we can start again?"

"I would be most honoured sir. And for the record I must tell you, I'm much too expensive for a man who can only afford Audi TT."

He smiled for the first time. Touché. Her eyes lit up and her hair shone in the last of the evening sun.

He loved the brass-necked cheek of this girl. He certainly admired her beauty and yet still he couldn't believe his…luck.

Fifteen minutes later he had convinced the owners of the Motu Kitchen – Whitianga's finest restaurant – that he genuinely needed a table for two and that the 'need to know' was a matter of national security. The owner Ian knew him well and answered his prayers.

He recommended a few great local wines to accompany her meal – she chose seafood and he the quail. They nibbled on some freshly baked bread, dipping it into an exquisite green virgin olive oil as their conversation, along with the wine, finally started to flow.

He'd extolled the virtues of the Lonely Bay 2012 Chardonnay suggesting that it would be a great match for her scallops, pancetta, black truffle and cauliflower, whilst he dined upon the quail roulade with thyme flowers. He was right, the wines' tropical notes and flavours of grapefruit, nectarine and peach complimented her scallops perfectly. She was in seventh heaven, having never dined so opulently in her life; at that moment she decided that from then on only the finer things would do.

Finishing the meal with a buffalo mozzarella panna cotta and local strawberries they sat back and for a while stared at one another. In the end he spoke first.

"OK. Why me?"

She faltered, trying perhaps to refine her English "I, I'm, look, I don't know. I saw you. You saw me. I am here, on holiday, a big girl, in a small country and I felt like some adult company. I like you straight from the first time. You call me whore and yet I still forgive!" She threw her head back revealing a perfectly formed neckline, hinting, for a brief moment at what lay below.

She emptied the last of a Taylor's port and allowed her tongue to linger on the rim of the glass as he finished a 12-year-old Bowmore malt whisky.

"And that's it? Just, how I would say, fate? Nothing more, you don't just want me for my car?" He winked to re-affirm that he was playing mind games with her.

"That? In Sofia they call it the…hairdresser's car!"

Convinced she had been talking to Big Stan he threw his napkin at her, although intended to be playful it caught her square on the chin, causing her to wince. She feigned injury long enough to draw him in and then she struck. A piece of panna cotta left her hand; it had been debated over for long moments after she had declared that she had finished, for the second time.

It flew, almost expertly through the air and hit him on the cheek, just below his left eye. And it stayed there. Neither it, nor its new host prepared to yield.

The resultant giggling from the pair attracted more attention than they had anticipated. Most of the female patrons despised her and the males simply looked on in awe, desperate to understand how this fellow male could attract such a mate. Most formed the opinion that she was his secretary or better still, his long-lost daughter. All were wrong as it happened.

He looked up and saw the proprietors Ian and Emily standing together, arms folded and tutting at his antics.

"Come on, it's time to go…I'm getting *that* look from the owners. You are bringing out the worst in me."

He paid the bill and apologised to the host who simply shook his hand and asked for his secret – in doing so earning him a gentle clip around his left ear from his wife.

She allowed him to walk her to his car, opening the passenger door he stopped.

"Sorry, I can't…I'm really sorry."

She looked hurt, almost upset. "But I thought we have the most wonderful night. I thought we…"

"Yes, yes, we have, it's been remarkable, in fact better than I could have ever hoped for."

He raised his hands up into the darkening sky before continuing "and seeing as though we'd never met until three hours ago and all was going well until I suggested that you were a high-class prostitute – well yes I too thought we were having a wonderful night. When I say I can't, I mean I can't drive; I've had too much to drink. Shall we walk?"

She readily agreed, not wanting the night to end. To date this had been the best night she could remember for a very long time. Where it would end she simply didn't know.

He locked the car which responded with a multitude of orange flashes which lit up the surrounding space – he walked away, quite frankly not caring whether it was there the next morning.

At sea a storm began to build, the heat of the day finally coming to a climatic conclusion; typical at this time of the year it would soon make its way inland, often accompanied by intense lightning and eventually, rain. For him it was not unusual, for her, it added to the intensity.

She slipped her shoes off and stepped onto the sand feeling the still-warm grains wrapping themselves around her painted toes.

An hour later, via a slow walk along the beach they arrived at *Spindrift*. He slid open the door and pressed an indigo-blue wall switch which initiated a set of low-light features in the kitchen. The light reflected off the industrial worktops and onto her face, creating an even more attractive view.

He opened a bottle of Roaring Meg pinot noir as she walked slowly around the lounge gazing at some photography; land and seascapes featured. They were simply framed and initialled.

"You know this photographer?"

"Carrie? Yes, you could say that. I practically taught her everything I know!"

"She's good. She was your girlfriend?"

"She…no. She, is, was, a very…" It was obvious he was struggling for words.

"She's an old…colleague who I haven't seen for a long time, but that's a long story and we haven't got all night, but all I can tell you is I owe her a great deal indeed and vice versa. I miss her enormously, but I made a decision to leave her behind; best I leave it that. By the way, make sure that photo is straight would you? Now if you like wine, you'll love this," he offered her the bottle to read as he selected two large glasses.

The deliciously dark red liquid was decanted into the glasses as she slipped off her shoes once again. She felt at home, any risk of harm seemed negligible.

"That is shame; I was hoping we would have…"

He looked, raised an eyebrow and continued pouring.

"Would have?"

"All night."

They moved from the industrial steel of the kitchen to the softer tones and furnishings of the lounge where he selected some music and turned the volume to a level that allowed them to enjoy both the selected disc and their own conversation.

He chose the red leather Danish-inspired armchair and she the more conventional cream coloured chaise longue.

She lay back on the chair and stretched out, allowing her summer dress to move gently up her leg. Thankfully his thought process was interrupted when she clapped her hands together like a teenager.

"Bruno Mars! I love Bruno…you love Bruno?"

"Well, I don't love him the same way as you might, but I happen to think his music is great."

"What it is with you men? Are you afraid to love someone because he is a man too?"

He was not quite sure how to respond to this but went with his instinct.

"No" he started to laugh "No, it's not that at all, it's just where I come from and where you come from, well, things are different."

"So, like I am a woman and you are a man no?"

"Yes, but…but Bruno and I well…" He was now completely lost and unsure which direction to head in and quietly she was enjoying every moment. "Look, shall we start again?"

She agreed, they chinked the overly large red wine glasses together which created an enduring mid-range tone.

"So, why me?" he asked, almost unsure if he wanted to hear the answer; at forty, here he was, at a point in his life when he had only just recovered from the last 'relationship', and God knows how long ago that was. Now he found himself, in his own home, alone with quite the most delectable girl he had possibly, probably ever laid eyes on.

He struggled to avoid her gaze, wanting to take a moment to admire her whilst not appearing to be overly lustful. She was as perfect as a Michelangelo sculpture, her skin exquisitely clear, her figure clearly honed by exercise; why even her hands were bloody perfect.

Her feet, recently benefiting from a pedicure were a foot fetishist's day dream and her legs resembled those of a runner, no, a thoroughbred, shiny from a recent gallop down a windswept shoreline.

As she wriggled about on his chaise he saw, for the second time that evening, that she was not wearing a bra; the image was beyond tantalising, her breasts were so perfectly formed that he only just managed to regain eye contact with her – his timing, as ever, immaculate.

"Why you? If I said I saw you arrive in your sexy sports car would that be enough?"

"No, not really, anyone can own a car like that – it's not an Aston Martin after all, is it?"

"No, Mr Bond, it isn't and if you were Daniel Craig you would, erm, what it is you would say - have me by now!" She giggled adding another dimension. When she smiled her nose screwed up; God if he was a foot and nose fetishist this was eighth heaven indeed.

"You haven't answered my question, please don't misunderstand me, I am incredibly flattered, but why a man who must be twenty years older than you. Why?"

"Thirteen."

"Sorry?"

"I am thirteen years younger than you!" She answered so quickly, so confidently that for the first time since they met he paused, acutely aware of who she might be, what she might want and whether in fact their meeting was indeed purely fortuitous.

"I look at your driving permit. See, it is on the kitchen top, by the sink, you leave it on the side, I pick it up and look. Simple. You are forty and I am twenty seven. It's easy, what is problem?"

She was right, he'd lived a life of caution, cynicism and downright mistrust – the job did that to you, but now he was at risk of ruining a beautiful evening and one which he would be the envy of his select group of friends. Now who was the Hairdresser?

"Sing to me!"

"What? I can't sing, I have never been able to sing and I'm not going to start now." He was most indignant, as if she had touched a nerve.

"But it is only song…sing with Bruno, he won't mind…"

And there on that balmy evening he found himself singing along to bloody Bruno bloody Mars, without a clue why and suddenly, for the first time in a very long time, he relaxed.

"Same bed but it feels just a little bit bigger now….."

"Our song on radio, but it not sound the same…" she teased him but encouraged at the same time.

"'Cause my heart breaks a little when I hear your name..."

She left the chaise and moved towards him.

For a man with so much experience – so much international experience of names and places, of culture, of people, of corners, light and dark, of time zones that most never knew existed, of training and sixth-sense responses he suddenly felt very inept, impotent and almost scared.

His wife was a redhead too and she had destroyed everything he ever held dear to his heart. Never again; until now.

She moved across the wooden floor, her bare feet skilfully carrying her lithe frame around the room as she danced in perfect time to the music, pretending to carry a bouquet of sweet-smelling flowers and feigning heartbreak.

He smiled 'My God she is good'.

Arriving at the chair she lowered herself to her knees and gently laid her head in his lap. He leant back slightly, hesitating for a second, then relaxed once more. He heard his heart beating and felt her presence against his legs. He could smell her hair, a mix of natural oil and a vague hint of something tropical – it couldn't be anything but passion fruit. He found that once again and for the second time that day his senses were focusing at infinitesimal level.

Her head remained in situ for a few minutes until it became rather too impossible to avoid his natural feelings towards her. He was a man after all. He continued to suppress these feelings until the intensity was such that he could no longer disguise or repress the increasing urges of arousal, an aroused state that he had not experienced since 'she' had left him. And now in the presence of this profoundly beautiful and intensely captivating vixen, he finally let go.

She looked up and straight into his eyes. She nodded as if endorsing that it was alright.

This time it was her outstretched hand that he took.

He stood up, picked her up in his arms. His strong hands gripped her hips, leaving imprints on her flawless skin; unable to turn back from the tide-like pull of this entrancing girl he seamlessly and powerfully lifted her up towards him, displaying a level of strength that made her gasp – his sudden display of authority and sheer potency had truly taken her by surprise.

She wrapped her legs around his waist, gripping like a vice to his hips. She let herself go now, her total body weight falling back towards the ground. He was ready for her, with one swift, fluid movement he directed her upwards again, where her face met his. Without hesitation she bit his lower lip.

She was his.

And he knew it.

With renewed vigour he carried her across the lounge to the chaise, lowered her gently onto it and then lowered himself, equally gently onto her. She kissed his neck and then began to open his shirt, kissing his chest, licking his throat.

Sensing that she was starting to take control he found himself wondering whether to let her – or do what he imagined most women wanted and overwhelm her with his own sense of power and control.

Somehow 'she' came flooding into his bloody mind again, yet every time he thought of her now it was with a sense of hatred and pity. She had her chance and now he had his. This made his decision easier; if she wanted to take the lead then what man wouldn't let her have her wish? And the truth was he loved her energy and sense of wickedness. He loved it very much. He found himself thinking 'Teach me things I don't yet know and whatever you do, do not spare the horses…please'.

This was quickly followed by another thought.

'And if 'she' so happens to be outside in the growing tempest, watching through the opening in the curtains, well frankly, fuck her, so much the better!'

He sat up and onto the edge of the chaise before standing. She knelt behind him; her slender fingers unbuttoned his shirt, slipped it over his head before dropping it onto the floor. His other clothes followed, as slowly, building the anticipation, she freed him from the restraints of the warm fabric until he was naked.

She paused, admiring him in what was left of the natural light. She caressed his thighs with her raspberry-red lips, licking them before gently blowing air onto the moistness of her kisses. It felt incredible.

The first flash of lightning lit up the room, creating intense brightness across the walls. It made her jump, she laughed; he laughed too and then pulled her towards him, reassurance – for the first time in a while he was back in control.

He held her for a moment then once more he picked her up – physically, but without obvious aggression. Her own feelings were now fuelling her desire to take things so much further than she could have ever had thought possible only a few hours before. He lifted her up and gently lowered her to her feet. She stood in front of him for a brief moment until he turned her around. He unzipped her dress, kissed the nape of her neck and slid the narrow straps off her shoulders.

A whisper of breeze entered the room, dancing around their intense bodies, cooling them momentarily.

The dress slid from her body, pausing as it traced every outline of her figure and finally onto the wooden floor. Without encouragement he placed his hands around her waist, lowered himself onto his knees and as he did so, he removed her white lace underwear, causing her to let out a gentle sigh.

As he stood, his hands traced the outline of her thighs, almost imperceptibly touching her pear-shaped behind as they continued their journey upwards. He stopped momentarily at her hips, his fingertips reaching around into the cleft in her pelvis, almost unsure of the reaction, almost out of respect he paused further until they completed their journey, purposely walking around the front of her body until they reached the silky smooth and final destination.

He placed just enough pressure onto her to make her inhale.

"Oh God, to the left, just……there."

Her own hands slipped behind her back; she teased him with her fingers, hearing his own response she took hold of him. He was intensely hot and the touch of her hands only increased the sensation.

A bolt of lightning struck nearby, this time accompanied by a massive clap of thunder. She grabbed him even harder, causing him to let out a loud cry.

"Sorry…I…"

"I don't care, please, don't stop."

She didn't, continuing to take him closer all the time until he forced the situation to change. Either that, or for now, at least, the night would come to an untimely end.

He turned towards her and once again picked her up, her legs instinctively locking around his hips. They were one now.

He walked with her towards the sliding door, slid it in its runners and stepped out onto the wooden decking. He could feel the grooves of the platform upon his feet as he guided her up against the outside of the door.

Her skin slid against his, moist with humidity from the effect of their actions. Her body left marks upon the glass that he subconsciously thought he'd never, ever clean.

Their rhythmic movements began in time with the distant pounding of the waves, with every few becoming more powerful, more intoxicating.

The seventh wave came all too soon, beating down upon the shore, before dragging the myriad grains back out to sea. He knew he had to control things.

Inside the house Bruno continued to sing, to no-one in particular,

"I gave you what you want, but you tossed it in the trash, you tossed it in the trash...I would die for you baby...but you won't do the same..."

If nothing else, the pulsating beat added to their increasing rhythm.

Another flash of lightning lit them up for all to see. He doubted anyone would be looking and right now cared little if they were. His movements were faster now, more deliberate and she mirrored every one.

The rain announced itself almost instantly as the palms and grasses began to hiss and sigh with the growing strength of the wind. The storm transformed quickly as the monsoon-like downpour rushed towards his home and across the surface of the water in the nearby moorings, causing the boats to quarrel with their restraints.

It finally arrived with a stinging announcement onto his back and into her eyes. Whilst she struggled to see, she wanted more. Her hair was now matted to her face, a river of water running down her body and over her breasts before continuing downwards. His hands left their own unique impression upon the glass as he let go of what was left of his inhibitions.

Whilst she apparently had none, this was a first for her and she hoped it would never end.

He kissed her throughout the downpour, their lips forming together, almost as if providing life-giving air. She placed her arms above her head and grabbed the top of the window frame willing him to penetrate her even more deeply.

She shuddered involuntarily as they reached a crescendo and screamed, biting deep into his shoulder to lessen the chances of being heard.

Sensing, incorrectly that she was afraid, or cold he lifted her up and into his arms, carrying her once more across the threshold, catching the door with his foot and dragging it closed behind him. Another hammering crash of thunder accompanied the door as it locked into its frame.

They stood for a moment in each other's arms, breathless but innately happy. She wiped her hands across her face, over her eyes and pushed back her auburn hair before placing them onto his own face and guiding the last of the rain down across his chest, over his stomach and pausing just long enough to cool him down – once more resulting in a gasp of pleasure.

The last of the storm passed *Spindrift* by, heading south until it would eventually run out of power.

He lifted her up, her wet body slipping at first until he added more pressure. As he walked from the lounge the two sets of damp footprints became one.

The music had finished, all that remained now was the indigo light on the Yamaha hi-fi, its blue glow matching the display of the appliances in the kitchen and illuminating the last of the Roaring Meg, now desperately clinging to the curves of the two half-filled glasses.

They arrived at the bedroom; he paused, leant backwards and pressed the wall switch with his shoulder, instigating the four stainless steel blades that were hanging from the ceiling. The fan began to rotate with a distinctive 'whop-whop-whop' sound and got up to speed until its circular motion wafted cooler air onto their humid bodies.

He got alongside the Californian king-sized bed and threw her onto the covers, somewhat harder than he had intended, but she cared not. She landed in the cooler, crisp Egyptian cotton and threw her arms above her head; once more indicating that she was his, to do with, as he pleased. He stood looking at her, waves of passion built up inside him; he was almost shaking with anticipation.

He beckoned her to come to the edge of the bed.

Pulling her towards him it was immediately obvious that he was ready to follow the path that they both desired. She took hold of him and guided him onto his bed and soon they disappeared under the cold fibres and into the shadows.

She spent the next hour kissing him, the scarlet coloured numbers on his bedside clock slowly changing, unseen. She slipped out of the bed whilst he lay staring up into the whirring, hypnotic fan blades, drunk on the moment and most likely still intoxicated by the taste of the wine. She returned, wearing just his favourite, crisply-ironed blue business shirt and an expectant grin.

All that was missing was a pair of dark-rimmed glasses; he laughed inwardly at his stereotypical fantasies, but quickly set himself straight – tonight, this girl would fulfil them all.

It was indeed as if all of his deepest fantasies had come true: Meet girl in bar. Fall out. Have make up sex: All in one night, all night long.

And that is exactly what they did. She was extremely practised in the finer art of lovemaking, initially in the bedroom and later, much to his delight, the lounge and finally, the kitchen.

Writhing around on the very same industrial, cold steel worktops that had earlier illuminated her face, she unintentionally left impressions of her exquisite body on the mirrored surface. Looking down at the burnished steel, their bodies were replicated in an erotic image that would probably never leave his sub conscious.

Totally oblivious to the fact that she had only met him that evening she lay on the cool surface, her back arched gently so that she could reach up and probe his mouth with her tongue.

Finally, in a moment of sheer alcoholic madness she poured what was left of the Roaring Meg onto her breasts and commanded that he remove it with his own inquisitive tongue. Like a highly trained Sommelier he savoured every note, every flavour, allowing the taste of her and the taste of plum, cherry and cinnamon to mingle in his mouth. He declared that it had honestly never tasted better.

As his tongue navigated its way down her stomach he stopped momentarily to admire a bright green jewel set into her navel. It was as bright as her eyes, and equally striking. He continued on his journey of discovery until they both arrived, exhausted, breathless and intensely sensitive.

They awoke an hour later, still lying on the steel bench. He climbed off, picked her up and carried her to his bed.

A few hours later the sun started to rise, heralding another crisp and impressive day. He opened his eyes, slowly at first, then completely. He had been having an R.E.M dream, the type that offers intensity; touch, taste, sound, pain, his eyes started to become heavy again and once more he dreamt of the girl, the mysterious Slavic beauty; literally, the girl of his dreams.

Waking moments later he was instantly aware that she was not a vision. She was as real as he was. Gently he turned, lifted the cotton sheet and in the half-light of the room could see her naked form, coiled around his own; tanned, taut and incredibly attractive.

In the lounge her summer dress lay on the Danish red chair, her shoes abandoned on the polished rainforest wood floor. His clothes were a reckless mess, for one so obsessively compulsive about his attire, he simply didn't care. What had she done to him? Who was this astonishing woman who had left mesmerizing images of herself upon his home?

Her breathing was rhythmic. He could feel it on his shoulders. It was incredibly calming and serene after such a frantic night. Without warning he sat up in bed.

"Christ! Who *are* you?"

She awoke with a start, almost in a panic, to see him stood in the emerging light; naked as he was the night before. Her heart rate was desperately trying to recover, to provide her with enough energy to stand. She staggered slightly until regaining her composure. Finally she grabbed the sheet to cover her exposed body. It was as if she regretted the previous evening, her face a mixture of shock and guilt.

She started to sob.

"What have I done? I thought I knew you. I leave, you want me to leave? I go, I get dressed and I leave, now."

He shook his head, put his arms out in an open gesture and encouraged her to walk towards him. His enigmatic smile and cool blue eyes persuaded her even more so. As she stepped towards him the sheet unfurled, once more revealing her arresting body, her bejewelled stomach and beautiful feminine self.

She stepped into his arms and he held her tight to his chest. It wouldn't be long before they returned to his bed but before they did he explained his outburst.

"Last night…"

"Yes, I know, I can't explain, I have never done anything so…I have no word for it…the lightning, the wine, the rain…" she replied, almost breathlessly.

"No, let me finish. Yes it was incredible, you, were, are incredible but……this is completely crazy…it's quite the most wonderful thing I have done for a very long time, but…"

"But what?" She could have easily slapped him.

"But I don't know your name!"

She laughed, "Well, then I don't know yours too!"

They stood there, perfectly naked, perfectly connected and perfectly ready to be finally, perfectly introduced.

She gathered her hair up onto her head in a temporary attempt to add some style and then playfully let it cascade over her amber coloured shoulders. She turned around, so that her back was towards him and then teasingly looked over her right shoulder.

The dimples in her lower back, were, he decided, beyond sexy.

"My name is Elena Dimitrova. My friends call me Ele. It means 'the light' in Bulgarian."

He kissed her with a gossamer touch; onto her nose and then, gently, her eyes, alerting her senses once more.

He guided them back into bed, where they would stay for the rest of the morning, exploring one another even further.

"Well Elena Dimitrova, my name is John Cade; but my friends call me Jack."

She grinned, placing her tousled red hair onto his chest; she took a moment to listen to his still pounding heart and spoke, in barely a whisper, "Hello Mr Jack Cade. I have waited a long time to meet a man just like you."

She would use his name many times over during the remaining few hours.

His run could wait; the beach would be there tomorrow.

Chapter Two

He was right. The beach was still there the next day.

But she wasn't.

He left the bed in a heartbeat, searching his home for signs that she wasn't a lurid, fascinating, intensely tangible dream.

He threw on a pair of shorts and the shirt from the night before, then moved rapidly about the property looking for evidence; evidence beyond the smell of her, the haunting echoes of her laughter and sighs of pleasure. The overwhelming sense that she had become a part of his life drove him to find her – she had entered it in a heartbeat, and apparently had left just as quickly.

With precision borne out of training he cleared each room, bedroom, clear, bathroom, clear, lounge, wait. Signs of her existed, her handprints on the exterior glass and more intimate impressions of her on the kitchen worktops.

Two empty glasses.

Congealed red wine on the cool stainless steel surfaces.

Her shoes by the side of the chaise.

Her shoes, by the side of the chaise.

He took a deep breath.

"OK, so this wasn't the best dream I have ever had? Now where are you, you incredible creature?" he offered to an audience of one.

He moved around his home, opening doors, looking outside, he took a moment to reflect upon the storm and what they were doing, just there, only hours before. He smiled, shook his head as if to clear it and carried on.

Now he called her name for the first time since the night before.

Nothing. So she wasn't hiding, a naughty child, trapped in a woman's body. Oh she was wicked alright, my God she was incredible.

He had no doubt that he would have never ended up wrapped around her, inside her, on her, as part of her, in a tropical storm – if she hadn't have offered the intoxicating encouragement via her touch, her whispers and those damned green eyes.

"OK, think this through, look at the options. One, she has had her wicked way and left. A one-night-stand with an older, more experienced guy and she has left; possibly with your wallet. Get over it. Two, she has left, but wants more, but doesn't know how to broach the subject – pursue her, yes follow her, find her, get her back whilst you still can. And your wallet too." Now more serious. "Three – she has been taken."

She had got under his skin, completely, utterly. Was he hooked like a marlin in the deep, clear waters of the ocean, fighting for its life, thrashing, spinning and trying to throw off the predator? So if it was a one-night-stand, could he just forget her?

Rhetorical.

Had she caught him, tagged him and released him? Or let him enjoy the fight and now just tipped him back into the ocean to die?

"OK, calm down, work this out, put some coffee on, relax, turn on the radio, but please don't sing, she's not here, so you have no-one to impress and for God's sake – don't dance man!"

He walked across to the kitchen, opened the cupboard and removed some Colombian Arabica, flicked the switch on the percolator - it made the very best coffee – and found himself removing two mugs from the top cupboard.

He nudged the soft-close door, knowing with some confidence that it would silently do its job, closing, whisper-quietly. Boy the Germans knew how to engineer things.

He placed the mugs on the island worktop. Stopping for a moment to admire the outline of her naked body, ingrained in the clinical metallic surface. Christ, how could he ever remove that?

He picked up his phone and thought about snapping a picture whilst he still could.

"Cade, you weird bastard what are you doing?"

He laughed at himself, something he'd been unable to do for a very long time.

"Perhaps next time you can film it for posterity?"

He shook his head again, still trying to remove the recurring video playback. He cursed himself for thinking such a thing. Give it a week.

The coffee started to bubble, filling the room with a heady scent, alerting his mind before it even reached his lips. Despite trying to be 'normal' he was distracted. "Where are you girl?"

A new song came onto the radio; a few lines permeated his sub-conscious until he became aware that he was singing along to it.

He laughed again, "I don't even know who you are Olly Murs, but your song seems to sum up my feelings right now."

"Where do I begin?
Should I tell you how bad I need you now?
Yeah, you're underneath my skin, but I'm confused, my head is spinning all around, oh!
I waited so long…
Please don't let me go…"

He repeated the last few words before turning suddenly. His hearing alerted to a new sound, deeper, a low snarl, an engine and a superior one too.

Instinctively he picked up both of the mugs and walked out onto the decking as a late-model gunmetal grey Porsche Cayman purred to a halt on his driveway, the thumping bass line to Cher's *"Believe"* disguising the familiar tick of a hot engine, the crackling of super-heated brake discs.

The driver was dancing inside, dancing like no-one was watching, but she knew that Jack Cade was of course watching. She wore a familiar dress; Bvlgari sunglasses concealed those bright green eyes, her dark red hair glistened, but nothing could disguise that beautiful smile. She raised both hands over the leather steering wheel, shrugged her shoulders and blew a kiss.

She was back. Thank God.

He tried not to rush towards her, like a worried father-figure or a schoolboy with a crush on his art teacher. He waited for what seemed like a lifetime as she exited the car, her wonderful legs revealed to anyone that was watching. She swung out of the Porsche and popped the bonnet switch. She leaned in, just far enough for a hint, a suggestion of bare thigh – and higher, to be offered to its one-man audience.

She lifted out a brown leather overnight bag, leaving behind a matching case. Perhaps stereotypically she stood up and swished her hair in the gentle breeze.

She was back.

"Good morning Jack Cade, you like my car? Now this is not a Hairdresser's car! One day, if you are a good boy I will let you drive it but I don't think you ready for its power…" she ran her hand suggestively over the bonnet, caressing the V line of the panel. It reminded him of the very same area on her body.

She stopped at the badge and pointed.

"She handles like a very bad girl; fun, exciting, flirtatious, daring, occasionally dangerous and very, very naughty. Always, she is naughty."

He smiled, a relieved smile, but one that he hoped wouldn't display a hint of relief.

"It's not about the car, it's about the driver! Coffee?" he beckoned to the outdoor loungers – probably the only furniture to have escaped the previous night's escapades.

"We shall see, later, tomorrow, we have race no?"

She dropped her bag on the deck and sat on the bed, flicking her shoes off.

"The best thing about the car? I drive it like I rented it!"

He laughed, hesitated then followed with a cautious "I've missed you."

She looked straight into his cobalt eyes, took a sip of the heady brew, breathing in its vapour before saying "I have missed you more Mr Cade. Sorry if I worried you this morning. I leave to go to my apartment; it is my last day there before I move on. I don't feel good there, there are some men who…"

"They cause you problems?"

"No, no, they just look at me when I go swimming, men from my home land."

"I would look at you when you were swimming Elena Dimitrova - you are a beautiful woman."

"I know."

"Modest too. Anyway, we never had chance to speak last night" he paused realising that they had hardly exchanged more than a few conventional words in nearly eight hours, "I was going to ask where you were staying but I didn't want to…be too…pushy."

She replied in her staccato English.

"Jack, be pushy person, I like that, since I met you I want to be with you more than any man, like you say last night, I not sure why we come together" she giggled at her choice of words, clearly it meant the same in Bulgarian too.

"Me too, me too. By the way Mrs Richards from *The Lofthouse* rang me to complain about our nocturnal activities, she asked that next time we give her fair warning so that she can view the whole show."

She blushed intensely before throwing a cushion at him, then stood and leant across to kiss him, affording him a perfect view down the front of her dress, all the way to those adorable legs.

She emptied her cup and asked a new question.

"May I take your shower?" she started to walk, then turned, "Jack, I want to stay - I know we don't yet know each other but I want to stay, is that OK?"

"Of course, how long for?" he asked, somewhat hopefully, hopefully not too desperately.

"Forever! No only joke, I must leave Monday, I have flight booked to Europe." She pulled a theatrically sad face.

Seizing the opportunity and suddenly fearing that she might leave his life as quickly as she had entered it he asked "Do you have to go? I make great coffee and I can cook too, I have a nice home, what I thought was a reasonable car and I'm only minutes from great beaches" he clicked his thumb and forefinger together and pointed at her.

"Your visa, how long do you have left?"

"Five months."

"Then why not stay – please?"

This was possibly the most reckless thing he had ever done, he'd met the girl twenty four hours before and now he wanted her to stay. She could be the world's greatest con artist, a travelling international thief, but he'd ID her in a heartbeat, wouldn't he?

Surely she hadn't exposed his gullible side? Right now if he'd been offered a chance to invest in a West African bank he would have taken it. 'Yes Mr Prince Sunday Blessings, you seem like a very fine man indeed, here is my account number and don't forget the PIN now!'

Reckless.

But something deep within him said she was trustworthy and his instinct counted for a great deal.

For a moment he started to recall the early days of his doomed marriage, albeit one that had started well. They'd met as young people, she was two years his junior, he'd just joined 'The Job' – or as everyone else not connected to the world of law enforcement called it – the Police Force. It was a force then, and he liked that. As it gradually became a Service he felt less inclined towards it.

They did what most newly-weds did, went out with friends, had what they thought was daring sex in daring places, struggled to make ends meet and slowly began to form a relationship. Sadly, like many in the law community it would be doomed to failure. Fortunately there would be no children as a result of the loveless union.

Long hours, late nights, stress and limited opportunities to take leave meant that they started to drift apart – in the relationship and in the bedroom. Of course 'she' blamed him for everything; low income, low morale and in her opinion at least, a poor sex drive. If they weren't at it like rabbits in the local park or trying to break into abandoned buildings to have frenzied sex, then frankly, she was not interested in him and may as well have been alone.

She hated that he was so suspicious of everything, everyone and all this did was build up resentment, on both sides, but insidiously on his. As the marriage had started to decay the rows become more prominent, more acrimonious – somewhat awkwardly in spite of a continuing sex life.

Somehow as much as she hated him from her side of the fence he clearly wasn't that bad and anyway, on his side he could always imagine he was doing it with someone else. That someone else was normally Kate Winslett.

Unfortunately try as he may he no longer loved her. He would look at her body, which ironically was similar to that of his favourite actress, but every time he moved his eyes slowly up her pretty impressive figure, it was her bloody face on Kate's shoulders!

He recalled one last argument before the inevitable separation occurred. He'd arrived home late – having been 'up north' on an investigation. He was tired, hungry and frankly just needed half an hour to unwind; whilst not a drinker, he could have done with a quiet one.

Within seconds she was confronting him.

"So, why did it take so long to get home, was she good? Where did you do it? I doubt it was outside, you are awful at that – so scared, so bloody suspicious of everyone Jack, never relaxed, good old Jack Cade, a man for all seasons but never around for his wife. Good old Jack Cade…"

It was evident that she'd beaten him to the bottle.

"You always look for the bad in everyone Jack; it's so bloody tiring, so fucking, mind-numbingly, unbelievably…"

"So leave. Pack your bags and leave. I won't stand in your way. Oh and for the record I have no one else. You were my first and only – the only one I thought I'd spend the rest of my days with. We made a vow, remember? The fact that I don't perform like a circus chimp every time you want to get your rocks off in someone's garden is hardly my fault, go join a swingers club for Christ's sake, at least then you'll be happy. No doubt you'll wear them out soon too – the poor bastards!"

"At least I'd be happy, I'd rather do it with three men that were enjoying me than one who thinks about that bastard bloody Winslett all the time! At least they'd be bloody relaxed!"

She stormed away as usual, normally upstairs to bed and the night would end once more with him in the spare room, staring at the ceiling and questioning his existence. He'd drift off eventually, imaging life on a remote island in the South Pacific being served tropical fruit by a redhead wearing nothing but Chanel No 5 and a smile. He loved redheads, hated blondes; she was blonde these days, 'upstairs' at least – the hideous cow.

Perhaps she was right? Perhaps he was suspicious of every one and every thing. A turn of events had certainly offered a period of calm, a chance to get away from it all and start again. Life had been good since then. He'd paid her off - the spiteful whore - and now at last, in the present day perhaps finally he was able to do as she commanded all those years ago – relax.

His guard was finally down and it felt extraordinarily good.

He watched Elena walk towards the bathroom, as she neared the door she loosened both straps on her dress and allowed it to fall neatly onto the ground, stepping out of it in one fluid movement she looked over her shoulder - did that thing again with her eyes - and walked into his bathroom, teasingly, deliberately perhaps, leaving the door ajar.

His instinct was purely animal but he knew he had to proceed with caution, so instead of following her with a hound dog expression and loitering outside the door, he remained on his lounger, which admittedly he'd repositioned 'just so'. Just so he could admire her in the large walk-in shower.

Moments later he was aroused from his daydream.

He'd lasted four minutes and twenty six seconds before he joined her. Four minutes longer than she had hoped for.

Later he wrapped a large chocolate-brown towel around her and a matching one for her hair. He knew how to appeal to the innermost needs of a woman – if he'd learned nothing else from 'her' it was that a few throw away lines, a couple of compliments and an occasional admiring glance were often all that was needed for a quiet life.

He wrapped another similar towel around his waist and walked towards the kitchen.

"More coffee?"

"Yes please. And I need to eat. My energy is…gone!" she giggled as she left the sauna-like bathroom, her handprints slowly vaporising on the smoked glass shower cabinet.

She arrived in the kitchen ten minutes later, her hair still damp but now much lighter in colour, revealing the true redness, a colour which truly appealed to him. Once more she was wearing just a pair of white knickers and one of his business shirts.

He found himself thinking that at this rate they would *never* get anything done. It made him smile – as if that was really a problem?

"What Jack Cade, why make you smile?"

"It's what make you smile."

"Nothing, what make you smile?"

"Don't worry, just a quiet thought, so what are your plans for today?"

He asked as he still didn't know enough about her to even begin to plan for the next hour let alone the rest of the day.

He knew how old she was, that her name was Elena and that she was in her late twenties. But why was she in New Zealand, and more than anything else he needed to know, still, why she was now sat on a chrome bar stool, in his kitchen wearing his favourite blue shirt?

"So my Bulgarian beauty, what do you do?" She looked at him, slightly confused, "I drink your coffee and eat your muesli, it's good, needs more fruit but you try some?" She offered him her spoon, laden with oats and dried fruit.

"No, sorry, what do you do for a job? Where do you live? Do you…have a boyfriend? Family? Why are you in New Zealand?"

"What are you, a Detective or something?" She laughed and threw a dried cranberry at him, it bounced off his cheek and into the sink.

Instinctively he grabbed it and like a schoolboy threw it straight back, down the front of her shirt.

She laughed openly, "For later Jack?"

"Something like that…so, come on, what do you do?"

It was as if she had skilfully negotiated her away around that particular question.

"Of course, sorry, you ask, I not tell. I am a secret agent for Bulgarian government, my grandfather was too. He taught me so many things; how to shoot, how to drive, how to kill a man with my bare hands, how to live in the forest, to escape, climb mountains, swim…"

She quickly became aware of his changing face.

"No silly, I work for Bulgarian government; I am Architect – a Planner for the future of our beloved country!" She emphasised the latter, almost as if she were delivering a speech to the Communist Party.

"So Mr Cade" her Bulgarian accent purred as she spoke, "what do you do?"

"Well, I too am a secret agent, but for the British government. They taught me how to shoot, to drive, to make love to beautiful women, to cook, clean and how, most importantly to hunt down Bulgarian Architects…"

She threw another cranberry at him. This one hit him squarely in the eye. He gave chase; they danced, weaved and ducked around the stainless steel island until she gave in. He lifted her over his shoulder and took her outside to the outdoor shower.

Pinning her to the wall he held the shower head to hers and demanded the truth.

"Your last chance Dimitrova. Tell me the truth or else…"

"Or else what Jack Cade…you wouldn't…it's your best shirt!"

She had a point.

Sod it.

He turned the water supply on to full, a powerful jet of ice-cold water shot out and hit her. She evaded his grasp and started to run but it was too late, he got her, gunning her down in cold blood. She disappeared around the corner of the building, squealing like a teenager.

It was quite the most ridiculous game he had played, certainly since he was twelve anyway, but it made him laugh, so much so that he sank to his knees, the damp floor and capillary action quickly making his shorts wet.

He looked up to see her returning, now on the counter attack, a bright green plastic bucket in one hand and a brush in the other. He knew that the contents of the bucket were destined for him; quite what she planned to do with the brush was anyone's guess. What was clear was that she was quite the sexiest-looking cleaner he had ever laid his eyes on.

With a deftly aimed shot the water left the bucket and hit him in the chest, she followed up with a swift one-two jab with the brush.

"How dare you say I have boyfriend! You are my man now! I should kill you with my deadly…brush! Tell me, what you do?"

She fell into his arms and they continued to laugh. Standing there, both soaked, both laughing, it felt for all the world like they were a married couple, except this time Jack Cade was enjoying the experience, and somehow he too had avoided the real question.

"I work for a company as a Consultant on information security."

It was almost true. He did consult. He also did many other things. His real expertise was using his many years of knowledge and importantly even more years of connections to hunt down people groups, to find the thorns in the sides of what was known colloquially as The Five Eyes.

She nodded pensively before hitting him with the brush, just a little harder than she had anticipated.

It was clear she wasn't happy with his explanation. The brush began to rise in her hand once more.

"OK, OK don't hurt me" he pleaded; in truth he could have disarmed her of the deadly cleaning utensil in a heartbeat, but why? This was fun.

"I spent some time working for the British government – my specialism was border intelligence, identity crime and people groups. There, now you know. I have told you something that not many people know. It had better be worth it."

What he had told her was about twenty percent of the total picture, but it was true nonetheless. His time with the British government spanned many years, covered many aspects of the criminal world and saw him trained by a number of Commonwealth nations. He was what many governments referred to as an asset.

It was what attracted his wife to him in the first place and yet Elena hadn't known this, therefore, in his mind at least, she had been attracted to his personality and devilish good looks.

The resultant full-on kiss showed that it was indeed worth it.

An hour later and seemingly content with their answers they were once again dry and dressed, he in a clean pair of shorts and a black Hurley T shirt, her in a different, but equally striking summer dress.

They walked along the road, away from his house, admiring the yachts and motor cruisers en route to the beach. He discreetly checked his watch – a stainless steel Citizen Nighthawk Eco-Drive – it was almost four in the afternoon. Where had the time gone?

They walked arm in arm along the sand as the chatter of Oystercatchers filled the air, their distinctive flight a familiar sight to Cade but enough to make Dimitrova stop and stare.

"This is so beautiful here Jack. I do not want to go home. I didn't before, but now…"

Her words were consumed by the pounding surf which threw up a silky mist, causing the late afternoon sun to refract, throwing rainbow-like colours into the sky.

He shouted back "So don't. Stay. We can work something out: live for now. I've spent too long looking over my shoulder and regretting things I have done, things I should have done. I have money; I can support you, even with your Architect's car…"

"I have money Jack, but thank you. I could get job here, no? I could work for you. I am very skilled, no?"

"Absolutely Moneypenny" he replied in a faux Bond accent. "Look, at least try and stay for a while longer, we could change your flight tickets, contact your department, tell them…I don't know, tell them you are ill and that you need constant bed rest!" He winked at her, earning himself the second slap of the day.

Over the course of the next few hours they walked the length of the beach. By the time they reached the town they were hungry, weary and ready for a break.

"Come on, let's go and see Big Stan, he owes us a drink."

"He does. Jack?"

"Yes, go on…"

"Everything I have told you is true, what I haven't told you is that I came here to do a particular thing, I can't explain what this is, but now, I don't need to anymore. It is done."

"OK." It was all he could verbally offer.

They walked into The Oceanside and up to the bar.

Big Stan appeared, a cloth over his left arm and an inquisitive look upon his face.

"Jack, how are you…both, today?" he asked, nodding to Cade's female companion with an encouraging smile.

"We are fine thanks Stan. Now, my usual and….a Pimms for the lady please, and make sure the recipe I gave you is followed, to the letter. Mint leaves, cucumber, orange…none of that kiwi fruit or pineapple! We'll be outside."

"Hello Big Stan, I have missed you, Jack tells me you find me sexy!"

She smiled a confident, radiant smile and flounced across the sun-bleached wooden floorboards, her hips gliding from side to side, fiercely aware of their one-man audience.

Cade beamed inwardly, knowing that his local landlord was furious with him, he'd got the girl alright, still not quite sure how, but he had and Stan, well Stan was bloody seething.

Cade felt more alive than he had done since the delectable Jacqueline Clark had asked him to dance at the sixth form disco and that, as he recalled, had been a significant moment in his journey to adulthood.

He tried not to stare at his newfound companion as they sat outside and watched the sun slowly align itself with the horizon, creating myriad colours that would amaze the gathered mix of local and tourist alike. All too quickly he realised that she was already staring at him, clearly she didn't care so why should he?

He paused for a second, "Seriously Elena, I know most rational people would think I am mad, but please stay. We have a few days; think about my offer. You don't need to work, you can't, but you can stay here on holiday. Over the next few weeks, months we could become really close."

Praying he wasn't sounding a little too desperate he chinked his glass against hers, causing the condensation to run off the stem and onto her radiant skin.

She licked the water from her wrist and looked up at him.

"I have known you for a long time Jack, we should get married."

It wasn't quite what he had anticipated, but honestly, given the view, given the amazing allure of her, given, well given the last few days, why not?

"OK. Let's do it!"

She looked bemused.

"Jack, I, like you so much but it was a joke, I only met you a few days ago, I'm sorry, I didn't mean to…"

He ushered her words away with a wave of his hand, almost embarrassed at his boyhood naivety.

"Of course, I understand, I was only joking too. Phew, thank goodness for that, that was far too close!"

He feigned a horror-struck facade but suddenly, deep within his psyche he felt that actually it wasn't such a ridiculous idea after all.

She stared out to sea thinking the same.

The spell was broken a short while later when a waitress delivered their food and a refill for the now empty Pimms glass.

After a few hours Jack suggested they should head home, he walked up to the bar to be greeted by Stan, leaving Elena to chat to some tourists.

"Christ mate, how the hell did you manage that? I mean you must be twenty years older at least, if it wasn't for me you wouldn't have stood a chance!"

"Indeed Stanley but there's no accounting for taste my good man, and if it wasn't for me, you wouldn't have a business, so what say you let me pay for the food and drink and if you are really good I'll let you keep your job. Oh and when your jaw has returned to its rightful place you can watch her walk off into what's left of the setting sun, conscious in the knowledge that only I know the answer to the next question upon your lips."

He nodded defeat, aware that all of what Cade had said was indeed correct. He had come into his life at a time when he needed what he called 'left-field support' and in Cade's case it was an impromptu meeting that resulted in his major investment in The Oceanside.

Stan had never questioned where the money had come from, content with Cade's story that he had been the victim of a messy divorce and a subsequent spell of good luck.

Frankly, he didn't really care, Cade had rescued him at the point of taking on water, of drowning, had steered the ship back on course and had seen The Oceanside become quite the most trendy bar and restaurant in town. In a short space of time his investment had been well rewarded.

Stan quite liked his car, albeit he would never admit it, he actually really liked Cade too, he was what the Kiwi's referred to as a 'good bastard', but above all Stan was completely captivated by his friend's companion.

"Twenty years older…lucky bastard…" he muttered as he wondered around clearing glasses from the tables and making small talk, all the while contemplating the answer to the question that only Cade apparently knew the answer to: "How? Lucky bastard".

Cade could tell that his new found friend was tiring – quietly he hoped that she wasn't too tired – so indicated that he would carry her along the beach on his back. He bent his knees and put his arms out ready to accept her legs.

Like a little girl she jumped onto his back and they started to run along the sand, the hissing of the outgoing tide doing its best to drown out her shouts of mock protest.

Arriving back at *Spindrift* he couldn't help admiring her car, but he wouldn't tell of course, that was tantamount to admitting defeat. A sideways glance was all she got.

"I see you looking Jack Cade, you love her, and you want her no?"

She playfully leant over the bonnet, allowing her hemline to rise just far enough to entice him towards her.

"I do, more than you can imagine."

And he did.

It wasn't until the next morning that he would explain his confusion over a light breakfast.

"I meant the car you bad Englishman!"

"Oh, really, how, terribly, terribly naughty of me." His fingers pressed to his lips in an attempt to be plausible.

On this subject he was incredibly translucent and she loved it, as much as she had loved the preceding night. This time things were a little less frantic, less daring, but very much more sensuous.

"Jack I have decided, I stay a few more days then I drive to Auckland and change my tickets, I stay as long as I can, perhaps Big Stan let me work as a Waitress. No?"

"No. Frankly I'd rather you worked for Hugh Heffner. I can find you some work, just not with Big Stan and it cannot be paid."

"Is Mr Heffner a friend of yours?" Her apparent naivety was incredibly attractive.

"No thank goodness, Stan is quite bad enough with his entourage thank you very much; I don't want you adding to it. So, what made you decided to stay a while longer?"

"You can say I am just stupid but I have your love in my first sight, in just a few a days I need you, so, if it makes you happy then yes I stay, until you or the government throws me out!"

He found himself chatting to her, comfortably, with an assurance he had perhaps never had with any female before. Somehow this woman was entirely different. He poured her a fresh coffee and discreetly cleaned the kitchen as she relaxed, now flicking through the channels on the wall mounted television.

"Jack, there is nothing on, your television is worse than ours, we should go to bed. Or go for run, or walk, or race the cars. We only have a few more days before I must go to Auckland, show me this wonderful place, then, we go to bed."

"OK, with such a list I need to prioritise and it's something I'm highly trained to do. If you want to see this beautiful place then we haven't got time to go to bed…"

She feigned disappointment.

"…but if that is what you want, then yes, I guess I can be persuaded at the end of the day!"

She beamed a sunny, carefree smile.

"We've eaten, so for a while a run is out of the question, besides you would never catch me, we've walked the beach a few times, so how about a drive?"

"Yes! I drive though, in a real sports car, no?"

"Yes OK, but only if I get to try her out too, you know, just to see if she handles as well as her owner, to see how she responds to my touch."

It was initially lost on her, but he knew that she somehow understood.

"OK, let's finish our coffee and you can fire up that beast, I have some errands to run in Pauanui, you'll like it there, lots of lovely houses, lovely people, a stunning beach and if you are really good, you can buy me lunch."

They gathered their things and headed for her car, he tapped his code into the house alarm system which responded instantly, locking itself down, waiting for the Master to return.

She was already in the Porsche.

Chapter Three

As he walked towards the Cayman she turned the key. He conceded, she sounded beautiful, animal-like, a discreet, yet sporty tone that hinted at its makers racing pedigree. This was a very nice car indeed, he was envious but desperate not to communicate this to her just yet.

Moments later they were out on the road.

Leaving the town she began to provide a commentary on the cars' engineering – he found this quite surprising, his own prejudice surfacing appallingly.

"You like the sound of the engine Jack? This one has 3.4 litre, six cylinder engine, the sports exhaust, makes it sound....sexy! She has seven-speed PDK twin-clutch automatic too, watch this!"

A deft tap on the steering wheel paddles selected third, causing the car to lunge forwards, gripping the road surface and launching it into a superbly weighted overtake of four other vehicles.

"Nought to one hundred in four and a half seconds Jack!" She was raising her excited voice, better to be heard over the raucous cackle of the engine as it kept pace with her lightning-fast gear changes.

He was impressed. The change-up was magnificent, even better than that on his own car, itself a revelation of engineering.

For a moment neither spoke as she concentrated on driving, really driving. He noted how she used the throttle to balance the car, expertly, holding off, trail braking and then reading the road, skilfully, almost playfully. She knew how to drive.

"I love her Jack. She is so, amazing. Feel that power. It excites me, almost as much as you excite me." She laughed at his puppy-dog expression. "It's OK Jack, I love you really."

Mile after mile melted away, bends treated with respect, straights treated with utter contempt, slower traffic passed in a moment. The combination of chassis, transmission and sheer refined power had him hooked. He loved the Audi, but he *wanted* this.

It had never once crossed his mind to ask how she had come to have it in her possession. Perhaps it should?

'Perhaps Jack you should just bloody relax for once in your down-trodden, cesspit-inhabiting life?' he found himself musing as she deftly threw the car from corner to corner.

As they made incredible progress across country he finally began to relax, no longer mentally, and at times physically braking for her. He hadn't been this impressed in the passenger seat for a long time.

The last time he saw driving this good – and at the hands of a female, well, that was a while ago and in another country.

She turned on the Bose eight speaker surround sound system. AC/DC's *Thunderstruck* rumbled through the multiple speakers, a perfect accompaniment to the performance of the Cayman.

Soon they were singing along to its chanting chorus.

"Thunder!"

"Thunder!" Elena threw a punch in the air to each chant, steering skilfully with the other hand.

Jack knew he couldn't match Brian Johnson's screaming, rasping voice so he didn't try, but inwardly he was belting out the tune.

He looked into his door mirror occasionally, old habits die hard.

As they had left Whitianga he had noticed a black Rolls Royce, not exactly the rarest thing on the road, but this was a Wraith; new to the country, extremely expensive and very, very powerful. It was a leviathan and it had his utmost respect; nearly two tons of motoring madness.

Since the very early days out on the beat, alone and always in the pouring bloody rain he'd been observant. Frankly if you weren't you we failing to do your job – and importantly in the worst possible case you would end up injured, dead or worse.

He smiled inwardly at the thought of being worse than dead.

'Cops eh Cade, half the time you don't want to be on duty and the other, well you're never bloody off!'

He was running a few memories around in his head of the 'old days' and tried to push the Wraith out of his mind. Life was good and right now it was quite frankly abso-bloody-lutely wonderful. Quite why this girl had entered his life he still wasn't one hundred percent sure.

Should he be suspicious? Should he check her out? That is more than he already had; one thing was for certain she didn't have too many hiding places left.

He took a deep breath, almost under his breath and let himself unwind.

Another look in the tinted passenger mirror rewarded him with an empty road; the Wraith had turned off down a farm track.

It was replaced by a bright red Volkswagen Golf R.

"Nice" he said out loud.

"Thank you Jack, you like my driving?"

"I do, sorry I was talking about the Golf behind us, very capable, very quick and half the price of this beast!"

"Yes Jack, but it's a Golf. Question, who is your favourite actress?"

"Kate Beckinsale for looks, Kate Winslett for acting" he replied without hesitation.

"OK, so I tell you to spend the night with me or Kate – you choose me right? Yes, it is same with Golf, very fast, nice car, but which one go in your garage at end of day – the Porsche. Anyway, it is being driven by a boy!"

Clearly unaware of the aspirant Bulgarian racing driver behind the Cayman's wheel the young male in the Golf decided it was time to try out his new steed and changed down to fourth as he applied pressure to the throttle.

Both cars were on the Tairua-Whitianga Road heading south.

As the Golf got alongside the Cayman the driver took a split second to look to his left. For some reason he had stereotypically expected to find an elderly, wealthy female behind the wheel, driving, like Miss Daisy, instead he found himself looking into the startling green eyes of a drop-dead gorgeous twenty something that he would have frankly exchanged his car and both legs for, in a heartbeat.

What made the event even more fanciful was that the anonymous female blew him a kiss, waved and then hurtled off down the road before he had chance to get past her.

He lunged back to the left hand side of the road and accelerated, coming up behind her quickly as she braked for a sweeping left hand bend.

Jack tried his best to remain relaxed, looking across the headland to the azure-blue Pacific Ocean.

"Lovely day for a race Miss Dimitrova!" he offered, knowing that she was now operating at a different level.

"Jack, I'm showing this boy how to drive" she responded a little too excitedly for his liking. Despite his years of advanced driving he knew that these mountain roads were unforgiving at best – equally he knew that a full-blooded Eastern European goddess was not to be messed with either. It would take a brave man to halt her progress.

The Cayman darted left and right, the Golf driver refusing to yield.

They approached the small hamlet of Coroglen, she left the braking until very late, double-tapped the paddle shift system and dropped the car from sixth to third, its engine providing the opportunity for her to make the change appear almost imperceptible, but above all intensely fast.

They flew over the Waiwawa River and soon got up to 130 mph. The car was capable of much faster and apparently so was its driver. Jack had warned Elena about the roads and the local Highway Patrol, who were, in his words 'less forgiving than the roads they patrolled' but for now at least she had erased his words from her immediate memory.

The joust continued for another twelve miles. To many it would have been an eternity, to them, a game, a game of Big Cat and Ferocious Mouse. Neither of course would admit to being the rodent.

The scenery reminded her of home but with the notable addition of the cobalt blue Pacific Ocean which was in her peripheral vision; hazy with occasional whitecaps, an ever-present mass of sparkling sapphire and pristine sandy coves which intermittently revealed themselves among the pine forests and plunging valleys.

Bends continued to be treated with contempt, straights shortened and hills ridiculed. She was enjoying every inch of the journey and the car seemed to be perfectly matched to any given command.

He conceded however that given the cost, his next car may well be the Golf, its own performance outstanding in such exalted company.

"Let him by, he's earned it, poor boy" suggested Cade with a wry smile.

"Never!" proclaimed Dimitrova with a pump of the fist.

At one point cade watched her slowly, provocatively lick her lips.

They dropped into the town of Tairua alongside its beautiful harbour, their speed now at a sedentary level and more in keeping with the environment. Jack switched on the radio. A song was playing, he was unsure of the singer, but he loved the words.

> "*Lady running down to the riptide,*
> *Taken away to the dark side,*
> *I wanna be your left hand man*
> *I love you when you're singing that song*
> *And I got a lump in my throat because*
> *You're gonna sing the words wrong…*"

The song finished, a local DJ announced that it was called *Riptide* by Vance Joy before going on to describe the weather for the next few days. Cade noted the title for another time.

Once through the town she opened up the Cayman again, but for some reason as they hurtled along State Highway 25 towards the wonderfully-named Duck Creek she slowed, placed her arm out of the window and allowed her challenger to pull up alongside her.

The Golf driver didn't hesitate for a second and soon they were cruising at a respectable eighty miles an hour, windows down and comparing vehicles. The air whistled by her window as she yelled to her opponent.

"I let you win!" she shouted to the good-looking male, a young European who had clearly done reasonably well for himself. Cade guessed that he had entered the world of Information Technology early in life and was now reaping the rewards.

Red Golf carried out micro-adjustments to his steering, desperate to avoid running off into the water-filled ditches that were an ever-present feature in this part of the world.

Designed to take the sting out even the most powerful tropical or winter storm they mirrored the road perfectly, adding safety but a hint of danger too – a driver, and particularly an inexperienced one, only had to place an errant wheel on the gravel to find themselves tumbling out of control and into a nearby field. The unlucky ones would meet their fate by careering down into a pine-filled gorge.

"I let you let me!" he shouted back, enjoying the automotive flirting before decelerating sharply to allow a large truck to proceed north.

He whipped the car back alongside the Porsche once more and this time noticed Cade. He nodded, as if in apology, perhaps for chatting up his...daughter?

Cade, ever one to skilfully read body language leant across and shouted "If you think she's a maniac on the road you should try her in the bedroom!"

Suddenly unsure of what he had got himself into the Golf driver nodded, smiled and floored the throttle, soon creating a healthy gap between the two cars.

"Jack! You scared him off. Anyway, he was a boy in the car so he would be a boy in the bedroom!"

Red Golf found himself pondering a few questions: Who was she? Why was she of such interest? And fascinatingly was that a roadside offer of a swinging session? That was a first! He might never know, but assured himself that whatever the outcome he had enjoyed the journey. Whoever the older guy was, for now, he was a lucky man.

The couple indicated left and turned towards the stunning town of Pauanui as the Golf headed south west towards Kopu Bridge and the inevitable drive North to Auckland. Dimitrova flashed her lights earning a double flash of the Golf hazard lights.

On the way to Pauanui he questioned her about her driving skills.

"Forgive me for asking but where the bloody hell did you learn to drive like that?"

She laughed openly "Jack, I intimidate you?"

"No, far from it, actually I found it to be a real turn on. Most women, with a few exceptions, can't drive a car like this, like…that." He nodded back to the Tairua Road.

"My father and my brother, they teach me. When I was little girl I learned on the family farm, my uncle, he had lots of land so we drive fast – everywhere!" she paused as if recalling a time in her past.

"But you would have had something much slower than this?"

"Of course, but I learn. I find a good-looking boy and make love to him for days until he introduced me to his father…"

"My God you slept with him too?"

She slapped his thigh "No naughty Jack, his father owned a garage!"

"Yes, now I understand."

"I don't think you do. His son was terrible in bed. So I had affair with his father, it was worth it to get to drive the Porsche 911 Turbo, a car so sexy I just look at it and have…" she ran a few words through her mind before completing the sentence "…orgasm."

She bit her lower lip for the rest of the journey which Cade found instantly sexy. She was desperate not to reveal that the story was almost entirely untrue. She had worked as a valet at Sofia Airport, deliberately as it transpired, so that she could drive the latest vehicles from the parking bay to the garage, her 'little detours' proving invaluable in her learning curve.

Eventually she would meet a man, they would become lovers of course but in truth she only ever wanted him for the car. His pathetic, lumbering skills in the bedroom were worth enduring for the chance to drive and Bulgaria, well it had some of the best driving roads, anywhere.

The truth was he was starting to read her like a book. Trained in NVC's – non-verbal communications – he could watch and observe, detect the slightest 'tell' and a blatant lie was nigh on impossible to miss. So why, he often asked himself, was he so terrible at poker?

Ten minutes later Elena parked up on Jubilee Drive and walked into The Lime Room, a local bar and restaurant.

Jack recommended the burger; simple, well done and wholesome, Elena followed his lead and they both had a fruit juice, it was clear already that neither wanted alcohol as there would be a fight over the keys on the way home.

After a few minutes a distinguished-looking male walked across the bar towards them. Lean and tanned, he had salt and pepper hair, swept back ever-so-slightly, Jaguar titanium-framed glasses perched awkwardly on top of his head allowing his Cornish-slate eyes to sparkle. They were one of his most disarming features and he used them very skilfully, particularly around the opposite sex.

He was dressed in a Ralph Lauren polo shirt over a pair of beige chino shorts. He wore deck shoes on his feet. The casual, yet classy ensemble was completed with a black-faced Omega De Ville wristwatch.

The male, who many women felt resembled a young Omar Shariff stood straight in front of Cade then held him at arm's length – as if to examine the goods he had just purchased and then drew him in for a very positive 'man hug'.

"John Cade, as I live and breathe; how are you young sir?"

"I'm well my friend; very well, it's bloody good to see you again. Allow me to introduce my friend to you. Elena Dimitrova, this is a very old friend of mine from the past, we cut our teeth together in the United Kingdom, meet John Daniel."

Daniel leant forward, picking up her right hand and placing a perfectly weighted kiss onto the surface of her skin. Some older men would not get away with it, but Daniel had made it into an art form, charming the ladies around the globe since before Jesus was a lad, apparently. His healthy looks and relaxed style belied the fact that he was nearly sixty five.

"Delighted to meet you John Daniel, Jack did not tell me he had younger brother!" which earned her an incredulous look from her man.

"Udovolstvieto da se zapoznaem Miss Dimitrova. I have heard so much about you. Tell me, what is a beautiful Bulgarian girl doing with an aging and neurotic Brit like Cade? You let me know if you get tired of him, I have a great business going here and could always look after you!"

He reaffirmed his intentions with a playful wink and a peck on her left cheek before succumbing to a deftly delivered flick of a tea towel from his hitherto unseen wife's hand.

"Ouch!"

Clutching his now reddening ear he continued "And this aggressive beast Elena is my wonderful wife of forty years, she's called Lynne. Lynne this is Jack's new 'friend'" he did that fashionable thing with the fingers of both hands to indicate speech marks.

Both John and Lynne conceded that Cade was a lucky man before Lynne offered Elena a chance to look around the restaurant and their adjoining home.

She took the subtle hint and left her new man to talk to his old friend.

"So my boy, you staying the night? A chance to knock the top off a couple? I've got a twenty year old Laphroaig that's just begging to be sampled. You up for it, or as I suspect do you have an altogether new hobby these days? My God she is *fabulous*, where…"

He interrupted his old mate. "John I haven't got a clue, she came into my life only a few days ago but we seem to have gelled so quickly."

With a wicked grin and the twist of a non-existent moustache Daniel gave him hell.

"Oh come on man, you expect me to believe that a drop-dead-gorgeous girl like that just walks into your life, shags you senseless, lets you drive her Porsche and then announces her undying love for you is actually genuine? Come on mate you are losing your touch. It's not your money, so what is she after?"

"You know JD I've got more money than you would imagine, things are going well, you know The Oceanside in Whitianga?"

"I do, you own it."

"Bugger, you haven't lost your skills have you, you crafty old fox!"

"Look Jack any man would give his right arm for a few nights with such a looker but be careful, you don't know a lot about her, you've spent years hunting Eastern European criminals, you know the syndicates, the top players, so why now after all these years do you roll over like a pup and let her get under your skin without a fight?"

"Fair point JD but, I don't know" he shook his head as if to clear it "she's just so special, we hit it off immediately – well after I accused her of being a…"

"Hooker, yes I heard! Nice chat up line boy, have you learned nothing from The Master?"

"Sounds like you have been talking to Big Stan, the loud-mouthed bastard!"

They laughed just like old times before Daniel changed the subject rapidly, seeing the women making their way back to them he took the opportunity to exchange some work-related information with his friend; it was after all the reason for his visit. He was too old for field work now but he knew he could rely on his old team mate to track down someone for another old acquaintance from the United Kingdom.

He laid out some paperwork on the bar table, turned a couple of pages and then said "Find him and there's a few thousand on the table. He's missing from Berkshire, his rather wealthy wife has reported him absent to the UK authorities - he's gone off the radar and she thinks he's shacked up with some equally rich bird here. This is a true case of hell hath no fury! Mind you seeing who he's with now one can hardly blame him; exquisite shape, great taste and probably twenty years his junior. I mean, who could be so lucky?"

He winked at Cade and indicated to a monochrome image "I've carried out the basics Jack but I can't be arsed to continue with it. The job's yours if you want it, if nothing else it will help you keep your hand in and avoid becoming stale. After all I'd hate for you to be taken in by a striking twenty eight year old redhead with a penchant for outdoor lovemaking."

"Christ is there *nothing* you don't know?"

John Daniel skilfully brought his protégé back down to earth as he beamed a huge grin and laughed a raucous laugh before clashing his glass onto Cade's. The women returned to the table, the early effects of a bottle of house red starting to impact upon their step. It had all the hallmarks of a fun day.

"I see you two have reacquainted far too quickly" announced Lynne Daniel, a grand looking woman with naturally dark hair and a slim and attractive figure, the apparent regular work in the gym aimed at hanging onto her somewhat playful husband.

"And I see you two have acquainted with a bottle of my house red!"

The foursome spent the next few hours chatting; chatting about the past but being careful to balance the conversation with the future, in their case the restaurant industry on the Coromandel Peninsula – a place that both Daniel and Cade had gravitated to from Europe.

If the truth were to be known Daniel always knew exactly where his pupil was, he'd sworn a debt of gratitude many years before and had made it his life's work to uphold his end of the bargain.

Daniel subtly tested the Bulgarian, probing questions being used to elicit some of her background.

"Smashing car Elena. I wish I could afford one like it."

"Yes, I am lucky, no?"

"You are, very. Just make sure Emerson Fittipaldi here doesn't wreck the damned thing!"

She laughed but honestly had no idea who he was referring to.

"It is just a rental!"

"Ah, I see. Well it's certainly nicer than the Toyota Corolla I normally end up with. Here, try this" JD suggested to Elena as a plate laden with lime meringue pie arrived at the table.

"We serve it with vanilla cream, and a heavenly tropical compote, really brings out the flavour of the limes, it's our signature dessert."

He was right, it was sublime.

The night came to an end with the two ladies hugging one another and promising to stay in touch.

"Look after him Elena, whatever you are doing keep doing it, he's not looked this good for years!"

"I promise I will. Tell me was he a good man to work with JD?"

"Yes, he was Elena." He was guarded and skilfully avoided the obvious question.

"And whatever you are doing for this old dog make sure you tell Mrs Daniel too as it's certainly put a spring in his step!" offered John Daniel as he sealed the goodbye with a firm kiss on her cheek and a playful, almost imperceptible tap on her bottom.

Cade hugged Lynne and promised to keep her updated on any news, then turned to his old friend as the girls walked to the car arm in arm and made small talk.

JD gave his second man hug of the day, but this time just before he let go Cade whispered into his friend's ear "John, have you seen a dark coloured Rolls Royce Wraith around here? Brand new? Dark windows? I haven't seen the plate, not got that close yet."

"No I haven't, sorry. You OK Jack? What is it?"

"Not sure mate, call it a gut feeling."

"You forget my boy we go back a long way, me more so than you. Old habits die hard. Now do me a favour, just watch yourself, you have picked up on this car…"

"And?"

"And I'm wondering who it is too, call it idle curiosity but I'm also wondering just who this sweet little spoonful of honey is with the red hair and the taste for expensive sports cars. Have you not had the same thoughts Jack?"

He had, but for some bizarre reason he found himself trying to separate them: the car from the girl, the girl from the car, the Wraith from the girl and vice versa. They could not be linked, he was just lucky that she chose him and as he had found in the past, you run with your luck.

Daniel hadn't noticed the Rolls but he promised he would keep a weather eye out for it and report back if he found out who owned it. He knew what such a feeling was and in Cade's world that meant one of two things: Trouble or worse.

"Do me a favour my boy. Let that gut instinct of yours guide you. Remember London. You have enemies in the East. And it's not as big a world as it was when we were growing up."

Dimitrova threw the keys to Cade announcing that she was in no fit state to drive. Cade winked at his friends, they knew how much he loved the road home and in a car like that it wouldn't take long.

"I'll ring you about that job JD. Catch up soon."

He poured his extra-feminine guest into her car and strapped her in.

The drive home was spectacular, the arctic-white headlights illuminating the way as he teased the Cayman back through the mountainous switchback towards his adopted town. He swept past late night tourists and locals alike, the Porsche eagerly consuming the road ahead. A row of camper vans, heading north and probably lost were dispatched in seconds, he accelerated so fast he didn't see the same red Volkswagen in the middle of the convoy.

As he surged on back towards the coast soon all he saw in his rear view mirror were the distant lights of Pauanui. In the valley below a stream of headlights from the convoy he had overtaken continued to snake around the steep mountain pass, a convoy that included the red Golf and at the rear a new arrival, the dark automotive leviathan that Rolls Royce had christened the Wraith.

Elena Dimitrova slept the whole journey, oblivious to the movements of the car and the contemplative silence of its driver.

Chapter Four

They pulled up onto the drive at *Spindrift*. The sensor lights lit up the driveway and the path to the front door. Hidden but noisy crickets called to one another as he opened the passenger door and scooped out his girlfriend.

"Come on Miss P let's get you to bed."

She stirred "Ooh Mr Cade you are so strong, I hope you don't take advantage of me..." she giggled a drunken giggle before slumping into his arms once more.

He navigated his way to the front door, put the key in the lock, walked inside and kicked the door shut with his foot. En route to the bedroom he nudged a wall light with his shoulder and tapped a familiar number into the alarm panel. Arriving at the bedroom he flicked up the duvet with all the skill of a Premier League football player and then placed her gently onto the sheets.

He slipped off her shoes but decided against the inevitable fight with her dress, sorely tempted though he was. Instead he rolled the duvet back over her now sleeping body and watched her fall into a deep slumber.

He pulled a chair up to the side of the bed and placed his now bare feet onto the covers and watched her for a full ten minutes. He marvelled at the colour of her hair, her skin tone and her sheer untainted beauty. He smiled to himself at his incredible luck. In a moment of madness this girl had entered his world, he had almost let her go and now, well now he was contemplating a possible future with her - the relationship felt that extraordinary.

But his instinct was yelling at him. 'This may be too good to be true'.

He was one hundred percent besotted and whilst he hated himself for falling so quickly for a member of the opposite sex, he somehow knew that this one was different.

As he watched her chest silently rising and falling, JD's words appeared in his mind "Be careful Jack".

He woke a few hours later with a start and realised that it had been a very long day, much longer than he had anticipated. He massaged his neck, got undressed and slipped under the bedclothes. She moved gently towards him to accept his embrace. They both slept better than they had done for years.

Morning was heralded by the frantic call of gulls in the nearby moorings; the arrival of a local boat with fish on board had ensured their eager and ravenous presence. It was a sound that Jack enjoyed; it reminded him why he chose to live near to the sea.

He rose before her and carried out his daily ritual. A wet shave, using some newly marketed citrus gel - it left his skin feeling alive - at least that is what it said on the tube. He then stood for a full minute with a volcanically-hot flannel on his face, a trick he learned somewhere exotic some years before.

He slipped out of his towel and into the shower. It was one of his major vices. The system allowed water to pour down from a rainfall fitting onto his body; the smooth, almost silk-like water washed over him, ideal for a morning when he had the luxury of time.

Today he switched the system to power out the water from a number of jets in the wall. The steamy liquid ricocheted off his body and onto the tempered, tinted glass. It quickly began to unravel the many knots in his damaged body.

As usual he was soon lost in the mist and began to formulate his plans for the day – he laughed as sometimes he would even write up his 'things to do' list on the glass door before erasing it with the shower head – old habits died hard. Leave no trace.

He was so lost that he didn't hear the door open. Somewhat startled he opened his eyes to make out the divine shape of his Bulgarian concubine.

She stepped into his arms and they both stood, taking in the sheer power and heat of the shower. It was a wonderful start to the day. He turned her around to wash her, gently allowing his hands to 'accidentally' explore the contours of her body once again.

She knew of course exactly what was about to happen and didn't resist in the slightest. It was her intention for this to happen the previous night and she felt a little guilty.

"Jack, last night, I…"

"Shh…I know, it's OK. We had a wonderful day, you were drunk, it was great to see you so happy."

He massaged her shoulders causing her to respond with moans of genuine pleasure.

"JD and Lynne think you are wonderful. Trust me, if he likes you, then you are doing really well!"

"I think he would like to be here now. To feel me do this…"

She lowered herself into the heart of the shower and onto her knees, her head disappearing into the enveloping, intense vapour. Within moments her whole body had vanished into the steam, but he knew precisely where she was.

Her skilful hands and mouth began to work on his body, taking him to an exquisite place in a moment of absolute pleasure, an act made all the more surreal by her almost complete physical absence.

For a brief second his mind reverted back to another time, 2004 to be precise, to a similar scenario but in a different place entirely. A different town, different hemisphere and an entirely different, completely dissimilar girl in fact – one equally passionate but now a distant, if not important and rather evocative part of his past.

Later, having slowly dried each other off, they moved through to the kitchen. Cade switched the faithful coffee machine on and opened the blinds. Elena was still dressed in a towel, a towel that could have all-too-easily been removed.

He smiled outwardly and found himself thinking that he was living a second honeymoon, although this time without the shackles of a marriage certificate. Should his internal alarm system be triggering? Should he just relax? Should, could, would, all words that he currently didn't have time for, choosing to exchange them, albeit possibly naively for 'here' and 'now'.

The weekend came quickly, for Cade it was another day in paradise – the joy of working when he wanted to, as opposed to years of having to work when work dictated that he had to.

The weather put on a truly amazing show so taking the opportunity to see her in a swimsuit he took her to his favourite beach. Like many men the thought of what she was like underneath those summer dresses, and even the smallest of swimsuits did something for him, making the journey towards the next level all the more, enticing.

He had the foresight to pack a picnic that would play tantalising tricks with her taste buds – the fact that he was so well connected to the local restaurant trade appeared to have escaped her grasp – and coupled with a chilled bottle of St Clair Riesling he was guaranteed to impress.

She had great taste and yet, and yet underneath there was something incredibly 'simple' about her, something intensely normal that made her all the more attractive.

The day was spent on the shores of the Pacific Ocean, she found herself thinking that there were worst places to be in the world – and she'd been to a few.

She slipped off her sarong to reveal a simple, elegant, dark blue swimsuit, cut to fit her in all the right places.

Laying on her front, on the blanket that he'd thoughtfully put in the bag, she sighed deeply.

"It's so lovely here Jack, the colours, the sounds, the emptiness is so, how you say? Yes, you say it is super!" She mocked his Englishness which earned her the instant punishment of a very chilled bottle between her shoulder blades causing her to yelp like a new born puppy.

She rolled over to greet his kiss, her tongue quickly savouring the freshness of the wine upon his own lips.

"Last one in is girl!" she announced, quickly up and running to the sea.

"You are so on girlfriend!" he replied as he sprinted past her, diving head-on into the surf. It was the first time he'd done so since she arrived on the scene; he'd missed it, but accepted that he'd been rather busy. He once more found himself thinking that the beach would be there when he was ready, but she could be gone soon.

For a man of such distinction and experience he suddenly felt like a love-sick teenager at the thought of her leaving, to the point of suggesting that if she didn't return he would go to Bulgaria to find her. He chose to leave that conversation for another time, for she was clearly enjoying herself and dragging her down to his level wouldn't be wise on such a fine-looking day.

They remained on the beach until the sun started to nestle onto the horizon.

"It's so beautiful Jack. What are those islands called? Can we go there tomorrow, you know, imagine that we are shipwrecked? We could pretend that we didn't know each other and make love all day!"

"A bit like we have been doing on the mainland then Elena!" he replied with a chuckle. "Is that what shipwrecked people do in Bulgaria?"

"Hey we have beautiful sea and beaches in my country too Jack Cade. One is called Sunny Beach, the other one Gold Sands, they are on Black Sea. I used to go to Burgas as a little girl, we had such good time. I will take you one day."

He put himself there for a moment; all too stereotypically he imagined a rundown sea front with faded colours and grey, miserable people. His mental picture was based not upon imagery from the internet or hearsay but first-hand knowledge.

"Is it as bad as I imagine?" knowing instantly he shouldn't have asked out loud.

"On behalf of Bulgarian people I am insulted by you Mr Cade and will only forgive you if you kiss me again, now, on this beach."

How could he refuse?

Twenty minutes later and still intoxicated on the moment she returned the conversation to the island.

"OK so fine, we don't go then…but I could wear coconut bikini…"

"You could, or we could wonder around naked all the time and I could catch fish and feed them to you. There are no coconuts over there on those islands, you need to head north or east for those; the main island by the way is called Motukorure Island."

"It is so special, what does it mean?"

He paused for effect. "It means the island of the beautiful redheaded maiden…"

"That is so lovely. A beautiful redhead, like me no? Take me there tomorrow Jack?" She had completely missed his playful embellishment.

"Can you swim that far?"

"No, but Big Stan has a boat in the harbour, he told me, he say 'Elena my love I take you to the island and we make love for hours'…"

"I bet he did. He can lend me his boat. I'll take you tomorrow."

And he did.

The next morning they boarded *Black Marlin* and slipped out of the busy harbour. Giving a wave to the Harbour Master on his port Cade waited a few minutes to fully exit the river mouth and then accelerated, the four stroke Hi Power Yamaha VF200 engine dug deep into the water and soon the pale, crystal clear water to their stern turned a vibrant, oxygenated white.

It didn't take too long to clear the harbour and head towards open sea. Within ten minutes they approached their initial goal.

"So there you have it, Motukorure Island, as you can see we can't land, it's too rugged, but I happen to know an island where we can; it's called Ohinau Island. Do you want to go?"

She did and confirmed her intentions by turning away from him and slipping one strap of her swimming costume onto the top of her arm.

"My God you are incorrigible woman!"

"Incorri-what?"

"…rrigible…it means persistent…"

"Per-what?"

"Sistent…it means…"

"I know Jack, I have English major – I know what persistent mean! I was teasing you and you love my tease, no?"

"I do, I love your tease very much Miss Dimitrova, now for God's sake cover yourself up or you'll have the bloody Coastguard after us."

"No Coastguard in New Zealand Jack, I checked." She grinned like an errant schoolgirl and flicked her immaculately preened eyebrows skywards.

He smiled as he once more got the boat up to speed and headed for Ohinau. The *Marlin* made good time as Elena leant out of the starboard side and allowed the pounding surf to throw wildly effervescent splashes of water onto her sun-kissed face; soon they were anchored up and ready to swim the short distance to shore.

Cade grabbed a dive bag – he'd thought ahead. Inside it contained the picnic he'd prepared, a blanket and a bottle of Oyster Bay Sauvignon Blanc. He knew she'd fall for its crisp tropical flavours and the alcohol seemed to relax what was left of her inhibitions.

She emerged from the surf onto the small and very private beach. He soon followed. The sun shone brilliantly – in fact it was incredibly hot and like any good Kiwi host he warned her of the intense damage that the sun could do.

"Make sure you wear this constantly!" He pointed to a tube of sun cream that he was using to cover his face and upper body.

He looked up to see that Elena was stood on the beach – in partial shade – but completely and beautifully naked.

"Rub some into my body Jack Cade – I don't want to spoil my swimsuit."

"For the love of God girl you'll get us arrested!"

"Oh Jack, who can see? If the Coastguard have big telescope let them enjoy it. Tell me you don't like and I will…." She thought for a moment before continuing, clearly trying to come up with an appropriate analogy, "Close the shop!"

The comparison didn't quite work but he knew what she meant and given what was on offer he was more than willing to browse a little longer. He went to speak then stopped.

"What?"

"I was going to ask if you accept American Express…but realised that particular conversation might head down a different path…and after all I'm a gentleman."

She didn't understand but smiled nonetheless. There and then she had not a care in the world. She was with a man she found incredibly attractive, on a beach in the Pacific Ocean, naked with a picnic and not a spectator in sight. What more could she ask for apart from a corkscrew?

"Come Jack, let us swim to the boat – we need a screw on boat."
She ran playfully across the sand and dived through a small wave. She
quickly popped up on the other side, and stood waist deep in clear
water splashing herself provocatively.

"Come on in, the water, is how you say? Fine?"

The view wasn't bad either. He went to run towards her, his dives
were impressive so he intended to show off, why not, after all it wasn't
everyday a man of his age got to swim with a mermaid was it?

"Oh no Mr Cade, there are rules in the sea, you have to be naked
too. Come on, take them off or I will swim away and go to Atlantis!"

"They won't have Oyster Bay Sav in Atlantis!"

She pulled her brilliant sad face once more then mischievously
looked up at him before starting to clap her hands rhythmically "Off!
Off! Off!"

He laughed, "Where did you learn that?"

"Oh come on Jack, I have been to strip bars too, Firemen,
Policemen, Doctors…now you can be…Information Security
Consultantman!"

"In for a penny…" and with that he whipped off his shorts and ran
straight to her, grabbing her around the waist and dragging her under
the waves.

He expected her to panic but instead found himself in deeper water;
an expert swimmer, he looked around, his eyes fully open and soon
focused on her face. It was clear that she was quite adept beneath the
water too. Her beautiful hair swayed in time with the pull of the current
as her arms and legs fought to stabilise her. A small shoal of silver fish
darted by her, almost brushing against her equally exposed body,
causing her to form the 'OK' signal with her right hand.

She smiled. At that moment she couldn't have looked more striking.

The water was cool, and it showed.

With their senses narrowed to sight alone they remained in the
crystal-clear ocean, watching, studying and admiring each other as if
players in an aquatic reverie.

Moments later she had to surface, so with a kick of his feet he
followed.

Gasping for air she swam back towards the boat, reaching it she
hung onto the stern, fighting against the gentle pull of the current. Cade
climbed aboard and as he did so she slapped his backside, so hard that
it instantly left a vivid handprint on his left cheek.

"I, young lady, have a very long memory!"

"So I see Mr Cade, the water is not so cold today!"

He shook his head, amazed at how, despite her linguistic challenges she managed to be ever-so-slightly smutty whilst being incredibly sultry too.

A quick search of the *Marlin's* many cupboards located a corkscrew, he walked to the stern and clutching onto it dived back into the ocean.

"Last one there makes love to the other!"

A race was once more the order of the day. A race, as it happened that neither minded losing.

It was quickly apparent that she could swim and without the resistance of a costume she was probably even swifter than normal. He deliberately slowed, sank beneath the waves and watched her graceful shape being propelled through the cool, clear cerulean water.

Luck was suddenly his favourite four letter word.

She got to the beach first and allowed the gentle surf to wash her onto the sand. He joined her and lay next to her. They remained in the surf for a while, staring up at the sky and joining together via just their little fingers.

She turned to him and placed a perfectly weighted kiss onto his damp lips; he reciprocated and within moments they were making love among the waves. It was stereotypical of so many movie scenes and yet so incredibly intense too. The waves did their best to encourage a natural sense of rhythm.

About a mile offshore other boats went about their business, heading to the best fishing spots, apparently oblivious to the activities on the remote island.

They lay there on that silica bay, panting, covered in a fine film of perspiration and both began to laugh. Being an eternal gent he covered her in a towel, gently drying her and reapplying sun tan lotion. As he did so he asked a rhetorical question.

"Elena, are we the luckiest people alive?"

"Yes" was all she could say.

"Oh, and another thing, is it just me or does sand really damage the knees and elbows?"

The sun was dipping below the horizon – all too quickly for Cade's liking, he knew he had to head back, despite being proficient behind the wheel the *Marlin* was a big boat and the last thing he wanted to do was run her aground.

"Come on you, let's go, we need to swim back to the *Marlin* before it starts to get dark."

Back on board he started the engine and prepared to pull away from their ocean hideaway. It was clear she was disappointed that they couldn't spend the night there.

"We don't have enough food, and you would soon get cold, I'm just caring for you."

"I know, but we could light fire and eat each other!"

Despite understanding what she meant the idea of being sacrificed to a naked, intoxicated, flame-haired cannibal did have a certain appeal.

They re-entered the harbour, Cade slowed the boat down to a walking pace and navigated to the marina on his starboard. Slowly they pulled up alongside the wooden boardwalk and towards berth 25.

With good fortune the skipper of the local pleasure boat *Coromandel II* managed to grab a line and skilfully tied her off, allowing Cade to steer her into the berth and shut down the engines.

"Evening Jack. Had a good day?"

"Absolutely Ron, beautiful weather."

"Catch much?"

"Oh a beauty; metre and a half long and she put up one hell of a fight, I played her for about an hour but I eventually got the better of her and managed to get her onto the beach."

"Nice, I'm sure we'll get to see the pictures one day. Have a great evening mate, catch you tomorrow. Oh and Jack…"

"Yes Ron."

"Make sure your tackle hasn't been damaged."

And with that Ron Wilson gathered up his belongings, shuffled along the wooden decking and disappeared into the dusk. He headed home with a broad smile on his weather-beaten face.

Dimitrova appeared at the stern "Jack Cade you are so naughty man, pretending I was big fish!"

She jumped down from the *Marlin* and into his arms. Her face was sticky with salt, her skin hot and slightly flushed from being exposed to the fierce New Zealand sun. He held her in his arms for a moment.

"Thank you."

"For what?"

"For giving me a sense of hope; for some amazing fun-filled days and above all Elena for making me the envy of this wonderful little seaside town."

She laughed, jumped up, putting her legs around his waist and whispered into his ear.

"Take me to see Big Stan; I have worked up appetite for his French fries, then after he has watched me eat every single one, slowly dipping each into his hot sauce you can take me home for a fun-filled night."

He loved her endless energy and how even her most conventional sentences became lines from an adult movie. It was her incredible innocence that he adored, it all made the thought of her leaving the next day so much harder to contend with.

Chapter Five

She leant on the granite work surface and smiled at him "Jack, I have to go to Auckland today. You come with me or I go alone?"

He paused, trying to think how to compose his words. Monday had come around all too quickly.

"Erm, I…"

"It's OK, I understand."

"No, no, it's not that I don't want to, I have a job to do for JD – it's what we discussed the other night, it won't take too long but I have to start today. I've got to go to Tauranga – it's about an hour south from here. I'll be there a few hours. I should be back before you, when you return why don't we go to the Motu Kitchen? It could be our five day anniversary!"

She laughed, agreed and said she understood. She took a mouthful of the hot coffee and wiggled off across the lounge floor, her towel deliberately beginning to fall as she got to the bedroom door.

"Oh Jack!" she called "this is your early gift for tonight!"

With the skill of a fan dancer in a burlesque nightclub she dropped the towel and allowed glimpses of her naked body to be revealed as he stood impotently in the kitchen trying to think of mundane household chores to complete.

He managed to resist the thought of her for a few minutes and then once more gave in. She had cast a spell on him that he was literally powerless to evade.

By the time he reached the bedroom she was dressed. A dark blue summer number, strapless but very tasteful, it really enhanced the colour of her hair which for the first time he noted she had put into a pony tail. Matching blue shoes completed her outfit and did a sterling job of accentuating her shapely legs. 'Christ even her legs are lovely' he found himself thinking as she playfully brushed by him heading to the main door.

"No, it's OK Jack Cade, you don't want me then fine, I go to Auckland where lots of men find me attractive!"

"Fine, go, see if I care!" He offered as a retort, a useless one but he had to offer something in what appeared to be a developing early morning fantasy role play.

"OK, fine, I will!" And with that she strutted outside, the top of those legs doing their level-best to shift the blue cotton dress from side to side in a hypnotic fashion.

Before she had even got to the driver's door he had caught up with her: a lap dog.

"I'll miss you; drive safely, please, not like the other night!"

"Me too Jack. I go into town and get some fuel first, someone has used it all, perhaps you meet me on the main road – we have race at last? My Black Panther against old lady Hairdresser's Car!" she mocked him earning a short, sharp slap across her shapely pert arse.

"I'll be twenty minutes, I'll see you alongside the airfield, bring your driving gloves!"

She lowered herself into the Porsche, the material of her dress riding up to reveal a glimpse of her thigh. His left eyebrow rose playfully.

She turned the key and selected reverse, slowly backing the car onto the road. With drive engaged she waved, blew a theatrical kiss and accelerated out of sight.

It was an enormous cliché, but he was missing her already.

As he walked back to the house he found himself thinking of the old days, the meetings with JD always did that, allowing the past to insidiously slip back under the radar.

However he wasn't consumed by the darker thoughts of his life and career but considering how his old mates would now look upon his life and particularly the latest additions with intense jealousy.

It made him smile for the second time that morning.

He changed, cleared a few things away; he was clean but far from Obsessive Compulsive – unlike his old team mate O'Shea – now she took OCD to an altogether different level. Rampant in the bedroom, fanatical about her work and fixated on cleanliness, it wasn't unheard of for her to shower four times a day, often alone.

He was back there again. Like so many involved in law enforcement he lived it, breathed it, and dreamt it. For a while he stood and rewound his own internal video, playing back the scenes that stayed with him. He'd dealt with a lot of what society would consider nasty people, but his adversary had left a scar, and not just a physical one.

As he went through his 'exit strategy', locking the house down, conducting a final sweep and then walking to his car he became aware that he was now laughing about the old days, about the people that formed a major part of his life, albeit they now lived in an unread chapter of a dusty book, lost on a dark shelf in a nameless repository.

'Only remember the good parts Jack…'

He jumped into the TT, placed the key into the ignition and twisted it gently to start her up. As reliable as ever the dashboard ran through its own checks before igniting the silky V6 which came to life with a satisfying purr.

He put the gearbox into drive and exited, turned left, then right and drove out onto the main highway. Moments later he arrived at the airfield, parked up and watched a Cessna 182 on finals, another fortunate holiday home owner flying in from one of the cities for a break.

He became lost in the moment, observing the intricate adjustments of the aircraft as it glided down onto the grass landing strip.

At the exact moment its wheels touched the runway a black Porsche shot by, a slender arm waving from the driver's window.

"Bollocks!"

Cade had been napping and she'd caught him square on the jaw. He hurriedly turned the key once more and engaged Sport. The Audi Launch Control ensured that it took off like the proverbial feline as he allowed the gearbox to take over. Although she was moving at a rate of knots he soon tucked in behind her.

A flash of his headlights and a wave of the hand indicated that he wanted her to pull into a lay-by. Unexpectedly she bought it and did as she was instructed.

"Old habits eh Jack, nice, you haven't lost your touch."

Now both of the German cars sat ticking over in the lay-by. He beckoned for her to join him. She left her vehicle and walked towards him, her dress fighting against a breeze in a Monroe-esque moment, causing a few male heads to turn as they sped past.

She got to the Audi and leaned in, a little too far, knowingly displaying her breasts.

"Is there a problem officer?" she asked mischievously.

"There will be if you don't slow down miss…" he countered.

"Well, are you going to punish me?"

"I might, if I catch you doing it again."

"Well, be here tonight at six o'clock, I will be coming through at two hundred kilometres an hour and if you catch me, you can discipline me. But only if you catch me!"

The fantasy was becoming reality – he knew she had a long journey ahead so reined her in.

"Look you take it easy on the way. Be careful, there are some shockingly bad drivers here. I miss you; it feels like I have known you forever. See you about six? Dinner's on me."

Still in role she curtsied and replied "Whatever you say officer" before strutting back to her vehicle.

He leant out of the window and called her back to his car.

"By the way Miss."

"Yes Jack, what?" For once she looked serious.

"By the way, I'm in the lead!"

With that he pressed the accelerator pedal fiercely and allowed the Audi to skip off the gritty lay-by, all four wheels fighting to gain traction on the loose surface. As the Bridgestone tyres gripped the smoother carriageway he was off, racing up to a set of bends and leaving the incredible girl in his wake, stood in the lay-by initially, but then running as fast as her spectacular legs and heels would carry her.

"Jesus Cade what have you done? She'll be…furious!" he provided a brief commentary on how things might have been in the cockpit of the Black Panther. He knew she would be angry, possessed almost, but he couldn't help being amused.

"But think of the make-up sex Jack! You can't lose! Worst case, you'll be covered in her lipstick!" He laughed at his own internal dialogue.

They retraced their steps from the day before although this time the cars were more evenly matched. He knew he was down on power but had all-wheel drive on his side, which when coupled with his superior driving skills meant a sure-fire win.

The cars ducked one way then the other, tyres scrabbling for grip, hands flicking left and right, dashboard needles responding in millisecond bursts, feet dancing on brake pedals, eyes peeled, ever-watchful on the road ahead.

"Time for a power anthem Jack" he announced to himself as he switched on the Bose twelve speaker system. Springsteen leapt from the front set as the E Street Band offered brilliant support from the rear. The New Jersey singer belted out *"Born in the USA"* as Cade played the drum section on the leather-clad steering wheel.

"I'm, ten years burning down the road…ain't got nowhere to go…"

His moment of indulgence with The Boss allowed her to tuck in very close to his stern and now the Cayman lay in wait, poised like a ravenous big cat, ready to pounce upon its prey, the Panther and the Gazelle.

Inside the Porsche all was quiet, no music to distract her, she was more than happy with the soundtrack the engine provided. She tapped the window switch for a second; all the better to hear the flat-six reverberate off the rocky walls of the pass that they were busy navigating.

Seeing a slowing group of vehicles ahead she sprang into action, a familiar double-tap on the paddles threw the car forward and in two seconds she was past Cade and the slower procession.

As they cleared the next set of bends he followed suit.

This was entertaining; nowhere near as pleasurable as seeing her spread-eagled on his stainless steel worktop, but fun, nonetheless.

The two Teutonic creatures continued to dance, the Mongoose versus the Cobra. They eventually slowed once they reached Tairua, baulked in heavier traffic she made faces at him in the rear view mirror and generally teased him. Nevertheless as soon as they left the town any flirtatious thoughts evaporated as they found themselves catapulted along State Highway 25.

His phone rang.

"Jack it's me, I win yes? We are up Duck Creek soon, I win, please, let me win…"

"OK, OK I can't believe I'm giving in like this, but yes, you win."

"Say it."

"Say what?"

"Say Elena Dimitrova is the greatest driver on the Earth!"

"I'm sorry, your s-s-signals are breaking up, I can't h-h-here you…"

"Jack! I know you can. Stop it. I win!"

"OK, yes, you are the greatest. Now go easy, not everyone wants to race you. Get to Auckland, change the tickets, buy some filthy underwear and come home. Deal?"

"OK deal, but I buy clean underwear? Love you Jack Cade, my sexy Information Security Consultant man. See you at six. Ciao."

She deliberately changed down a gear to make the most of her farewell; the Cayman dropped itself onto the road, grabbed the tarmac and tore off up the gradient on State Highway 25A towards the Kopu Bridge. Between the two lay one of the best driving roads in the world.

Cade indicated left and turned towards Whangamata. He slowed, looked right for as long as he could and watched the 'Panther' slowly blend with the horizon; he contemplated following her, an extra chance to spend time with his newfound lover, but decided it smacked a little of over eagerness.

Instead he slipped the TT into Sport and settled in for an aggressive drive to the coast.

Today was a good day and with any luck it would be an even better night.

Chapter Six

The Boss had finished his pounding anthem about Vietnam. Jack switched over to the local radio whose cheesy DJ reminded everyone to put out their recycling and remember the roadworks on State Highway 25A.

"Clearly they forget to inform you about the bloody roadworks on the Tairua Road my friend!" He muttered this to the radio, as if, by chance that would make a blind bit of difference.

He slowed to a halt behind a Ford Transit van; in stereotypical dirty white it had had a typically hard life. He smiled – his days of sitting on British motorways in traffic jams were a thing of the past. If this were such a road, behind such a van the door panel would have been inscribed with the classic line 'Wish my wife was this dirty'.

There were some things he really missed about The Motherland.

Meanwhile about fifty feet in front of him a bored-looking road worker stood holding a 'Stop/Go' sign which was currently bright red. He couldn't see any reason for his presence so assumed the chaos was around the next corner.

A large freight truck had stopped in front of the Transit.

Cade's phone rang.

"Jack my boy, JD here, just seeing if you are en route to Tauranga?"

"I am indeed you old fox, I'll try and drop in for coffee on the way back. Elena has gone to Auckland, trying to change her flight; it transpires that she truly loves me. Give my love to Mrs D."

"Indeed, it's only Day Five Young Jedi, tread with care…"

Cade cut him off in mid-flow.

"Anyway, tell me, anything new on our amorous Brit – the one I'm trying to gather Intel on in Tauranga?"

"No my lad, nothing new, you've got the address and vehicle details. Just see if you can get that Canon of yours whirring away and capture some damning evidence."

"Will do John."

"Right I must go, got a game of golf with Sharon."

"Sharon?"

"It's a long story my boy, a long story!"

"Aren't they always Daniel, OK, I'll drop in later."

"Good man, catch up then."

Cade paused - then spoke, JD picked up a rise in tension.

"John, the other night Elena and I had a race with a young guy in a red Volkswagen Golf – a flash one."

"And?"

"And it's behind me…"

"And…So what" It was a classic intelligence question.

JD was from the old school who believed that if asked a question six times you always got the answer. Four more to go.

"And I'm not sure mate. Maybe just me but…"

"Jack?"

The cell phone had dropped out of coverage, no other plausible explanation for it. He'd ring back.

The Golf had rolled forward, so far that Cade could no longer read the number plate. The same male was behind the wheel, this time however he looked 'different'.

Something in Cade's sub-conscious kick-started a familiar cycle of training; of muscle memory, apprehension and a return to the old days of surveillance and counter surveillance.

He cursed for allowing himself to break the habit of a lifetime and get too close to the Transit. He felt trapped.

Looking right he saw a steep rocky bank and to the left a previously unnoticed even steeper hillside lined with dense vegetation, trees, ferns and bushes. He discreetly released his seat belt and leant into his glove box, all the time trying not to take his eyes off the Golf. He ran his fingers around the void until they latched onto the non-slip surface of an ASP baton. Why he had it was his business, but right now he was glad he did.

"Why is this traffic not moving?" He mused, all the while trying to look relaxed. His senses were spot on.

The Golf rolled forward again and only stopped when its bumper made contact with the Audi. The Transit's brake lights suddenly went off and it rolled forward about two feet. The doors started to open.

Instinctively he drove the Audi forward and jammed the doors shut. He'd damaged the TT but he knew it wasn't catastrophic.

"Shit, I knew it, this is wrong." He punched JD's number on speed dial.

"Go."

"Get the local boys to my location now – you know roughly where I am. Three vehicles, one white, one red and one HGV, I'm boxed in, road works somewhere approaching Staircase Road. John they only sprang up today. Tell the boys in blue there's been an RTA, be vague, be anonymous and don't tell them how many involved. I don't like it John, I'm going active. It's them….John, look after Elena."

JD knew not to argue, knew that his student was well trained and knew this would end in tears.

Before Cade exited his car he carried out a rapid evaluation of his surroundings: Golf behind, one occupant, Transit, at least one in the driver's seat and possibly more in the back – for now they were trapped. The Truck plus one - or maybe two on board and lastly a road worker with a stop and go board.

In every sense he was outnumbered.

The Road worker moved towards him, placing his hand underneath his high visibility orange vest.

Cade's inner dialogue immediately saw it and announced it - "Gun."

The Transit door started to open.

The window of the truck lowered and suddenly a heavily tattooed arm appeared. It grabbed the road worker by the hair and dragged him into the door with such violent force that he collapsed onto the tarmac.

Cade saw it, acknowledged it and made his decision. So far the whole incident had taken twenty seconds.

He ran to the Golf, pulled the driver's door open and struck the male occupant in the face. He was holding the ASP in his right fist and by doing so had created a formidable weapon of opportunity.

His decision was perfect. The male was immediately stunned but had not let go of a Glock pistol that was now sat impotently in his lap. Cade hit him again, and again. Sensing he needed to escalate things further he dragged the male from the car. As he did so he slammed the heavy door onto his head. Looking right he became aware that the truck was reversing. Having little time to observe what was unfolding he turned his attention back to his newfound enemy. As he did so he heard a horrendous collision.

His foe was trying to rid himself of a low-level concussion but failing dismally, struggling to get off his knees. Cade swung the ASP back behind him and as he did so he heard the familiar metallic swoosh as it engaged.

Now three times longer it became far more useful and in Cade's hands far more potent. Continuing the rearward arc he gained momentum before he began to thrust the metallic bar forwards and straight at the driver's throat.

The ASP contacted just below the Adam's Apple – fracturing the cartilage instantly and rendering the driver incapable of any further action. He gasped for air, both hands clutching at his neck. His eyes bulged, the hunter now the hunted and rapidly drowning in his own blood.

Cade no longer considering the driver a threat, reached into the VW, picked up the Glock and placed it down the front of his trousers.

Seconds had passed, he ran towards the Transit but realised what the dreadful noise was. The truck had reversed into the transit door. The timing, for Cade at least, was highly fortuitous as the Transit driver had been trapped, rather hideously as he tried to escape. He too was gasping for air as the door, rammed firmly into his ribcage, ensured that every breath would be one towards his last.

Cade carried out another rapid evaluation. Golf – down. Transit – possible threat. Road worker? Unconscious. Truck – unknown? Friend? Or foe?

He walked towards the wagon, his senses at the highest state of readiness. He removed the Glock, his thumb connected with the magazine release as he walked, but then due to a lack of time he paused. Normally he would whip out the magazine and check it; instead he looked at the polycarbonate holder as it sat in its housing. Sixteen rounds indicated - one possibly up the spout. He gently dragged the slide backwards on the familiar Austrian weapon and revealed the last round. The whole process took seconds. He walked quickly; ensuring each footstep was deliberate, offering a strong platform should he need to start firing.

He could hear activity in the back of the Transit. Whilst the doors were closed he felt relatively safe. A muffled voice shouted something vague but he wasn't in the mood to reply. If they were friendly they would wait.

He darted around the front and looked in through the passenger window. Clear. There was no obvious doorway from the cargo area to the cab. Whoever was in the back was going to have to remain in situ until he decided what to do. Fortune favoured him further as this model had no sliding side door.

He grabbed the ignition key, ran to the rear and locked the doors, adding another level of security then pocketed the key.

Gun at the high-ready he approached the truck and pushed the weapon out in front of him, looking tactically over the sights straight at his target – the least likely to offer any opposition.

"Driver, show me your hands or I swear I will shoot you!"

One huge heavily tattooed hand appeared on the window frame, followed by another, although this time un-inked.

"Good. I'm coming to talk to you, stay where you are and leave your hands exactly where I can see them. Do as I say and you will not be harmed."

He walked up to the truck, arcing out into the road and in doing so allowing himself an earlier view of the cab. He was greeted by the nervous face of an old friend – The Seaweed Collector.

"Talofa Filemoni – my Samoan Warrior. You OK?"

Despite his enormity he looked petrified and stammered slightly as he replied "Talofa, yes boss. I am good."

"Thank you brother, you did really well. Look my friend we haven't got long, I don't know what happened here but it's not good. They are not after you or your family. The way I see it we have only a short time. The driver of the Transit is dead, it wasn't your fault; he would have shot either one of us, probably both. We are friends, yes?"

The warrior had a thousand yard stare and was clearly frightened.

"Filemoni concentrate, I know about your background OK? I know you are on parole for murder, I also know that even the authorities had a lot of sympathy with you; if it was my child I would have done the same. Now look, we have to act quickly here or we are both in a whole heap of trouble. It's a quiet road but we need to move and we need to move now. OK?"

Cade hoped that keeping it simple would help. The warrior was slow but he wasn't stupid. He was also incredibly strong.

"We need to move brother. If they catch us you will go back to prison. And I will join you..."

He nodded, apparently now very aware of the need to act swiftly and in unison.

"Get the truck about a hundred metres down the road and put it across both lanes, when you've done that get back to me."

He did exactly as he was told. Meanwhile Cade bundled the dying Golf driver back into the driver's seat. He was almost dead and certainly beyond help. Cade had no sympathy. He quickly checked his pockets, the door bins, visors and the glove box. Empty.

He decided it was pointless asking him any questions as the damage he had caused prevented him from saying a word. He was about to shut the door when he heard a faint buzzing sound. He stopped and drilled down on the source. It was a phone in the drivers back pocket. He leant him forward and removed it.

He slid his thumb across the screen of the Galaxy, incredibly it had no PIN. His luck, just possibly had changed.

Three missed calls, one voice mail. It could wait.

He checked the hatch area. Empty.

He switched the ignition to the right and started the Golf; he turned the steering wheel to the left and released the handbrake. It started to roll, gaining momentum until it broke through the low level shrubbery on the edge of the verge. It hurt him to watch it begin its last journey – a great car, just a poor driver.

It commenced a hundred foot descent into the valley below, a tree-lined area known locally as bush. It was dense and unforgiving; the further down the hill the vehicle travelled the more it became enveloped into the shadowy canopy and in just a few moments it had disappeared. By the time the authorities located it the driver would be completely beyond medical intervention. If indeed they ever did.

"OK boss, I'm here. I did good yes?"

"You my man did bloody good. Now, the same with the Transit. Get him into the driver's seat. He's dead OK, no need to worry, his spirit was bad, it's gone and he can't hurt you. Here, catch the key."

The Ocean Harvester caught it deftly then picked the unidentified male up with one hand, placed the other onto his chest and lifted him into the driver's seat. He followed Cade's instructions to the letter, turning on the ignition and turning the heavy steering fully to the left.

"Now get him into the passenger side!" He indicated to the road worker who was still unconscious, a vivid wound still bleeding on his forehead. The Samoan didn't realise it but his initial action had not only stopped Cade from being shot – it had also fractured the man's skull.

Once they were both in the cockpit area Cade issued another instruction.

"Now push brother, push."

Between them they got the vehicle rolling, slower than its German counterpart, but rolling nonetheless.

The faceless voice started to shout again and struck the door panels aggressively.

Cade checked his watch. Twelve minutes, incredible. It felt like hours. He knew where the local police had to travel from and just hoped they weren't any closer. He could not believe his good fortune that another car hadn't joined them from behind.

The Transit picked up speed. The rear occupant started to hammer on the side panels and began to yell something which the Samoan could not understand. It sounded 'foreign'. To Cade it was instantly familiar – Romanian, and it wasn't very pleasant.

The muffled heavily-accented voice soon began to plead with Cade.

"Let me out and I will not tell anyone, you will be OK. Do it now or I will kill you." Cade thought the initial offer was quite charitable but the latter confirmed to Cade at least, that he was dealing with another member of the team, not some unfortunate kidnap victim.

"You heard the man? Now push!"

As with the Golf the Transit soon gathered pace, but its weight ensured that it careered down the hillside in much more spectacular fashion. It was probably travelling at about twenty five when it hit a large rock and began to tip, inertia soon ensured that it rolled onto its roof and slid down the incline, faster and faster until it too disappeared from view. En route to the forest floor a number of significant branches demolished the windscreen and bonnet.

Unlike Hollywood the vehicle did not burst into flames, it just came to a halt among the dark, dank undergrowth that began to consume both vehicles almost instantly. Tree fern fronds wrapped their velvety fingers around the new arrival. The impressively wide trunk of a native Kauri tree jammed against the rear doors entombing the rear occupant who, along with his driver now fell silent.

It wasn't unusual for vehicles and even light aircraft to disappear into this terrain and to never be seen again. Occasionally and often only by pure luck one might surface many years later when discovered by a hunter.

"Get back to your truck. Say that I ran into the back of you, you are not injured and that we are exchanging details. Say that I am going to contact your boss and tell him it was my fault. OK?"

He kicked a few branches across the verge, covering the exit marks of both vehicles. He looked at the front grill of the TT – it was buckled, the offside headlight was shattered, leaving polycarbonate crystals on the surface of the road. The back of the car was practically unmarked.

"Boss."

"Yes."

"I'm scared. Scared that they will take me back to prison."

"E te iloa a'u?" He asked the Samoan if he knew him – at least it was as close as his basic Samoan would get to the question.

"Yes, you are good man; you own the restaurant with Big Stan."

"That's right Filemoni I am good and I will look after you. Trust me like you have never trusted a man before? I cannot explain here, but I will look after you – and your family. OK?"

The warrior nodded.

Cade slipped the Glock from his waistband and after a gentle wipe of the grip and slide threw it as far as he could, down into the canopy below, it dropped so far he never heard it land.

He put his hand out in front of him. The warrior took it and then pulled cade into his chest, typical of an island greeting, albeit one heavily influenced by the USA. They were in that modern male embrace when a silver Toyota Corolla came around the corner, no doubt a rental, followed by a local Highway patrol car which whipped around the tourists and pulled up behind them, the first patrol car on the scene. The driver pulled his vehicle across the road and illuminated his federal bar.

He got out and as he did so he announced his arrival to his communications operator. His distinctive blue uniform with matching blue body armour and a high visibility yellow tabard was completed when he placed his forage cap onto his suntanned head.

"G'day. So what's happened here folks? Anyone injured?"

The warrior looked at Cade.

"Good morning, thanks for coming officer, appreciate you've probably travelled a long way – I tried to ring to say we were both OK. No-one's fault, the driver here stopped to let a tourist vehicle through – he was on the wrong bloody side – and it all happened so quickly I didn't have chance to stop. My car is damaged, the truck is obviously fine. I guess we are both lucky?"

"Indeed. Bloody lucky mate. I've known of cars going off these edges and never being found."

He rubbed his bearded chin and had a brief look around. He observed a sprinkling of glass on the road surface among which were a few flakes of black paint, almost invisible to the untrained eye. The tailgate of the truck was so dirty and rusty that he wasn't surprised to see a lack of evidence.

"OK, here's what I'm going to do. Normally I would be looking at issuing you with a ticket for careless, Mr?"

"Cade, Jack Cade." They shook hands.

"OK Mr Cade as I say a ticket – but given the circumstances I'm prepared to give you an official warning, no-one hurt, no damage to the truck, the only damage I can see is to your vehicle. I take it you have exchanged details?"

"Of course, I'm fully insured, so if the company needs to claim it can. The driver has all my details too."

Cade looked at the Samoan.

"Again my friend I am so sorry, I just couldn't stop, you sure you are not injured?" It was fair to say that a locomotive would have struggled to injure him, he was so vast.

"No boss, I'm fine, thank you for everything." He looked at the officer "Can I go now boss? I have things to deliver."

The officer nodded approval.

Cade shouted "Mate – if you need anything you know where to contact me – anything at all."

The warrior smiled for the first time in a while and walked pensively back to his truck. 'Thankyou boss.'

The officer took a basic photograph of the scene – he'd have to submit a straightforward crash report and with his current workload it would be as basic as it could be, clearly this was one to file as quickly as possible.

The traffic was starting to back up behind the Corolla and as he was as keen to open the road as he was to get his breakfast the Constable got back into his Holden Commodore and cleared the job with his communications centre.

As he was about to drive away Cade shouted to him. He looked in the side mirror to see that Cade was holding a Stop/Go sign.

"This was in the middle of the road officer, probably what the other vehicle swerved to avoid?"

"Yep, happens now and then, they leave all sorts of crap behind, do me a favour, throw it onto the verge by your car and I'll get someone from Highways to come and pick it up. Thanks. Drive safely."

Cade assured him he would, as he walked once more through the longer grass erasing evidence as he did so.

He got back into the Audi, turned the key, it started first time. He shuffled awkwardly, realising he still had the ASP in his right hand pocket. He removed it and placed it back into the glove box. He looked over his right shoulder, indicated, saw a courtesy flash of the Commodore's headlights and then drove off down the hill towards his destination. The Highway Patrol vehicle followed him.

Within seconds the Commodore driver illuminated his red and blue lights, Cade slowed, instantly thinking that somehow he had missed something, something critical. Instead the officer indicated right and accelerated fiercely to overtake him, the twin exhausts rasped as the car changed to third and with a wave the officer was gone, off to his next call of duty, his previous commitment now a number on a computer waiting for his Sergeant to file, his breakfast getting colder by the minute.

Chapter Seven

A few kilometres ahead of the Cayman a familiar yet sinister apparition appeared on the lesser-used Puketui Valley Road, a detour which allowed access to the small village of Puketui and mirrored the winding path of the beautiful Tairua River.

The four-wheeled ghost whispered to a stop allowing the driver a commanding view both right and left. Evoking beauty of a different type, the vehicle, a black Rolls Royce Wraith – the most powerful Rolls-Royce in history, sat quietly, its potent 6.6 litre twin turbo-charged V12 engine barely audible above the nascent breeze that encouraged the nearby forest to life.

Behind the Pantheon grille sat a 624 bhp engine, more than capable of powering the 2800kg beast from standstill to sixty in 4.6 seconds.

The two door leviathan contained four people, none of which were visible as the heavily-tinted glass denied the casual observer a view into the opulent cockpit.

In the left rear seat a beautiful woman sat, flicking idly through her iPhone. Five foot something with distinctive features and a shocking head of black hair she was what most men would describe as stunning.

She dressed beautifully too; a Stella McCartney outfit, black, sensational and completely inappropriate for the current terrain, her matching black shoes lay on the cream carpet. Sitting next to her was a male, in his thirties, shaven head, much of which was scarred and a mathematically perfect jaw. He wore dark grey clothes; shirt, trousers and shoes, the only hint to fashion being an Omega Seamaster wristwatch with a black face, white hands and a distinctive orange bezel.

The driver was around fifty. He had hair that at one time was Raven black but now so faded down the centre he resembled a skunk. And he hated how people reminded him of the fact. He had black soulless eyes.

One, the left, had a glassier appearance than the other, it was almost too perfect. His left eyelid was deformed, burnt and cruelly twisted. Unlike his colleague he didn't wear a watch. He hated being reminded of the fact that he had to live another eighteen hours until the dawn of a new day, when once more he was expected to exist again. He had money. He had, at some level, power, enough to cause concern among even confident men but this was never enough to quell the overwhelming and almost constant desire to step off a precipice or in front of a fast moving vehicle.

He was once advised, quietly, that he made a drizzling start to a Monday morning in January, without an umbrella, actually look appealing.

Sinister, muscular and malevolent – he epitomised the cinematic image of a very bad person. He had not always been that way, many years before he had been described as a weakling, puny or even diminutive, albeit he didn't know what it meant.

He smoked, much to the annoyance of the front seat passenger.

As he raised his hand to inhale the smoke his cuff rode slightly revealing a vivid scar underneath which lay the remnants of a blue mark.

The Passenger was more than just along for the ride. To anyone watching it was clear that he was in charge and despite saying very little everyone in the car knew this to be the case. He wore a charcoal Viktor & Rolf suit which would have seen little change from two thousand dollars. Underneath he had a pink Bertigo Puyol shirt, again expensive and as with the car, very flamboyant – arrogant almost but undeniably stylish. His ensemble was completed with a pair of Ray-Ban Aviator's: Classic eyewear that never left his face.

The male leant gently back into the ivory leather seat; his head resting onto the illustrious double R logo. He looked forward, his face reflecting back at him in the dark veneer. It was beautiful, the work of a master craftsman and yet as sinister as the occupant. A subtle stainless steel pinstripe followed the contour of the dashboard, drawing the observers' eye to the monitor lid.

The lid, which opened to reveal the on-board computer system, was inlaid with a replica of the Spirit of Ecstasy – the feminine icon so familiar to the marque. The whole experience cocooned the occupants in a state of luxury, of incredible comfort and safety. It was for all intents and purposes a gentleman's club, an ocean-going yacht and a symbol of intense wealth – an icon for the uber-rich and stylish.

The female slipped her phone into the side pocket and sunk into the supremely comfortable seat, its supple, seamless leather encouraging her to sleep. As she slipped into a darker world she ran her fingertips over the Canadel panelling, each delicately curved section felt exquisite to the touch, each oriented at exactly fifty five degrees. Behind her shoulders the leather was joined by chromed bullet tips, gathering the material together, hinting perhaps at the immense speed of the vehicle. It was attention to detail beyond which most mere mortals could only dream.

It was such a pity that the occupants lacked the overwhelming class and sense of breeding of their anthracite carriage.

The Passenger moved his right hand towards the rotary controller. Mounted in the central section of the vehicle the controller's crystal glass surface allowed him to run his index finger across it, in doing so inscribing a letter, a letter that allowed him to commence a search on the advanced satellite navigation system, search of an address, a technical issue on the vehicle or a phone contact. To a man who paid such an obscene amount for his suits it impressed him enormously.

He ran his digit over the glass, with three simple strokes painting a letter A onto the surface.

The phone started to dial, the signal soon leaving New Zealand and racing across the globe.

"Salut Alexandru…it is me."

"Salut Stefan, how are you my brother? I hear the weather is wonderful where you are, you should stay a few days more perhaps?"

"This would not be necessary my friend, our work here is soon done. I have but one regret".

"And that is?"

"That I must give this very special car back to its owner!"

The faceless male laughed, he knew The Passenger would enjoy the car; after all he had one of his own except his was the polar opposite of the obsidian monster, being almost entirely white.

"Leave it at the airport my brother; put the keys on the roof, whoever finds it can have it. Let us hope it is someone who will appreciate it. Clear the on board memory and physically wipe it clean. We can always get another."

In the Romanian city of Craiova The Jackdaw pressed the red button on his cell phone, disconnected The Passenger and rolled over in his palatial bed to finish what he had started. The two sixteen year old girls either side of him appeared not to care what happened next. They were sheltered, fed, given alcohol and the level of drugs in their system quickly allowed them to forget about the brutal reality of their naked existence.

If they were any older than eighteen he simply lost interest.

The Jackdaw lit an American cigarette, laid his head back on the sumptuous pillows and cackled like his ornithological namesake as his female concubines went about their work feasting upon him and in doing so earning another meal, another bed for the night and another sordid infusion of Class A drugs.

In the Rolls Royce The Passenger dropped a small pair of Nikon binoculars onto his lap.

"She is coming. Wait. Wait. Go on my word, and not a second before!"

The Wraith was now poised like a cobra waiting to deliver its final cargo of venom, but The Passenger had a plan that would make everything appear to be normal, above board and realistic, at least as 'normal' as things could be, given what was about to happen.

Dimitrova was accelerating along 25A. Her hi-fi was off. The sheer enjoyment she received from listening to the car was music enough.

Second, third....back off, trail brake...exit...third, fourth: the car was a revelation and she was absorbing every minute detail, every sound, every vibration and every contact with the road.

Despite Cade's warning's she pushed the car a little harder, and checking her rear view mirror she could see she was alone, the road ahead was clear and not a Highway patrol officer in sight.

If she was stopped she had a number of methods of distraction that had never failed. Men were weak, the world over.

Her right foot depressed the accelerator and the Cayman dug its heels into the tarmac before aggressively catapulting her forward.

She even started calling out the speed as it rapidly increased.

"80 – 90 – 100 – 110...120....come on Cayman, faster girl!"

At the rate she was eating up the miles she would soon be through the gorge and out onto the Hauraki Plain and in an hour, with limited traffic, she should be sitting in the airline offices of Cathay Pacific.

She further calculated that four hours after that she could be sipping Pinot Noir in Cade's bedroom wearing nothing but Chanel No 5 and a smile.

She deftly reduced her speed as she banked around the sweeping left hander, again the road was clear. An open road with a car to match; every girl's dream, at least it was one of Elena Dimitrova's.

She suddenly became aware of her cell phone vibrating. Looking down for a moment into the passenger seat she could see it was a familiar caller. She smiled – she would tease him by making him wait.

Cade sat in a lay-by dialling and redialling. As his phone tried to connect he recalled the Galaxy that he had seized from Red Golf.

He recovered it, his thumb quickly slid across the screen before heading to the voicemail section.

"For messages press one…"

He pressed One and waited, apprehensive but fascinated about what he might learn about the man who had tried to kill him and more importantly, why.

Was it even him they were after? Had he just been, ironically, in the wrong place at the wrong time?

The message initiated.

"Marko, it is me, salut. I trust all is well with your business? We are about to execute our delivery at this end. I have assured Jackdaw that you have closed the road and dealt with the obstruction. It has been a pleasure my brother. See you at home."

Cade listened intently, running the words around in his head, like a recipe that was missing an ingredient.

A growing sense of nausea filled his stomach and then a chilling realisation.

"Shit, they are going for both of us. The Wraith. The bloody Wraith. Christ Elena answer your fucking phone girl. Now!"

Cade started to sweat, a fine bead appeared on his top lip and he could taste the familiar tang of adrenalin upon his tongue. Whatever had happened here today was clearly for a reason, whether it was targeting him, her or a combination was an unknown. He'd been away from all of 'this' for a long time, so he quickly formed the opinion that his new found love was the target. And now she was alone, vulnerable and in need of urgent help.

He checked the messages. One was innocuous, the other two far more sinister.

'Marko – Monday morning – close the road as we talked about. Make it look real. Deal with the traffic problems and remove any evidence.'

'Marko. Your wages are in the bank. Bine facut.'

The second message was clear and ended with 'well done'.

He was rapidly putting two and two together and coming up with…four.

He pocketed the phone and started the TT and without checking his mirrors spun it around in the road. With a full throttle and a skilled driver the Audi planted itself firmly onto the carriageway and tore back towards the State Highway.

With his left hand Cade kept hitting redial. He cursed for not setting up his hands free.

Dimitrova looked down at her phone again. "My dear Mr Cade you really want me! I will taste all the better tonight."

She turned the hi-fi on. *Happy* by Pharrel Williams was playing.

In her stilted Bulgarian she sang along, after all she was and hadn't been this happy for a very long time.

Cade got to the main junction and hammered the TT out onto 25A almost over-correcting. He didn't count the speed increments; his concentration was total, absolute and focussed. The six speed sequential gearbox propelled the little black car along the road as if it were its very last journey. The V6 screamed in protest but did exactly as its German engineers had designed it to do.

"Come on, answer the fucking phone! Please. Dear God answer the bloody thing."

His request for celestial intervention was a rare one but he meant it.

Somehow he knew that even at maximum speed he would never catch her, she would be miles ahead now, but at least he could get close enough to talk on the phone and get her to pull over. What he would do then he hadn't quite thought about – he'd do that when the time arose. If.

Dimitrova stormed around the long, beautifully cambered road. At 120 she was going far too quickly, but the car and importantly the moment was just so right. She was even happier than a few moments before.

She had just had a flashback – back onto the stainless steel worktops, the wooden decking, the thunderstorm and the incredible lovemaking in the rain with a man she had only just met and yet, honestly, and very much against all of her plans, a man she could easily spend the rest of her days with.

A heat haze rose from the black carpet highway that stretched out in front of her. The jolly, almost nonsensical music filled her ears, her phone's unanswered vibrations continued and she pushed on, her mind now divided between driving and the intense daydream pleasure being skilfully delivered to her by her older lover.

As the bend started to straighten she was immediately blinded by the rising sun which had now announced its presence over the top of the ranges. She instinctively flicked the sun visor down and slowed – just a touch.

The Cayman backfired – to the uninitiated it was a fault – to the skilled driver a sign that she had released the accelerator momentarily and as she had done so, the engine ran rich causing fumes to explode in the exhaust system resulting in the familiar refrain of a rally car – an audible, clacking, staccato sound.

It was enough to distract the Bulgarian redhead for two seconds and that was all The Passenger needed. He'd planned this over, and over again. It had to be delivered with the precision of a Swiss watch. To the second.

"Now!"

The Wraith exited Valley Road straight into the path of the German sports car and then it simply stopped. It was a calculated move and not without huge risk to both sets of occupants. The way The Passenger saw it, had enthused about it, it was them, or her, and he knew who would win.

His most calculated risks were never that in his eyes. Calculated yes, but rewarding, always.

Dimitrova looked up to see the Wraith. For her it wasn't about familiarity, more a case of instant, gut-wrenching survival. Everything she had ever learned about the art of driving happened in the next eight seconds.

One: she braked. Two: she began to rapidly decelerate. Three: she looked for an escape route. Four: she started to steer to the left. Five: she made contact with the gravel at the side of the road. Six: she over-corrected.

Seven: she closed her eyes.

Eight: she listened; listened to her life unravelling in hundredth of a second bursts.

First all sound stopped, then it started again, quicker this time and more aggressively. Her tyres scrabbled, fought and battled with the changing surface, in doing so letting out a cacophonous racket, like the Gates of Hell had just opened after ten thousand years.

The engine, that beautiful, balanced incredible engine roared disapproval as the gearbox changed down, bang, bang, bang: and then her own sounds; anger, fear and aggression, all at once, all in a terrifying split second.

To the onlooker this was an accident, the Wraith merely entering onto the road, careless at best; the Cayman, travelling far too quickly. The poor driver of the Wraith didn't stand a chance, the driver of the Porsche, even less. This was the plan. This was the brutally simple highway execution of the Bulgarian: Elena Dimitrova's last defiant act.

Inside the Porsche almost all sound had stopped. The car had over corrected, or rather Elena had over corrected, everything she had ever learned, practised and re-practised had gone. As the front nearside wheel had dug defiantly into the gravel the weight and sheer momentum had caused it to lurch, pitch forward and become airborne.

It remained upside down for only moments, long enough for her beautiful auburn hair to allow gravity to play its part. Instinctively she hung onto the steering wheel, as if by chance it would make the slightest difference. Her knuckles whitened, her pure white teeth ground together, her jaw muscles locked. Her screams never came.

The Cayman's roof landed onto the carriageway, the noise was horrific, like nothing she had ever heard. The sheer roar of pristine metal on the road surface was beyond description – The Four Horsemen of the Apocalypse had visited.

War, Famine, Pestilence and Death; they stood with her on that lonely highway and encouraged her to join them, slowly, deliberately beckoning her.

Perversely when the journey appeared to be over she found herself relaxing, almost accepting her fate. At that very instant the driver's side struck a colossal rock, crushing the cockpit and its simply beautiful occupant. She heard no more, felt no more, cared, no more.

The Cayman was now on its side, Dimitrova's pristine head lay on the road surface, the driver's window long destroyed. Blood started to ebb from an unseen wound as she began her unwilling journey into another life.

Drops of scarlet trickled onto the tarmac and mixed with myriad cubes of the blue-green remnants of a previously pristine windscreen.

All that could be detected of life was the smell of blood which mixed rapidly with an assorted cocktail of vehicle fluids to form a heady concoction of man and machine.

A small, almost imperceptible shape appeared on the road. A Fantail, a native bird, pretty, with subtle colours and a mesmerising flight, flitted here and there before landing next to her.

The local Maori considered the bird a harbinger of death when it entered their home, but here on this impressive day it was just a curious passer-by, dancing from tree to tree, fern to fern and closer than any bird would normally dare to go. It was bold, brave and delicate and as such it was familiar with the girl that lay before it.

The nosy bird became alert and flew away as a whisper quiet vehicle pulled up next to the Cayman. It landed on a nearby tree branch and watched, inquisitive but quickly uninterested, it soon darted off into the darker canopy of the forest seeking shelter and food.

A pair of black, highly polished and very expensive shoes exited the vehicle, carrying their owner along the road until he reached the shattered remains of the car.

He squatted down onto the highway and looked into the cockpit. He placed a probing index finger into a developing pool of blood, rubbed it between his fingers and raised it to his nose. The metallic smell had always fascinated him. He massaged his fingers together until the fluid became a dry mixture; minute pieces of it dropping onto the road.

He positioned his two fingers onto the wrist of the dying female, checked for a pulse and looking down at the scene, nodded gently, and then smiled. He looked up at the intense sun and for the first time removed his sunglasses. He was heterochromic. One of his irises was brown, the other hazel. It was a rare condition but one that made him very distinctive.

The male fumbled around inside the cockpit of the Porsche, careful not to damage the sleeve of his much-cherished suit and conscious of the pain that visited him, a legacy of a past injury. His hand settled on a small brown bag, not dissimilar to a laptop bag. He pulled at the strap and released it from the wreckage.

Elena Dimitrova fought her greatest battle; to remain calm, quiet and for all intents and purposes, dead. However she observed everything through the opaque veil of her auburn eyelashes.

As the anonymous hand brushed by her face she opened her right eye a fraction. The last thing she saw before she slipped into unconsciousness was an indigo blue tattoo. The tattoo was simple, beautiful and memorable.

The tattoo's owner stood, brushed down his suit, as he did so cutting the palm of his hand on a minute sliver of glass. He wrapped a handkerchief around it and walked briskly back to the Wraith. He turned, took one last look and got in. The door shut with a reassuring clunk. The Passenger looked at the driver and nodded.

With cold-hearted, simple, cynical ease the driver pulled up alongside the debris. He lowered the window and was about to flick his still-lit cigarette into the pool of fuel that had seeped onto the surrounding road and verge.

"No! What are you, an idiot? We leave nothing behind, not even a cigarette butt. You call yourself trained? I should have you exterminated. Now do your job and drive, and don't talk to me until we reach the Motherland."

The driver was angry, he knew he could deal with this conceited fool but chose to leave that for another day. He accelerated until the Wraith disappeared from view, leaving her behind to take her last breath.

In the illuminated ashtray the Marlborough also faded and died.

Inside the cockpit The Passenger took a moment, staring in the tinted door mirror at the disarray behind him, and then made a call.

"It is done." It was the agreed term – cold, blunt and in no need of embellishment.

He placed his phone back in his pocket, sank back into the glorious leather and fell asleep.

Behind him the shaven-headed male leant across to the female and placed his hand underneath her dress exposing her breast. He felt it for a moment, marvelling at its shape and fine alabaster colour. She didn't resist.

"I wanted to see how excited you were. Your heart is there somewhere." He smiled, considering himself further up the food chain than the female, and therefore able to have, or take, whatever he wanted to.

"Well, now you have, remember where you fit in the greater scheme of things. Take your hand away before I call The Jackdaw. If he hears of your behaviour he will cut it off and feed it to you, piece by piece."

Clearly the threat was something he considered her capable of carrying out so he quickly retracted his hand. As he did so he revealed a mark on the inside of his wrist. He too had the tattoo.

It was the same symbol that Elena Dimitrova saw before she tumbled into oblivion, she would remember it for what remained of the rest of her life.

The Wraith was out of sight now, heading north, its occupants preparing to carry out their last act in the Southern Hemisphere.

The curious Fantail landed once again, hopped across to the dying female and sat next to her, encouraging her into the next life. Its distinctive chirping failed to raise her from her darkest slumber so once more the diminutive bird fled, back up into the relative safety of a Totara tree.

Half a minute away a sleek black vehicle hurtled towards the scene, its six speed DSG gearbox changing down rapidly as it decelerated alarmingly, coming to a halt across the carriageway, its brakes ticking, screaming hot and glowing as red as the darkening scarlet pool only feet away.

Cade opened the door of the Audi, clutching onto his phone. He ran the few short steps and dropped to his knees. He saw the worst possible image: the girl was lying motionless, her immaculate body now shattered, almost beyond recognition.

Countless such experiences should have allowed him to go into overdrive – triage, action plans and decisions.

Stop – Think – Plan.

Casualty, Obstruction, Witness.

Think, think, think! Do SOMETHING.

He took a deep breath and lay down onto the road.

He spoke quietly at first then raised his voice.

"Elena, talk to me, please."

Nothing.

"Elena, don't move, I'll get help, dear God don't die. Just…don't."

It was possibly the most banal statement he'd ever made but unusually he was lost for words.

His phone rang.

"Jack. It's me. Sitrep. Now."

JD knew that he needed to kick start Cade's muscle memory or he would never get the information he needed.

"Erm, stand by John. Stand by. Just…stand by."

"Jack, focus my boy. What has happened? What do you need and where?"

"John, she's gone, dead. On State Highway…the car is beyond recognition. It's hit a large rock, she's bleeding heavily. It's too late. It's them John, I know it is. It's them. They've got her and I let them. I let those evil bastards kill this beautiful person…" he drifted off.

"Jack, for Christ's sake stay focused. You could be in danger here too. Think back. You know you need to move. Is she alive?"

"No."

"How do you know?"

"I don't, she just looks dead. John I've seen enough…"

JD cut him off "Forget that, check her signs Jack. Do it. Now."

Cade leant into the cockpit, brushing windscreen glass from her face; the whole interior stank of black powder – the result of multiple airbags firing in unison.

He placed his index and second finger onto her throat. Nothing. He quickly found her wrist and repeated the action.

"JD I've got a pulse!"

"Right, good, talk to her, tell her that we are sending help."

Cade put the phone on the tarmac road surface and lost the signal to his friend and former manager.

"Elena, don't leave me girl, I need you far too much. Think of the times we have had together, think how many more we are going to have. Breath slowly, help will be here. JD is sorting it out."

He was. He'd already started to dial on another cell phone. He knew the correct language and elevated things rapidly.

An air ambulance was needed, yes there was plenty of room on the carriageway, yes the local police would be there to assist; yes, yes, yes.

Cade stared at her intently, trying to imagine life without her. As he looked his eyes glazed over, to a point where he almost missed it.

He looked again, her lips were forming words.

He leant in further, glass shards digging into his chest and causing multiple minor wounds to bleed on his chest and spread across his shirt.

"I'm here, speak to me."

She moved her lips but there was no obvious sound.

He placed his ear up to her mouth.

"The…" she hissed, her lungs barely able to force enough air over her tongue to shape the words.

"The w…"

"OK, the water? Yes, we will go to the beach again, I promise."

"The w…" It was evident that even this action as exhausting her.

She was unable to move so instead directed Cade with her eyes, her beautiful sea green eyes.

He looked but could see nothing. Think man, for the love of God think. What is she trying to tell you?

"A wave…?"

Again, her eyes flickered and indicated to her arm.

He looked, studying every minute part.

He looked deep into her eyes, eyes that showed a weakness now, the last few moments of life ebbing away like the very wave she kept referring to.

"OK, this wave, it's important, yes?"

She closed her eyes, deliberately then opened them.

"That's a yes?"

She did it again.

"Do it twice for no."

She complied. They now had a simple, basic code. It was a start.

All he had to do now was ask the right questions. Surely, it wasn't that difficult, after all, he'd made a career out of it.

"Right, the wave, it's important?"

She blinked once.

"Something to do with your arm?"

Again an affirmative.

"A wave, on your arm?" It seemed ludicrous, but it followed so he went with his base instinct, adding inflection to the word arm.

She blinked one long, purposeful blink.

"A drawing?"

One blink.

"A tattoo?"

A series of positive blinks followed. This was important.

His phone rang.

"JD I'm busy…"

"Listen, medics are en route, expect some noise in the skies John boy, but hear me when I say I think you need to leave and leave now. Trust my instinct. Go!"

"But John…"

"Just go. She's in the lap of the gods now Jack and I think you have to do the right thing for her and for yourself, you need to somehow disconnect from her and, if your gut feeling is right, from what she may be connected to. This is history coming back to haunt you, us, I have a bad feeling my boy. It's them Jack. Now either go or so help me I'll drive there myself and bloody drag you away."

Cade pressed the red button on his cell phone. Even as the call ended he knew Daniel was right.

He looked back at Elena one last time. It would be the cruellest departure.

Something made him stop, to take another precious moment.

"Is the tattoo linked to who did this to you?"

Yes.

"Were they in the Wraith, the Rolls Royce?"

Yes.

"The red Golf?"

Again, yes.

"You are going to pull through this, just try to breath and rest. I will find them, somehow, but I need a start. God I wish you had told me more.

He looked back at her, her eyes were now closed.

He shook her, contradicting every rule in his damned training.

She came too with a start. Her eyes now wide open. Alert again, more so than before.

"Somehow give me a clue beyond the tattoo El, try, please. For me, for your family, for whoever it is you care about."

This time her expressive eyes indicated left as once more she battled to maintain consciousness.

"The case."

He looked into the shattered remnants of the sports car. Handbooks, tissues, a drinks bottle, make up, a cell phone, sections of plastic and fabric; dark, twisted pieces of bodywork all combined to create a catastrophic and confusing mess and somehow she wanted him to look beyond it and find what it was she was trying to tell him.

He hunted with his eyes. It was pointless. He moved further into the cockpit, pressing down on her already torn body, causing her to exhale what was left of her oxygen, to moan gently and begin to cry, but he knew he needed to continue.

His fingertips searched, here and there and back again until they stopped on a small case that had been jammed under the passenger seat.

It was the case that she had had with her from the first moment she had arrived at *Spindrift* – in what seemed like months ago.

He wrapped his fingers around the strap and started to pull but it was stuck fast, wrapping its own defiant tentacles around the wreckage, refusing to yield.

He turned gently to her and looked into her eyes.

"Is it the case?"

She whispered "Yes…take it." She exhaled "Go."

"I need to move your left leg, I'm so sorry…"

"Do it Jack, go."

Despite the fact that she was clinging to life, her sense of urgency had a profound effect upon him, so he grabbed the strap and pulled, at the same time pushing her hideously bruised leg to one side.

She screamed and somehow used the energy to shout out two words.

"His eyes!"

It was lost on Cade for now but it would one day drift out of his sub conscious and act as a guide, steering him along the path to retribution.

He extracted himself from the cockpit as carefully as he could, slowly pulling the case towards him. His face brushed across hers. He placed his lips onto hers and kissed her, knowing now that she could never reciprocate.

Her exquisite face was covered in dust and minute fragments of glass, her encrusted lips were arid, all that moistened them was a single tear.

She continued to murmur; just eight words were all that she had left.

"I love you Jack Cade…."

She swallowed painfully, her throat crackled and then she continued.

"The Seventh…"

Her lips, a mixture of rubicund lipstick and insidiously developing cyanosed cells were trying to mouth a new word.

She exhaled, unable to form the word. In her mind she could hear it, as clear as she could hear her mother's voice, her grandmother too.

"Come dear girl. We are waiting for you. There is nothing to fear."

Her eyes closed and her head dropped to one side.

He shuffled out of the wreckage, kissed the tips of his fingers and placed them pushing against her cooling skin, brushing them across her face before he stood and walked as quickly as he could to his car.

He was able to make out a collection of sounds, a car engine, being pushed to capacity, a siren, a throb of blades, somewhere in the distance. Noise travelled a long way in this terrain, it could be twenty miles away or just over the next crest.

His old boss was right. He needed to detach himself from the scene, from the event and especially from the elevated risk that he had found himself embroiled in.

'Not good Jack. Not good in any way.'

The faithful TT started once more. Its sole occupant, darker now than its exterior colour, engaged drive and accelerated along the empty road until the ruins of his anticipated future lay in the past, a disappearing image in his rear view mirror.

He shook his head and said to no one in particular "The *Seventh*. The *wave*, so what? So what are you trying to tell me?" He continued to say it as he left her. It helped to focus his mind on driving, as quickly as he could without attracting attention.

"The Seventh…" Her lips had made a peak, with a circle at the centre, as if she was blowing out a candle or trying to whistle for help. The two words could be separate, but equally connected.

Desperately she gasped, "It is what he…calls them…now. Al Saptelea Val."

"The Seventh…?"

His eyes darted to the rear view mirror, attracted by the arrival of flashing lights and frenzied activity. Another response vehicle hurtled past him, also heading into the chaos, the Doppler effect of the sirens waking him from a daydream.

"Wave."

Overhead the rotors of a bright-red and yellow air ambulance chopped at the sky, announcing its arrival and the hope of salvation.

He nodded approval and let out an exhausted sustained breath. He looked back at himself in the mirror; his eyes reddened enhancing the intense blue of his irises.

This time they were not passionate, flirtatious and alluring but livid, angry and cold.

What was it his Sunday school teacher used to say?

"Know thy enemy…against the spiritual forces of wickedness in the heavenly places."

Oh, he knew them alright, now all he needed to do was work out the how, and the where, then the when and the who. The why would hopefully never be asked as he intended to leave little, or better still no trace of his intended pursuit of sustained and hideous retribution.

Such a shame he had to work within the boundaries of the law. Every now and then he wished, like many of his colleagues that he could be a normal man in the street, driven onto a path of vengeance that even the harshest of judges would understand.

He knew them alright. Of course he did. He'd spent years hating them.

The Seventh Wave.

Chapter Eight

He returned to *Spindrift* to find JD waiting for him.

He got out of the Audi and walked towards him.

"Come here my boy, give me a man hug."

In the past Cade would have taken the arm and bent it up his back or whipped it around into his favourite judo arm throw, but he didn't want to kill the old bastard so decided against it, besides, frankly, he needed a bloody hug.

Daniel held him for a moment.

"She'll be fine John…she'll be fine."

"She's dead JD. How do you associate that with fine?"

Daniel raised a hand and gestured to speak but Cade cut him off.

"Sorry mate, I tried, God knows I tried. I…it's them isn't it? Has to be. Christ I've been blinkered."

John Daniel wasn't sure why his pupil was sorry but he could clearly see the combination of anger and sorrow had already taken its toll.

"Come on my friend let's get you inside, I'll raid your cupboard, you've got a bottle of *Dark Storm* in there somewhere I recall. Looking at the state of you it seems appropriate."

He found the bottle of Talisker single malt, eased the cork out of the slender neck and let some of its contents empty into two crystal glasses.

Daniel held up one of the glasses and encouraged Cade to take it. When he had he chinked his own against Jack's and took a moment to savour the deep, dark tones. It was his new favourite, the heavily charred taste rested upon his palate for a second, an ocean of spice and smoke.

The distiller had intended to recreate a full blown storm at sea and although that perhaps sounded a little melodramatic it captured Cade's mood entirely.

The Seventh Wave meeting The Dark Storm.

"So, now what?"

Cade looked at him. Almost unable to speak he began to sob uncontrollably, but somehow through his tears he said "Now? I find the bastards that did this and end this once and for all, that's what I do."

"Jack, this is not the movies my friend, people will get hurt and most likely that means you. And if that means you it means me too, and my loved ones. Right now you are angry, and as we know anger does not allow you to focus. If you are going to embark on some frenzied counter attack, then you will need help. And we may have to cash in a few favours."

Cade nodded, wiped his tears away and clashed his glass against his teachers.

"Too fucking right I need help."

"But what you need to do first is start to formulate a plan and as we all know Jack plans need detail, fine detail: a start point, a beginning, a middle and an end. And right now I don't see that you have anything other than a whole pile of twisted excrement and the intense love of a Bulgarian girl, who it needs to be said appeared out of thin air and will be OK by the way, I'm convinced of it."

Cade shook his head pitifully.

Daniel ignored it. "So, correct me if I'm wrong my boy…" he swallowed another mouthful of the whisky causing him to shudder "…but do you have anything?"

"I've got this." He raised the small case up onto the stainless worktop. It landed, allowing dust and glass to scatter across the previously pristine steel.

He unzipped the brown leather carrier and opened the case up to reveal its contents. The array of items inside made him stop in his tracks and caused JD to let out a long wolf whistle.

"Well, well, well what do we have here?"

"John, I haven't got a clue. Look, can we do this some other time, I can't concentrate now."

"Jack, they, whoever 'they' are, targeted Elena, you could guess why but you may be wrong, but this is too close for comfort. Think man, think about your past and if I'm only half right you are a potential target too. You know this, I know this and sure as eggs are eggs old son, they know it."

Cade nodded, almost defeated.

"It's them Jack. It's them. Now we have to formulate a plan to get you out of here and fast."

"Where oh great sensei?"

"No time for sarcasm Johnathan…" he replied with equal disdain.

"Fair enough, I deserved that. Where?"

"Where you can switch back into operational mode, where you have more 'friends' and where you can strike out like the cornered cobra that you currently are."

"And where would that be?"

"Why Britain of course."

"But…"

"But nothing, it makes sense and you'll thank me if you really want to do this. Besides I've already booked your seat. You travel to Hong Kong for a few days, chance to meet up with an old friend. Seat 11A, CX198, leaves Auckland at 13:20 tomorrow. Then another CX flight to Heathrow. Any questions?"

"How much?"

"You don't need to know."

"How did you pay for it?"

"You don't need to know."

"How did you know my credit card number?"

"Ditto."

Daniel smiled, knowing full well that his apprentice could easily afford the business class seat he'd recently booked.

"Now, let's get you sorted out, you need to pack and arrange for this place to be locked down. I'll get Gerry to come and tend to your garden, but I'll make sure the window cleaner never touches that one."

He pointed to the large glass patio door, still resplendent with the two cheek impressions and handprints from a few nights before.

Cade smiled and then broke down once more. It was deliberate on Daniel's part; he knew that somehow he needed to grieve or he would never be able to function.

Daniel sifted through the contents of the case, inhaling, tutting and making a few notes in his head. He would study it all later.

"This? This is something alright. Why she had it is another wholly different something. What we do with it is…"

"Let me guess JD? Something else?"

Cade sat on the kitchen bar stool, staring out of the window, looking at the distant mountain range and wondering just which part of heaven his beloved redhead was inhabiting, and which bar she had walked into.

"Make sure you look after yourself and Lynne JD."

His pocket vibrated, it was enough to drag him back into the world of the living. He fumbled for the Galaxy, forgetting for a while that he even had it. The message icon indicated that a new one had arrived.

He slid his thumb over the screen and read the new communiqué.

'See you at home. Well done my brothers. Jackdaw will reward you well; our part of this exercise is also complete. Travel safely, until we meet again. Stefan.'

He showed JD the screen, and then the other text messages.

"Can you do anything with this phone before I leave?"

"No, but I know a man who can, besides, you are coming back with me tonight. Lynne and I will take you to the airport, it will look less obvious and if they try anything en route, well, she's got a mean left hook!"

Cade smiled for the first time in hours. It had been a long day and yet the whole process, chronologically had taken just minutes.

He found himself thinking how minutes had changed his life, just days ago, and now a few more had changed it back again. He had the next few days to dwell on this and for once he was glad he was booked into a single seat on the Hong Kong-bound flight. He would use every minute to study the brief that his old friend was to write up that evening.

"Come on my good man; let's get you and this little case of goodies to my place – oh and Jack..."

"Yes…"

"Bring the Talisker!"

Cade spent the next half an hour packing whilst his old friend garaged the Audi and locked the rest of the property down. He walked around to a neighbour and informed him that Jack was heading overseas, the result of needing to tend to an uncle who was seriously ill. The neighbour being a kindly soul agreed to look after the place until he returned.

With his Samsonite packed and a carry-on bag loaded with a laptop, cables, phones and a couple of different wallets he walked through the house, closing doors and mentally saying goodbye.

He paused in the bathroom and for a moment found himself back in the shower, the steam enveloping them both and the undeniably wonderful sense of arousal that he had experienced at the hands of a woman he had truly fallen for.

He shook his head, quelled the rising acid in his throat, spat the contents of his mouth into the sink and watched it rinse away. In a short time he was stood with Daniel on the driveway.

"Ready?"

"Yep, ready as I'll ever be mate. Come on let's go."

They got into Daniels' 'boring' RAV4, belted up and moved off.

"Keep an eye out for that bloody Wraith John," said Cade even though he suspected it was now long gone.

"Roger that, will do, you know it's probably parked up at the airport by now?"

"I do, but call me paranoid, let's not let our guard down. OK?"

"Agreed." And with that JD patted his long-term friend on the thigh and accelerated through the town, back out onto the open road and towards home.

They arrived at JD's home after an eventless journey, the only highlight being when Cade looked out across the dense, dark green tree canopy to his left and wondered quietly just how long, if ever, it would be until the Golf and the Transit would be located. He hoped they died a long, slow and rather irritatingly painful death.

Moments later he was asleep.

If JD was able to study Cade's eyes he would have noticed the REM activity that led to him surfacing from his dream with a start.

"You OK?"

"Yep, just a bad dream. I could see those stunning eyes John but I've missed something…"

"It will come to you Jack, just be patient, possibly somewhere over the Pacific, but it'll come to you, the mind has a clever way of surprising itself!"

Daniel's words were lost; Cade was in a deep sleep once more, somehow trying to reconnect to his departed soul mate.

They arrived at JD's home, decanted and met up with Lynne.

She stood arms out wide and didn't say a word.

Cade stepped into her embrace and fought back his raw emotions.

"Platitudes Jack, platitudes, and therefore pointless. Come on, I've got a great lasagne waiting to be devoured. You need to eat more and drink less, you look terrible." She looked at her husband who winked and shrugged his shoulders.

"We only had one love…and it was for medicinal purposes…"

"Indeed, but this man needs to stay focussed and Messrs Talisker and Bowmore are hardly going to help are they?"

She was right of course but being right wasn't always what people needed to hear, especially after the loss of someone so dear.

"I'll be fine Lynne, promise, I'm OK."

"OK? And what exactly does that mean?"

He laughed "Darling I haven't got the foggiest, but somehow I'll be OK."

She tutted and walked him into the kitchen.

"Eat this and we'll talk about tomorrow. Dip the sourdough into the sauce, it's delicious. John tells me you are booked and ready to go, what are your plans?"

"Honestly? Not a bloody clue, but JD has been putting a few things into place. First and foremost I need to get there, find somewhere to create Base Camp, reunite with a few old friends and sift through the wreckage of the last few days. I also need to find out who I'm dealing with and if the basic intel that your husband has gathered is correct then the UK is the best place to start my hunt; if I'm going to be staring down the barrel of a gun it would be quite nice to know who's likely to pull the trigger."

He took a mouthful of the pasta and nodded.

"This is great Lin' just needs a touch more pepper."

He deserved the slap but it made him smile if nothing else.

Contrary to her early guidance they opened a bottle of Rabbit Ranch Pinot Noir and got to work demolishing it, along with the meal.

"Once I've sorted out a few things in Hong Kong I'll head to London and see what I can dig up. At least I'll be on familiar ground and..." he paused for a moment.

With an over-laden forkful JD looked at Cade and said "You know she's gone Jack, I told you didn't I? Just try to put her in the back of your mind if you can, get on that plane tomorrow and head down a new path, for now, it's all you can do. You cannot afford to go anywhere near her now. You, or rather we need to abrogate you of any connection to any of this. I'll make some discreet checks with the authorities and let you know if I hear of anything new. As soon as I do, you will."

He nodded, all the while staring out into the blackening Pacific Ocean, wondering what the last week had been all about and whether in fact it was all actually quite as real as it seemed to be.

Outside, in the main restaurant a sound stirred him from his daydream.

"What's that, or rather should I say who?"

"Oh, they are a country band – we got them here on recommendation. Lynne loves 'em, called *Cooper's Run*, very talented bunch, all locals and trust me, they are the next big thing in country music..." he paused "Oh and Jack, the lead singer is simply gorgeous!"

Lynne interjected "Yes Jack, he is!"

They all laughed. For Cade it was a blessed release, for JD a sign that the pressure cooker had just released a small percentage of steam; for now at least that would be enough to assure him that his protégé was unlikely to erupt.

"Come on old son, let's take what's left of this and head down to the bar. You'll love them, it will do you good, and that my lad is an order."

They gravitated towards the bar where the band were now in full swing, singing a combination of classic country and their own new track called *Summertime*.

Cade allowed himself a moment to bathe in the sound, JD was right, the lead singer was heavenly but for Cade there was only one woman in his life, and besides her partner looked all too rugged.

Would he ever hear them play again? For that matter would he ever return to New Zealand? Or, as the natural pessimist in him suspected would another series of events guide him along an unknown and perilous path?

Within twenty four hours he'd be embarking on that journey. He could spend the rest of the night going over the plan, again, and again, but instead settled on raising a glass to the band and began to think about Elena as his right foot unconsciously tapped along to the music. Try as he might he couldn't stop, each time he drifted off, recounting the last few days, the lyrics to their song haunted him *"Down a dirt road, where nobody goes, our little secret, that nobody knows…"*

He awoke with a start, the song was still in his head. Christ, it wasn't a dream. It was hugely real, dangerously tangible and deeply disturbing.

He tidied up his bed, ever the disciplined individual and headed for the en suite. The shower finally woke him; the steam filled his lungs and breathed new life, untying myriad knots in his back and neck and seeking out the tiny cuts on his chest. As he stood in the cubicle he slowly wrote her name on the tinted glass and then watched the letters bleed, one by one, before fading away.

Drying himself off he noted a few more knocks and scrapes, evidence of the preceding day, adrenalin had forbidden his body from reacting to them. They would heal, far quicker than his mental scars.

He said out aloud 'She's gone.'

Lynne called out to Cade that breakfast was on the table. He smiled; it truly didn't matter how bloody terrible you felt, the smell of bacon in the morning was unbeatable. He placed his shaver and other bits and pieces into his case, twisted the combination locks to 385 and tapped the lid.

As he walked out of the room he looked back at his case, "See you in Hong Kong".

Chapter Nine

The RAV was loaded up and with a nod Cade bid goodbye to the exquisitely beautiful Coromandel Peninsula, an area that for a while at least he had called home.

They soon arrived at the intersection for State Highway 25A, Daniel indicated left and accelerated. His pace quickened. Cade knew why, it was obvious that his old friend was in a hurry to pass by the site where the events of the previous day had unravelled.

As they drove by the location all that remained of the horrific scene was a single black line on the road surface, a score mark deep in the tarmac that veered sharply to the left and a hundred metres further on a neatly swept pile of auto glass; clear, red and amber in colour it sparkled among the dreary grey pieces of tarmac bringing life to an otherwise generic vista.

Where the Cayman had come to rest a single white rose was propped up against the rock.

"JD stop the car!"

The Toyota came to an abrupt halt as Cade left the passenger seat and ran back along the road. Lynne went to follow him but her husband stopped her.

"Leave him, he needs to do this."

Cade reached the site in seconds, crouched down and with complete deference touched the ground upon which his lover had lost her fight. Tears ran down his face and onto the floor, quickly evaporating and blending into the dusty surface.

He reached towards the rose which had a small ivory-coloured card attached to its stem. He turned it over, upon the reverse it simply said "Until then."

His reserves of rational thinking were depleted. The words could have meant many things, however right now, none of them made any sense.

He placed the rose carefully back onto the floor and walked back towards the RAV 4. Opening the door he took one last look before getting in and asking his friend to drive on.

Two hours later after an eventless run they pulled onto the forecourt of Auckland International Airport. He exited the Toyota and took his case from Daniel. He turned to Lynne and accepted the inevitable hug. She quickly got back into the car, better that way than showing her obvious feelings to a man who simply didn't need such emotion.

He looked at JD.

"Thank you for everything. I'll wait till I get to Hong Kong before I read the report but I know it will be typically thorough. I've got the hard drive in my carry on and the documents are in the case. Once I've met up with a couple of our old friends I'll be in touch. Did you run your eyes over the papers last night? Are they what I think they are?"

"I did. And yes, I think they are as significant as we both imagine. What she was doing with them is anyone's guess Jack. Why she had them is another and what this group want with them is yet another. I took the liberty of copying them, they are locked in my own personal safe. The original is safer still. Until or if we need them."

"Thanks boss. Look after Lynne and keep an eye out on my interests won't you John?"

He nodded and offered a hand.

Cade took it and as he did John Daniel pulled him towards him and held him close for a few seconds.

"Remember everything, forget nothing and for God's sake come back alive Jack. Oh and this is for you, a gift from Lynne and I, she insisted on getting you something. I told her not to bother…"

He took the small package and placed it in his pocket.

Daniel smiled "I'd open it if I was you, you'll need it to fill out your departure card.

"Nothing like a surprise JD!" said Cade as he opened the small square package to reveal a Fisher Space Pen, stainless steel, in the shape of an elongated bullet. Along its flanks were the words *'Kia kaha'* – Cade knew it meant Stay Strong, an oft used Maori phrase; simple but appropriate for what lay ahead of him.

"Now don't lose the bloody thing, took me ages to find it. I remembered you had one back in London in the old days, I never forget when Jason Roberts gave it to you as a leaving present and gave the infamous speech…"

Cade started to laugh as his friend relived a story he had told many times before.

"…about the pen being developed by NASA, how it was researched by the Americans for years, how it could write under water, on grease and upside down and even in space and you said…"

"The Russians took a pencil!"

"You did Jack, you did and it still makes me laugh. Right piss off and ring me when you get chance." He patted him on the back and let him go.

As Cade walked away he turned once more. Lynne Daniel had composed herself and blew a kiss which Cade returned with gusto. He shouted to Daniel "I'll ring you mate unless I get lucky at Happy Valley again, then…well then…I might not!"

Cade turned, crossed the road and into the departure lounge of Jean Batten Airport, its official name, commemorating the female aviator who landed there in 1936. To Jack she was a genuine heroine and one who he had researched before he first travelled to New Zealand.

He was dismayed to learn that she had died in a Majorca hotel, as a result of complications following a simple dog bite; at the time he remarked to anyone that might have been listening 'all that way, alone, battling the elements and her own limits of endurance and she succumbed to a bloody dog bite.'

A strikingly beautiful woman who had courageously travelled the world, endeavouring to make a difference; she had succeeded but her lonely, anonymous death in a corner of the globe so far from home was incredibly poignant to Cade. He patted a bronze statue of her as he walked into the Departure hall.

"Hello sweetheart, look after me during my travels."

He slipped inconspicuously into the Business Class lane of Cathay Pacific and greeted the ground staff member in Cantonese whilst handing over his passport.

Having answered all the obligatory questions he placed his hold stow luggage on the conveyor belt, accepted his boarding pass and said farewell.

He stopped at a nearby pillar and leant on a glass shelf, filling out his departure card with his newly-acquired gift. He hesitated on the section which asked how long he would be out of the country. Optimistically he ticked one month.

Moments later he was at the New Zealand Customs Service primary line, handing over his passport and departure card. The young female officer scanned his travel document, checked her recessed screen for alerts and seconds later handed back his British passport.

"Enjoy your trip Mr Cade, see you in a month."

He'd often marvelled at just how approachable the local Customs Officers were. He'd met a few in his time and he regarded them highly.

He placed his carry-on luggage into a grey plastic tray along with his watch, some coins, a belt and his paperwork; leaving the package of documents in his check-in luggage was a master stroke as he knew that at any international border they would attract attention.

Moving through the magnetometer without incident he smiled at the Aviation Security Officer and collected his items, placing the tray back on a growing pile.

The airport was getting very busy, the main Asian flights were starting to fill, departing the Land of the Long White Cloud for Singapore, Bangkok, Kuala Lumpur and Hong Kong.

He had a few moments to spare so walked towards the duty free area, his intention being to price up another bottle of *Dark Storm*, JD having successfully depleted his last one.

As he made his way to the store another Customs Officer walked towards him.

In his twenties, six foot three and all too handsome he had a dog with him, a shimmering ebony-black Labrador who was paying a little too much attention to Cade's bag.

"Excuse me sir, can you just step to one side please?"

He did and without fuss.

"Thank you. My dog is trained to detect a number of commodities and he has indicated on your carry-on bag – is there anything you need to tell me before I commence a search of the luggage?"

"Well, I can tell you that I have nothing to hide if that helps – what is he trained on?"

It was a fair question and the officer didn't hesitate with his response.

"Drugs sir, oh and cash."

"Well officer I certainly wouldn't be carrying drugs, I've spent years targeting narcotics operations and as for cash, yes I've got an amount in my bag, I'm heading to Hong Kong for a few days and I owe someone some money, call it a debt of gratitude, it's New Zealand dollars, about a thousand, I can show you."

He did and as he did so the officer praised his dog and gave him his favourite training aide – a soft rubber toy. It clearly meant more to him than finding any drug or amount of money.

"He's a great dog" Cade offered.

"He is sir, very, I'm a lucky man to have him as a partner – he's more reliable than most humans that's for sure!"

They both laughed. Cade's was genuine, he missed the days of enforcement, and here he was talking to a genuinely decent young officer who was trying to make a difference to his adopted country.

"Where are you from?"

"Originally? Nottinghamshire, England."

"Well, well. I thought I picked up on the accent. I was originally from Kent, moved north, spent a while at East Midlands Airport myself, worked closely with your UK colleagues and the local police".

"Really? My old man was a copper in Nottinghamshire."

"Would I know him?"

"I doubt it. Left there in 2003 – works here now."

"Small world isn't it?"

"It is, unless you have to paint it."

They laughed and Cade put out his hand.

"Jack Cade, thanks for doing a great job for our chosen country."

"Thank you. I'm Andrew and this fine young Labrador is called Ajax. As you say, small world, travel safely Mr Cade and let's make sure he doesn't indicate on you on the way back in!"

"I'm stopping off at Happy Valley, trust me, he won't! And…" He sighed "I may not be back."

They parted. Cade had enjoyed the brief interlude; it was a form of escape from the rawness of very recent events and being airside in an international airport gave him an even greater sense of security.

As he picked up a bottle of his favourite malt Ajax the Lab had picked out a new target, a Chinese male who was protesting far too much for both Cade and the canine hunter's liking.

He walked along the departure pier until he reached Gate 9. Despite having access to the Business Lounge he simply couldn't be bothered. He'd dine in style soon and unlike the majority on board could genuinely stretch out and relax. He placed his bag on the floor and sat down. An attractive brunette smiled at him so he returned the compliment. On any given day he would have been as interested as any male, but not today, not tomorrow and probably sometime never.

He tapped his jacket pocket; passport still there. He could relax. In ten minutes the Menzies ground staff started to call for Business Class passengers to board. Cade was one of the first on the Airbus A-340 – the other members of his exclusive club had all diverted to the nearby lounge for drinks and nibbles. Cade had been more interested in meeting a wet-nosed narcotics hunter and besides he knew he would be treated like royalty on board.

He greeted the In-flight Service Director in Cantonese and was shown to his seat.

His luggage tucked safely in a compartment at the side of his seat he slumped into the overly large chair and buckled up.

He had an eleven hour flight ahead of him. Unlike a normal journey of this type he would not be watching countless films but instead prepared his laptop for a briefing from one of the best in the business. As soon as they were in the air he would switch it on and start reading JD's briefing document.

The aircraft soon filled, people further back fought with their far-too-large carry-on luggage and huffed and sighed at the thought of spending eleven hours next to someone they didn't know and really couldn't be bothered to engage with.

Cade smiled and said internally "Thanks for spending my hard-earned cash JD – very much appreciated."

He meant it.

He had often marvelled at how humans could sit quite so close to one another, for hour after hour and in some cases, never speak.

As he pondered on the foibles of the average human being CX198 taxied onto Runway 19 at the eastern end of the terminal and started to roll forwards, gathering speed. Cade looked out of the window and could see the terminal racing by to his right, to his left, the sea.

The 340's Rolls Royce Trent engines thrust the aircraft down the runway until almost imperceptibly the pilot eased back the yoke and they were airborne.

Cade could soon see the beautiful Hauraki Gulf beneath them with Auckland at its centre, the famous Sky Tower vying for attention on the skyline.

As soon as the seatbelt lights extinguished Cade drank his complimentary Moet, set his chair to recline and kicked off his shoes. He unzipped the carry bag and removed the laptop. In seconds he was knee-deep in a mass of data which JD has added a sound file to. Cade plugged his Bose noise-cancelling headphones into the computer and started to listen as a member of the crew offered him a top up.

"Greetings Jack my lad; I thought I'd offer you a sound file in case there were prying eyes on board. By now you will be thanking me for upgrading you to Business and trying to fathom why the pretty girl-next-door brunette who smiled at you found you even vaguely attractive."

Cade smiled. It was a wild guess on his mentor's part but a good one nonetheless. He continued to listen.

"Now, the events of the last few days have been a mixture of many incredible things and I know your head is spinning at ten thousand RPM, but you have to try to focus. What I'm about to tell you will help. Down in that case of yours which is by now freezing away in the hold is a mixture of documents, a huge collection of business cards, computer data and importantly, a significant collection of passports. Hit next."

Cade looked around. No-one was remotely interested so he eased open the laptop to reveal the screen and what he saw made him extremely interested.

The slide showed imagery taken from the business card folder. Whilst there were indeed hundreds of cards there was a single theme – they all belonged to Diplomat's, Consul's or Ambassador's and almost without exception they all hailed from countries in Africa and all appeared to have the same address on them: Quartier Rubens, Block C2

1040 Bruxelles, or more simply, one of the most significant branches of the United Nations.

He shook his head. "Elena what were you wrapped up in girl? Was this stuff even yours?"

JD had filmed the documents and as the camera ran by each one he picked out some common themes – he knew that Cade was a qualified Document Examiner so threw in phrases that were important.

"Look here, a Diplomatic Passport in the name of Noel Sankara, which matches this business card and this birth certificate and this set of passport images. Interesting eh?"

Cade scanned the documents.

"By the way Sankara is probably linked to the famous revolutionary from that part of the world, Thomas Sankara. Anyway, that's beside the point. Where was I? Ah yes, see how they react to UV? Indeed, the Intaglio printing is of a high quality, the UV thread is spot on, the watermarks react as they should, the micro-printing is a work of art, security threads, they even have optically variable inks…Jack they look bloody good and do you know why?"

He paused, awaiting an answer that would never come, as if he were engaged in a face to face conversation with Cade.

"Indeed, because they are genuine, that's why!"

Cade continued to cast his eye over the footage which played in front of him, checking the quality of the printing and not doubting for a second that these travel documents were as his friend had stated, nothing more than bona fide passports. The question was why did Elena have them?

"OK, so we know that the passports are genuine and she's got thirty and each is accompanied by supportive data as you can see; other documents that support their integrity and give weight to them being genuine. The business cards are probably kosher too. I've run a few checks on the names; it transpires that none are reported stolen. The countries are all on the fringe Jack, there or thereabouts places that you and I would most likely never visit and in the main places most normal folk have never heard of."

He started to reel off a list.

Benin, Burkina Faso, Burundi, Comoros, Djibouti,

There were other better known states but the majority were small, almost anonymous.

"Jack, Interpol confirm that all the docs are technically live but most haven't been used to travel since arriving in Belgium a while ago. In theory the owners work in the UN community – or at least purport to. My biggest question, my greatest misgiving is…"

He didn't need to ask it. Jack was thinking the same thing.

Why? Why Dimitrova?

He could ask the question ad nauseum. He did. But the answer never came. Clearly this spellbindingly-pretty girl was not all she seemed – but still he felt that she was genuine, on-side, possibly now with an agenda but definitely an ally. Had she stolen the case? Or, rather had she been given it by someone else? Were the contents and their true value even known to her?

What stayed in the forefront of his mind, haunted him the most, was John Daniel's final summing up.

"Jack. I can begin to explain a lot of what makes this group tick. We've skirted around the peripheries of them since we first met. We know they are well organised, at times unpleasant and in the main, I hate to say it, successful. In essence they are no different from any other organised criminal group in what drives them; greed. But what is in that case adds up to something else. False or genuine passports, stolen to order, possibly for identity or financial gain. My instinct tells me that our target intended to use these to gain some credibility on the European or even world stage. That's the easy part. The bit that I don't get – don't yet understand is the document that is in your hand luggage in the last unmarked envelope."

Cade thought back to the large manilla covering – he'd ignored it, dismissed it as a copy of an official document that only a solicitor would ever be able to interpret.

"You probably opened it, gave it a cursory flick through and put it back. I did too, on the first run. But late last night I read it again. Jack, it's not just a document, it's dynamite in the wrong hands and for now I encourage you to keep it close hold, like it's a part of you. I've held the original as you know, you have a copy. But guard it as if it were able to destabilise a government. Because quite frankly, it could."

The Cathay flight was cruising at five hundred and fifty miles an hour, crossing the vast expanse of water that was the Pacific Ocean. People had settled in to their in-flight entertainment and had polished off the first meal. Cade had been offered a very passable fish dish; red snapper and a choice of steamed seasonal vegetables.

The dessert was a heady concoction of tropical fruit which cascaded off a heavenly cheesecake. These were followed with the freshest of coffee, served in a china cup and a choice of handmade chocolates. It was as good as any meal he had ever had. Either that or he was exhausted and simply didn't care. Either way he knew there would be breakfast in eight hours and on-demand food from the Galley only a button push away.

As a final nod to a hedonistic form of travel he was offered a choice of either a dessert wine or a spirit. He could have had both but as a nod to his dear old friend he chose a twenty year old Bowmore.

He savoured each drop before allowing the staff to clear his table. The electric motors on his seat soon made light work of turning the already comfortable chair into an even more relaxing bed. He stood up for a moment to stretch his tired legs and looked along the infinite alloy tube that now skipped across the night sky, heading for Papua New Guinea.

A few people, those who were awake at least, looked back at him, clearly despising him for his good fortune. Their grey, almost lifeless faces stared impassively. He had some sympathy, having travelled many thousands of miles in the rear end of such aircraft, escorting waifs and strays back to their homelands, he knew just how hard international travel was. It was anything but glamorous.

His sympathy ended soon after he pulled the covers over his cooling body and laid his head onto a goose down pillow. Within minutes he was asleep.

He woke with a start many hours later after an incredible, dreamless sleep.

"Good morning ladies and gentlemen this is your First Officer Tony Baker; we are about two hours from Hong Kong where the temperature is currently twenty nine degrees. Soon the crew will be serving you breakfast, which will consist of either a cooked or continental meal, I hope you enjoy it as much as we just have."

It raised a few weary titters of laughter. Everyone else in economy wanted to eject the smug bastard as they were almost guaranteed not to get their first choice.

"Finally as we approach our destination, on behalf of the crew I'd like to thank you for flying with Cathay Pacific today, we do appreciate you have a choice. The Captain, Michael Wilson and the rest of the team wish you safe travel if you are heading onwards from Hong Kong."

Cade couldn't believe how much he'd slept. The combination of the previous week had obliterated his sleep patterns. He rubbed his eyes and accepted a hot flannel from a very attentive Steward.

Daylight had arrived as they skipped across the South China Sea. An hour and a half later, with a favourable tailwind they approached one of the busiest airports in the world – Chep Lap Kok or to give it its more common name, Hong Kong International.

Chapter Ten

The A340 touched down at its home port without drama, onto the Northern Runway and was soon rolling along the taxiway towards Terminal One before arriving on time, on block at Gate 30.

It was at times like these that Cade appreciated the benefits of travelling in style. He thanked the crew in both Cantonese and English, collected his belongings and left the aircraft, leaving behind the usual seething mass of litter, stale air and quietly bristling, exhausted economy passengers.

In less than twenty five minutes he was outside the terminal and in a taxi heading along the North Lantau Highway towards one of his favourite destinations. He nodded quietly, wishing that she was here to share it with him.

They crossed the Tsing Ma Bridge, offering a magnificent view across to Hong Kong Island and its crowning glory, Victoria Peak. All that stood between the two was a swirling, darting mass of interwoven highways and tunnels, bridges and interchanges. It was a simply brilliant lesson to the world on how it should be done.

Once more he found himself admiring the determination of the locals to move the city into a well-earned place as one of the most vibrant and successful on the planet.

They cruised across Stonecutter's Bridge which scythed through the immense container port before veering right onto the West Kowloon Highway. Cade took in the familiar sights and begun to smile, he was back in a place that some years prior had become, somewhat unexpectedly, responsible for his financial independence.

The taxi bypassed the toll booths and soon they were making great progress under the harbour. Cade's driver skilfully negotiated the numerous lanes, amongst myriad other red and white taxis which were as 'Hong Kong' as the famous Star Ferry. The cars jostled for position with their peers, with tour buses, delivery trucks, motorbikes and the now ever-present Mercedes Benz, BMW's and Rolls Royce's. Occasionally a Lamborghini would dart by, a break from the monotony of the boring luxury saloons, twelve cylinder engines rasping, clawing at the air and ricocheting off the immense skyline. And yellow – just to buck the trend.

A blue Wraith whispered by, the mirrored glass shielding the occupants from the intense heat and prying eyes. Cade shuddered involuntarily, blaming the air conditioning all the while knowing that the very image of the British icon would forever make him think of the past and what might have been.

It wouldn't be the last Rolls that he would see; in a city which claimed more owners than any other he would soon turn a blind eye, just like everyone else.

Soon they re-emerged into the stunning sunshine and entered Connaught Road. Five minutes later they arrived outside the iconic Mandarin Oriental Hotel. It had been a trouble-free journey and thankfully, almost anti-socially it had been quiet. Conventionally Cade would have made the effort to strike up a conversation in the local dialect, but not today.

As he exited the cab, having settled his bill, Cade noted that the Concierge was already directing staff to collect his luggage. A few Hong Kong dollars were exchanged and Cade made his way to reception, pausing for a second to wipe a thin veil of perspiration from his forehead.

It didn't matter how many times you visited the more tropical climes they never failed to surprise you with their innate ability to drain you of your energy in moments. It was a way of life for many, but for Cade it was something he only ever intended to experience for a few days.

The usual details were exchanged for a key card and six minutes later he walked into his Harbour room. His luggage was waiting. It was almost perfect; all that was missing was a green-eyed playful redhead. Despite the superb view and wonderful facilities he felt empty.

He acquiesced, accepting that he was alone, fired off a text to JD and threw his clothes into a laundry basket before stepping into the shower.

The glass-walled room offered a brilliant view across Victoria Harbour into downtown Kowloon, the tallest spires of which were lost in the familiar haze.

He luxuriated in the hotel-supplied Hermes body wash as the multi-headed system got to work unravelling his tired and over-stressed muscles. A good ten minutes later, with the glass and mirrors obliterated by steam he wrapped a thick white dressing gown around himself and stood in the window.

He knew he needed to eat, but first had to make a few phone calls. As he walked towards his phone he flicked a switch on the Nespresso machine.

The number on Cade's phone connected and started to ring.

It was answered in fewer than two rings.

"Ni hao"

"Wai"

"Hóunoih móuhgin"

The voice on the other end of the phone went quiet for a second, as if the owner was trying to place the caller's identity. He was.

"It has indeed been a long time…but forgive me, I can't quite place you…"

"Ngaw serng ngaow!"

Cade had deliberately informed the anonymous voice that he was feeling a little unwell. It was unusual but it broke the ice and allowed the missing piece of the jigsaw to fall quickly into place. With a mixture of surprise, delight and deliberately spoken English the voice responded.

"Well my dear Mr Cade, it has indeed been a long time since that happened. Fuck me Jack where you been all these years. Where are you? Talk to me!"

"In a room overlooking the harbour at the Mandarin Oriental, give me time to finish this coffee and I'll even think about coming to say hello my good friend."

"Cade, forget the coffee I've got a bottle of Glenmorangie in my filing cabinet."

"So you kept it all these years, I'm impressed!"

"I made a promise that one day we would finish it off. I tell my staff that if one of them so much as touches it - I kill them!"

They laughed. It was good to hear the voice of an old friend and as he was a Chief Inspector in the Royal Hong Kong Police it was even more reassuring. If he had been followed at least he felt safe in a city where theoretically he was as much a foreigner as anyone from Eastern Europe.

"Get out of that free dressing gown Cade, put on some clothes – but try to look stylish, I'll have a car there in twenty minutes."

The phone disconnected. Cade knew better than to argue, as tired as he was he needed to meet up with Kwok-Leung Tsang or as he was often known by his Anglicised name, Andy. It had been far too long and they had a lot of catching up to do.

When they had last met Tsang had been a newly-promoted Chief Inspector, Cade was keen to find out how his career had progressed. He sipped his coffee and selected some clothes, lightweight chino trousers and a smart-casual shirt. He sat at the teak desk and opened his laptop, connected to the wi-fi and entered the Hong Kong Police website.

He let out a low whistle as he read his old friend's biography. It transpired that Andy had indeed progressed. He had served mainly in crime units at regional and headquarters levels for most of the early stage of his career.

He drank more of the intense, hot coffee and continued.

Between late 2006 and 2010 he was seconded to the Interpol General Secretariat in Lyon, France as a Liaison Officer. Cade knew this part. Subsequently, he was promoted in the organisation as Deputy Director heading the Interpol Asia & South Pacific Branch.

The site explained that after returning to Hong Kong, Tsang worked as a Senior Superintendent in the Drug Squad until promotion to Chief Superintendent in 2010 when he was posted to the Security Wing. He was now knocking on the door of the rank of Assistant Commissioner and had been tasked with heading up the newly formed Organized Crime and Triad Bureau.

The web page explained that the Bureau investigated complex organised crime and serious triad offences and worked with international enforcement agencies to exchange intelligence, and as the site succinctly put it, to 'neutralise illegal activities'.

He smiled and said out aloud "Right up your street Andy my old son, right up your street."

His bedroom phone rang. The female voice announced that his car had arrived. He travelled down to the Lobby in the gold coloured lift, leaning on the brown leather-panelled walls as his ears adjusted to the change in pressure, exited quietly into the dark wood hallway and waited for a man in uniform to arrive.

"Well look what the cat dragged in, if it is not my old British friend Jackie Cade!"

The voice was Tsang's and the reference to Jackie Chan was not lost.

Cade spun around and dropped into a mocking martial arts pose, knowing that whilst he was relatively proficient he would have lasted but a moment at the hands of Andy Tsang.

Tsang was lean and had looks that belied his age, he was immaculate in a dark navy suit, white shirt and scarlet tie with a matching handkerchief peeking out from his breast pocket. His black leather brogues were startlingly clean.

They exchanged a fierce handshake and looked one another up and down before announcing mutually that they looked well.

"You've done well Andy; I've been reading your bio. All rather impressive Acting Commissioner!"

"Thank you Jack, it's good to see you again, been a long time, too long, how have you been?"

Cade explained that life had been good since they had last met but Tsang sensed that something was missing.

"Have you eaten Jack? You look tired, come on I know a great restaurant and I'll even pay!"

"OK, is it far?" replied Cade.

"No, in fact it's walking distance."

Tsang laughed, walked to the Concierge and handed him his car keys knowing that they would be looked after. Tsang's face was well known, despite it being a city of seven million people.

"This place has a number of Michelin starred restaurants, but I know somewhere that is going to be dearer to your heart old chap." He mocked Cade's accent "Come on, we have some serious eating and catching up to do. Afterwards we can hit the town if you are still up to it!"

Tsang had lost none of his appetite for the finer things – his current salary and status in the region meant that he was living a very pleasant lifestyle, but instead of walking into the French restaurant they entered the infamous bar known as The Chinnery.

Named after the famous British artist George Chinnery, the bar epitomised an old English gentleman's club, complete with deep upholstered armchairs, green leather banquettes and warm wood panelling.

It offered something rarely seen in the world of celebrity chefs and on-demand catering; a laid-back alternative to fine dining restaurants, offering traditional British cuisine such as bangers and mash, fish and chips, and steak and ale pie.

Rather rebelliously it was exactly what Cade fancied. He placed his order for the fish which was a Haddock fillet fried in Boddingtons beer batter and home-made chips and sipped, much to Tsang's amusement on some mineral water. He was pacing himself.

The Chinnery was also home to one of the world's largest collections of single malt whiskies, with over 109 varieties it was a challenge for even the most ardent drinker.

Tsang ordered pan-fried John Dory with new season vegetables served with a mussel and clam broth. He had acquired a European palette during his time in France.

The food arrived and Tsang and Cade began to put the world to rights, covering off the past as quickly as they could. They had first met in Lyon when Cade had also been seconded to the Interpol General Secretariat, he as an Investigator, his Chinese counterpart as a Liaison Officer.

He beckoned the waiter to the table and ordered a couple of drinks, he chose a Johnnie Walker Blue Label – a rarity in many countries, whilst a protesting Cade decided upon a fifteen year old Aberfeldy, a drink he had not been able to sample for many years.

It was good to be in Andy Tsang's company again. He clashed his crystal glass against his counterpart's and proposed a toast.

"Let us hunt down the bastards and make them pay!"

"Agreed!"

Tsang didn't realise that Cade had a specific group of bastards in his sights but was always willing to raise a glass.

"Gam bei!" announced Tsang.

"Cheers" replied Cade.

Over the next few hours he outlined what had been happening. He painted a remarkable picture of the amazing woman who had entered his life and who had left it so abruptly.

Tsang could see his friend was starting to struggle to say the words and so steered him skilfully away from the subject, for the time being at least.

Cade returned to the theme briefly and then explained the two main reasons for returning to Hong Kong.

"Number One? Going through Los Angeles is such a pain…Hong Kong is so much easier! No, seriously Andy I need to pick your brains on who I might be dealing with. I may need your help, if that's OK? I think I've inadvertently stumbled across some of our old sparring partners from Romania, they are linked into so much of my past and now, well now they feature in my future too, oh and Number Two, to give you this."

He leant across the table and placed an envelope into Tsang's hand.

"Suggest you open it at home, it's all above board, but I owe it to you for that suggestion a few years ago at Happy Valley. It's Kiwi dollars too, worth more at the moment!"

As he opened the envelope and examined it contents Tsang cast his mind back to the last time they were together and began to smile.

Cade had travelled to Hong Kong in 2006 following his unexpected 'career break' from the British Police, he also recalled there was an issue with his wife, Penny, yes that was it, Penny, attractive girl apparently, but slightly unhinged.

He remembered how Cade had been desperate to start a new life, one without the bitterness, but still be able to hold onto the brighter parts of his past.

Back then they were working on an operation targeting an Eastern European crime syndicate; it was all coming back to him now. Cade had taken a career break after calling his boss a...what was it now? That's right, a complete fuckwit. Andy Tsang had never heard of the phrase before but would use it from that day onwards.

Cade had left Britain and arrived in Hong Kong en route to the Southern Hemisphere and had offered to act as a consultant to the HKP, surprisingly for free; he felt so passionate about the damage that a select group of Europeans were doing and wanted to make a difference. Tsang remembered thinking that Cade was either mentally ill or a spy. He soon learned that he was in fact neither, just a decent man who cared about right, and wrong, and besides he was willing, in a city driven by financial gain, to work for nothing. He probably was mentally ill.

Together they had spent a few weeks hunting a couple of European targets who were believed to be in Asia and despite the odds being stacked against them they succeeded.

Two of the most wanted Romanian financial crime targets had been apprehended trying to leave Hong Kong Airport. They were in possession of masses of personal bank information, obtained using a system that had previously not been observed in any part of the world.

They saw Hong Kong as a honey pot and stripped it bare. Or at least they had until the cold determined hand of Andy Tsang had landed upon their shoulders as they stepped onto a late-night Lufthansa flight bound for Munich.

Tsang and his team were lauded as international thief-takers and although, deliberately, Cade had not been mentioned in the press coverage that followed, both Tsang, his bosses and importantly Cade's old management team knew that he was heavily involved in the capture.

Cade was offered a law enforcement key to the city.

The night that the pair was convicted saw Tsang and his team celebrate by hitting the town, painting it red and every other possible shade, descending upon The Chinnery to almost clear the top shelf and eventually after being asked politely to leave they ended up at Happy Valley an iconic location of its own making.

As the team left the Mandarin Oriental the managers gathered to count their gains; never before had their prized collection been so brutally attacked. The night would enter into local folklore and would never be repeated. The last round alone, bought by the poor

Englishman was valued at over two and half thousand Hong Kong dollars.

However the poor Englishman was now a part of that team and as long as Tsang was in the Hong Kong force he always would be. They were poured into taxis and made their way to the famous horse racing stadium.

Their spontaneous fleet was waved goodbye with a promise that they would be needed later, the drivers accepted, quite readily, that they would not be paid for their services; it was, if you like a way of life when dealing with government agencies.

"Come on Cade! This way, there are six races left, bring your wallet Englishman – I have friends in low places, let us see if we can win back what that last round just cost you!"

Cade was amazed at how sober his Chinese counterpart appeared to be; he was an absolute professional in the station but utterly ruthless in a bar, Cade simply couldn't keep up and was starting to stagger a little, his speech was slurred and his eyes glazed – the classic signs of drunkenness.

They all paid their minimal entry fee and wondered into the racecourse, the home of the Hong Kong Jockey Club and arguably one of the most impressive horse racing venues in the world.

Cade shook his head to clear his senses and looked at his surroundings. He was amazed to see upwards of twenty thousand people, all there for one thing, to gamble.

The course was surrounded by magnificent skyscrapers, dramatic hills, apartment blocks and graveyards. People came from across the island and mainland China just to have a chance to increase their wealth. For many risking a month's wages was worth the gamble, with an outside chance of changing their lives forever.

"So Cade, how much are you going to bet? I've had some inside information…" he tapped the side of his nose and started to laugh.

Cade was desperately trying to rid his body of alcohol so gave his wallet to his colleague.

"I'm off to the gents Tsang. Put it on *Alimony* in the first, *The Other Woman* in the final race and…oh I don't know Andy, it's your call – put it all on for all I care. Stick it on one of those quilena things." He laughed at his own inability to pronounce a simple word.

Tsang held his right hand up to his mouth and shouted "You mean a quinella! You win if you get a combination of first or second. Sure, I'll sort it out my friend. If we win you owe me a thousand bucks!"

Cade waved his left hand, caring not one jot about what Tsang had just said.

Tsang took the bulky wallet, opened it and by some coincidence handed over the equivalent of a thousand pounds. The old woman behind the counter didn't flinch, wrote down the bet and gave Tsang his slip before attending to the never-diminishing queue.

Cade staggered off to the gents, making his way haphazardly through a sea of excited punters heading past him and back towards the racing. The smell of the course was unforgettable, the sense of anticipation palpable.

He entered a cubicle, pulled down his trousers, sat on the cool seat, leant against the wall and almost instantly fell into a deep sleep.

Outside the toilets the noise was intense as eager race goers urged on their chosen steeds; it was like a highly organised, highly disciplined riot but with huge sums at stake and absolutely no need for the slightest police presence.

The second race had finished with *Alimony* thundering into first place, clouds of vapour emitting from its fiery nostrils as its jockey egged it over the finishing line to roars of approval from the eclectic mix of locals, tourists and expats.

Cade woke with a start, finished what he had never begun and left the crowded facilities, making his way back up a flight of concrete steps to where he last remembered seeing the team. He had also just recalled how much money he had actually put into his wallet when he left his room at the Oriental.

"Jack, we are over here!" Tsang yelled through the crowd.

Cade apologised to all and sundry as he made his way, rather awkwardly towards the squad "I'm on the way my men, I'm on my way!"

It all seemed so safe; Hong Kong was and still is a very safe haven. Or perhaps it was because he was in the company of a successful police unit who had an almost legendary status for their ability to apprehend criminals.

He made it to Tsang's side as the third race commenced.

"Sorry Andy I got a bit lost."

"You won! The old girl made it home in first place; you are up three thousand already."

Cade could only smile, a few thousand Hong Kong was not to be sniffed at. For now the wallet was empty but for a few bank cards, a driving licence and a white betting slip on which his future appeared in Cantonese.

Green Eyed Monster came home a close second. Cade was slumped over the railings and hadn't even realised that his winnings were slowly, exponentially growing.

As they stood in virtual daylight a British Airways 747 cruised overhead, on final approach to the airport, affording its passengers a brilliant view of the event below.

Back on the ground Cade was finally sobering up, he had plied himself with bottled water from a nearby vendor, much to the amusement and feigned horror of his newly adopted team who declared him a 'British lightweight'.

Despite his lack of alcoholic athleticism he was attracting a lot of attention from the group; Constables, Sergeants and Inspectors, all good men, loyal to the fight and now it seemed very loyal to Cade.

"They are a great bunch Andy, they seem to like me?"

"Jack, that horse coming in second just put your winning's up to twenty thousand, of course they like you!"

He was now sober. Very.

"Twenty? How? Why"

"Jack don't worry, you'll end up losing it all, we always do. Have some fun while you can – then later, you can leave here miserable like everyone else!"

"And it's *Admiral's Lad* from *Quartermaster*..."

It was all Cade needed to hear; another first. He was every problem gambler's nemesis. He knew two tenths of sod all about horses, let alone racing them around a track and yet here he was staring down the barrel of...how much?

Actually, he hadn't even begun to work it out. As his overpaid Chinese bookies' runner had announced, all too flippantly, he'd lose it all anyway.

But what if?

"*Golden Jubilee* by a nose from *Aardvark*!" announced the excited commentator.

"Jack, *Aardvark* is one of yours, check the slip. You need two more. Get ready to buy another round!" Tsang gestured with his right hand feverishly jabbing at the indecipherable names on the simple paper slip.

He was correct. It was. This was now getting a little too surreal. And Cade was now a little too sober. He needed a drink.

"Come on Andy I need a drink. I can't do this; I've never risked so much money. This is by far the most stupid, reckless thing I've ever done since that time in 1999 when Penny convinced me to..."

"But you need to watch. How are you going to let your grandchildren hear of how the Great Jack Cade won so much money in the Orient?"

Cade was as persistent as he could be and led them to a nearby bar from where he could both drink and observe.

"Grandchildren? At this rate I won't be around to have them, I'll have suffered a premature death from a heart attack and in my dying words I shall blame you Tsang!" He raised his glass once more "Cheers."

"You need to start living Jackie boy" said an animated Tsang. He raised his glass "Gam bei – come on – follow me."

Moments later they were at the finish line, ushered through the manic crowd by a Steward who had spotted the important visitor among the throng.

A few of the unit had joined them and were now as animated as their boss.

They watched the amusingly-named *Kinky Sect* cruise across the line, a leisurely second, a long way behind the winner but it mattered not. It was the penultimate winner Cade needed. Money was no longer on his mind, now it was all about putting a very large finger up at his former partner – if he won a reasonable sum, at least enough to help him live the next stage of his dream, then so much the better.

"And they are off!" The commentator announced the list of runners, almost breathlessly, introducing each as if he had his own personal fortune resting on the result. Perhaps he did?

The front runners thundered past Cade and his growing entourage, the combined effect of so many intensely-bred animals, the exotic location, the baying crowd and the potentially large amount of money, now poised on a financial cliff top made it one of the most outrageous things that he had ever encountered and he'd encountered a few.

He was feeling intoxicated by the experience and as the pack began to splinter, allowing the front six to make a break for the finish he took a long, deep, deliberate breath. Each exquisite animal strained to stay ahead of its peer, ligaments tauter than a long bow's drawstring, looking fit to burst; nostrils flared, eyes widened, hooves rhythmically drumming onto the dew-laden turf. He could smell the turf, feel them approaching, the growing vibrations manifesting themselves through the damp grass and into his own body. It was incredible.

He couldn't hear now. He didn't need to. He still had his eyesight however and that allowed him to watch *The Other Woman* come sensationally from behind, romping home to a resounding first place.

He punched the air, throwing his plastic glass sky high, its contents disappearing into the night. He was now laughing too; the irony of the winner coming from behind was certainly not lost on him. It was a personal moment of sheer delight; complete and incredible delight.

"Give me your betting slip Mr Cade, I will get one of my men to collect your winnings, you want cash or a cheque?"

"Hang on Andy, how much are we talking about here? I need a moment to clear my head. Jesus H Christ this is mental, categorically barking bloody mad."

He broke the rules and hugged the future Commissioner, who allowed it for a while then broke free so he could shake Cade's hand warmly before saying "I think we need to go with Sergeant Chung and collect your winnings. You need a police escort to ensure one of my guy's doesn't run away with your bounty!"

"One and a half a bloody million. Five bloody hundred thousand, and a million, exactly three halves of a fucking great million Andy. Five…" He was unable to articulate his thoughts and making no sense whatsoever. Tsang grabbed hold of both of his hands.

"I know, I know. You owe me Englishman!" He was genuinely delighted. Ten minutes past by and with cheque in hand and a growing group of new friends Cade watched as Tsang rounded up a fleet of taxis and once more poured his men into them.

The red and white convoy sped through the night towards the Tsim Sha Tsui area of Kowloon and their intended destination, The Intercontinental, a hotel made infamous by the many celebrities and very important people who had chosen to stay there.

They arrived fifteen minutes later. To their right a thriving mass of bars, restaurants and the ever-present tourists, cruise ships and the green and white ferries, each in its own way endeavouring to keep pace with the never-ending demands upon them. Bus doors hissed as they opened and closed, collecting and delivering thousands to and from the Ferry Terminal.

The door opened to the hotel and Tsang's team made for the bar. They were soon joined by an entourage of attractive women, all resplendent in evening gowns, gold, scarlet and green, immaculately made up and quintessentially exotic, especially to a Westerner like Cade.

Tsang stood on a small chair and announced to his team and their new-found concubines, "Ladies, gentlemen, I give you our colleague, our friend and our personal banker for the first round, Mr Jack Cade and his new friend *The Other Woman*."

The crowd cheered and started to place their orders. In the past Cade would have been a little concerned about how he would pay for such a gesture, given that his cheque hadn't even begun the journey to his account, but Tsang had already made 'arrangements' with the General Manager, assuring him of Cade's credentials.

They drank their way into the next morning when Cade and Tsang were tipped into the back seat of a patrol car with a warning to the somewhat perplexed officers to never discuss the moment again. It was

Cade who was the more sober on this occasion and who managed to utter the word Mandarin before passing out.

At nine o'clock the following morning he woke, startled by a shaft of light penetrating the heavy curtains. He blinked twice then rubbed his eyes with his balled-up fists.

He had not been that drunk since 1992.

He pushed his tongue through his arid lips and heard them crack apart. He tried to swallow but failed. He needed a drink. He needed water.

He shuffled around the room, trying to regain his bearings. He fell forwards over his suit, cursing whoever it was that left it there. He then began to replay the previous night.

Hotel, Andy Tsang, Happy Valley, a bet, a win and finally the Intercontinental where his last memory was seeing two exceptionally beautiful but decidedly upmarket whores diving naked into the pool with the Chief Inspector's men, who had clapped repeatedly until Cade stripped off and joined them, entering one of the world's most exclusive and expensive swimming pools with an uncharacteristically pathetic dive.

Legend would later have it that he took both girls to a room where despite their best and most skilful intentions, semi-naked and partially aroused he passed out; again.

He opened the curtains a little wider and delved into the deepest recesses of what was left of his mind and recalled being handed a cheque. He peered through partially erupted eyelashes and saw that it was propped up on his bedside table. He was somewhat incredulous. Despite his best laid prejudices it was still there.

Perhaps the girls had been honourable after all? Try though he might he simply couldn't remember where he and they had parted company, but wherever it was it wasn't with his cheque.

It was a simple cheque too, printed on Hong Kong and Shanghai Banking Corporation paper, made out to Mr Jack Cade to the sum of $14,430,492.90 HKD.

"Dear God it wasn't a dream. Jesus! Look at that, would you look at *that?*"

He heard a low-level moan from the bathroom. He rubbed his hands across his arid face and tried to process the sound. As he walked he blew his own breath into his hand, it stank and reminded him of an estuary at low tide.

There was that moan again.

"Great, I brought one of them back with me, this is really all I need right now; in-room dining with a high-class escort and an awkward conversation over breakfast. Tsang is going to be dining out on this for years."

It was all coming back to him, a tsunami of vivid information that plunged him back into the preceding evening. As his sub-conscious once more began to rewind and replay he started to feel a little nauseous. He sat bolt upright and made the decision to head for the bathroom.

He almost made it too, aiming to reach the sink but instead throwing up a bilious, bright-green cocktail, the remnants of the final round - complete with a partially digested cherry - straight into the enormous bath tub. It exited his body with a vengeance, reminding him with each convulsion why he hadn't drank that heavily since 1992.

The smell was atrocious, itself enough to upset the equilibrium of a hardened street dweller.

He clung onto the side of the bath, knuckles whitening with each miserable moment. It was only when he commenced the third set of convulsions that he realised that the bath had an occupant. Curled up in a spare duvet and resting his head on a few borrowed goose down pillows lay the next Commissioner of the Royal Hong Kong Police. He was, fortuitously oblivious to the events of the last ten minutes.

Quite how Cade was going to break it to Tsang that he had evidently vomited all over himself was something he wasn't exactly prepared for. It took a full ten minutes in the shower to come up with a plausible story and one which whilst not exactly happy with he was going to have to stick too for rather a long time.

Hindsight being what it was he now considered consuming a continental breakfast in the company of a voracious whore to be far more palatable than what he had done.

Tsang would eventually rise from his vitreous sarcophagus. He was appalled at his condition and apologised profusely to his friend who was incredibly charitable about the whole event, even offering to send an urgent request out for a new suit, it was he said the least a colleague could do.

And so it came to pass that Cade and Tsang would become lifelong friends. Their debts now settled they would remain in touch when and wherever they could and if ever Cade was to pass through the region he was instructed, on pain of death, that he must visit Tsang and his team.

As he farewelled Cade at the airport a few days later Tsang wondered where their individual paths would head. They did indeed make a pact to stay in touch and Cade assured him that once he had arrived in his intended destination he would send a message.

Cade had explained that he had chosen one of the most remote countries on the globe to escape to, a chance to leave his problems behind and start anew. With the benefit of his unexpected equestrian windfall he could invest in a business and soon gain permanency in his adopted land.

It was the least Tsang could do to wish Jack Cade every success. Tsang knew he didn't need luck but he wished him continued good fortune nonetheless, he shook his hand warmly then turned sharply on his heels and walked back to his car.

Neither could have known that it would be years until they saw each other again.

Those eight years had flown by at a rate which alarmed both the Chinese and the British officer. It seemed that with the passing of time a little wisdom has been implanted too.

Both men decided against a repeat of The Great Night of 2006. Tsang for the sake of his career, Cade because he was just too exhausted; both physically and emotionally. Besides that bastard Tsang would lure him back to Happy Valley and lose his entire fortune. Instead they agreed that once Cade had caught up on some sleep they would meet the next day.

Cade heard a knock at his door at eight in the morning. It was the international police knock but he checked the spy hole anyway. Tsang was smiling ridiculously through the glass, knowing that Cade would be looking back at him. It raised a smile as Cade opened the door.

"Good morning double O – I have a new mission for you, should you choose to accept, this tape will self-destruct in five..."

"Tsang, if you are going to force your way into my bedroom at this ungodly hour at least have the decency not to mix up your film lines!"

"Good to see you have lost none of your edge Jack! How did you sleep? Better than last time? Vomit on anyone?"

He stopped for a moment and looked at Tsang "You knew?"

"Of course I knew. I am an international law enforcement officer Cade, I know everything and anyway it would have been rude to turn down your offer of a nice new suit!"

"Bastard! You are an absolute cad sir. Why I should take you outside and..."

Tsang dropped into a cat stance, ready, quite evidently to provide Cade with proof that he had lost none of his skills in close quarter combat.

"...and?"

"And buy you breakfast. Come on, my treat this time." He playfully slapped him around the side of the head but was quick to create some distance. Like two highly trained schoolboys they continued sparring until spotted by a hotel employee. Tsang immediately reverted to type leaving Cade to grin like an idiot. It transpired that no matter where you travelled in the world cops were underneath it all just overgrown naughty boys.

They made their way to the Mandarin Bar and Grill, crossed the marbled floor and stepped onto luxuriant mushroom coloured carpets that sank beneath their feet. Tsang smiled and nodded to the Maître d' who showed them to a table overlooking the harbour, it was perfectly placed to allow cautious conversations as each table was shielded by hardwood and lightly frosted glass screens.

They ordered tea to start; Cade tried Ceylon orange pekoe whilst Tsang preferred Lapsang Souchong. Cade followed with Eggs Benedict leaving Tsang to choose a more traditional local dish of dim sum and scallop congee.

As they waited for the food they began to discuss how Tsang could assist Cade with his evidence gathering.

Thirty minutes later Tsang finished his meal, wiped his lips and placed his napkin on the heavy cotton tablecloth. He took a moment, realigned the remaining cutlery neatly so it all faced in the 'right' direction, placed the condiment set together, wiped a few crumbs onto the floor and then looked up.

"So Jack, tell me more about this Seventh…Wave."

Chapter Eleven

"Where do you want me to start, it's a hell of a long story?"

"Dare I say it?"

He didn't need to. Cade started at the beginning.

"I first came across the wider issue of Eastern European financial crime years ago, I stumbled across it to be fair, call it luck. It was before we first met in Lyon."

Tsang nodded encouragement, sipping his second cup of tea.

"I met a female, don't I always? Anyway she had an agenda and taught me a lot about the ability of 'her people' to infiltrate and exploit the financial sector. At the time I was amazed at their ability to adapt, but typically, within my organisation no-one else was interested."

"But they are now." It was a statement. Tsang knew full well how brilliantly ruthless these particular groups were, especially those from Romania.

"The sad thing is Andy that they give so many good Romanians a bad name. I've met some truly great people as part of my extensive enquiries, they despise the criminal element, but as criminals go you have to admire their dexterity, it's almost as if they have taken skills learned under the Soviet regime and allowed them to flourish, and this has benefited only one group."

"And let me guess, at the top of the food chain…the Seventh Wave?"

"Quite possibly, quite possibly indeed, to be honest it's an educated guess on my part but I doubt I'm far from the truth. I have a list of names here, but most appear to be nicknames or incomplete. I've also got an extensive collection of diplomatic passports and identity documents. It all adds up to something, but what?"

"Give me the nicknames first; I have no doubt that the diplomatic stuff is genuine. Why your girl had them of course is another question altogether."

He had not heard her referred to as 'his girl' before. Who would have known quite how far the relationship would have gone; reason, season, forever and all that. Either way he was grateful for the intensely brief chance to experience her.

Pointing to his Samsung tablet Cade indicated a few of the names that JD had loaded into it, along with his own findings and a few open source search results.

"OK – the first is Jackdaw – it's got the ring of a leader. Then someone who calls themselves The Passenger, there's a Marko, a Stefan and an Alexandru, George, and a name beginning with C, some are common names in that part of the world but the nicknames…"

"Leave them with me, I will get my team to run a wider search of the 'net, we'll use TOR and see what's lurking in the shadowy world shall we?"

Cade nodded. He knew that Tsang was referring to The Onion Router – a network favoured by the criminal underworld – and for that matter law enforcement teams too. It allowed anonymity by virtue of its multiple layers, just like an onion. For all intents and purposes a user could disappear within a few transactions. The irony that it was created by the governments that now struggled to police it was not lost on either of them.

"Let me have that phone you recovered too, I'll get my Electronics lab to clone it, see if we can drag anything new out of it. You appreciate that all of this is off record, very unofficial? I know I shouldn't have to say it, but you understand?"

He did. He appreciated it too. Since leaving the thin blue line he had lost none of his skills, just some of his contacts and their ability to gather information. He still had a huge amount of friends however and these would prove to be very useful.

"So, do you have a theory or any idea why this group have chosen you, Miss Elena and above all New Zealand?" He paused for a moment and made a mental note to ask another question.

Cade responded in chronological order.

"Firstly I genuinely think I am only involved because of Elena and equally the connection to New Zealand is…"

"Elena? Of course and you must have been asking this question constantly? This reminds me Jack. When my people start their quest for data, information and potentially for intelligence they will need to look at her too. Is that OK?"

He understood fully, the difference between information and intelligence wasn't lost on a career police officer either: Intelligence was information with value added. It was how he had been taught and he'd never forgotten.

He hoped that Andy Tsang's team could find out more about the group and why they were doing what they were doing, all of which equated to intelligence.

"Come on, let's get to the office and see what we can do to start the ball rolling." Tsang stood and checked his appearance in the reflection of the sight screen whilst Cade added the meal to his account.

Twenty minutes later they were sipping green tea in Tsang's impressive office at No 1 Arsenal Street in the Wan Chai District. It would have been quicker to walk but Tsang needed his discreet, dark blue BMW 5 Series within close proximity – besides when you had reached such lofty heights why not benefit from the perks of office? And a parking space in a city such as Hong Kong was as much of a perk as a black credit card.

Cade found himself staring out of the window whilst his friend responded to an urgent phone call. The view was magnificent, across Victoria Harbour straight into downtown Kowloon where ferries criss-crossed, darting here and there with their constant supply of passengers. To the left of the Star terminal Cade witnessed some highly effective parking as the local pilot and crew of the Cunard *Queen Victoria* ensured she was berthed without so much as a scrape. At 964.5 feet long she was no longer considered a leviathan of the high seas but Cade uttered out loud that he wouldn't want to park her.

"Sorry Jack?" asked a now attentive Tsang.

"Oh nothing, just talking out loud. Saying I wouldn't want to park that beast."

"Indeed, she and her sisters come here quite regularly. You should book to go on her, you might meet the woman of your…"

He stopped himself mid-flow.

"Sorry Jack, I wasn't thinking, I apologise."

"No need, you were at your relaxed best Andrew, please don't change. Now, talking of the high seas, how are we doing on Operation Wave?"

"We will need a few days but some very interesting news has come back from our Document Examiner, he concurs with you, the passports and papers you have are all genuine. All we have to do now is probe; push a few doors open, gently at first. When do you head to the UK?"

"In twenty four hours, so whatever you can find between now and then will be useful, after that I'll be online or on the end of my phone, day or night."

"Look Jack, there is one thing that is concerning me, why England when this group are sitting in Eastern Europe?"

"Normally I'd give you ten out of ten for that one Andy but it's easy. A few years ago I would agree, to hunt a Romanian criminal first one had to head to Bucharest, but not anymore. These days the nucleus of their tactical financial activity can be found here in Hong Kong, or embroiled in Boiler Room Scams in the Philippines or Thailand but the strategic brains are to be found in London and a few other provincial cities, and that is where I operate best."

Tsang knew not to argue; when it came to European crime syndicates few people had better knowledge than Cade and Cade found himself wishing he was still attached to his old team, which would at least give him a fighting chance – and importantly with the weight of the law being on his side. However despite the immense skill that he knew he possessed Tsang couldn't help but be worried about where Operation Wave as he called it might lead.

Tsang's phone rang again.

"Yes, I understand, thank you, good work."

He looked at Cade and smiled "We have a small breakthrough; it transpires that your girl is actually called Elana Dimitrova, a small but possibly important difference. It could equally be what you call a typo. Her death was reported in the New Zealand papers whilst you were in the air." He continued, trying to be matter of fact without appearing callous "Bulgarian tourist killed in single vehicle crash, police appeal for witnesses et cetera, et cetera. I'm so very sorry Jack."

Cade resisted the urge to break down in front of a colleague – it was one of those jobs that often frowned upon such human reaction, instead he offered a simple nod of the head and said "Thank you, at least I know now."

"If however there is some brighter news then I can also confirm that we think we have located The Passenger. My electronics team have been running a data miner over TOR for hours; for a while we found nothing then quite literally out of the blue, well, to be accurate, hazel, we traced him."

"I'm not with you, how can you link an open source search to him?"

"Technically…it wasn't open source Jack, but as you English say, needs must. In your very early recall of the events in New Zealand you talked about how Elena had mentioned a man with two different coloured eyes?"

"I did…"

"Yes, you did indeed. I never knew but the condition is called complete heterochromia, it isn't extremely rare, about ten or so in a thousand and even some famous people have it. Sometimes it's hereditary or caused by disease…"

"And…" Cade was becoming a little impatient.

"And in the case of your Passenger it turns out that an old girlfriend of his posted a picture of him on Facebook. Simple! Where would we be without social media Jack?"

"You are kidding? An international assassin with his imagery on Facebook, it's unbelievable Andy. Show me."

"Ah, well that is the thing, it was deleted but we have the text that went with the image. We knew we could possibly obtain the original by executing a warrant in the USA but we would have to provide Facebook with some compelling evidence that we weren't just…on a fishing expedition."

Cade understood and besides the fewer footprints the better.

"Any moment now I should receive the data from our lab. Have some more tea."

Cade motioned to his bladder signifying that it was fit to burst "Perhaps later, thank you."

A small electronic announcement indicated that the data had arrived – it was a noise quite familiar to Cade as it had been occurring on average every minute, an indication of just how busy Tsang was. It was also a gentle reminder that Cade needed to allow him to return to normal.

"Can you send it to me? I can see how busy you are."

"Jack, I am extremely important these days. This will be written off as international partnership building with the Five Eyes – and you know how important that is to my leaders!" He grinned, paused and then turned the large computer screen around so that Cade could clearly see the text.

'I long to see my beautiful man, to hold you and kiss those lips, to touch your strong body and to look into your special eyes. It is like looking at two men at once. Much love Stefan. Maria xx'

"OK it's a start, but now all I have to do is trace a female with the most common first name in Romania and a male with…"

"Yes, yes I know, a male with a common name…but Cade you forget you are dealing with the Hong Kong Police Department now, not some group of Kermit's!"

The error made Cade laugh, in fact he laughed out loud. It was a much needed pressure valve.

"It's Muppet's but you made me smile, please, go on."

"Of course, a brightly coloured talking frog isn't everyone's idea of an international thief taker…"

He paused and looked at Cade. They both said exactly the same thing in an exaggerated French accent before collapsing into fits of laughter, "Unless you mean Francois Les Incompetent!"

Chef d'Escadron Le Compte was a senior man at Interpol back in the day – as incompetent as he was good looking, he made a habit of infuriating everyone he worked with and yet had one of the highest capture rates in the organisation. He was, it was once said, a capable Clouseau and his trademark fluorescent green ties soon gave rise to the Kermit moniker.

"If you get stuck Jack give him a call, you never know he might have forgiven you by now!"

"I shall, Jesus that was funny, so funny I forgot to get an answer to my question. How do you know who Stefan is?"

"Relax. It is easy. Maria is Maria Antonescu, twenty six years old, petite with bleach-blonde hair and according to most of these historic images she spent most of her time in a bikini. As you can see she is very pretty, in this picture she is posing, perhaps a little too closely with her best friend Ana Dumitru, also in her early twenties and equally beautiful."

"They are and I suppose our friend Stefan had the pleasure of both of them?"

"One can presume so Jack."

"Presume, surely the Hong Kong Police are more confident than mere conjecture?"

"Indeed, as you know we work on fact; black and white, never grey and as we both know knowledge is power. In Stefan's case it meant taking the power away from the lovely Maria and in turn her friend."

Cade responded with a puzzled look.

"Both dead Jack. Found at an out of town rubbish dump near Craiova, naked with their throats cut and their eyes were surgically removed and left hanging on their cheekbones, hardly very romantic."

"And indicator that they had seen too much?"

"Possibly."

"Go on."

"We couldn't locate Maria's original Facebook homepage but rather fortuitously the bereft family of Miss Dumitru kept her page alive as a tribute. Within six links to that page was an old photograph of this man…"

Tsang pointed to a muscular blond-haired male who was sat between the two females. "Clearly his parents lacked imagination. His name is Stefan Stefanescu, and our good friend Stefan just made his first schoolboy mistake. He arrived in England a few weeks ago via Dover, local Border Agency staff had a good look at him but he was clean".

"And?"

"And his blue Audi A6 passed through the City of London Automatic Number Plate Recognition system an hour later. You were right. He's in London Jack."

The frigid, complex and impassive eyes stared back at him. Cade took a while to absorb the new-found information, leant forward slightly and mumbled something under his breath. It was an opening, a small start but a start nonetheless.

"Come on, it's been a long day, we need to eat again, an army marching on its stomach and all that, let us return to your hotel and run up an even larger bill!"

He nodded and smiled an exhausted smile. It was the least Cade could do.

En route they covered off the successes to date and formulated an action plan for the next phase.

Tsang quoted a few stats from a report he had been reading before Cade had arrived.

"I have taken the liberty of printing off a copy for you. It's the latest UK Serious and Organised Crime Strategy, it will keep you company as you fly over Russia en route to your Motherland. As you will see the Brits have a few concerns; terrorism, drugs, people trafficking, firearms, cyber and acquisitive crime. It's all gone to hell in a handcart since you left Old Boy!"

"Tell me about it."

Tsang continued, missing the irony.

"The UK forces believe there are somewhere in the region of five and a half thousand organised criminal groups operating on their mainland and many more offshore. The combined impact of fraud and acquisitive crime is considered to be upwards of ten billion. That's a lot in any currency Jack. And it means that you alone will never be able to resolve it."

Cade replied "Do you honestly think I plan to single-handedly swing into London, take out the leaders of these groups with a double-tap to the head, make love to countless beautiful women and be home in time for tea and medals?"

"No of course, but I suspect that is your wish."

It was, but life on the law enforcement side of the fence had taught him that you could not win every battle. You started with small victories: talking to people, building up your HUMINT, talking to people, gathering information, turning it into intelligence then slowly, deliberately you either disrupted or destroyed the networks. In some cases this meant cutting off the Hydra's head all the while unaware of another newer, more insidious one emerging quietly behind you.

"The report suggests that over half of the crime issues stem from the drug trade but I suspect that your Seventh Wave is somehow wiser than this. After all, why dip your toe in the same pool as everyone else when there are bigger fish to fry?"

Despite the mixed metaphor Cade knew what Tsang meant. If half of the world's criminal organisations were profiting from drugs then surely there must be another avenue to exploit.

"The passports?"

"Sorry Jack, what do you mean?"

"Sorry, I was thinking out loud, perhaps the passports are a link to this? Could they provide some level of credibility perhaps? A way of showing prospective investors that they can be trusted? Is it blackmail? Or are they just stolen like everything else?" It was clear that Cade was tired. A good night's sleep might offer some clarity.

"I don't know my friend but what I do know is that your old colleagues are trying to deal with it all head-on. It's all about disruption Jack – in the first place at least. Then gathering intelligence, and finally striking the key targets. It's all part of what they refer to as CONTEST: a system of targeting those at the bottom and top of the food chain, in the hope that the middle order will collapse. They used it initially for counter-terrorism, now other areas too. Their aim is to pursue, prevent, protect and prepare."

Tsang's almost photographic memory was impressive, Cade found himself wishing he would accompany him to Europe. So much so that he asked him.

"Andy, come with me to Europe. I can pay you any expenses."

"Jack, this is becoming too personal. I am worried about you. I alone cannot help you but you have my word my team and I will be just a quick phone call away should you run into a brick wall. I understand that your 'Operation Wave' is actually already underway; in the UK it is called NEXUS."

Cade's face took on a puzzled look, he had only been out of the game for a relatively short time but it was a game which changed, as fluid as the enemy it pursued, and those that failed to keep up were swept away like autumn leaves in a wintry gutter.

Tsang carried on, "I have put together some files on the current ops in Britain; I think you need to combine these with what you already have and see if you can get one step ahead, at worst at least you will be on that level playing field that you Brits are always referring to."

"Thank you."

"My pleasure, now, when you arrive back in London I know you will be meeting up with some old friends and I have no doubt that Mr Daniel will have organised some of this, but I must ask that you look up someone else from your past too, he can help you more than you realise."

"Who?"

"This man" Tsang handed his cell phone over to Cade who struggled to recognise the image at first.

"No? It can't be, is it?"

"It is Jack, your friend and mine, Jason "Ginger" Roberts or as he's called these days Detective Chief Inspector Roberts. I have already made contact, he's looking forward to seeing you again and I quote, 'a cup of Rosie and a game of arrows', whatever that might be."

"Good God, Ginger Roberts a DCI, who'd have thought it? Last I heard he was a Detective Sergeant at the Yard with a career goal of never going any higher."

"Well it turns out that he has and his team have exactly what you need. Maybe time to cash in a few favours?"

They arrived back at the Mandarin, entered the restaurant, ordered their meal and an accompanying glass of Mascara de fuego, a newly imported Chilean Cabernet Sauvignon. Both men admired how the rich red liquid clung to their glasses before chinking them vigorously together and dining in relative quiet.

When they had finished Cade wiped his lips, placed down his napkin and raised his newly acquired glass of Macallan from the Fine & Rare collection. The bottle Cade had selected was from 1974. He examined it and decided after a moment that it had matured somewhat better than he had during his own forty years.

"To the next Commissioner of the Royal Hong Kong Police. May he always be successful, a great friend and occasionally sober!"

Tsang replied "To a man I admire enormously, one who epitomises everything that is great about British law enforcement. Sadly, he cannot be here tonight!"

"Touché, my friend, touché, your comedic timing is as exquisite as ever."

An hour later they stood in the lobby, hands firmly gripped in a strong handshake they promised to remain closely in touch, with Cade agreeing to update his old friend and colleague as often as he was able. With the goodbyes finalised Tsang turned around and walked swiftly to his awaiting car.

As he reached the door he stopped and turned around, he bowed gently "Good luck Jack, watch your back and remember who your friends are."

Cade returned the bow and walked away.

He later left his room and entered the nearby lift. As it carried him down to the lobby he removed a small magnet from his carry-on bag and ran it over his electronic hotel door key. It was on old habit designed to eradicate his personal data from the card, the result of spending years hunting financially motivated criminals.

He paid his bill without questioning any of the numerous transactions, collected a small parcel from the Receptionist and approached the Concierge.

"Would you do me a great favour?" He motioned to the bottle of 1974 Macallan. "Ensure the rest of this gets delivered to this address with this note?"

The Concierge assured him he would carry out the duty himself, recognising immediately the recipient's details, he knew how important he was to the hotel and besides having friends in high places was more advantageous in Hong Kong than an annual pass on the Star Ferry.

Cade shook his hand and walked to his taxi.

The note was brief and to the point "Sir, keep this until the next time we meet. JC"

Within three quarters of an hour he was outside the International Terminal. As he exited the car and paid his bill he noted storm clouds on the horizon; a dark almost sinister bank of anthracite and green heralded the first few large spots of tropical rain which started to hit the concrete walkway as Cade turned his back on Hong Kong and entered Terminal 1.

He arrived briskly at the Cathay Pacific Business Class desk and checked in for flight CX239 for London Heathrow. With his luggage labelled and already en route to the baggage make up area airside he took his boarding pass and placed it together with his maroon-coloured passport.

"Thank you Mr Cade, Gate 67, your flight is on time and leaves at 14:35. Thank you for flying Cathay Pacific. Have a safe journey."

Chapter Twelve

The Boeing 777-300ER eased off the ground, climbed steadily over Guangzhou before continuing a north-west journey towards Mongolia and the great Gobi Desert.

It would soon reach its operational height and become as fuel efficient as a jet weighting nearly three hundred thousand kilos could. Its General Electric GE90 engines had the airliner cruising at over five hundred knots and before too long it would clear mainland China and begin the remainder of its twelve hour journey to Europe.

Cade settled into his more than comfortable seat, accepted a drink and chose his in-flight meal. Whilst the other passengers, both economy and business also selected their in-flight entertainment he opened up the package that Tsang had handed to him and started to digest its contents.

Tsang had lost none of his incredible ability – he always had a tremendous eye for detail and as a Briefing Officer Cade always thought him only second to himself.

The briefing package had a yellow Post It note attached to the front; the note was lined up perfectly with the edge of the A4 paperwork.

"Jack, as discussed here are some notes, my team have made me proud. I told them this work was immensely valuable and for a friend of HKP. I suggest you read it once en route to London and then once again when you first wake up. It was great to catch up after all these years – it seems impossible to think it was so many years ago. Stay in touch, keep safe and let me know what you need. AT."

He turned the first page and began to read. It was a deep read, not one of those lightly-skimmed, can't-be-arsed affairs. The data that the report contained could save his life and therefore it took on a new dimension.

Whilst he held no respect for the members of the Seventh Wave he did respect their skills and abilities.

The report commenced:

Jack, as we discussed, since October 2012, the Metropolitan Police and British Immigration have been running a joint operation known as Nexus: the aim of Nexus has been the sharing of tactical, operational and strategic intelligence to identify foreign national offenders at the point of arrest.

The police and Immigration have been working very closely with a number of international and domestic partners and other international policing agencies such as Europol and Interpol.

It would appear that a group of Eastern European criminals formed a syndicate in the early 2000's and then became fractured due to different goals and leadership ideology.

This is when the group we now know to be The Seventh Wave (hereafter referred to as TSW) formed.

TSW headed down the 'more is more' path very quickly, targeting high value commodities such as vehicles, jewellery and watches but soon found that their biggest hurdle was groups that were very similar to their own – there was no appetite at the time for a shared economy.

As a result TSW headed along a new avenue – financial crime. This developed during the mid-2000's and in turn gave birth to Boiler Room operations, ATM attacks and point of sale offending.

The latter areas were insidious. They were seen by many as 'victimless crimes' and yet, according to our Senior Analyst, they were responsible for millions of pounds of international fraud, most of which was occurring under the very nose of the Met Police. A direct consequence of this was the establishment of the Dedicated Cheque and Plastic Crime Unit.

The DCPCU consists of officers from the Met and City of London Police and for the first time they are receiving backing from the banking industry and have begun to work in conjunction with the Insurance Fraud Enforcement Unit. This team was again industry-funded; they had realised that their losses were not centred on general claims but fraudulent claims. This is an interesting development – given the historical lack of cooperation by law enforcement and bank officials.

Secondly (and this will interest you when you consider what Miss Dimitrova left you) the Metropolitan Police Project known as Amberhill was set up to collate and analyse data specifically connected to forged, counterfeit and fraudulently obtained genuine identity documents that were recovered during police operations.

Since it was implemented MetPol have built a database of some 80,000 false identities and documents.

Where MetPol have been successful is in sharing. As opposed to Need to Know – they have adopted a Need to Share policy and this is becoming widespread throughout British forces. Again, according to my Analytical Team this has helped your old colleagues detect and stop crime. One estimate refers to a saving of three million pounds in only one year.

Now, where things have really changed is how the government spend that money – they no longer lock it away in an account to gather dust, afraid of the public's perception, they utilise the proceeds to go on the offensive. HKP are doing this too, in fact you will find this method of counter-attack occurring throughout the world of law enforcement.

Taking your collection of passports into consideration you will be interested to note that the Serious Organised Crime Agency has begun to issue a series of alerts to government organisations – these relate to travel documents. Only recently they issued alerts pertaining to nearly five hundred fraudulently obtained genuine passports and some of these relate to Diplomats and Consuls.

Note the importance of 'fraudulently obtained' documents Jack. We both know from our past that passports were often altered – the fewer alterations the better – but they were altered nonetheless. Complete false documents were rare but photo-substituted items were turning up at ports around the world on a daily basis.

In Europe these were often seen in the form of Scandinavian passports, assisting former refugees from the Middle East – the holders had entered countries such as Norway, Sweden and Denmark, attracted by their positive welfare schemes, but they then learned of new opportunities in lowland Europe and the United Kingdom.

Italian and Greek passports on the other hand helped Romanian, Bulgarian and Albanian nationals to enter the European Union.

In the USA they were obviously facilitating the migration of Mexican and South American nationals across the southern border and in the Far East/Pacific Region we were seeing Chinese passports in the hands of North Koreans and a swathe of Malaysian, Thai and occasionally Singaporean documents. In addition to this, Indian passports were heavily abused; however these started to die away as the newer chipped documents began to circulate.

The biggest remaining risk was the use of fraudulently issued South African documents – corrupt officials issuing genuine documents – so completely genuine that no Document Examiner would ever detect anything wrong – because of course they were genuine. This facilitated widespread fraudulent travel by members of other African nations.

Cade knew a lot of this already but it helped to provide a broader picture of global events. The report continued:

So what? These passports were being used by criminals and illegal migrants to secure employment and gain access to financial products and services. But where they also targeted their host nations was in the area of benefit fraud and this has unravelled into an almost 'viral' state.

Offenders used the documents to travel within Europe and commit a variety of criminal offences. The aim of the British initiative was to offer prevention rather than a cure – as a result many businesses were able to use the information to protect themselves from online and direct financial attack.

What really changed the entire picture was the entry of former Eastern European states into the European Union. This allowed nationals previously locked down by their countries' historical status to travel freely, not just within Europe but also across the world, right into the heart of vulnerable countries that allowed visa-free access to the EU.

As a direct consequence places such as Australia and New Zealand – previously immune, started to note low-level but growing cyber and financial crime risks. This is of course where Dimitrova joins the equation.

My Analyst suspects that TSW were heading to New Zealand with the intention of opening accounts, accounts that would on the face of it be legitimate but with a sinister background and intention. It is entirely possible that smaller nations in the Pacific were being considered as target destinations for money laundering – away from the prying eyes and grabbing hands of the larger Western government law groups.

Furthermore whilst in New Zealand it is suspected that a small number of Seventh Wave agents or associates of the group were instructed to hunt down and kill Dimitrova.

Whilst uncorroborated it is likely that this is linked to her being in possession of valuable documents and data incriminating the group.

Either that or she had knowledge of something far more damaging.

Cade sat up and read the last paragraph again before continuing.

Therefore in summary Elena Dimitrova is known to be connected to the Seventh Wave via a 'liaison' with one of its key players. It is the assumption of the Analyst that she was in possession of harmful evidence that would close down the TSW's operations' globally, impact upon the operational practices of her home nation – and – this is purely supposition – undermine governments.

Further, Dimitrova is loosely linked to a number of higher-level diplomatic entities from both Europe and Africa.

In summary it is the belief of my staff that her international movements, financial transactions and associations indicate that she was either a part of the group or a member of a law enforcement/government organisation.

At the foot of the report Cade read what would become the most haunting aspect of the entire briefing.

**Footnote: Of note a wider search on Europol's system and the archived files of the Bulgarian Committee for State Security have produced a new area of potential investigation.

In the late nineties it was popularly thought that much of the post-Soviet era organised crime was instigated and carried out by members of the organisation.

In 2002, Bulgaria's former Interior Minister General Atanas Semerdzhiev was found guilty of destroying 144,235 files from the Durzhavna Sigurnost archives. A number of criminals were investigated at the same time however none were prosecuted (or at best their cases never progressed beyond an early aborted trial).

A wildcard search of a number of 'accessible databases' has found the following matches to the current investigation:

Alexandru/Stefanescu/m/Romania - 13/10/1969 – Stefanescu has countless associates but only two recorded links to females.

He has a number of nicknames. The Crow, The Raven, The Magpie, The Jackdaw.

The link terminates with this nominal:

Nikolina/Elena/Petrov/f/Bulgaria - 06/07/1970 - alias Nikolina Elena Stefanescu

An uncorroborated hit has identified a link to both Petrov and Stefanescu.

Elena/Simona/Petrova – approximately 1988 - it is possible that this information has been extracted from health records.

Both Stefanescu and Petrov are shown in a number of Intelligence Reports held by various European police forces and thought to have been actively involved in the wholesale theft of luxury European motor vehicles.

Lower-tier intelligence indicates a period of sustained domestic-related violence at the property of one Alexandru Stefanescu, with the repeat victim being Nikolina Petrov.

Source documents suggested at the time that she was trying to remove herself from the relationship as a result of the persistent violence and repeated affairs conducted by Stefanescu. She had provided the local police with evidence to implicate him in a widespread operation targeting Volkswagen, BMW and Mercedes vehicles in Spain.

The Madrid Police commenced an investigation which indicated that a fleet worth 10 million Euro's had been stolen, re-birthed and shipped out of the country into Poland, the Czech Republic and Romania.

They initially located Stefanescu but his case did not proceed. The files do not offer an explanation. It is possible that some level of corruption was involved.

A source document suggested that Stefanescu may have been the subject of an assassination attempt. Given his status, wealth and social standing this is plausible.

The fact that the source suggests he was poisoned is not in keeping with conventional European offending.

It is suggested that Petrov may have been involved.

Petrov was never found.

In the margin Tsang had written in pencil *'Hell hath no fury like a woman scorned...'*

The report concluded:

It is the recommendation of the Analytical Group that any investigation into TSW commences in 2002 and examines the link between the latter two names. Key risks are luxury items, documents and financial crime.

A strong possibility exists that government officials are either complicit in this offending or have been blackmailed.

He sipped on a cup of Earl Grey tea, trying to allow the information to process and then slowly placed his cup onto its matching saucer. What was he missing?

He closed the file, sank back into his seat and turned the reading light off. Around him every other passenger was either asleep or watching the latest thriller through bloodshot eyes.

The twin engines of the Boeing continued to carry the aircraft across southern Russia, their constant hum acting as an inescapable narcotic. His head began to nod.

Sleep encompassed him quickly and he soon found himself drifting on the sparkling waters of the Pacific Ocean. The powerful outboard of the *Marlin* had stopped and the effervescent actions of the propellers had ceased, the remaining white gaseous bubbles hissing to the surface of the azure ocean. Cade drifted the boat towards the shore, dropped the anchor and dived into the cool water.

He surfaced seconds later, wiped the saline from his eyes and looked up at the stern. This time however his new-found soul mate had gone. He could no longer hear or see her and began to panic in the water, fighting against a new and stronger tide that enabled the *Marlin* to slowly but inexorably drift away.

He fought the waves, battling each one until the boat and the island had vanished. He was alone in the greatest ocean on the planet.

He awoke with a start, as if his heart had stopped. However he could hear its beat above the constant roar of the jet engines and feel it deep within his chest.

Without hesitation he opened the folder once more and read the report from start to finish. As he reached the end of the document, the missing piece of the story dropped into place like an errant and elusive part of a childhood jigsaw, one previously lost in the dark and slightly sticky recesses of an old, much-loved sofa.

An uncorroborated hit has identified a link to both Petrov and Stefanescu.

Elena/Simona/Petrova – Birth: approximately 1988 - it is possible that this information has been extracted from health records.

Unexpectedly his mind returned to *Spindrift* and that almost inconceivable morning when he first met her, after making love for God knows how many times she had laid her head on his chest and in a barely audible whisper she had murmured, "Hello Mr Jack Cade. We meet at last."

He played and re-played the sentence, dwelling on the last part. His head was nodding now, four or five times before he conceded and fell into a light sleep.

"We meet *at last*…Jesus Christ, of course, she knew who I was. How naïve am I?"

He was awake now. He clapped his hands together.

"Nikolina Petrov, East Midlands Airport! I knew I recognised those bloody eyes. It wasn't Elena that was linked to Stefanescu it was you, you're her mother! You clever girl."

He felt foolish, isolated, angry but euphoric. As stunning as she was, his exquisite redhead had played him like the *Black Marlin* Big Stan's boat was named after.

Was she using him or running to him for help? He explored his mind, eventually recalling his words of support so many years prior.

The passenger in seat 10A rubbed her eyes and glared at Cade through the half-light. He had woken her up.

Frankly, he didn't care.

He didn't care at all.

Chapter Thirteen

Cade had re-entered the much-needed world of deep, uninterrupted sleep and had spent so long in it he had missed another meal and the chance to fleece the aircraft of a few more of its luxuries. Despite this he felt good, refreshed and as if he had been given a new lease of life.

He walked the short distance to the bathroom, locked the door and splashed some cool water onto his face. He looked in the mirror; looking back he saw that his face was drawn, lifeless and grey. This was the result of international aviation, time zones and the impact of the last week. It was more than most men could or should ever have to contend with.

He dried his face slowly and pumped moisturiser onto his palms before rubbing it slowly into his skin. He could hear his old Metropolitan Police colleague Jason Roberts' voice.

"Moisturiser, you poofter, moisturiser is for girls my son, girls."

He smiled, added some more and rubbed it deep into his skin. It was a trick taught to him by an all-too attractive Australian cabin crew member many years before.

He took his shaver from his travel bag and slowly, deliberately removed the overnight growth from his face before adding a final amount of the luxuriant fluid onto his skin. The last drop was applied just to piss off Roberts. He slapped his face in a vain attempt to apply life to his wilting body.

The intercom hissed slightly before coming to life and waking those that were still asleep.

"Ladies and Gentlemen this is your Captain speaking, we are heading into an area of clear air turbulence, as such I would like you to return to your seats and fasten your seat belts. Thank you."

Cade knew better than to argue, he recalled seeing an American woman collide with the roof lining of a 737 once as it travelled over northern Scotland. The first collision took the wind out of her but the second, as she clattered onto a seat and smashed her head against an unwitting passenger's knee made sure that Cade always followed the Captain's orders.

As he strapped himself back in he looked at the GPS map on his TV screen – below him, many miles below him, the settlement of Bila Tserkva passed by.

He'd never been to the Ukrainian town and most likely never would either but whenever he flew he often wondered what was happening far below him.

Who lived there? What were the houses like? Who was guarding that disused Soviet Air Force base just to the north west of the map? Was the parkland as pretty as it looked from that glistening metallic speck in the sky?

Before he had had time to digest these thoughts the Boeing had travelled another hundred miles, ever closing in on its destination; on board a familiar aroma drifted through the cabin indicating that it wouldn't be long before breakfast was served and for once he was hungry.

Two hours later they were over Rostock in northern Germany and heading on a course between Hamburg and Heligoland. The remnants of breakfast were being cleared away as the sun began to climb slowly above the horizon, announcing its presence on board, teasingly distributing shafts of light through even the smallest gaps in the visors.

Cade could feel the airliner starting to gently descend, to their left the Dutch coast with its endless dunes and to the right the North Sea with its battalions of wind turbines harnessing the air currents that flowed through the natural throttle point that separated Britain from mainland Europe.

The enormous white blades rotated and churned, stereotypically not unlike Cade's mind. He too found that his thoughts were whirring, spinning and diverging from one notion to another.

What would greet him when he returned to his homeland? In fact who would greet him and importantly how? Would his old friends and colleagues come to his aid and make good on their long-forgotten promises? Would he ever see his adopted home again?

These thoughts allowed him to drop back into a half-sleep once more as the white, green and red Triple Seven cruised into the Thames estuary heading straight for London and one of the busiest airports in the world.

Cathay flight CX239 held in a pattern for ten minutes, drawing a bright green circle on Cade's in-seat TV screen and then another in an almost perfect figure of eight. The shape and colour reminded him of

Elena's eyes; either that or he was genuinely much more tired than he dared believe.

Below him the wealthier suburbs of London were waking to a new day, leafy streets and multi-million pound properties in isolated bliss only miles from poverty, chaos and heartbreak.

Richmond gave way to Hounslow as the Triple dropped through the sky, now flying along the path of the Staines Road. Droplets of condensation energetically rushed backwards across the portholes, providing a reminder that although the aircraft felt as if it were almost stationary it was still travelling at over a hundred and fifty miles an hour, but now slowing at a mile per hour, per second.

Three hundred, two hundred, one hundred, seventy, fifty, thirty, ten and she was down, her rear wheels contacting with the concrete and throwing thick plumes of acrid rubber smoke into the air. The crew began to reverse the engines as the massive wing spoilers combined to bring the aircraft under control.

Within minutes they were taxiing towards their air bridge and Gate 24. He was back on British soil and for the first time ever he felt lost and vulnerable.

As he left the aircraft the familiar twang of a Londoner brought him back to earth, he instantly felt less isolated and strangely empowered by one simple greeting.

"Alright chief, you look lost, do you need an 'and?"

"No I'm fine thanks pal, just getting my bearings, been a while, but nice to be home, how are The Gunners doing?"

"Awful mate, but better than United, so it can't all be bad!"

Whoever he was he had made Cade's morning, there was some sense of belonging that he hoped gave him an advantage on home soil. His comfortable feeling changed in a heartbeat when a swarthy-looking male collided with him as he raced to get to the baggage carousels.

"Hey mate, steady, got a plane to catch?" Cade offered to the rapidly disappearing individual.

The male turned and stared at him, long enough to unsettle him but short enough to avoid colliding with an oncoming golf buggy that was being used to carry an elderly lady to a Monarch Airlines flight.

Cade hadn't seen the male on his flight and to be fair Heathrow was massive, he could have come from anywhere, and importantly be heading anywhere. He decided to switch off his overactive, tired mind and switch on his cell phone.

'Welcome to the United Kingdom' announced the text message as other notifications started to broadcast their presence. Three missed calls were also showing.

He ran his finger over the screen and entered his PIN. The first voicemail was a courtesy call from his local bank manager, offering various ways in which Cade should invest his money. The second was from Elena.

"Hi Jack Cade just me phoning to say I am missing you and can't wait to be with you again later, even though you drive like girl I think I love you. Ciao baby."

It stopped him in his tracks. He moved to the side of the terminal walkway and paused, took a deep breath and tried to continue, but the voice and the nature of the message tore him in two. Despite this he listened to it again. He realised that the call had been made prior to her death and that somehow it had been drifting through cyber space ever since.

The last call was from JD.

"Right then Young Jedi, by now you should be in Blighty and safe and well. Check your emails dear heart and let us know you are safe. Lynne asks if you've still got your pen and to tell you she misses you terribly. Me on the other hand I don't miss you at all you miserable little shit. Catch up soon lad."

It was good to hear from the old bastard.

He deleted the first and last messages but saved the second into his vault.

He passed through the Smart Gate passport control without incident and set out towards the Baggage Hall at a fast pace, if nothing else it was a chance to stretch his legs.

Heathrow was its usual self: busy.

He collected his luggage, did a sweep of the baggage hall for the male he had bumped into earlier and satisfied that he wasn't anywhere to be seen moved off to join the building torrent of passengers who were heading towards the final hurdle, the UK Border Agency checkpoint.

He had nothing to worry about and nothing to declare – other than enough stolen passports to keep him in an interview room for days.

He left the Customs Hall and walked out into the main arrival's area. He was met by a sea of faces, all shouting and gesturing for attention, waving pieces of card or professionally made notice boards, none were for him and none were expected.

Cade estimated there to be around five hundred people, most legitimate, some clearly not, milling around looking for an opportunity to strike, to steal from the unwary, the tired and vulnerable.

Cade, in true law enforcement style, hated the lot of them.

He walked briskly towards the Hertz car rental desk, with a computer print-out in hand. As he was about arrive at the desk he became aware of footsteps approaching quickly and then heard a voice behind him.

He stopped, suddenly very aware of his surroundings, watching the petite brunette behind the counter to see if her facial expression changed; was it unexpectedly attentive enough to provide Cade with a warning.

He was ready, the minute hairs on the back of his neck stood up and his right hand discreetly balled into a fist.

He turned around and instantly released his grip from his suitcase, let out a breath and begun to laugh. Stood in front of him was a forty year old European male, about five foot eleven with a good head of blond hair, cut short but thick enough to allow a gentle quiff at the front. He had grey-blue eyes and a clear complexion, almost pale, no doubt the result of many years of being on a strictly vegetarian diet that evidently consisted mainly of chips, crumbs of which were clinging precariously to his chiselled chin.

The male wore a grey suit, white shirt and black, rather superb brogues, but his ensemble was finished off with an orange tie, as bright as the navel orange Cade's grandmother used to give him each Christmas. The tie had a double Windsor knot and sat almost half way up his chest in homage to a bygone era.

The male was chewing the arm on a pair of silver framed, blue-tinted Ray Bans.

"Alright my son, fuck me you look rough, anyone would think you'd had a long flight. I bet you've spent the last few days up to your nuts in Chinese hookers? Fancy a cup of Rosie me old China?"

Cade put his hand out which was immediately greeted by the warm hand of Detective Chief Inspector Jason Roberts, or as he was affectionately known, Ginger.

"Do you know what? That is the single best offer I have had in days!" replied Cade.

"Good, well come on then you great Nancy, some of us are busy, and if you think I'm paying for it you've got another one coming!"

As they walked towards the rear of the terminal Cade realised he hadn't collected his rental car.

"Leave it. I'll get you some wheels, besides we've got some catching up to do my old mate, rather a lot as it happens. How's JD?"

"Fine, same as ever, living comfortably on his pension and running a nice little business in a stunning location, what more could you ask for?"

"A shorter bloody flight!" replied Roberts with his hand held out in front of him in an aircraft shape.

Roberts slapped Cade across the back and plipped the remote on his Ford Mondeo which was double parked in a bus bay.

"Sling your case in there but watch out for the radio kit – very sensitive that my son. Doubt you've seen anything like it where you've been. I hear they have carrier pigeons over there still."

"You know I'd like to say you've lost none of your acerbic wit but I'd be lying, by the way Andy Tsang sends his best wishes."

"Andy Tsang! Bloody hell, well take me back in time why don't you. What's he up to now, apart from his nuts in a Far Eastern whore?"

"Eloquent as ever Ginger, eloquent as ever. Actually he's likely to be the next Commissioner of the Hong Kong Police."

"Fuck off is he. And I'm likely to be the next Queen of frigging England, get away with you; honestly you're pulling my bleedin' chain."

Cade replied "Trust me on this Jason, I've just spent a few days with him in Hong Kong, his team managed to iron out a few creases and direct me along some paths that I hadn't considered beforehand." He sighed; it had been a long flight.

Through all the banter Roberts could see his colleague was exhausted.

"Listen me old China what say I drop you off at your hotel and you catch up on some kip and we'll meet tomorrow? Where are you staying?"

Cade pointed to the hotel across the dual carriageway "Just there as it happens!"

"Nice, bit upmarket for you isn't it?" replied Roberts as he skilfully hurtled across both lanes and into the main car park.

He exited the car and tossed the keys to Cade.

"Don't break it, it's one of our old ones but if you ruin it I'm in the doghouse. He flicked his fingers together in a style often displayed by Afro-Caribbean men and turned on is heels, across the car park and got into another equally anonymous vehicle, a grey Ford Focus with a well-built Jamaican sitting behind the wheel.

Cade knew he was tired as he hadn't seen it at the terminal.

The Focus pulled up alongside Cade as he emptied the boot of the Mondeo. The passenger window slipped silently down into the door frame.

"Jack, meet Dave Williams, good lad, first black lad on my team in fact, joined me back in 2004 and I'd have plenty more if I could get them, great dancers all of 'em."

Cade placed his tanned hand into the larger and darker palm and greeted Williams.

"Dave, ignore your senile boss. We've already met, back in Oh Four if my memory serves me well?"

"We did boss, we did. I try to humour him. But often fail. It's a miracle that we've stayed together quite so long."

Roberts threw back his head and laughed, "Christ has it really been ten years David? Where does the time go? No, really, where does it go? Clearly I am an amazing boss or you'd be back on Traffic by now…and don't forget I can make that happen like that." He clicked his thumb and finger for effect.

"Anyway Cadester see you tomorrow ten o'clock sharp – you know where we are? You all over it?"

Cade nodded and shook hands with Roberts once more before walking into the foyer of the Sheraton Heathrow and checking in.

Minutes later he walked into his room, closed the blackout curtains and made the mistake of laying down on the king sized bed which consumed him in a matter of seconds.

He woke six hours later, took a blisteringly-hot shower, slapped on some Givenchy Neo and staggered to the restaurant for breakfast only to learn that it was four in the afternoon. Jet lag was indeed a bitch.

He grabbed a light snack and read the local national papers whilst drinking a pint of Theakstones Old Peculiar, a beer he had not tasted for a very long time.

The headlines were no different from the rest of the world; chaos, mayhem, sleaze, political posturing and gossip, but on page three he noticed an article on an Eastern European crime syndicate that had been identified by the Nottinghamshire Police, a force about two hours north of London and one dear to Cade's heart.

The article explained how the group of Romanians had arrived into England a year before, initially set up their operation in London but then relocated to the East Midlands when the local police became too proactive. They then commenced a widespread series of thefts of personal data via Automated Teller Machines or ATM's and electronic point of sale terminals – often called EFTPOS.

The victims were generally, blissfully unaware that they had been targeted and often failed to act until their accounts had been stripped bare by which time the offender had long gone, often leaving the donor country with the data held on computer portable devices and posting them via courier to their own countries for use or sale to the highest bidder.

Technology was changing at such a pace that it was always difficult to keep up – but it was one thing the financially motivated crime syndicates did well.

'Staying only one step ahead of us would be a luxury' a senior police spokesman was quoted as saying the *Telegraph*.

The syndicates recruited from within their own society but also had great success in exploiting low income students who were, as luck would have it, incredibly gifted in the world of Information Technology.

Paying them one US dollar per transaction seemed like slave labour however things were put very much into perspective when the sheer amount of transactions were considered.

These relative 'kids' were tasked with number-crunching, literally taking the account details obtained by the onshore teams and feeding them into the internet to buy goods which would then be sold on at a profit. Ten thousand here, five there, it all amounted to a multi-million dollar operation.

From deep within a provincial city, bang in the middle of England, a group of students did just that and within no time their operation became so fruitful that they divided into cells and soon their associates were setting up the same operation in Leicester and nearby Derby. Each cell in turn spawning more cells until practically the whole of the United Kingdom could almost reach out and touch them – but they were always more than one step ahead.

Because they were students they lived en masse, either in flats or in 'two up – two down' accommodation, often sharing wi-fi connections or even better cruising around the city streets until they managed to either find an open system or hack into one. Once online they would conduct their transactions with the original victims none the wiser and the international banks banging their collective heads against a hypothetical wall.

The article elaborated on the police operation, causing Cade to shake his head as he took another sip of the hop-laden brew. Surely the last thing the authorities should be doing was play their hand?

But Cade also knew the power of public opinion and education. If a few victims passed on good practice techniques to keep their accounts safe then perhaps they too could become as viral.

For the authorities it was now about prevention.

On the very next page, next to a dubious article about Prince Harry, Cade saw another crime-related report, this one related to Boiler Room scams. He found himself shaking his head once more. It was literally everywhere. These types of victimless crimes abounded, and who could blame the offenders really? Why would you conduct an armed robbery on a jeweller for a few Tag Heuer watches when you could rip off an online dealer for far more and at far lesser risk?

He continued to read the article.

'Police could not provide the number of prosecutions or investigations linked to the reporting, saying such investigations were long term 'and may take many years' quoting the shadow justice spokesman Andrew Lamont, 'And given the sheer number of transactions that are being reported, thousands of innocent people are being affected. Quite what the government are doing about it is a matter of great conjecture.'

On the opposite page was an article about technology which discussed the virtues of 'contactless' smart debit cards. The system was spreading across the world and whilst it would take a long time to reach third world countries it was already having a huge impact upon retail spending habits – and crime trends.

The cards worked via a radio frequency chip and meant that the legitimate owner could quite simply buy something and pay for it with a wave of the card over a reader at the checkout. In principle it was a great idea, simple in fact and for the financially-motivated teams yet another opportunity to exploit as they set about working with their own intelligence gatherers and engineers to work out a way to extract critical data from the cards – some were even reporting successes by using the newest breed of smart phones to hack into the data held within the heart of the cards.

Cade finished his drink and wondered back to his room, as he did so his phone started to vibrate in his pocket.

"Jack my boy, how's things in the Motherland?" It was JD and he was as ebullient as ever.

"Have you met up with Ginger yet? How's the weather? Good flight?"

"Christ JD how many questions? But off the top of my head yes, not bad and great, glad you spent my money wisely. Hey John…"

"Go ahead over."

"What do you know about the passports? Any news? Anything out of our old friends? Other than what I found out from Andy and his team?"

"Bloody hell what a hypocrite I counted at least three questions then too! OK, in chronological order: the passports are confirmed stolen, they are legitimate and they have links to every despot country you can think of, but as yet no-one knows why they would have been in Elena's possession. Two, I'm pretty sure Mr Tsang's findings reflect ours and three, you know bugger me Jack I can't remember what the third question was!"

"Senile old twat!" replied Cade lovingly "you were going to provide a link between the documents and Elena."

"Thanks, it's the middle of the frigging night here remember, I got up to use the bathroom and decided to ring you. Glad I did with comments like that! Anyway I'll get onto that. You'll be pleased to hear the weather here is sublime, cracking sunset last night. What's your plan for tomorrow?"

"Wake up, eat breakfast and head into town in a dubiously-loaned section car."

Daniel laughed as he put two and two together and came up with the correct number. His own days as a Chief Inspector came flooding back to him, and if he were in the same position as Roberts he'd have 'accidentally' leant him a car too.

"OK my friend, take it easy and report back for Christ's sake or her indoors will kill me. By the way, check your emails. Out."

And with that Daniel was gone.

After a night of fractured sleep Cade woke, showered, shaved and splashed on some Givenchy Gentleman; the sting soon passed but the fragrance would last all day.

Cade walked out into the car park, got into the aforementioned dubious Mondeo, let the wipers clear the early morning dew from the windscreen and then drove off onto the Colnbrook Bypass and into the early morning rush hour.

It was just seven o'clock and he'd already been awake for four hours. He left the bypass after travelling along the busy A4 and headed towards the even busier M4 – one of the main arterials that would take him into the heart of one of the busiest capital cities in the world. Hong Kong seemed peaceful by comparison.

He cursed the remnants of jet lag as he took a very brief glimpse in the rear view mirror, his eyes were bloodshot and his head pounded, his neck throbbed as he managed a cursory glance over his right shoulder before seeing a quick double flash from a Jaguar behind him, he acknowledged the courtesy with a double flash of his hazards and joined the M4 where he sat for the next hour.

He switched on the radio to hear the ever-popular DJ Chris Evans on Radio Two. He was chatting away to a vicar about the impact of crime on a community in Somerset, or somewhere, Cade wasn't really paying attention.

He slid the window down and tried to get some fresher air. It was a mistake as in seconds he was consuming the fumes of a thousand other motorists, all heading inexorably into the 'Big Smoke'.

He passed Chiswick and Earl's Court before continuing along the A4 and into Kensington. If he had wound the window down again the smell would have changed, this time it was money; pure, unadulterated wealth.

He turned onto the A319 and headed towards Grosvenor Gardens. With the absence of traffic the journey would take five minutes – today it took half an hour. He stopped, turned the radio down and stared out of the left side passenger window.

He was looking at an eight foot high wall, topped with a six foot high barbed wire fence. To the uninitiated it was just that, a bloody great wall with a fence on top, surrounded by mature trees. In reality it was the perimeter fence for Buckingham Palace.

Cade was now in the wealthiest part of the city, with some properties attracting prices in excess of thirty million pounds. It was obscene and whilst some of it was legitimate Cade knew that squirreled away behind the facades of those glorious Edwardian properties lie some of the richest and most powerful people on the planet.

A chill ran across Cade's shoulders causing an involuntary shudder. Perhaps within striking distance lay the answer to his conundrum? Or more likely it was seeing a familiar vehicle grill appear in his driver's mirror?

A silver Rolls Royce slithered by, its engine barely audible. It was certainly Rolls territory and to see a Wraith in these parts was like seeing a Toyota in any other city – almost common and certainly not worth turning a head for. However this particular road-going ocean liner was a Phantom, driven by an enigmatic Chinese male, no doubt the Chauffeur to the exquisitely attired and equally mysterious oriental female in the rear.

The Phantom turned at the next junction and whispered away, out of sight and out of mind. Despite the urge to drive along The Mall Cade resisted and headed straight for Dacre Street SW1, turning left and left again by the cycle shop and only stopping when he came across the rear entrance to New Scotland Yard.

Another hundred metres and he would have seen the iconic revolving sign – but he'd seen it before many times and besides, when Roberts had rung him half an hour earlier he'd told him the kettle was on, and right now he needed a cup of tea, nothing else, just good, old fashioned tea.

He put the window down on the Mondeo as an armed security guard walked towards him.

"Good morning Mr Cade, we've been expecting you, just park her down next to the silver van please sir. Here's your ID, wear it all times, we are on a raised alert status. Go to that back door over there. You will be met."

He drove fifty metres, parked between two silver Ford Transit vans and switched off the engine, got out, stretched his legs and grabbed his bag before swinging his ID into place, straightening his tie and walking to the rear reception area.

He stood by the door for a few moments until Detective Constable Dave Williams appeared. He placed a large hand into Cade's and shook it warmly.

"Morning boss. The Governor asked me to pop down and pick you up. By the way, ignore what he says, I'm a crap dancer. I understand you and the Guv go back a few years?"

"We do, we do indeed Dave, ten or so actually. Oh and by the way you are most likely a far better dancer than he is. You know the phrase dance like nobody is watching?"

"Uh-huh."

"It was invented for your boss."

As they entered the lift Cade started to brief Williams on his background, the journey he had made over the last ten years and how he and Roberts had first met.

"Jason and I met in 2004, I came down to the Yard on secondment from the East Midlands, expecting to spend a few months here, and as they say the rest is history."

He was almost finished as the doors opened onto the tenth floor revealing a hive of industry; Detectives, Analysts, all moving around quickly, none rushing, but all with people to see and places to go.

Stood in the middle of the office melee, arms pointing here and there was an animated, brown-suited Jason Roberts.

Brown suit, brown shoes, beige shirt and his trademark orange tie with an impressive double Windsor knot. Somehow he carried it off.

Detective Chief Inspector Roberts was in the middle of a briefing – it was the bedrock of his business day which started with a seven a.m. briefing and continued throughout the day – each piece being linked back into a continuous cycle of brief and debrief.

This particular morning was no different as the head of the Dedicated Cheque and Plastic Crime Unit covered off the Word of the day, overnight occurrences and finished on a good news story.

"A recent major success for the Unit is that it has successfully dismantled a major organised crime group involved in ATM criminality. A total of fifteen suspects have been arrested, with many thousands of compromised card numbers recovered together with numerous items of equipment for use in ATM crime. This is one of the largest operations undertaken by the Unit since its inception and work is continuing to identify and disrupt other organised crime groups involved in this method of operation. We are all over it people."

As he spoke Roberts became aware of a new arrival in the unit. Without being distracted he continued, however as he finished his briefing Roberts spun around and pointed straight at Cade and held up his spare hand, as a Traffic Officer would to stop vehicles.

The office went deathly quiet.

He looked straight at Cade who stood with his hands held together at waist height. He looked immaculate in a dark navy Jaeger Italian wool suit, white shirt and red tie, a black Jaeger metal buckled belt connected the whole ensemble and last but by no means least a highly polished pair of black Oxford brogues.

Worn discreetly on his cuffs was a pair of blue and gold US Secretary of State Protective Detail cufflinks – a gift from 'a friend' and clearly a gift with provenance.

"Ladies, gentlemen, Liverpool supporters and the rest of you that simply don't fit into any category whatsoever, it is my honour to present this rather dapper man who goes back a very long way with both me and this department. He was involved in policing before Jesus was a lad and 'e's forgotten more about Eastern Europe than most of you have 'ad for breakfast. Don't ask how a northerner ended up working here, it's a long story and one normally left for cheap novels. But I'll let you into a little secret. This man was in the right place at the right time and used his skills to influence. There's a lesson for you lot right there. For one or two of you he'll be very familiar..."

Roberts tapped the side of his nose as he looked around the office at his adoring audience. In a corner of the room an anonymous female looked up and nodded once at Cade and then carried on typing. As she did so she smiled, almost imperceptibly but she smiled nonetheless.

"My old friend and a bloody nice bloke too, former Inspector and now Mr Jack Cade. Help this man as much as you can please – and learn from him. Please, learn from him or I shall be putting my size ten up your rings!"

Roberts beckoned him over as a stereotypical short-skirted female approached and handed the boss a mug of steaming coffee.

"Where are the bloody biscuits? Christ how does this office function sometimes?"

The same female returned swiftly with the office biscuit tin and opened the lid. Roberts placed his hand into it whilst he sipped the piping hot black coffee with the other. Seconds later he produced a ginger nut biscuit, held it out in front of him as if he were examining a piece of faeces and then threw it across the office with a flick of the wrist. It ricocheted off a heavily distracted Detective Sergeants' desk and broke into a hundred pieces.

Roberts shouted "Who", to which the entire team responded in a Michael Caine-esque voice, "puts bloody ginger nuts in with the custard bloody creams?"

Cade smiled, it had been years since he last heard that mantra; whilst in many ways so much had altered, it also felt, with some relief that in fact nothing had changed at all since he and Roberts were last together.

Where those years had gone God himself knew, but it was good to be back. In fact, it was great.

Part Two

Summer 2002

Chapter Fourteen

Nottingham, England.

Cade slipped off his shoes. It had been an intensely long day at the office.

The office in question was the notorious Meadows Police Station, right in the heart of the English East Midlands city of Nottingham, next door to the main railway station and only minutes away from once-rare, now mounting Yardie-centred black-on-black, drug-related drive-by shootings.

These were some of the first in the country and the reason why the local force, Nottinghamshire, were providing an armed response capability, to quell the fears of the neighbourhood and support the girls and boys out on the streets, who as luck would have it were armed with no more than good looks, verbal reasoning skills and a wooden truncheon.

Cade had been based at the Meadows since moving from a nearby station in a far nicer part of town, where even the criminals were generally more pleasant and easier to deal with.

He'd started his career in 1994 at the age of twenty as a uniformed Constable, trained at one of the Home Office District Training Centres near Coventry and had been posted to a town thirty minutes from home.

Home was a three bedroomed semi in a quiet rural village which was as far removed from life in the Meadows as the Florida Keys were from downtown Harlem.

He'd met his wife ten years earlier when they attended the same school but had avoided marriage until 1998. They didn't have, and were unlikely to ever have children. It was a good thing for the marriage was somewhat unconventional.

He had enjoyed his time as a front line police officer and although the news that he was transferring to the Meadows was greeted with horror – as it was seen back then as a 'punishment station' he lived to hold the place, its better quality residents and the staff that policed it in great esteem.

Cruelly injured in 1999 when set upon by a hissing, spitting Hepatitis-laden drug addict he had found himself temporarily office-bound. Whilst he despised the addict for what he had done he also knew that he had inadvertently shaped the rest of his career as an Intelligence Officer.

Ronald Brown, an emaciated, odoriferous and drawn man in his fifties was a familiar sight at the Central Railway Station, he loitered there often and had the appearance of someone who eagerly dressed in the dark, such were his dubious colour choices.

Whenever the British Transport Police were on duty somewhere else in the region it fell to the local boys in blue to respond to his regular antics.

It was a cool Wednesday evening in March when a 'three-nines' call had been made from the railway station platform. A mother of two, en route to Grantham had witnessed Brown exposing himself to a group of women. He was apparently drunk and 'on something'.

'Whisky Uniform One' – the local emergency response car was dispatched – and as luck would have it they were outside the station in seconds, as they were about to head out on their evening patrols.

On board the car was an experienced Jack Cade and his partner and new-found closest friend, a fresh-faced Constable called Vince Johnson.

The Constables arrived at Platform Two, informed the Control Room that they were on site and that they would follow with a sit rep - an update.

The 18:00 to Derby was due to arrive.

Cade and Johnson approached the staggering Brown in a classic military pincer movement, one from the left and the other from the right; they'd done this before and knew that taking an arm each soon reduced the risk of being punched. In doing so they reduced the risk to themselves, the public, and despite what some people thought a bad move, to Brown himself.

Johnson took hold of the right arm but as Cade went to put his own lock on Brown dropped to his knee causing him to roll over the top of his shoulder, across the cold stone platform and onto the track.

Despite wearing body armour he landed with a hefty blow, knocking the wind out of his sails and cracking his temple onto the highly-polished silvery-blue rail. As if that wasn't troublesome enough he also sustained a few bruised ribs and a fractured wrist.

At that moment a few injuries, serious though they may be, were completely irrelevant. Down on the diesel-laden tracks Cade lay on his back, thrashing around like a turtle stranded on an isolated beach and struggling against the body armour that was meant to protect him.

His senses were now scanning on multiple levels; to his left an open train track, to the right his colleague, struggling with the drunken, drug-fuelled Brown and to his front a twenty tonne diesel locomotive, slowing, but still travelling at thirty miles an hour as it arrived into the busy station.

Cade could see the damned thing approaching, he swore he could almost smell it and he could certainly hear it. Being at track level made him reconsider a few things and despite being in an unconventional marriage, with an unconventional wife he was buggered if he was going to call it a day on that by-the-second-colder Wednesday evening.

He turned and pushed off the sleepers with his left leg and instinctively took hold of a leather-clad hand that was offered to him.

Grabbing the hand and propelling himself to the edge of the track he felt the side of the Inter City 125 graze against his Kevlar armour as more hands grabbed hold of him and pulled him upwards, onto the platform and out of harm's way.

Vince Johnson was sat on top of the foul-smelling Brown, having been joined by his namesake, local beat officer Pete Brown. The leather gloved hand belonged to none other than Sergeant Andy Jenkins, who would dine out on the rescue and medal-less event for at least the next twelve months.

Cade was taken to the local hospital by a traffic car and spent the night on a general ward in the care of a charming brunette called Caroline.

Getting home the next day he was greeted by his partner in crime.

"Now then Jack, how you doing? You were lucky you know. You do know don't you?"

Cade knew, it wasn't his first lucky escape but he was hoping it might be his last.

"The lads send their best wishes and the boss said he'll pop and see you as soon as he can. They sent this."

Johnson handed him a bottle of Johnnie Walker. It was the standard Police Federation gift – even if the recipient had a drink problem or a heavily sclerosed liver the gift was the same.

Cade looked at his friend and said "Vinnie, I'm done, I've had enough, that was just too close for comfort."

Johnson replied with a misplaced joke "Well I heard that Brown was a sleeper agent who had got onto the wrong tracks and that he was expressly wrong…"

"Do you actually think you are funny?" Cade asked rhetorically.

"Well I used to…" replied a wounded Johnson.

"Seriously mate, I'm done. I know Penny doesn't give too shits about me but I've got to think of my future. The Chief Super rang me this morning and offered me a secondment onto the Intelligence Unit. I know what you are thinking, but I'm taking it, you'll find another Hutch."

"That's as maybe, but I love being Starsky and it won't be the same. But if you need my blessing, then I understand pal, we'll still be friends right?"

Cade replied with a wink "Absolutely not, I can't bear the sight of you, get out and don't come back."

Johnson knew his colleague well and also understood that despite a love for policing the time was right. Knowing Penny as he did the chances were that she'd probably kill them both if he managed to talk Cade into staying on the frontline.

Cade knew immediately that he would miss his partner, a former printer with an enviable physique. They'd worked together for such a relatively short time, but policing an inner city area made you hard, devoted, loyal and above all it taught you who to trust. And he trusted Vince Johnson with his life. They had enough stories to tell – enough Cade said for an entire book. Perhaps one day he would get around to it.

And so in the late autumn of 1999 he returned to work, still slightly injured but ready to take on a new role.

Cade joined the Local Intelligence Officer on the Monday morning, raring to go and keen to fill his sponge-like capacity for knowledge. He spent the next three years with crusty veteran Derek Kay and learned the art of intelligence; how to cultivate sources, exploit data and extract solutions from hypothesis. This was all pre-internet and as such was very much by the book.

What the book didn't know Kay had made up. He was a legendary figure in the Nottinghamshire force and had played a part in the arrests of grandfathers, fathers and sons, often from the same families. With twenty nine years and a few months under his belt he was due to retire.

Cade quickly became known for his ability to cultivate informants, to gather information and turn it into intelligence, above all he knew how to get results. He almost single-handedly ran the unit when Derek Kay did eventually leave the force. Cade knew he had large boots to fill but proposed and delivered new systems, created new methods of gathering information and soon became the go to person in the station and later on the subject matter expert on the Division.

He forced the organisation into the 21st century, kicking and screaming at first but they rapidly gained a reputation as one of the front runners in intelligence led policing. Whilst the senior staff took the credit everyone knew who was responsible for creating the foundations and building a capable and effective team.

If you wanted to know the answer about something, somewhere or someone, you paid a visit to Jack Cade.

Cade's professional life meant that he could study for his Sergeant's exams and in less than six months he was not only ready to take them he passed with a higher-than-average mark, all of which attracted attention from his old Shift Inspector Tom Jackson.

Jackson was an ex-military man and had an eye for skill and raw talent and despite knowing that he would be losing one of his best men he recommended Cade for promotion in 2001.

A role as a frontline Response Sergeant followed which Cade both enjoyed and excelled at. He was fully fit and raring to go. He hated his wife more than ever, but somehow they managed to live a life of complete separation, the twain never meeting.

Despite enjoying the role Cade often found himself harking back to the world of intelligence. He'd set a few benchmarks at District level but knew he could go no further, unless he moved or left the organisation. What he needed was a parallel shift and it would arise at the most unexpected time and location.

Chapter Fifteen

Cade was at a rare social event, made even rarer by the fact that he was with his wife.

It was the late spring of 2002, he'd had his stripes for a while, had a great section and a reasonably supportive boss. Professionally life was 'OK'.

It was his Shift Inspector Grant Cooke who had invited him and Penny to an early season barbeque. Cooke was a good looking man, in his mid-forties and fitter than most men half his age. He had black, shiny hair that appeared almost entirely natural. He also had a reputation as a hard bastard; worked hard and played harder. But above all he had a roving eye which normally settled upon the fairer sex and rather fortuitously he had a flexible and adventurous wife.

"Bring some beer and wine and make sure you bring that gorgeous wife too! You are welcome to stay the night" his boss had announced as the two men had gone their separate ways after finishing a set of nights.

"Will do boss, see you Saturday."

In truth he really couldn't be bothered. It was a work event and as such the topic would all be about work. As it happened he couldn't have been further from the truth.

The weather was simply beautiful as Jack and Penny arrived. He parked his blue Ford Focus ST outside the imposing, modern but almost anonymous four bedroomed home.

He suggested Penny should go ahead as he collected a few bags from the boot. By the time he had slammed the tailgate Penny Cade was being greeted enthusiastically at the front door.

She had never changed; the life and soul of any party and effortlessly attractive to the eye. She always made the most of her more than ample figure and today was no different. A simple summer dress, white with red Hibiscus flowers splattered over it, it was slashed up the leg and plunged, just enough to reveal her good-enough-to-dive-into cleavage.

Above all, she knew how to work a crowd, and if that crowd was predominantly male so much the better.

As Cade walked towards the house a former colleague arrived and eagerly wanted to show off his new acquisition, a bright red Subaru Impreza. Cade, a keen driver was soon sat in the driver's seat and probing the switchgear and trying out the gearbox.

"What do you think Jack?"

"Nice Phil, we should have a race sometime!"

"Indeed mate, but perhaps another time, that car is like a wife to me, talking of which, you brought your missus tonight?"

"Yes, she's gone inside, to be honest she doesn't need me around, she's at her best with a crowd."

His colleague popped the bonnet on the WRX and showed off the engine. As Cade looked at the impressive layout his workmate looked longingly at the house and involuntarily licked his lips. It was clear that Phil Clarke's mind was on other things.

In an apparent change of heart he threw the keys at Cade.

"Take her for a spin, try her out, it's good to compare wives!"

Cade laughed and agreed.

"I'll be ten minutes, keep an eye on Penny for me, make sure she moderates her alcohol, she tends to get a little bloody wild if not."

Fifteen minutes later Cade returned to 26 Beech Avenue or as the sign on the driveway said, *Sycamore Lodge*. He parked the Subaru and locked it. He was impressed, she handled very well indeed.

He knocked on the door but getting no answer walked into the hallway without being greeted, he could see that Penny was already holding court. He knew she hadn't missed him at all.

He also knew how she liked to flirt and with five men around her in such short time it neither surprised nor shocked Cade to see her clearly holding court and very much on form.

He took a moment to study her for she was oblivious to him even being there, enjoying the undivided attention from Section Two, the off duty Armed Response Group.

He knew why he had fallen for her a few years before. It was for the same reason that every man in that immaculate but stereotypical home, complete with its bespoke Canadian Maple kitchen now couldn't take their eyes off her.

She was playful, quick-witted, flirtatious and bold. She had an amazing head of bright, blazing red hair too and Cade, well he was an easy target for a redhead.

She was trim, in all the right places, looked after herself and was the archetypal suburban bored housewife. When she and Cade first met she had come out of a tempestuous relationship but one which she endured purely for the physicality of its sex life. Her ex-partner would beat her during lovemaking and she loved it, got a kick out of it and made endless excuses for the bruises and the barely visible flinches each time she put pressure on her battered body.

One day it became all too much, he overstepped the agreed limits and she called the police.

Cade was the first officer on the scene, offered her advice and a comforting arm. The rest as they say is history.

They fell deeply in love, the sex was quite incredible, more than he could have ever had hoped for. She was voracious, daring and almost reckless. But no matter what he offered, attempted or tried it was never enough. So he pushed the boundaries, further and further until he was finally able to satisfy her.

Weeks became months and without warning he asked her to marry him and much to his surprise she agreed.

Penelope Roberta Stephens became Penny Roberta Cade.

It was a friend of the Groom who announced on that all-too-forgettable Saturday and for all to hear that she'd become Penny R Cade and it was clear from her ferocious glare that she despised the friend and somehow her new husband too for not defending her honour, but more so she was furious about the cheap link to a seaside amusement hall.

She didn't speak to him until the next morning, having successfully evaded his every wedding night advance.

The next day they flew to Tenerife on honeymoon and made love each day, and every night, leaving little time for sightseeing. It was on Day Nine that she suggested that they invite the young American couple from the adjoining apartment to join them and from that moment Cade knew his marriage was doomed.

Life continued 'normally' when they returned, but she never allowed him to forget how much she wanted to experience two men at once. It came up in almost every conversation in the bedroom, skilfully, brutally she steered Cade down the same path again and again until one day he relented.

It was an unmitigated disaster and for Cade being a serving police officer not without risk. But it was that very risk that excited Penelope Cade.

The very next evening she convinced her husband to break into the newly-completed show home that had been built at the end of their road. She announced her desire to have sex with him in the unfinished bathroom – she said she wanted it in the bath; dusty, dirty and completely, unashamedly naked.

"But what if we get caught?" Cade asked, almost pleadingly.

"Then they'll have to join us darling" she replied with a teasing wink.

Going against his better judgement he agreed. They found an open door and made their way upstairs under the guidance of Cade's cell phone, it throwing out just enough light to navigate by. In minutes she was ready and as usual took the lead.

Whilst he tried to maintain a level of covertness she screamed her lungs out in ecstasy, awaking the neighbours who alerted the local police.

He knew he had to put an end to this – but at that moment the key was to escape and leave behind no evidence. They hid in the garden until the coast was clear. He prayed that the attending staff would be inept and not find them. His wishes were granted. Meanwhile she adored the whole experience and confessed later that she wanted to be found.

He had started to hate her, albeit the sex was indeed almost absurd, he found that her constant demands were, despite what most men thought, beyond control. It was no longer fun.

From that day they made a pact, without a word being uttered, to travel along different paths. Penny continued to manage what she saw as a boring job in a mundane role within a tedious Building Society, hunting for new conquests whenever the chance arose, whilst Cade busied himself with work and more work, volunteering for any overtime that was going.

He knew he would miss her 'her' but not 'them' and despite desperate attempts to avoid the inevitable he knew she would soon leave him, or kill him in the process.

In the hallway of *Sycamore Lodge* he stood alone, watching her select her prey, dancing and weaving like a Siren, luring her next conquest onto the rocks. She threw her head back in laughter revealing straight, ermine-white teeth, a sleek neck and a glimpse of what lay beyond that enthralling cleavage.

She was tactile, stroking one or two of the men with her long, manipulative fingers before sipping elegantly from a glass of champagne, her tongue darting onto the strawberry that clung to the side of the glass.

"Jack, welcome, what took you so long? Penny has been entertaining the troops, come on in and meet the gang" announced Cooke as he walked from the kitchen to the hallway.

"Come join us in the kitchen, I've got food to cook so grab yourself a drink. All the neighbours are here so don't worry about the noise. I hope you both brought your swimming gear?"

Penny turned and feigned surprise when she saw her husband stood next to her.

"You didn't tell me Grant and Julie had a pool darling, I haven't brought a swimsuit – oh my God that means I'll have to go in naked!"

She held her fingers up to her lips in a faux display of shock. It worked for everyone except her husband.

He knew she was already well on the way to being intoxicated and for Penelope Cade drunk meant an impending display of wildness and complete lack of self-control.

Cooke's wife, an artist of growing repute had skilfully sensed an air of unease and had asked Cade to join her in the lounge, stating convincingly that she had been working on something that might interest him.

As she entered the room she asked for his opinion on a new watercolour that she had embarked upon. She seemed the most sober of the group and therefore, perhaps unwisely, he trusted her.

They spoke for half an hour about her work and his and how her husband valued him. She laboured on the point that he wanted to help him progress through the ranks. Cade was sold and listened intently. He either deliberately or naively missed the encouraging and mounting sexual signals on display in the room.

Out in the garden the party became louder as more and more alcohol was consumed, the men became more adventurous, the women more outrageous, pushing their own and each other's boundaries, playing drinking games and slowly becoming less bashful. Two of the female neighbours were now in the pool and kissing one another openly.

It was now obvious that as parties went this was far from conventional. Blue diamond-shaped pills were being handed out, an apparently welcome change from vol-au-vents and run-of-the-mill finger food.

Cade was deliberately sober and was evidently alone in this experience. People that he counted as colleagues were now starting to overstep the boundaries that both life and career had imposed, choosing different partners and gradually engaging in more and more shameful behaviour.

The combination of alcohol, Tadalafil and bravado had reached a tipping point. Another ten minutes and it would be too late. He was far from a prude, but this, was just something else.

Julie Cooke thanked Cade for his advice and stood to leave but then turned and slipped her dress straps deftly from her shoulders. It slid effortlessly to the ground revealing nothing but a pair of high heeled black shoes and a provocative smile.

"Do you like what you see Jack? It's all yours. Penny's fine with it."

Cade had seen enough. For him it was career suicide and besides she wasn't a natural blonde.

He pushed his way past her and through the house, beyond the various groups and found his wife. Her dress was hanging over the pool fence, her shoes thrown across the garden, her nude and very wet body now surrounded by three men, including his boss, all of whom were getting to know Penelope Cade rather too intimately.

He squatted down at the side of the pool and called her towards him.

She turned around, looked at her husband and laughed.

"Come on in babe, the water's lovely."

"Penny, get out. Now! I won't ask again." Cade stood up, endeavouring to add some control to the situation.

"No Jack I want this. Come on admit it you do too. Go and choose someone, I'm having too much fun. You can fuck me later, but not until these gorgeous men have had a turn. You can be last and by then I'll be more than ready for you."

She was drunk, but very capable.

Cade was incredulous, he stared at Inspector Grant Cooke, his luxuriant black mane now swept back over his head, the substantial gold chain around his neck fought for attention with his heavily-matted chest hair but it was his hands that were the busiest of all, just below the waterline playing with his wife's incredibly buoyant breasts.

"Go home Sergeant Cade, she'll be fine, we'll all look after her. She's in good hands. We'll make sure she gets home in the morning. But for now we have some games to play."

Cade could feel adrenalin coursing through his veins, anger manifested itself as bile, boiling up into in his throat and scorching his skin and yet despite all of this he also sensed a battle lost. He was outnumbered, outgunned and alone with a group of people that were supposed to set the rules.

He knew he had to at least try, or be seen to stand his ground. If he simply walked away this pack of cackling hyenas would ensure he was cruelly swept away, brushed under the carpet and forgotten.

He felt betrayed by everyone there.

"Cooke let my wife get out now. I want to take her home before it's too late."

"Too late?" asked Cooke, almost mocking Cade "The night is still young my friend, still very young and besides, it's Sir. Don't you ever forget that?" He looked at his staff member through pitiless conker-coloured eyes and then returned to examining his wife in great detail, taking turns with the other officers who were by now more than acquainted with her.

Penny Cade shouted to her husband to change his mind – gave him one last chance, but it was far too late; as far as he was concerned their marriage had ended there, and then.

And as far as Cade knew his career had ended that evening too.

He left *Sycamore Lodge* with its annoying kitchen and inferior watercolours, exited the front door, leaving it wide open behind him, hoping in vain that someone would wonder in and steal the incongruous sluts' jewellery.

He walked across the immaculate front lawn and lashed out with his right foot, expertly knocking the head off an annoying and welcoming gnome before finally arriving alongside Phil Clarke's pride and joy.

The Ford key in his hand wasn't like a normal ignition key in that the end of the shaft was rounded, but as it dragged along the bright red metalwork of the front wing, driver's door and rear quarter it made an intensely satisfying sound. Small pieces of the paintwork fluttered to the road surface and blew away in the evening breeze.

Cade plipped the lock on the Focus and got in. He was about to put his seatbelt on but decided against it, instead he left the car, walked up to the Impreza, had a cursory scan up and down the street and realising that the immediate neighbourhood was probably preoccupied with his wife spun around driving his right foot into the passenger door.

The noise as it caved in was a dull thud but the damage was significant.

Cade felt better, it was an analogy, albeit a strange one, but he felt that he had kicked his marriage into touch too.

He got into the ST, turned the ignition key and drove off.

He drove unnecessarily for twenty miles at speeds well in excess of the local limit. At least the car was reliable.

His mind was whirring with minute detail of what his wife was doing with men who he trusted and respected. Eventually he pulled over into a lay-by, powered down the window and breathed in the cool countryside air. Try as he might he couldn't rid his mind of the graphic imagery that haunted him.

It would be a long time before he could trust another woman, let alone a nymphomaniac redhead, and he knew he could never trust his boss again. He had to move on, both personally and professionally. That bastard would pay, somehow.

The following morning he would be sat in front of his Divisional Commander, a man who he genuinely respected and admired and who had previously provided him with some robust career and personal advice.

Now a Superintendent, Tom Jackson was the only work-related friend Cade felt he had left. He hoped and prayed that Jackson would listen to him and understand why he needed to leave the force; above all he needed an act of kindness, understanding and rational support.

He walked into his office at D Division DHQ, closed the door behind him and started talking.

After five minutes Jackson picked up his phone and dialled his Executive Assistant and in his broad Nottinghamshire accent said "Make sure I am not disturbed Louise and bring us two strong cups of coffee, bugger it, bring the biscuits too."

He looked at Cade and shook his head.

"I don't think you are telling me the whole story here old son."

He wasn't, but fifteen minutes later he had.

The Superintendent got up and walked around the office. His knuckles were whitening slowly.

"This is not good Jack, not good at all, Christ, as if we haven't got enough enemies out on the streets. Did Penny get home OK? Are you OK? Bollocks, can you imagine this getting into the papers."

Cade said nothing for a few moments. Jackson allowed him the moment he needed to compose himself.

"I'll have that bastard Cooke by the throat when I see him" Jackson almost spat out the words, clearly more angry than Cade who had spent the previous twenty four hours trying to vent, to allow the venom to escape.

"Join the queue boss, thanks, but no thanks, you have a Division to run and I somehow need to start again. I'm not entirely sure where, perhaps another force, I may even leave altogether and certainly whatever I do it's as a single man. Believe me I ran almost every possible scenario through my head last night, from murder to arson, with that callous bastard tied naked to a chair in the middle of the fire and slowly burning to death whilst that fucking slut of a wife sat next to him..."

"Very sad Jack, a really pity, she's a cracker that one, there's not a man in this station that wouldn't want to..."

He stopped himself, like a freight train trying to avoid a pram.

"Jack..."

"It's OK boss, I understand, you meant nothing by it. It's OK, really. Help yourself."

Jackson removed his anthracite-coloured French Connection glasses and placed them on his desk.

He looked Cade in the eye. "Jack, you've been let down by the very people you love and trust, let me see what I can do to get you back on the road to recovery. I need to make a few calls. Grab a couple of sick days – we owe you that at least and stay in touch. Leave Cooke to me, his day will come. Meanwhile, talk to no-one, and I mean no-one. Oh and Jack…"

"Sir?"

"For the love of fucking Mary Jane do not burn his bloody house down. Take him to another force area and kill him by all means, I don't need the crime stats at the moment!"

Cade smiled a thin smile and agreed "Noted Sir, give my regards to MJ."

Cade left his old boss nibbling on a biscuit and running his spare hand through what was left of his hair. He walked out into the rear courtyard got into his car and drove home.

He turned the key in the front door, opened it and found his wife sat on the stairs. She looked exhausted, sober and yet slightly arrogant.

He placed his wallet, phone and keys on the hallway table and walked into the kitchen, flicked the switch on the kettle and took a mug out of the cupboard next to the fridge.

He heard her walk into the room as he finished making himself a strong cup of black coffee.

After clearing her throat she started talking first.

"Jack, I…"

He turned around, took a sip of the hot liquid and then wrapped his hands around the cup which provided a sense of comfort. When the heat was almost too much he placed the cup down and ran his burning palms across his face, screwing them into his eyes. It felt good.

He let out a long sigh and then began.

"Penelope, gather your things together and prepare to leave. Take everything; I don't want one single reminder of you in this house, nothing. You've got until the end of tomorrow. I'm going away for a couple of days, it matters not where I am going but when I get back you will be gone. I hope it was worth it?"

She started to cry.

"Save that for the divorce hearing my love, I gave you a fair chance to walk away but you let your whore-like nature win in the battle of head over heart. If I were you I'd get booked into the local clinic too, that lot have probably got more STD's than a Hyson Green hooker. Now, if you don't mind I've got my coffee to finish. It's hot, wet and steamy, a bit like Grant Cooke likes his women."

He knew it was petty but it felt bloody good.

She started to talk but Cade held up his hand in protest.

"Seriously Penny, the clock is ticking; I've started my life from scratch as of today. You need to as well. If you need a room you could always swing by *Sycamore Lodge*, I hear they've got great facilities and the hosts are most willing to accommodate guests."

He walked out of the door, entered the ST and drove along the main A52 and an hour later entered the Peak District National Park.

He pulled up onto the front of the iconic Izaak Walton Hotel, checked in and minutes later set out for a walk through the picturesque and breath-taking countryside that surrounded nearby Dovedale.

He revisited a childhood memory by navigating across the River Dove, using a set of slippery stepping stones to get from one side of the river to the other. He then walked through the wooded ravine and upwards, climbing steadily until he reached the top of a thousand foot high limestone hill known locally as Thorpe Cloud.

Once at the summit he paused, took an extended deep breath, the crisp, clean air filled every fibre of his lungs. He turned slowly, taking in the entire vista until he had returned to his starting point.

It was one of his favourite views and whilst he stared out onto the horizon he wasn't sure where his life would head, but he knew that it would now travel in a new direction, one without her, the rampant, selfish bitch, and one which might eventually find him happiness.

He sat down on a rough, blustery outcrop. As the wind whistled around him, antagonising him like an unseen spectre he started to plan the rest of his life.

Chapter Sixteen

His phone rang.

He ignored it. Whoever it was would wait and if it was that important they'd ring back.

Later when he got back down to the hotel he entered the bar and selected a ten year old Macallan from the top shelf. He added a hint of water allowing his skilled palate to clearly detect the Bourbon casks that gave it its light flavour; hints of heather honey combined with dried fruit and walnut to provide him with a welcome and warming end to the best of days.

He found a chair by the window and whilst looking out onto the rugged green hillside opened his phone and dialled into the voicemail service.

"Jack, Tom Jackson, I don't need an answer now but how do you fancy setting up a new team at East Midlands Airport? It's an idea that's been floated by the joint Chief Constables including ours, Leicestershire and Derbyshire. They think the airport with its rapid growth and comparative easy access is now a risk entry point for organised criminals. As luck would have it I was on a phone conference this morning and the Chiefs were canvassing for a good man to run the intelligence team. Naturally I put your name forward. There's no nepotism here, but the job is yours if you want it. Give it some thought and get back to me. Cheers."

He closed his phone and mused upon the idea as he sipped the liquid amber, savouring each mouthful, combining each burst of flavour with a new thought. He was almost at decision point but decided to have another, if nothing else it would help to erase all thoughts of his shattered marriage.

He approached the bar and met the radiant Elizabeth once more.

"I see you wear many hats" he said without an agenda, although she was delightful to look at; probably mid-twenties, nearly six foot, smoke-grey eyes and incredible silky blonde hair which was tied neatly into a pony tail.

Cade soon found himself captivated by her and as he was the only customer asked if she minded if he sat at the bar.

Whether she was exhibiting the virtues of a perfect hospitality worker or just happened to feel relaxed around him Cade would never know. At that very moment he found her enigmatic smile, attentive manner and her warmth to be a refreshing change and that was all he needed to begin the road to restoration.

"Can I buy you a drink – I have no agenda, none at all, I'm just trying to be pleasant."

She replied "Of course, that would be marvellous, to be honest with you I could do with one, it's been a hellish long day so it has."

Her voice washed over him, replacing the scotch with an altogether more beneficial result.

She selected a glass of cool, crisp Pinot Gris, it was a New Zealand vineyard that Cade recognised instantly. He'd travelled there a few years before and had grown to love the place, if nothing else it was a chance to extend the conversation

Both Cade and the vivacious Elizabeth were most comfortable with each other and a casual observer would have been easily fooled into thinking he was trying to seduce her; nothing could have been further from the truth.

She could have laid her admittedly taut body on a pristine sheepskin rug in front of a roaring pine cone fire, in a cabin deep in the woods and he would have simply, but respectfully declined; perhaps another day?

"So, Mr Cade do you know New Zealand well?"

"You are very observant Miss?"

"And you don't need to know!" she replied quickly but with that mischievous smile.

He felt like a cave diver – entering a dark void, knowing that to do would increase his risk, but somehow unable to back away.

"Touché, I shall retire hurt to my seconds and allow them to stitch up my wounds…" he feigned a hurt Labrador puppy face.

"No, no I was joking honestly I was."

"And me too, I must apologise, it's the nature of the job." He replied casually but with an olive branch attached.

"So, what do you do? Let me guess?"

"After you my lady, you have three guesses and the winner gets to choose the prize."

She was visibly excited and even more attractive "Oh dear God I love games!" She clapped her hands together, a sweet little girl in the body of a vixen.

"OK, guess one." Asked Cade, now enjoying the moment, they were still alone and as the evening was progressing it looked likely that he might be her only customer.

"OK, OK…er I know, you are a secret agent so you are!"

"No."

"But you'd have to kill me if I was right, right?"

"I would but I'd do it really slowly…" he was flirting now.

"I bet. OK, guess two, a Heart Surgeon, you have nice hands and inquisitive eyes."

"Better that than the other way around" he replied with a wink.

She laughed with real vigour and replied "Hell, you're a very naughty man Mr Cade," before leaning across the bar and punching him playfully on the arm.

"Please, call me Jack."

"If that's OK I will, Jack Cade, interesting name, very famous in British history you know?"

"I didn't."

He did.

"Oh yes, he was a real rebel, Shakespeare wrote all about him, I learned about him at uni, but that was a few years ago now. Are you a real rebel Mr Cade?"

He brushed the question to one side "Come now, it can't have been that long ago that you were at university?"

"I'm twenty six and not a day younger – and you?"

"Twenty eight and feel many, many days older."

They chinked their glasses together and carried on chatting about Cades' day, how he had revisited a boyhood dream and climbed the famous peak.

She looked at him squarely in the eye "Tell me, did you walk it, or run?"

"I walked it, only a fool would run it, or someone incredibly fit."

"Then for sure I'm a fool Mr Cade or, in your words, incredibly fit."

It was her turn to wink and now she was flirting. Her skin flushed as her hungry eyes held his gaze for just long enough to create a connection.

They continued chatting about random things, where she was born, how she came to be in Derbyshire, in the middle of nowhere in an old English country hotel and all the while somehow Cade managed to avoid the third question.

Eleven o'clock came all too soon and sticking firmly to the rules Elizabeth Delany placed a damp towel over the beer tap handle, rang a little brass bell which seemed to toll forever, and finally reduced the light in the bar to a bare minimum.

With that enigmatic smile she announced that the evening had come to an end. Cade drained the last of his Macallan and handed her the glass.

"Thank you Elizabeth, you have helped restore my faith in human kind today. Whatever your hopes and dreams are I trust they will all come true."

He placed his hand across the bar. She leant on the bar and placed her hand into his. Her handshake was firm and warm.

"And you Jack and you. It's been a pleasure, who knows perhaps one day we'll meet down under? Goodnight, safe travels, sláinte!"

With that she raised her own glass and emptied it before walking behind the bar, turning on the glass washer and switching off the lights.

A few more patrons were arriving back into the lobby, tired from a day's walking on the nearby hills. Delany conducted herself with the same easy charm that had captivated Cade as she ensured they had all they needed and then locked the main door and switched the answerphone on. It was a nightly ritual regardless of occupancy.

She made one last sweep around the lower floor and headed upstairs to her own room before another early start, where once more she would rise with the lark and attend to the guests. It was as if she was the only staff member, she certainly did the work of three people and for half their wages, but she got to meet interesting people and the sanctuary that the place provided was both timely and much-needed.

She opened her bedroom door, removed her clothes and slipped into an oversized shirt. The cotton felt cool against her skin. She cleaned her teeth and walked towards her bed. As she sat on the edge she realised that she hadn't asked the third question. That bloody good-looking Cade had got away with it.

"I bet he's a spy!" She laughed at herself before getting into bed and pulling the duvet up and over her face. It had been a long day.

Ten minutes later she was still wide awake.

"Damn it, I need to know. I can't sleep unless I know."

Breaking the hotel rules and her own strict code she quietly left her room and walked along the corridor towards Room Eight.

Cade was sat in his room, it wasn't entirely to his taste, but it was in keeping with the period features of the hotel. He was looking out of the window and across the valley. The moon was impressive; clear, bright and doing a remarkable job of illuminating the surrounding countryside. Despite his solitude he didn't feel lonely.

He stared at the rolling hills and began to wonder what Penny was doing. He hated himself for thinking about her, but it was intensely difficult to rid his mind of her image and their marriage. He hoped she was as miserable as he was.

He thought he heard a gentle tap at the door.

Penny evaporated from his mind as he concentrated on his surroundings. He heard it again. He walked quickly into the en suite and grabbed a towel, wrapping it around his waist before approaching the door.

Unlike most modern hotels the door didn't have a spy hole so he opened it revealing Elizabeth Delany in an old fashioned but all-too-sexy cornflower blue nightshirt. Her blonde hair was down now and cascaded like a waterfall over the material and across her milky-white shoulders until it reached the midway point of her back.

He was momentarily unable to speak so she started the conversation in a whisper.

"Hello Jack, look this is not something I would normally do, trust me on this. But I got into bed and I couldn't switch off."

"So, is this your third guess Elizabeth? You think I'm an Electrician?"

She giggled, trying desperately to restrain her laughter, feeling suddenly like a mischievous pupil on a summer vacation, discovering the perils and delights of boys for the very first time.

"No silly, I can't switch my mind off. You never allowed me the third guess. So, can I?"

"Can you what?"

"Can I bloody guess man?" she hissed "For the love of God you are not making this easy, so you aren't."

He stepped into the doorway.

"Look, do you want to come in, you look incredibly suspicious stood there; however looking like that it's fair to say that you would also raise the overall rating of the hotel, however you might just get sacked too! I'll get some clothes on, come in."

She paused, this was completely against everything she had ever stood for but she felt safe in his company. He'd been the perfect gent, but perversely, she felt like the filthiest, most immoral woman alive.

She walked into his bedroom, closing the door quietly behind her before speaking.

"Jack, I, look I don't know what to say..." her voice was very slightly quivering, a mixture of nerves and apprehension.

He walked towards her, knowing that somehow it was wrong, placed his arms out in front of him and said "Then don't say another word."

The moonlight sent shafts of clear light through the Georgian window frame; the curtains were wide open, allowing the lunar radiance to pick out the finer detail in the inviting bedroom.

Elizabeth Delany was true to her word, this wasn't normal behaviour for her but as she pulled Cade's towel from his toned body she was already pleased about her decision. It dropped to the floor with a dull thump. Cade was already undoing her shirt, button by button until she was able to pull it over her head revealing herself to him.

The moonlight created an incredible image; two beautiful people, naked and entwined and the only sound being gentle sighs and Irish words that Cade neither understood nor replied to.

Their lips met for the first time, she swallowed hard and then again, she was slightly awkward, but becoming more aroused by the moment. The body that Cade had seen when he first arrived, clothed in corporate and uninteresting colours was now revealed; exquisitely shaped and honed by an active lifestyle; her hip bones were prominent, acting as a natural guide, her skin was as smooth as satin. Her small, excited breasts tensed in an instant as his inquisitive tongue flicked across them. Her toned behind flinched as his strong hands grabbed at her, lifting her slightly off her toes and up to meet him.

In seconds he was inside her, her legs wrapped around his hips as he walked her towards the window. With three simple steps they were in the bay of the window, her naked back pressed up against the glass. To a hunter, plying his trade in the nearby moonlit valley she would have been the most magnificent sight; ethereal, beautiful and wanton.

Her tongue fluttered around his mouth as he reciprocated, her sighs were becoming more pronounced and he knew that it would not take long to reach a pinnacle. He tried to slow down and she sensed his hesitance.

"Jack, stop, turn me to face the window."

He gently eased her to her feet, allowing her to turn around.

She bent over in front of him, her hands upon the window sill, her hair falling downwards once more and covering her face. His tanned hands were evident on her pale skin as he wrapped them around her hips. With an exquisite feeling he was where they both wanted him to be, but now she was much noisier.

Her Irish drawl became more apparent as with each driving movement she cursed him, said she hated him and said she would never forgive him, she was constantly stifling her desire to scream, but all the while begging him not to stop.

"Oh God Jack Cade I hope someone is out there watching this!" and with that she screamed silently, biting her hand to avoid detection.

He stopped. His body was pulsing with pleasure. He too had reached the summit for the second time that day and once more he was breathless, exhausted but undeniably content.

She turned, stood up and wrapped her arms around him; he could clearly see her in the reflection of the glass. She had discarded any concern of being seen and it made her deeply attractive. She kissed him fully on the lips then walked across the bedroom floor and picked up her shirt.

"Look. I have to go. I want to stay. But I…have to go." She was still breathless.

"Elizabeth…"

"Yes?"

He nodded and smiled, still in a state of partial arousal his body was silhouetted against the window, his own breathing slowly recovering. In a pathetic gesture all he could do was create a kiss and blow it across the palm of his right hand.

She caught it and playfully pretended to lock it into her heart. And with that she left his room and closed the door behind her.

The following day he felt a sense of elation and sadness. Had he exploited that beautiful woman from the Emerald Isle? Or had they both needed an outlet and with more than a hint of luck had providence brought them together?

Or, perhaps, did they both just want sex? Questions, questions and the answer appeared to lay deep in his slightly troubled conscience.

He walked into a more crowded bar area the next morning. Tourists that he hadn't seen the night before packed the bustling restaurant, eager for a traditional English breakfast.

He was staring into his tea cup when a familiar voice brought him to his senses.

"Well good morning Mr Cade and how was your night?"

He smiled, looking straight at her gleaming grey eyes as every other diner continued to eat, oblivious to the nuance and interplay.

"Well I got to sleep eventually, I have to say the room service was just perfect, better than I have had anywhere in the world. Thank you."

"The pleasure was all mine. Thank you for coming Mr Cade."

He brushed his hand against hers, almost imperceptibly. She pulled hers away; perhaps already sub-consciously building a wall to protect her from the inevitable departure.

He finished his breakfast, dabbed his lips with the napkin and placed it upon the table.

He stood, turned around and walked to the reception, settled his account and left.

As he drove out of the gate and bid goodbye to the Izaak Walton he convinced himself that occasionally things did indeed happen for a reason. He indicated, glanced momentarily, turned right and never looked back.

It was a fantasy stop-over in an idyllic part of the world made all the more incredible by the events of the previous night – and yet.

He was verging on turning the car around and heading back, to apologise or perhaps to take the 'relationship' to its next phase, but he knew it wasn't feasible and 'besides' he said out aloud 'who was the victim here?'

He resigned himself to the fact that he had in fact been the prey of a lustful and rather wonderful girl with smiling eyes and the body of an athlete and that when all was said, and all was done he was the hapless gazelle to the imperious lioness.

"What a way to go!" he offered to the only other voice in the car, the iconic Terry Wogan, who was busily chatting on the radio in his own inimitable Irish style and introducing the next song.

"And this is especially for Jack if you're listening; it's The Eagles, and *One of those nights*."

He took his eyes monetarily off the road and looked in the rear view mirror; surely not?

At the Izaak Walton Elizabeth Delany carried on with her duties but with an intimate sense and a smell of a man she might never meet again. She felt nothing but elation. It had been wonderful, but now she cursed for not arranging to meet him again. The breakfast room was empty now; staff cleared up and prepared for the much hoped for lunchtime rush.

Lucy Foxton, a sixteen year old waitress with chestnut hair and vanilla skin skipped around the room, collecting occasional tips and cleaning each table in turn until she got to Cade's. She brushed the crumbs into a napkin and scrunched it up before throwing it in the bin.

Written on one corner accompanied by a single kiss was Cade's cell phone number.

Within the hour he was back in familiar territory. Life had already returned to normal and already he hated it. He started to regret leaving the Peak's quite so soon.

Despite being told to take a few days off he pulled into the back yard at the Divisional HQ and almost ran up the stairs to Tom Jackson's office.

If nothing else that pretty Irish girl had refreshed his mind and given his ego a sizeable boost.

As he turned the corner he became aware of another set of footsteps coming hurriedly down the stairs. He looked up, it was Cooke.

"Jack my boy, how are things, feeling better? I hear you were not well, good to see you back in harness." He smiled a smug almost overly-confident smile.

Cade had two choices: grab his boss by the throat, hold him up against the wall and throttle the life out of him or walk on by, rising above the situation and gaining the higher moral ground.

He chose the former.

Without a moment's hesitation he launched a hand straight for Cooke's throat, pulling him towards his outstretched kneecap. Cooke's stomach clashed with the much harder, bony structure and he was instantly winded.

Despite being a hard bastard Cooke was now very much on the defensive, he was dropping to his knees and desperately trying to regain some control over his breathing when Cade rammed his foot straight into his testicles. To an onlooker he was converting the winning penalty at a rugby match, the kick was equally deliberate, delivered with the accuracy of an international Fly Half.

Cade's instep struck the right testicle, causing it to almost burst against the pubic bone. Pain shot through Cooke's hips and up into his stomach causing him to feel instantly nauseous. The combination of the two rapid blows had been highly effective.

Cade stepped back slightly, aware that his boss could easily grab his feet and tip him back down the concrete staircase. Fortunately, it being the service exit it was unlikely to be used by anyone other than the Traffic staff who parked their vehicles immediately adjacent to the door.

Cade knew that he didn't have long before they were discovered. He could hear more activity in the adjoining corridor: Footsteps.

He placed his hand onto Cooke's hair and grabbed a handful, pulling his face up to look at his own. Cooke was still reeling from the hammer blow and was unable to feel the localised pain in his scalp.

"Trust me, we are nowhere near even, but that is a start. If you are half the man you think you are you will never discuss this matter again. You owe me at least that for what you have done to me."

He dropped his head, allowing him to breath in, each breath filling his lungs with oxygen and reducing the searing pain between his legs.

He slowly got to his feet, using the wall and railings as a guide.

Cade could feel the rage building again but knew he had to stop or it was likely that one of them would end up in hospital. He took a deep breath and looked at Cooke before adding "It's over Cooke. We are done."

As Cooke launched unexpectedly at Cade he chose possibly the worst time to commence his retaliation. Unmarked and visibly the aggressor he played straight into Cade's hands. Cade had become aware of the presence of another person in the stairwell, if it was one of Cooke's section then he was in deeper trouble than he thought, however fortune was on his side.

"Inspector Cooke what the fuck are you doing? Stand down man, stand down NOW!" It was Tom Jackson.

Cade was struggling not to respond but had allowed Cooke to land at least one punch to the left side of his face which was now starting to swell. He staggered slightly, adding to the effect of the slightly staged, ever-so-slightly harder than expected assault. For Cade it was painful, but perfect, for Cooke, possibly the end of his career.

Cooke regained his composure "Sir, this is not how it looks, Sergeant Cade and I were having a discussion and things, well, things got a little out of hand, I'm sure he would agree, wouldn't you Sergeant?"

Cooke glared at Cade through letterbox eyes, his nostrils flaring and his lips pursed over his teeth. He was ready for round two but the referee had called an end to the fight.

Jackson turned to Cade.

"Sergeant I saw Inspector Cooke attack you, do you wish to make a complaint?"

Cade rubbed his cheek bone, which was now angry, tender and red before responding to the question.

"And ruin a man's life sir? No, only the very weak would operate like that and you know me well enough...no, thank you I don't, it's clear that Inspector Cooke and I can no longer work in the same station though."

"Indeed" replied Jackson "Indeed. I don't need this sort of animosity between two of my most senior hands. Christ only knows what started this Grant but so help me it bloody well stops, here and now. Do I make myself clear?" He barked the words straight into Cooke's face leaving microbes of saliva on his forehead.

He had made himself extremely clear. Cooke was defeated, but in his own arrogant way felt like the victor.

Cade left the station and after a swift phone call met up with an old foe.

They had sparred many times but David Francis also had a level of respect for a man who he once described as 'the very best of the bunch' and for Francis that was a compliment indeed.

Francis was a fifty eight year old criminal, a brilliant burglar and ex-soldier. He'd left the Intelligence Corps during the end of the Northern Ireland conflict – The Troubles.

A man born in North Kent and with the areas' distinctive twang still present in his now softened accent he had trained to a standard that most Mitty-esque characters could only fantasise about. What Dave Francis didn't know about surveillance and counter-surveillance, intelligence gathering and source handling wasn't worth knowing.

He had left a fractured home and become a boy soldier, initially signing up in an Infantry role with the Infantry Junior Leaders Battalion at Shorncliffe Barracks, Folkestone.

After months of training and physical endurance he had made the final grade. Posing on a bright afternoon with a few of his new found friends, his tie askew and a broad smile on his face he looked as if he didn't have a care in the world. The photographers' index finger clicked away, his thumb winding on the film on his trusty Canon SLR before taking another group shot, this time with the few family members that had made the journey.

Sadly he quickly came to the attention of his senior command staff for the wrong reasons.

'A fine soldier in the making…but lacks commitment.'

However an observant Non Commissioned Officer had noted his potential to assimilate information and made a call to the nearby Templer Barracks, the home of the School of Service Intelligence.

The SSI took a quick look at his personnel file and declined him.

After almost two more years of firing, stripping down and firing again every weapon he could lay his hands upon, then repeatedly running, frenziedly at inanimate mannequins and stabbing them with a bayonet he was finally considered a fully trained soldier – with no war to fight. And he became bored.

Until he was sent to Northern Ireland.

It was in The Province that he really learned his craft, killing became all too easy, a thrill, and one which needed to be replicated on his leave days. He turned to drugs in order to provide something approaching the sheer high that stalking prey – on their own soil – had given him.

He unwittingly became the target of the Special Investigation Branch who conducted their investigation with the utmost vigour and pride. Drugs were not welcome in the modern British Army – and therefore neither was David Francis.

Never one to believe in the fabled six degrees of separation he did concede that Lady Luck may have been on his side when he was able to avoid the hell that was the Military Corrective Training Centre, Colchester, Essex.

Colchester was where all British servicemen who had committed criminal acts were sent to finish their time in the military – but not before enduring a certain level of humiliation and what some saw as Draconian treatment. Private 32979006 David Edward Francis would have adored it, frankly, the harsher the better.

Colchester also provided training, a way to steer its people back onto the correct path in life. By some means Francis had avoided both the internment and training.

The same NCO who had made Francis his own pet project a few years prior happened to return to Francis's regiment and spotted him in the mess.

"You are coming with me Private. No arguments. You are heading to Templer. Do I make myself clear?"

His rasping, intense Glaswegian accent enforced his meaning and Francis knew it was a fight he would lose.

Within months he had made a name for himself again, but for the right reasons.

'Private Francis is a natural collector of intelligence."

These were the kind of words he needed to assist him in finally achieving something, something that he not only enjoyed, but was good at.

"He is recommended for secondment to HUMINT Branch.'

From here he developed skills that would lead him into some of the world's most closely guarded secrets and some not so.

Northern Ireland was where he cut his teeth, on more than one occasion. He worked with the regular army and plenty of irregular ones too, in their day, special, but unknown, still hiding behind a veil of much-needed secrecy.

He would serve in the Northern and Southern Hemisphere, in obvious conflict zones and some, less apparent. He rose quickly through the ranks, never achieving a commission, but in truth that suited him – better to gain respect as an experienced Warrant Officer than be quietly mocked by your peers for wearing pips, and not having a clue about leadership.

Above all, he learned to capture information at a rate that most of his peers could not compete with.

After years of travelling around the world, free of charge and forgetting about more places of interest than most would ever see he made his first poor judgement call in years. An old service friend had left the Intelligence Corps a few years prior and had set up what he called a consultancy business. Mercenaries in any other language.

Francis was lured by the promise of obscene pay packets and a chance to re-engage with a tangible enemy. Despite the thrills of working in the Intelligence Corps he missed the raw, tactile brutality of inflicting pain.

He headed to Africa and immersed himself among the horrors of a war without conventions.

He lasted two years. A year longer than most.

Returning to the United Kingdom with a back pack full of memories and a carrier bag full of US dollars Francis drifted onto the wrong path and began to consume alcohol at an alarming rate.

His family members turned their back on him, society gradually stepped over him and ultimately he even lost respect for himself. He had initially returned home to Kent, a place he once called home. Then, facing continual rejection he caught a train, rather randomly to Nottingham, on the off-chance he might find his old service partner 'Mad Dog' Micky Hilton.

He never did locate him. Heroin had found Francis first and left him as a shattered wreck in an abandoned railway arch, a victim of the mental savagery of exposure to urban warfare and the inevitable drug and alcohol addictions that followed.

A number of unsuccessful suicide attempts had left him battered and scarred way beyond anything that two tours of The Province could ever achieve.

He first met Constable Jack Cade in the late nineties, by which point he was a ragged, dishevelled shell of his former self.

Cade had visited his home one November evening; every other member of the force had done their level best to avoid visiting the dark and damp flat Francis called home, recording a dubious-at-best 'no reply to knocking' on the job sheet. But Cade could see something unique in the eyes of 'Frank' Francis. He had obtained the details of yet another 'attempted burglary' to Frank's home and was about to close his pocket book when among the squalor and heartache he saw a solitary dog-eared, unframed colour photograph clinging to the edge of the beige-tiled sixties fireplace.

It was Francis in his 'Number Ones'.

Purple and green Northern Ireland and blue, white and green South Atlantic campaign medals accompanied some NATO ribbons that Cade didn't recognise. His family were stood proudly at his side as the shutter clicked on the photographer's camera on that long forgotten homage to the unsung hero of a distinguished career.

They were happier days indeed but ones littered with bitter conflicts and complex and deadly exploits the like of which many men would never have experienced, let alone survived.

"You know Mr Francis if you need a chat with a friendly soul then you can just ring me, you don't have to keep making up reports of burglaries."

Francis looked at him through bloodshot eyes and shook his head.

"Is it that obvious kid?"

Cade stopped in the doorway and asked Frank if he fancied putting the kettle on. He did as it happened and their friendship grew from that day on.

Cade's ultimate goal was to get Francis clean once more, back to the proud man he was before heroin and in turn the bastards that dealt it to him had deprived him of a life.

Cade grew to trust the former Warrant Officer and even gave him a few simple tasks, for which he rewarded him; enough cash to buy a single beer and the rest in the form of food. No point in setting him up to fail.

Mission after mission saw Francis providing quality intelligence and he never once let Cade down, never once betrayed him, slowly regaining his confidence and despite disappointments here and failure there he had a glimmer at the end of the tunnel, a future again.

Francis would later confide that Cade was the only true friend he had had since leaving the services. And heroin or not he was able to see through the haze of drug-induced bouts of depression to realise that he would be a lot worse off without him. Strangely enough he had not suffered a single burglary since.

In turn Cade protected Francis, continuing to provide him with nutritious food and regular health check-ups, but above all a solid, reliable foundation on which to rebuild his tormented life.

He had called in to see his old mate to inform him that he was moving on, leaving the force and explaining why in graphic detail. Without solicitation a devastated Francis offered to help. He'd met Cooke many a time and despised him. Hated him in fact and that bunch of cowboys he swanned around with; good looking, swaggering bastards all of them.

"Just give me the nod Jack my son and we are on."

He left Francis with a deadly glint in his graphite eyes, a sparkle of life that he hadn't seen before and one that had he been on the wrong side of the fence would have scared him.

Sergeant Jack Cade packed his kit away the next morning; placing it reverently into cardboard boxes he labelled each and wondered when he would ever see or need the contents again. He then sought out a number of individuals he cared about, said his farewells and handed his locker key to the Administration Officer.

"Cheers Jean, it's been a pleasure."

The normally-reserved Jean Wilson stood and hugged Cade. She told him she would miss him enormously. "The boss asked to see you before you go. Take care Jack; you are one of the good guys. Everyone knows about Cooke, his day will come. I shouldn't say it but I hope he gets chlamydia. Look after yourself."

He tapped on the Divisional Commander's door five minutes later. "Sir."

"Ah Jack, just wanted to say farewell. You are a bloody good man and the team at the airport are looking forward to working with you. I will ensure your staff file is written up appropriately and Cooke's too. Leave that piece of shit to me. I never did like him; in my day we would have made him walk the line like the bloody cons…" His mind wondered back to the heady days of policing the proud Midlands city in the seventies and eighties.

"Thanks for everything boss. I see this as a new chapter, a new beginning. I've spoken to a solicitor about a divorce, in a way I'm going through two at once. I won't let you down, thank you for believing in me. Please give my regards to Mrs Jackson. Here, this is for you."

He slid a sealed manila package across the desk, popped up a quick salute and said goodbye.

It was half an hour later when Jackson had cleared his mail tray and opened the envelope.

As the contents fell out he shook his head. Cade was good at his job and the intelligence world had just gained a new champion. He stood, closed his door and locked it.

The imagery was condemning and final. Each video showed Cooke engaged in varying degrees of sexual deprivation, occasionally with his wife and always with girls clearly much younger than himself. In one grainy shot he was with three women, one was his wife who was blindfolded and unceremoniously duct-taped to the headboard by her wrists as two provocatively-dressed school girls, at most only fifteen, sixteen at best performed with each other and Cooke.

The obvious signs of social drug use were also very apparent.

The images were evidently taken from a corner of a sordid motel room by an unseen device.

It was enough, it left Cooke without any excuse, legal or moral and Jackson now had him firmly in his cross-hairs.

He rubbed his eyes, partly through fatigue, partly to erase the images.

The last disc slid quietly into the drive and engaged.

It was CCTV imagery, taken at various points around the city of Nottingham. Each file showed Cade, either in the process of shopping, visiting restaurants or travelling in his car. The timeline on each set of images provided compelling evidence that Cade was never anywhere near Cooke's chosen motel and therefore completely unconnected to any of the surveillance that had been illegally conducted.

Jackson had a beaming smile on his face.

"Clever boy Jack, I pity your next enemy."

He slid the discs back into the envelope before sealing them and placing them in his safe. Job done.

Chapter Seventeen

Cade slept well over the weekend. His estranged wife had left the marital home, heading back to live, in the short term, with her parents in Kent. She'd soon refer to herself as Penny Stephens again and frankly that suited them both.

He travelled west along the A453 and arrived at East Midlands Airport ahead of schedule. He located the police station, parked up and introduced himself to the Front Counter Clerk.

"Good morning, Sergeant Cade to see Superintendent Curtain."

"Ah yes, we've been expecting you, the boss asked me to get you to unload your stuff. I've got you an office, when you are ready let me know and I'll let you back in, then I can sort out access cards and other bits and pieces. Do you need a hand?"

"No, but thanks, best welcome I've had at a nick for years!"

He meant it. Within twenty minutes his belongings were in the new office and to his surprise it was an office with a fabulous view across the runway. It was a little tired but the view made up for it tenfold.

He was finding a home for his clothing and equipment when he became aware of someone stood in the doorway.

"Great view isn't it?"

The voice belonged to Superintendent Eddie Curtain, or as he was known affectionately 'Mad Eddie'. A man with a fearsome reputation for fun, hard work and catching criminals, Curtain was a career cop three years off retirement but with the stamina of men half his age.

Despite having a full head of well-groomed white hair he still looked in his forties, slightly tanned, by virtue of a holiday home in Southern France, fit and an almost permanent smile. His positivity was legendary.

"It is sir, thank you, better than I expected." He held out a hand and introduced himself.

His new manager replied "Call me Eddie in here Jack, but boss, sir or whatever the frigging hell you like when we are in company. Jacko told me all about you and that's why you are here. He told me you are a bloody good operator son, and that is what I need, oh and someone who can make a decent cup of coffee. How you fixed?"

"In an instant boss, give me five minutes to find the kitchen and I'll get it sorted, where is your office?"

"I'm kidding you daft twat, grab your mug and bring it with you, we'll have one together then I'll give you the grand tour. When we've done I'll get Steve Hazard to get you out and about, set you up with a Civil Aviation pass and get you through a few doors. It's gonna be a busy week old son so hang onto Stu's coat tails. He's one of my best Sergeants, can shoot the balls off a fly at fifty yards, but he knows sweet Fanny Adams about intelligence, that's where you come in."

They visited the kitchen and got two decent-sized cups of coffee, Curtain stole a chocolate biscuit from an open packet as they gravitated back towards his office. Whenever they bumped into people the boss introduced Cade to his new colleagues.

The next one was five foot eight – squared.

"Stumpy this is Sergeant Jack Cade, top man from Nottinghamshire, been seconded here to set up a decent Intelligence Cell, when you've got a minute you'll have to show him that file you've got, the one with the Eastern Europeans. Jack's got a real interest in their growth in the UK and the connections to organised crime."

They walked further.

"Brian, meet Jack Cade, number one man from across the border, here to sort out our crappy intelligence gathering systems, I reckon you and him would get along fine." He pointed to Brian Watts' collar number before adding "Remember that number Jack, damned good Constable is Brian, submits more intelligence than the rest of the buggers put together!"

Watts shook Cade's hand and promised to call into his office once he was settled in.

Cade couldn't help noticing that Watts' collar number was 100. Clearly someone in the stores had a sense of humour.

Getting from the kitchen to Curtain's office had so far taken twenty minutes, but Cade felt good about the place already. It had a homeliness which was tethered to a sense of passion and pride. There were photographs of the various teams scattered throughout the corridors and crests from visiting law enforcement teams from around the world.

"So boss, do you have any female staff here?"

"Absolutely, one's a real looker, the other one, not so, but hard worker and popular with the lads. So to speak."

Cade was relatively 'old school' but still found it strange that women were isolated within what was deemed by many to be the modern era of policing.

As they reached the largest office in the station a male appeared from a stairwell. A rugged looking ex-Royal Marine he had a thick head of blond hair, swept back out of his bright blue eyes and almost stereotypically chiselled features.

He was wearing the standard black uniform of Magnum boots, combat trousers, polo shirt and black body armour. A Glock 17 was strapped to his right thigh and an H&K MP5 was sat on his chest. Extra magazines for both weapons were placed strategically on his webbing.

He wore an inordinately large wristwatch.

Clearly unafraid of being identified, his name and collar number were embroidered in white on a black patch which sat on the right side of the vest.

"Steven, meet Jack Cade" Curtain said, acting as an intermediary.

"Good morning Jack, Steve Hazard, heard a lot about you from a few old team mates at Notts, I was there from 94 to 98. Your reputation precedes you – and that is a good thing." He winked, encouraging Cade to relax, he'd been slightly on edge about anyone discussing why he had left his old force.

"Boss, if you are happy I'll take Jack out and about, show him the ropes?"

"Spot on Stevo lad, and don't forget to show him the shackles and chains too!"

They all laughed although as they walked to the car park Cade hoped his new boss wasn't quite as kinky as his old one.

They both got into a marked patrol car, the wipers brushed away the early morning dew as Hazard turned the key.

"He's a cracking boss Jack, work hard and play hard and you'll be fine. I reckon you've landed a brilliant job here, we need someone to set up some new systems, the world's a smaller place since Nine Eleven and there's too many bastards trying to get into my back yard – and for these four walls only, I haven't got enough ammo for all of 'em."

He did that fashionable action with the fingers of both hands to indicate speech marks before adding "Don't get me wrong I'm all for equality…"

It was clear he wasn't but the recent flood of migrants from Europe and North Africa had already started to impact upon his Motherland, so perhaps it was a reasonable attitude to have?

"They're flooding across the fucking border pal, Eastern Europe, North Africa, West Africa, East bloody Africa, Russians, Jamaican's, Trinidadian's, Asian's, in fact if they end in 'uns then they are coming and they are starting to arrive 'ere in numbers."

Cade threw out a few searching questions and a couple of generic ones; "So where's home? How many kids do you have? Been here long?"

He soon grew to like Hazard's approach, it was direct but underneath the weapon-clad exterior there was a warm soul and a great sense of national pride and well-placed humour. Hazard steered the Mondeo estate into a parking bay and asked Cade to follow him.

Having been issued with his Airport ID cards Cade now felt a sense of ownership; he also had a strong feeling that the work he was recruited to conduct would define him.

Forty minutes out of East Midlands Airport a blue and white Boeing 737 was cruising over the English Channel, steadily reducing height and speed and joining the countless contrails that zipped back and forth across the busiest shipping straits in the world.

Beneath them another 737 was dropping quickly, heading into London Gatwick. To their left another and to their right and higher, a 747-400 climbing now and heading out towards France, then Eastern Europe and the Middle East before arriving ten hours later in Singapore.

On board the Thompson charter flight the crew were clearing away the remnants of a meal, stowing the cabinets in the galley and ensuring the cabin was prepared for a safe landing.

It had been an eventless flight, leaving Spain, crossing France and up over the channel towards one of the quieter British international airports.

As the aircraft was almost full the crew had earned their salary once more, pampering to the whims of all and sundry and presenting an apparently never-ending smile.

In the galley one of the crew was taking a moment to catch up with a colleague. Kirsty Bell a Derby girl, born and bred who never thought she would get to travel the world was relating what she called a gut feeling to her crewmate and best friend Emma O'Brien, a hazel-eyed Liverpudlian with a sharp wit and an eye for detail.

"Did you see that guy in 29C? The way he was looking at the blonde girl next to him, made my skin crawl. Seriously what does he look like? Reckons he's some top DJ from the resorts, offered me a free ticket to his next gig. Says he's the next big thing."

O'Brien replied in an accent so thick it could be cut with a machete, "He's certainly big and he stinks too, poor cow having to sit next to that, if it's not Lynx its Kouros and if it's not Kouros it's…"

"B.O!" replied Bell with a giggle.

"Anyway, she's beautiful, Russian I reckon or Polish. Those Polish women can be dead gorgeous, fancy having to sit next to him. I saw her writing a note to him at one point, she looked worried so I asked her if she needed help. She said no but I could tell something was up, I'm dead clever me, our Craig reckons I should've been a Detective."

"A defective more like!" offered Bell which was rewarded with a playful slap.

O'Brien continued "No, seriously mate I think she's upset about something, she had tears in her eyes, she looked really worried, like she was frightened, but I didn't want to push it. I'm sure she will be alright."

The girls agreed, checked their hair and make-up, put on their uniform jackets, ran through some pre-landing safety drills, spoke to the In-flight Service Director via the comms system and strapped themselves in for landing.

In seat 29B a curiously pretty blonde woman sat staring straight ahead at the cockpit door, partly willing the pilot to land and equally eager for him to turn around and fly somewhere else entirely.

She had boarded the flight in Spain on a Russian passport which was good enough to fool the best of Document Examiner's. The photograph had been substituted skilfully, the laminate hardly broken and only visible to the well-trained eye under a really decent microscope.

Everything else about the travel document said genuine; stitching, holograms, ultra violet ink, print quality, watermark, all except the fact that the owner – or at least the person using it – was not the rightful holder.

With a timely smile and a pre-selected male border official she would make it work, make it appear legitimate.

What the outside world could not see was the inbuilt dread, the trepidation and the untold fear. Heading to a place she didn't know, from a place she had to escape from, leaving behind a raft of high-value possessions, all of which were conditional upon being beaten, abused, used and vaguely, strangely, loved by a man she no longer had sufficient words to describe.

She had also, on the face of it, abandoned her daughter.

Twenty minutes later Cade and Hazard were drinking the second cup of coffee of the morning as they stood in the control tower at the southern end of the airfield watching a Thompson Holidays 737 arrive from Malaga.

The pilot jostled with the wind shear, skilfully straightening the aircraft and aligning it with the single main runway just seconds before he put it down, a little too heavily, onto the airstrip.

Cade watched the Air Traffic Controllers, impressed at their quiet and unassuming manner. East Midlands was, according to the ATC Officer, hardly a busy airport in comparison to Heathrow but it had enough traffic to make it interesting at times. As he said interesting he too did the thing with the fingers. It was obviously fashionable. Cade made a mental note not to do it.

They left the tower and drove a few miles criss-crossing the airport, using taxiways and crash gates to navigate until they reached a bridge over the M1, one of the busiest motorways in Britain.

Hazard left the car and asked Cade to follow him. As they reached the far side of the bridge they stopped. Attached to the bridge was a plaque.

The airport had gained global attention in 1989 when tragically a disabled inbound British Midland 737 had lost power and struck the steep embankment of the nearby motorway killing forty seven people. It was only seconds away from landing.

They both took a moment to read the inscription before Hazard spoke.

"It's what defines the village and the airport Jack; it goes someway to explaining why the people that work here are as passionate as they are. My brother worked for Leicestershire Police at the time, he was one of the first workers to get to the scene. It was a bloody mess that's for sure."

He leant forwards and tapped the plaque gently before walking away.

Cade took a moment to watch a 757 Icelandair flight arrive. The noise of the twin engines was immense as the crew skilfully approached the runway. The sky crackled as the aircraft flew directly over Cade's head. He felt like punching the air, it was a great feeling to be so close to something so dynamic. He was hooked from that moment on.

Hazard was sat in the car, smiling at Cade's enthusiasm when he received a call on his portable radio.

He pressed the car's horn, summoning Cade who jogged the short distance and got in.

"Looks like your first job Jack! That Thompson flight we saw land from the tower? Well Customs have some source info about a likely passenger on board; they'd like our advice and assistance on a few things. You up for it?"

"Marvellous. Let's go. This is why I'm here Steve, come on put those blues on!"

Despite the combined enthusiasm of a couple of mischievous school boys they knew that they had to negotiate the airfield according to the rules, so even with the aid of a highly visible patrol car it still took a good ten minutes to reach the terminal.

Cade turned to his new colleague.

"Steve, can I borrow a pen and something to write on!"

Hazard replied "Bloody brilliant, no pen. Mad Eddie said you were intelligent!"

"Shut up and give me your pen before I shoot you!"

"Listen smart arse the pen may be mightier than the sword, but not much outruns a round from an MP5; your call."

Again, Hazard delivered the line with humour and esprit de corps uppermost in his mind. He beckoned to Cade as they reached the first Secure Area entry.

"After you pal, let's see if that card can open a few doors for you."

It could, in minutes Cade was being introduced to Danny Bingham a young thick-set Customs Officer who had climbed swiftly through the ranks. His uniform epaulettes displayed three gold bars and a hoop which lead Cade to guess correctly that he was a Chief. At thirty three he'd done well and as Cade was about to learn he'd achieved the rank with a sprinkle of good luck, hard work and an abundance of passion for a workplace that he would describe as 'a daily cocktail of risk versus consequence'.

Cade stood with his team mate and Bingham, watching the passengers arrive into the search area. They were in an elevated operations area behind tinted glass, allowing them to observe undetected the various souls highlighted by diligent staff for further intervention.

"This lot have arrived in from Alicante, Palma and Malaga. They are our main feeder airports, but we are starting to see an expansion, further out into Europe and even the southern states of the USA and Mexico."

Cade continued to watch, fascinated at the body language of some of the selected passengers. Some were openly confused, others slightly aggressive and the majority, whether it was small or great had something to hide.

"With our passenger numbers being in the three million plus category we can afford to be selective Jack but we know a few still slip through the net. We've got some new technology and of course the dogs but we rely heavily on human interaction – there's nothing better, but I guess I'm preaching to the converted?"

"In a way Danny yes, but I've come from a different world of law enforcement, so I'm here to learn. Consider me a sponge, in its literal not biological sense and we'll be fine. I have a real interest in people groups, you know, those from countries that the UK has never really either understood, or worse thought they had and were a million miles short of the mark?"

Bingham understood entirely. He'd cut his relatively junior teeth further south in the Port of Dover on the southern-most tip of England. It was to be his making. He learned quickly about how individuals and groups could exploit the system, import and occasionally export the choicest commodities and above all make a very successful living.

The key commodity through Dover was what loosely fitted into the duty free category: alcohol, tobacco and similar goods.

What Bingham was looking for whilst stood with Hazard and Cade was a different set of commodities.

"We are looking for cash Jack, and party drugs and any indicator that someone is being illegally brought into the country. We obviously work closely with Immigration which is why Terry has just joined us."

He introduced Cade to Terry Barker a career Immigration Officer who, so legend had it, could sniff out an asylum seeker before he or she so much as boarded the plane in a foreign port.

"Thanks for coming Terry, Jack has joined the Airport Police as an Intelligence Officer, I think you two will get along just fine. You talk the same language already. He's got a current interest in Romanian offenders, perhaps you can explain Jack?"

Cade outlined why he considered Eastern Europe to be a threat region, careful not to sound xenophobic he picked apart his message, highlighting how it was the few Romanian's, some, but not all of gypsy origin that were starting to harm the homeland.

"I need to try to get the message across. If we start low and aim high we'll get there Terry but it may take a number of years to succeed. No-one, with the notable exception of the present company and a few of my old bosses seems to want to listen. These folk are adept at using computer equipment and some are bloody brilliant with numbers, combine that with a smattering of Soviet training and street craft and as they say Robert's your mother's brother."

Barker paused for a second, a puzzled look on his face and then spoke.

"I get it, Bob's your uncle! Yep you are spot on Jack, good to have someone on board that thinks the same way. I was reading the Office for National Statistics blurb the other day."

Cade interjected "Christ, you know how to live!"

Barker continued, either ignoring or missing the sarcasm "they are starting to record inbounds from the former Eastern Bloc but it's not enough, the system is fractured at best, give it ten years I predict we'll be half a million out."

It was a sobering thought for those gathered in the glasshouse.

Barker continued, in a groove now and clearly enjoying having a new audience.

"The issue is Jack that we, as in the government, are concentrating on the big fish, the largest airports, you know, Heathrow, Gatwick, Manchester, but the buggers are getting in through here and Leeds and Stanstead, we are more porous than a Dutch dyke and I'm not talking lesbian."

Danny Bingham was tapping data into a computer terminal, trying not to laugh and attempting to check the Customs and Excise intelligence system, looking for cross matches or alerts, either those linked to passport movements or previous intelligence records.

Cade was looking over his shoulder, learning a new system and comparing it to the relatively archaic Police National Computer system that he was used to.

He pointed to a name in the flight manifest which for no reason appealed to him.

"So, taking that name there, can we search across our systems, police check, Immigration check and Customs? You know, all cross-matching and coming up with an intelligence picture?"

It was Barker who replied first "Sadly not Jack, one day I'm sure and I hear it's not too far away but for now, I'm sure you've heard this already, but it's human intelligence that wins, that and taking a punt now and then, seeing a gap and trying to fill it."

Cade nodded, encouraging more.

"Our source intel tells us we are looking for a redhead today. Why not have a go, pick a passenger out there and get Danny to run them through their system, use that telephone there to run a PNC check and I'll do the same. Like I say, sometimes it's about taking a risk."

Cade embraced the challenge and looked down the list, trying to match it to the person stood in the search area.

"OK, Geoff Pullen, UK national, 17th July 1961, seems to travel a lot between here and Ibiza. I'm going for party drugs; tanned, wearing a red tracksuit and sporting a recently pierced ear, he looks like an aging DJ! And above all, he's a redhead!"

Danny Bingham almost yelled "He's not a redhead, he's ginger!"

The team laughed but knew Cade probably wasn't a million miles from the truth.

Cade said "Ah yes but ginger people are survivors; tough, adaptable and unique."

Terry Barker commented "Well ginger or not he's a Brit, so no real interest from me, so I'll watch; I see the dog had a bit of interest but didn't indicate, so if he had drugs then he hasn't anymore, but let's give it a run. Over to you Danny boy."

Bingham spoke to a search officer and allowed Cade to prompt him with a few questions, it was an experiment and Mr Pullen was the guinea pig.

They watched from behind the surveillance screen as Pullen was ushered to a search bench and started to see his suitcase emptied out with military precision onto the stainless steel table. Pullen was impassive, apparently most at ease and possibly overly-confident.

Twenty minutes later the search was over and the best questioning techniques had failed to elicit anything from the forty one year old British national who was now getting packed and ready to leave for home in nearby Derby.

"Sorry Jack, you can't win them all" announced Daniel Bingham. We'll try again with the next flight, if you can hang around?"

Cade was highly motivated "If that's OK with you Steve I'll spend an hour here, things are all new and it's a good chance to network?"

Hazard was happy, it meant he could relinquish his responsibility as a mentor and get back out to what he enjoyed the most, quietly terrorising airport workers who were, to his mind at least, trying to run the gauntlet by moving illicit goods back and forth across the air/landside boundary.

"Give us a shout when you are done. Here take this radio; I've got another in the car. I'm Sierra Two Zero if you need me, you're India One."

With that Hazard stepped out into the search area for all to see, stroking the blued metal surface of his MP5 as he walked passed a group of young males, all evidently returning from an overly-taxing stag weekend in Spain.

Cade asked if he could follow Geoff Pullen for a short distance, something was gnawing at his intuitive mind and he wasn't about to let it end without a result.

He exited via a side door and skilfully merged with the passengers from a newly arrived flight and one or two stragglers who had been indecisive at duty free or detained by border authorities.

Cade took the chance and started speaking to Pullen as they both headed to the arrivals door.

"Sir, Airport Police, can you join me over here please?"

Pullen was on the defensive immediately "Listen pal, I'm not being funny but your lot 'ave all just about taken turns in shoving their fists up my arse and they found nothing, do you hear me, fuck all, now, if you don't mind I'd like to get home to me wife and kids."

"Of course I don't mind Mr Pullen, although I doubt you've got kids, and for the record I didn't see one forearm enter your rectum, but maybe I wasn't paying attention, but you were, Geoff. You were."

He stared directly into his eyes, noting that Pullen was unable to hold the gaze.

He left the last part of the sentence hanging, using his name to emphasise that this was about two people and one issue: Jack Cade, Geoff Pullen and whatever it was that Pullen was hiding.

"Now as I am sure you know we can do this the easy way…"

"I know, the hard way, which are you, good cop or bad cop?"

Cade replied "Both – and it's a deadly mixture. So what's it going to be, another few hours in my custody back at the station on suspicion of you exporting Ecstasy to Ibiza in the lining of your jacket to satisfy your youthful audience or are you going to tell me what's on your mind?"

Pullen sighed and shook his head "You know what kid you are good, I'll give you that, but if you think I've got half a pound of crack up me poop shoot you can think again. I'm not into that shit."

Cade laughed at Pullen's language which in turn caused the suspect to buckle slightly.

"Sir, I suspect you carry it in your jacket pocket, front left to be precise, not in an altogether darker and damper location."

"Christ that's all I need a copper with a sense of humour. Come on kid, let's walk out to the car park and I'll let you into a secret. I'm not carrying anything son, honestly, but you are right, I have got something weighing heavily on me mind."

Chapter Eighteen

Pullen appeared to ease in Cade's company; he wasn't sure why as he had spent thirty years of his life just on the wrong side of right when it came to the law. He liked people to know he was a little unconventional, daring almost and he felt this added to his sense of mystery, especially with young and attractive females who he had been spending a disproportionate amount of time with lately.

The reality was that most found him to be bordering on repulsive and only associated with him for his money and ability to provide them with party drugs.

He had an advanced case of Athlete's Foot, an improving case of Impetigo and a quite terrible body odour that was compounded by the daily activity of emptying an entire can of Lynx Voodoo all over his armpits, bulbous stomach and profusely sweating ginger crotch.

It was fair to say that in his presence Cade felt overly attractive.

To compound things it started to rain.

Pullen threw his much-loved and dog-eared suitcase into the boot of his white 1990 Vauxhall Astra, nodded for Cade to join him and got in. He turned the engine on as the interior had quickly fogged, the now present odour of a failing air conditioning system blending with Pullen's own unique signature.

Pullen pointlessly switched the wiper blades onto full and turned to Cade.

"Right, now I'm not sure why, but I trust you, so here goes."

Cade nodded attentively, unsure what was going to follow. This was what he joined for.

Pullen cleared his throat and coughed causing particles of dark brown highly-adhesive phlegm to collide with the windscreen and hang there, testament no doubt to his forty a day habit.

"Now it's like this kid, I was sat in seat 29C right, the girls always upgrade me as I travel so much, I'm what you call a frequent flyer, any road, on the way home today I was sat next to a lady."

He smiled a knowing smile and continued.

"Now, my educated ear told me she was a Russian, and I don't mean she was in a hurry neither!" The joke failed to raise more than a snort from its audience.

"Now, what's wrong with that Mr Pullen? I hear you ask, albeit you didn't." The conversation was clearly going to take a long time and Cade was beginning to wish Hazard would turn up and shoot his new-found friend in the kneecap.

"Well" Pullen continued "The point is she was gorgeous, I couldn't take my eye off her, so me being me, you know DJ Pullen Power, that's me", he skilfully handed a business card to Cade, "well, I thought in for a penny, so I started chatting her up."

"And?"

"And she tells me she's a Bulgarian, on the run from her boyfriend, he's some big unit in a gang over there, living in Spain though, into all sorts, mainly moving girls around Europe and stealing top-end motors. So I get chatting and after about an hour I've got her eating out of my hand."

Cade offered an airline-related pun "Did she have the chicken or the fish?"

Pullen continued, clearly on a roll.

"Forget that hombre, that's Spanish by the way, she didn't eat, I 'ad her dinner, but after she slept for half an hour she talked, non-stop until we landed, said she was heading to London and that she was on the run from some bloke called Jack Dawes."

The rain was now persistent, entrapping Cade in the faded hatchback, its cloth seats sagging and suspiciously damp.

"Jack Dawes? Who's he? Any idea?"

"I have and that's where you come in officer."

Cade was unsure where the conversation was heading but felt compelled to ask the obvious question.

"Go on."

"I will thanks. Look it's like this I've got a couple of parking tickets and I wondered if you could, you know, see your way to getting them sponged off?"

"Expunged?"

"Ay, that an' all, expunged."

"No."

"Fuck you then."

"Geoff and we were doing so well, OK, I'll see what I can do, give them to me."

Pullen replied "How did you know I've got them in the car?"

Cade, swift as striking cobra replied "Because Geoff you keep every other fucking thing in here, it's a mobile dustbin, a health hazard and a bloody death trap too. Give me the tickets and keep talking before I arrest you for something."

"Cheers Jack."

"How did you know my name?"

"It's on that ID card round your neck, I may be fat but I'm not thick."

"Fair point, right, now we've been introduced do carry on before I lose the will to live."

Pullen, happy with his new law enforcement friend now continued with gusto.

"By the way, you've got a rather big Glock too."

Cade replied "We've only just met Geoffrey; bit soon for such talk don't you think?"

Perhaps it was a good thing he'd seen the pistol. If Cade threatened him at least he knew he meant business?

Pullen seemed completely unperturbed by the firearm and carried on "You know what Jack me old mate, I like you. So anyway I said to her did she fancy coming back to my place to listen to me House collection, I love it I do, I base myself on Norman Cook, my mates call me Slimboy Fat!"

He punched Cade on the shoulder causing a look that said 'if you do that again I will cut your foot off and shove it up your arse'.

Pullen, valuing his ability to walk got the message and carried on.

"I know what you are thinking Ace, did she say yes?"

Cade was starting to feel nauseous, the damp, the stench and the overpowering bullshit were all combining to form a heady cocktail.

"Please tell me she said yes?"

"No, she didn't but she gave me this and then just walked off, she got into a taxi about two minutes ago, I was watching her in my door mirror, you know like that Jason Bourne would. I've just seen her head off in a white Mercedes. I got the registration too!"

Pullen handed an envelope to Cade. He opened it immediately and tipped the contents out onto his lap. There were six pieces of paper.

Two photocopies of birth certificates, two of passports, a business card belonging to some despot Ambassador from a place Cade had never heard of and what appeared to be a hand-written note on an aircraft sick bag.

Cade read the note twice.

"My name is Nikolina, I am not a bad person, but I know bad people. I have a good life, expensive jewellery, cars and holidays. But it is wrong. I do this no more. I am afraid. I need to claim asylum. Help me, my life is in danger. Please. Give to Police or person you trust."

He turned to Pullen and said with an air of urgency "So, why didn't you give this to the Police like she asked you?"

He replied, equally urgently, "Because I don't trust the police and I thought it was her phone number, you know, for later…" His eyebrows arched to emphasise his anticipation.

"On a fucking sick bag? Are you mad?"

Pullen got the impression that Cade was unhappy. He turned to him and said "I get it hombre, that's…"

"Yes I know, Spanish." Cade cut him off callously.

"I get it; this is that counter espionage shit isn't it? And she's a spy. I knew it, she were gorgeous an' all. I could have made it with a bloody beautiful Russian spy."

Cade had had enough.

"Geoff, you are forty, fat and you smell like a pair of three week old Y-fronts that frankly even a tramp would avoid. You smother yourself in bloody Lynx to mask the smell but it's never quite enough, another two cans might do it, but honestly it's like trying to hide an aircraft carrier under a…carrier bag!"

Pullen, thick-skinned as ever said "So, what are you saying Jack?"

Shaking his head Cade replied "I'm saying you're a prized twat, I wish I'd never got in the car with you and right now you are lucky I don't arrest you for obstruction. That woman's life might be in grave danger."

Pullen looked genuinely disappointed, sad almost.

"OK, I'm sorry Jack, alright? I didn't get it. I trust you, which is why I gave you the note. I put my own needs before the life of a beautiful girl. She was blonde and pretty and trim. We were a match made in heaven…"

Pullen drifted off into a world of lurid fantasy, the only sound in the battered Astra being the asthmatic fan and the occasional squawk of the perished wiper blades.

"She had a little blue tattoo on her wrist. I couldn't see it but I knew it was sophisticated. And she smelled of Chanel No.5. Classy like, dead classy. Me, I still favour that Kudos, it's a classic fragrance…"

As the sentence hung in the air it abruptly changed the situation for Cade, he could smell it too. Chanel No. 5. It was on the envelope.

He looked into his lap. He knew that the simple white unwritten envelope was empty but he still picked it up and opened it. Inside he saw a fine, long, single hair. It was red.

Forgetting himself entirely and importantly forgetting who was behind the wheel Cade yelled at Pullen "Follow that bloody car. Now!"

Pullen was in seventh heaven. It was the first ever order from a copper that he was willing to obey.

Cade grabbed the Motorola radio and keyed the microphone.

"India One, Sierra Two Zero."

Hazard was walking through the Departure Lounge, eagle-eyed and alert, smiling at a group of Norwegian students, all of them female and as luck would have it all sensational on the eye. Unusually he was so engrossed he missed the call.

"India One, Sierra Two Zero." Cade repeated his message, this time with a hint of urgency.

"Go ahead." Hazard replied, hoping it wasn't anything that was about to drag him away from his current commitment.

It was.

"Steve, I need some back up. Remember that Customs' target?"

"Yes over."

"Well it's a she, not a he, and she's in a white Merc taxi heading east, probably towards the M1. I think she's in danger. I'm with the original target in a white G plated Astra. Get control to ring me on my cell. Get someone else mobile as soon as possible and I'll give you directions when I've got them. You are looking for a white 200 series Mercedes with Capital Cars on the door. It's got a five minute head start on us. Out."

"10/4 en route."

Hazard hardly knew his new team mate but he knew his background and if he was asking for back up, then he needed it, it was the same the world over. He ran through the terminal, flashed his ID card across a reader and burst out onto the tarmac, running another hundred metres to his Volvo T5. He stowed the MP5 in the gun safe, jumped in and gunned the throttle.

Cade's radio hissed again.

"India One from Uniform One." It was Watts.

"Go ahead."

"Boss I'm en route with Uniform Two, confirm south or north on the M1?"

Cade took a second: Stop. Think. Plan. It was an old model for decision making but it had never failed him yet.

Why would she head north?

Pullen, now almost an old hand at policing shouted to his partner.

"Jack, she's heading south remember, London, to get away from Jack Dawes."

He was right, God bless the little fat ginger fucker. Cade conveyed the message.

"M1 south gents, south, white Mercedes 200. Capital Cars. Can we alert Leicestershire in case this is not a kosher taxi?"

"It's already done boss!" came the reply from Watts' team mate Stumpy.

"OK, remember I am in a white, unmarked Astra, belongs to a member of the public. Don't ask why but he's driving, just make sure you give him some room when the time comes. Out."

The Astra was already running so Pullen slammed it into reverse and accelerated aggressively. The resultant collision as they demolished a set of luggage trolleys made the bemused car park occupant run for cover.

Pullen was unfazed; wiping the driver's window and windscreen with an old sock he felt one hundred percent in control.

Cade just shook his head.

"Geoff, pull over."

"It's Geoff Pullen!" He laughed as he eventually selected first and floored the aging throttle. The front wheel drive Vauxhall scrabbled for traction. Somehow its Dunlop tyres, long past their best, wire carcass hanging from the front left and smoother than the proverbial baby's backside somehow got the white elephant under way.

With a partially flattened trolley now attached to the tow bar they were nothing if not obvious.

Passengers grabbed their cell phones, pushing their luggage and loved ones to one side and screamed into their handsets for the police.

Pullen was now navigating through a grapefruit-sized porthole in the misted up screen and using his dilapidated horn to warn passers-by.

Cade supported him by using the other sock to clear the glass.

"Stop the bloody car Geoff before you kill someone. Geoff. Geoff. Stop!"

"Sorry mate but I've waited years to do this and besides, no-one knows Tracey like I do?"

Cade was wondering who Tracey was when he first spotted the yellow fibreglass car park barrier. Pullen hadn't, either that or he was now so focused on catching the girl he chose to ignore it.

The Astra struck the barrier at forty miles an hour causing it to explode and Pullen to bellow a *Dukes of Hazard* war cry.

They were sideways now, sliding across the damp tarmac, negotiating the first real test for the aging Vauxhall. Pullen skilfully corrected the drift with a flick of opposite lock which in turn caused the contents of the back seat and floor wells to be instantly redistributed into the front of the cockpit. A thunderous crash to their right was the result of the trolley hitting a road sign.

Cade made comment about the paperwork but Pullen was oblivious. He then remarked that being in the Astra was reminiscent of living in a skip.

"But so much worse and dirtier too!"

"Reminds me of a girl I once met in Ibiza," replied Pullen shamelessly.

Cade looked down to see a pair of stained, greying, women's knickers and a festering Macdonald's burger wrapper had made their way into his lap.

He held the size 24 Marks and Spencer lace knickers up with a rusty spanner which had also appeared on his seat.

"Seriously, did any female ever wear these?"

"So that's where they got to!" replied an eager Pullen.

"Those are my favourites, belonged to a fat lass from Bristol called Tracey. I named the car after her. We did it in that seat after a flight back from Magaluf."

"Left here, left. Down there!" ordered Cade rubbing the windscreen with the underwear before ejecting it out of the passenger window.

"Good job I've got more where they came from" said Pullen as he weaved through the traffic with the skill of a getaway driver.

He continued, quite casually, "I've got Bikini, Thong, Midi's, Short, Brazilian, Shapewear, black, white, red and my favourite…"

"Where the hell did you learn to drive like this?" Cade bellowed, now unable to put the passenger window back up again.

"Getting away from you bastards!" replied Pullen with a punch of the air.

John "Jack" Cade was questioning where the back-up was as they screamed down the slip road and onto the ever-manic M1 motorway. He pulled down the passenger visor and looked into the mirror, wondering how life had come to this.

Here he was in pursuit of an enigmatic Bulgarian redheaded criminal, a helpless passenger in a decrepit Vauxhall and unwittingly at the hands of a ginger knicker thief.

He promised himself that one day, somewhere in the not too distant future he would have a better life, less complicated and far more rewarding. He also decided that Geoffrey Pullen would play no part in it.

He put the visor back up, unable to look at himself any longer.

The visor fell off and soon joined the knickers somewhere on the hard shoulder of Britain's most iconic highway.

Despite it's almost Neolithic status the Astra soon got up to speed as a casual, yet slightly paranoid glance from Cade revealed they were doing over a hundred miles an hour. It was fine whilst they were moving but he decided that if they needed to stop in less than half a mile they would die a horrible soiled-lingerie-laden death.

"There! Middle lane. Lima Alpha Zero Two," shouted Cade as they hurtled down the outside lane, blue smoke pouring from the exhaust.

"India One from Sierra Two Zero."

"Go ahead, vehicle sighted, registration Lima Alpha Zero Two…partly obscured by a tow bar but it's our car Steve."

"Roger, with you in one."

Cade knew that universally police staff underestimated their response time so expected them to be at least five minutes.

He placed his left hand out of the gaping chasm that doubled as a window and grabbed the passenger door mirror, trying to adjust it so that he could observe his colleagues coming up behind them, he knew they would be approaching at Warp Factor Five so wanted to warn Pullen.

Without the merest hint of surprise Cade saw the glass break into three pieces, clinging onto the frame rather than letting go and whistling back down the road, joining other bits and pieces of unrecognisable urban waste.

Pullen didn't see the two Volvo's in his rear view mirror but he saw what looked like three in his passenger side.

He yelled "I'm suing for that, and the visor and those knickers of Tracey's…"

Decelerating from a hundred and forty Sierra Two was now alongside and talking to Cade on his radio.

"Jack, get Fatboy Slim to back off we'll consider a TPAC if this thing doesn't stop."

"Roger, understood. I don't think we'll last much longer!"

Cade had been trained in Tactical Pursuit and Containment manoeuvres and knew how deadly they were in the wrong hands.

"Geoff, back off now, let the professionals take over, you've done well."

Cade saw the Red Mist had cast a worrying veil over Pullen. It was a look he knew all too well. He'd seen it in the best of police drivers but now it was on the face of an overweight northern Disc Jockey. It was, to say the least, not very promising.

"Geoff, back off. Now!"

The driver of the Mercedes looked into his own rear view mirror and smiled. In his late thirties Gabriel Cazaku's luxuriant black hair had started to prematurely grey. A long-term employee of an anonymous

Romanian business man, based in London, whose name he never knew, he was paid well to deliver the cargo from the airport to his office.

No questions.

Upon first seeing the police vehicles he exhaled, hoping they weren't after him; he knew that his passenger was important; perhaps the authorities had identified her? If that was so then they were both in trouble.

He decelerated slightly, trying not to bring attention to himself.

The patrol car lights illuminated once more and the white Astra slowed.

"Good, they were after that old Vauxhall," Cazaku whispered under his breath as he pressed send on a pre-formatted text message.

He moved to the centre lane and cruised at eighty miles an hour, a hundred metres in front of a large articulated truck.

It was also a white Mercedes but infinitely more powerful, however it had no connection with Cazaku. It was laden with potato crisps and bound for Oxford.

On the inside lane another white Mercedes 200 with the partial registration Lima Alpha Zero Two was keeping pace with the wagon. It also had a tow bar.

On board the second car, a fifty five year old Eastern European male handed a magnetic sign to his passenger. The sign was exactly the same size as the plates that adorned the white taxi a hundred metres in front of them. It had written upon it 'Capital Cars' and a randomly plagiarised phone number.

The driver and passenger depressed the switches on their tinted windows and fought briefly against the wind, which buffeted against their arms, causing them a short-lived sense of unease as they placed the plates onto the driver and passenger door panels. The fit wasn't pin-point perfect but it would serve a purpose.

The driver rang Cazaku.

"Ready?"

"Ready."

Vehicle Two accelerated along the motorway and joined the centre lane about fifty or so in front of Vehicle One. At the same time Vehicle One braked, darted to the left and tucked in behind the relative safety of the artic.

To the regular motorway user it was two similar cars travelling in the same direction. To the trained eye it was automotive ballet. The only person that saw it, and thought it unusual was Chris Tring the driver of the heavy goods vehicle.

He sensed something untoward but soon carried on listening to Radio Two, begrudgingly eating a banana – he was determined to keep up his new health regime, at least until the next truck stop.

In the outside lane Hazard and Watts arrived on scene, lights and wailer's activated and ready to carry out a stop. Any resistance would be met with the TPAC manoeuvre.

For once Pullen obeyed Cade and hung back. Cade had told him that if he interfered he would be shot in the face. Pullen believed him.

"Sierra Two Zero, India One."

"Go ahead."

"Leicestershire are on the other carriageway mate, miles away, do we wait or do this now? Your call."

"It's a taxi Steve, I don't expect any issues, let's give it a tug. On your word, we'll hang back now just to the rear of the wagon but be ready to assist once the circus comes to a halt. Let's keep this clean, I've got a member of the public on board and I have a bad feeling about this."

In time honoured fashion Hazard replied "Yes, Yes. Will do."

Hazard took over the stop, the artic slowed, Tring, a balding man in his early fifties and one of the oft-named Knights of the Road was quick to observe the action. He'd seen it all before. He gave a wave to Stumpy as they eased by him and got a thumb's up in return.

Now safely behind the Mercedes, Hazard flashed his headlights and pointed to the driver to pull over to the hard shoulder, Watts gently edged ahead of them, allowing Johnson to reinforce the instruction with a positive hand gesture.

The taxi driver nodded and started to drift to the left hand lane but then accelerated enough to cause the pursuing cars some concern.

Cade spotted it too.

"Geoff, pull in behind the wagon, something's not right."

They were covering the ground quickly, in less than half a mile there was a slip road, off the motorway and onto the A512 Ashby Road.

Pullen eased off the throttle and lined the Astra up behind the articulated lorry.

Quarter of a mile.

Cade's radio came to life, it was Hazard who was now using the Force radio which was repeating onto Cade's personal set. His tone changed, more professional now.

"Hello Mike Two November Lima this is Sierra Two Zero – Airport: On your channel."

"Sierra Two Zero from NL we are aware of your pending vehicle stop, local units en route ETA ten minutes, continue your commentary, over."

It was routine procedure.

Cade saw it first. Ahead and to his left was a Sales Representative in an orthodox blue Ford Focus, he was munching his way through a sandwich oblivious to what was happening ahead of him.

Immediately to his front was a white taxi. As they were about to pass the slip road it accelerated and shot left causing the Focus driver to spill his lunch onto his pinstriped trousers. His right hand hit the horn and then followed with a familiar hand gesture.

The taxi negotiated the rumble strips, unseen to the patrol cars. Cazaku had made it. Fools!

"Shit! Go left, go left!" barked Cade.

Pullen not wanting to disappoint his newly-acquired best friend did just that, throwing the Astra across the median strip and almost off the road. Whatever he used, will power, Jedi Mind Technique or just good, old, fashioned luck he managed to maintain a straight ahead course and kept pace with the target vehicle as Cade yelled into his radio knowing that he only had a minute to repeat off of Hazard's main set.

"Sierra Two Zero! We've been had. Your vehicle is a Trojan Horse. We are behind the correct car. It has the female in it."

Hazard and Watts were conducting the stop and were now fully aware that Cade was right.

Hazard shouted above the traffic noise "You two sort them out, Leicestershire will be here in a minute, let them realise you are armed, I'm off to back up Jack."

Watts gave the OK sign with his thumb and forefinger and got the driver out of the car and onto the embankment whilst his barrel-chested colleague watched the passenger.

It took less than a minute for them to realise that they would need Language Line as neither appeared to speak English. Watts suspected otherwise but sat the driver onto the damp grass and waited patiently.

Hazard was now using all his driving skills and going against everything he stood for by reversing at high speed up the hard shoulder. The Motorway Communications Centre had seen events unfolding and had put a warning up on the preceding matrix boards but drivers still hurtled by him.

He reached the slip road and put the T5 into first and rammed his foot into the floor well, the 2.3 turbocharged engine catapulted the Volvo along the road and he was soon back in the chase.

He was wringing out every bit of the two hundred and forty seven brake horse power available, navigating through traffic whilst trying to track down Cade and the Astra.

His radio sparked into life, it was a distant signal but he was still nearby.

"Sierra……..Ashby Road…….golf…"

It was enough. He turned left and hurtled along the A512 towards the Leicestershire town of Ashby. It was a single-lane carriageway but with the advantage of speed, warning equipment and training he was soon travelling at over a hundred miles an hour.

As he approached a group of cars he would place the Volvo into the centre of the road, watch for a gap and accelerate, drifting back to the left and out once more. Doing this he was both safe and making progress. It was how all the best police drivers were taught.

"Snell's Nook Lane…" It was Cade again, his signals once again clear.

Back on board the Astra Pullen was in seventh heaven. He was driving his 'Tracey' harder than ever before and in a sense should have been the pursued, not the pursuer, such was the stereotypical appearance of his vehicle.

"Easy mate, doing well but just hang back, Steve will be on us in seconds." Cade offered advice as well as a warning he knew how quickly things could go wrong. He suddenly laughed.

"Bloody hell Geoff, this is only Day One!"

Pullen was too focused to understand.

"Jack I reckon it's gone up there, to the right, towards…."

He read the brown sign.

"…towards the golf course."

Cade had a good hard look ahead of him, he couldn't see the Mercedes. It was either travelling far in excess of their speed or it had indeed turned off.

As they approached a set of traffic lights Cade pointed right.

"Go right mate, go right."

Pullen had been correct and the fresh traction marks that the Mercedes had left on the road and across the central reservation offered further evidence.

The two cars sat in the middle of the opposing lane with their drivers shaking their heads in shock endorsed the notion completely. One, an elderly lady with a face as white as her newly permed hair just pointed in the direction that Cade had chosen. It was all she could do.

"Snell's towards Nanpantan Steve, think we are heading for the village, possibly via the back roads to Loughborough."

Hazard heard Cade's comms this time, nice and clear, he knew he was close.

"You stay down or I will kill you!" Cazaku hissed through nicotine-stained teeth.

He was a proficient driver but despite his own beliefs he knew deep down that he would not evade the hunter for long. He would head for the golf course where a white Mercedes would not look out of place.

To make things a little more even he threw the first taxi sign from the car which clattered into a young Chestnut sapling, which like all of the others on the lane was in full bloom. Having scarred its tender trunk the sign dropped into the long blades of the grass verge and disappeared.

In the back a terrified redheaded female hung onto her seat, strapped in and screaming at her captor.

"Let me go. Please. I will tell my boyfriend that you were kind, let me go and you will be OK. Still have job, still have money. Stop the car!"

It was a repeated phrase and one she had been yelling since they veered off the motorway.

She had leaned forward as he had braked sharply coming off the motorway. She was somehow intending to attack the driver, to force him to stop. Despite the aggression showed by the female he effortlessly pushed her back into her seat with a strength that belied his diminutive size.

Now she looked for weapons of opportunity.

Nothing.

Chapter Nineteen

The Astra was flying now and in the mirror Pullen could see the Starship Enterprise approaching, piloted by Sergeant Steve Hazard.

Cade saw him too.

"Steve I think he's ahead of us, there's nowhere to hide."

"Received Jack. Let me get by you so I can open the road a little, I think we've got local Plod joining us too."

There were open fields either side of them which reduced the feeling of speed and made Pullen go even faster. He felt like he was setting the world on fire until a gap allowed the pursuing T5 to pounce, in third gear and turbo spooling it stormed by them, causing them to rock slightly in its wake.

The air crackled and stank of sulphur from the catalyst as the low profile tyres scrabbled and fought with the road surface, propelling the car ever-forwards.

The topography altered now, bramble-filled hedgerows lined the route. Starting to fill with an abundance of autumn fruits they were complimented by Cow Parsley and Willow Herb. A single telephone wire was strung from pole to pole and a solitary Skylark left the ground to commence its airborne aural assault.

As they travelled up a slight gradient the road kinked gently to the left where a two-bar metal fence was peering out from the vegetation, which in turn covered a dried up stream that normally ran under the road.

Beyond that were signs indicating a speed limit change and another warning of children at play. It was for all intents and purposes indicative of countless English villages, all it seemed sharing the same glorious summer's day.

The high-speed, raucous approach of the Mercedes was all that stood between this image and perfection.

Behind it and now leading the way was the first Volvo, followed by the rapidly-expiring Astra and a mile behind that a local Leicestershire Police Ford Focus that had seen the circus arrive in their particular town. Unfortunately as they were monitoring a different channel the two section staff on board were oblivious to why they were there. However like any hungry cops they were desperate to join the pursuit.

The convoy entered the outer margins of Nanpantan and slowed slightly, despite still travelling at seventy. The risks were now much higher.

The local force car was now trying to get the Astra to stop. Somehow the wires had been well and truly crossed. Quite why the Airport T5 wasn't forcing it to stop was beyond the two eager Constables.

All three cars thrashed past the green sign for the Longcliffe Golf Club and continued onwards towards the centre of the village missing the fresh traction marks on the road surface.

The taxi had now entered the outskirts of the course and was being driven at a slower, more appropriate speed, better to avoid detection.

Looking around in the rear the female knew she had a chance to escape, possibly her only chance, but somehow she needed inspiration.

A song was playing in the background. She asked if he could turn it up. She liked it, she said.

"Ha I like this song too lady, it's what I do to you if you try to run. I am fire starter! I tie you to tree, cover you in petrol and burn you alive!"

The *Prodigy* song was now much louder, for some reason Cazaku felt very much in control, so much so that he started to sing along in his strong Romanian accent. To an English ear it sounded ludicrous, to the singer, pitch perfect. He had taken his eye off of the situation.

She had seen her opportunity. In the carpeted centre tunnel of the car was a console in which was an ashtray and a cigarette lighter. She moved her right knee forward, pressing into the lighter until it engaged in its housing and rapidly started to heat up.

Now she was singing along too.

He laughed. He felt very powerful; he could feel himself becoming aroused. He believed that he could have this woman, the boss would never know and besides she'd never tell. It was more than her life was worth. With the hunters now pathetically searching elsewhere he could relax. Maybe she found him attractive? Perhaps he could try his luck?

It had been a long time since he had a redhead. They all said that blondes were more fun, but he knew the truth.

He saw an apparently disused lane to the right leading to a field and about quarter of a mile away a ramshackle wooden barn. She was his for the taking and with the music playing as loud as it was no-one would hear. No-one would care.

He grinned and made sure the central locking and windows were deactivated. He released his seatbelt and unlocked his door. He eased his trouser belt buckle a few notches.

He turned right and accelerated causing a trail of dust which whipped away in the breeze, soon erasing all evidence of their journey.

He heard a slight click, somehow his ears were attuned, he wasn't sure but it sounded familiar; then another similar noise.

The music played on.

She knew now that one way or another she was going to be harmed, either eventually at the hands of the man she pretended to love – and that would be a brutal and thoroughly inventive ending – or in the short-term at the hand of his hideous agent, a male with evil eyes and sinful intentions.

Not again, she simply couldn't contend with another lustful male. What sort of signal did she evoke?

She detested the thought of him being within arm's length let alone closer and more intimate; closer where she could smell the tobacco on his breath and hear his dominant words mocking her as she succumbed to him, eyes tightly closed but very aware.

She fought back the urge to vomit as she dug deep within her resolve and prepared for the fight of her life.

Contrary to what her heart was telling her, she knew that she had to do everything, hideous though it may be, to allow him to get close enough to carry out his act. In a moment she concocted a plan.

For Cazaku the situation was empowering – the Hawk and the Sparrow. He looked in his mirror and smiled, it was an attempt at seduction but it was so pitifully short of a romantic gesture it was awkward and pointless. It was lust and power, nothing else mattered now.

He heard the clicking noise again. But it was too late. Her seatbelt was undone. She grabbed the metal lighter, now glowing amber-red and with her left hand arced around his head and rammed it deeply into his left eye.

She could smell the burning hair and flesh instantly as the innocuous steel cylinder burrowed its way into the damp, soft tissue.

Cazaku screamed a hideous scream.

The car was out of control and ran along the track towards the barn. The front end of the Mercedes crashed through the outer walls of the building, striking an old cattle trough and bending back the three pointed star and everything beyond it.

The damage appeared to halt at the door pillars but despite being a low level impact it was severe.

It finally came to an abrupt halt after colliding with a stout wooden pole which had held up the building for a hundred years.

Cazaku lurched forwards; his face struck the laminated windscreen with a dull thump causing it to starburst. A small circle of bright red blood filled the centre of the beautifully symmetric pattern.

He slumped back into the worn driver's seat, immobile, disfigured and bleeding.

The woman had jammed her seatbelt back on moments before the crash; it had saved her life and her startling good looks.

She had held onto the lighter, possibly as her only weapon. Feeling for the first time like she was in control she engaged the small device back into the housing, letting it heat up once more before leaning over the motionless driver.

With the residual heat she pushed the lighter into his wrist, burning the indigo ink and disfiguring the tattoo. It burned so deeply that it bled. It brought him to his senses. But he could scream no louder.

No-one would hear.

No-one would care.

The woman got out of the car and ran across the adjoining corn field towards a solitary oak tree until she was physically unable to run another step.

She sank to her knees and fell into the crop, disappearing from view. She wrapped her hands around her head and tried desperately to prevent the escape of any sound that would identify her location.

The tree stood like a sentinel, silhouetted against the field, watching over her, its leaves whispering back to the corn, which danced and hissed a reply in the rising sultry breeze.

A small black bird flitted across the top of the corn and landed skilfully in the tree above her. It strutted up and down the lowest branch, its glossy black feathers running across its head and blending with its lighter, purple-grey nape. Its eyes were clear with deep lustrous black pearls at the very centre.

It was an intelligent bird; gregarious, curious and a natural survivor.

It called out to a mate somewhere in the nearby woodland.

"Chyak, chyak…"

The call gave rise to its name. This particular bird had brought with it a message.

The Jackdaw was telling anyone who would listen that there was a storm on the horizon.

Chapter Twenty

"Steve, something's not right. My instinct says we've missed them." Cade said into his radio. He was calm, experience did that to you, but he could almost chew the adrenalin.

Pullen looked exhausted.

Cade turned to him, "Well done mate, you did really well, now, please, get out and let me drive this bloody death trap."

Pullen was too emotionally and physically drained to disagree.

They were swapping when Hazard pulled up alongside them. They were joined by the local car.

The section staff took one look at Cade, armed and very motivated and knew it was best not to ask, their ASP batons were no match for what faced them.

The introductions were quickly made. Cade gave a one minute briefing before the larger of the two local staff, a Yorkshireman known affectionately as Brownie spoke up.

"Now boss, call me old fashioned twat and all that…"

Cade replied "You are an old fashioned twat. What have you seen?" He was a step ahead of Brownie or at worst running at the same speed.

"We entered the village a little slower than the Volvo and it was at the point where the speed limit changes that I noticed a set of marks on the road – back at the golf club turn off."

"And?"

"And they weren't there this morning my love."

There was no accounting for the observation skills of the good old fashioned British village bobby.

They were back in the Astra in a moment followed by Hazard and Brownie, now looking to get his first collar of the month and if luck was on his side he could make the arrest and hand it over: all the glory, no paperwork and a nice bit of skilfully created overtime.

Hazard had spoken to Watts. Neither male in the second Mercedes was talking, demanding consular support and feigning a lack of English.

Cade threw the Astra back along the road until they reached the side lane to the golf course; he turned left and gunned it once more. Tracey was an old heap but somehow he could see her appeal.

They reached the farm track and instinct took them towards the barn. Hazard continued onwards towards the club, covering all their bases.

Overhead the distinctive throb of a Eurocopter could be heard.

Pullen looked up and saw that its distinctive blue and yellow livery meant one thing; it was the North Midlands Air Support Unit – call sign Oscar Hotel Eight-Eight.

The Observer on board had dialled into Cade's channel and was now guiding him towards the barn. His idiosyncratic 'pilot's voice' came over the airways as clear as if he was stood next to him.

"Unit on the ground be advised that we have visual on an old barn about quarter of a mile to your north. So far?"

Cade responded "Yes, yes, en route. My call sign is India One."

He looked at Pullen. "He thinks this is a job car!"

Pullen laughed, at last able to relax "Never, not my Tracey, I think she's as fucked as her namesake was in Ibiza. I may need a new model."

"Easy tiger. This isn't over yet, no time to relax – cigars and fat ladies and all that." Cade warned.

"India One, Eight-Eight, we think there is a vehicle in the barn, some heat imagery but difficult to confirm. To the North West in the corn field near a tree is another heat source. Suggest one unit takes that over."

"Roger Eight-Eight, Brownie, can you and your crewmate take the barn, use caution. Wait for Sierra Two Zero to join you. I think my target may be in the cornfield, I'll go after her."

Hazard had pulled up with the local car and was informed that another area armed car was en route. The situation was back in control.

"India One continue in that direction, object is stationary, one hundred, ninety, eighty…yep towards the tree." The Observer was watching the ground whilst the Pilot kept the chopper in a precise hover enabling him to watch the barn. They transmitted imagery back to the Leicestershire Force Control Room and an Inspector watching the event develop, feeling a little uncomfortable that his own staff were not in control.

Cade had left Pullen at the car and was walking through the golden field at the centre of which and clearly untouched for years was an Oak tree.

"India One target is moving on all fours towards the tree, appears to be female, good heat source, good visual, caution she is holding something in her left hand."

"Is it a weapon?" asked Cade.

"Unsure India One."

Hearing the last, Cade instinctively released his Glock from the Safariland triple retention holster. His index finger intuitively ran alongside the right side of the cold metal slide.

He had no need to rack the slide, he knew exactly how many rounds he had in the magazine and there was always one ready. It was pointless carrying it otherwise.

He continued forwards, pistol at the low ready. If the target threatened him he would come up into the aim and carry out a voice command over the top of the sight. If she presented a firearm he would shoot her. He had no one to go home to now but he still wanted to go home at the end of the day.

The corn was so ripe it whispered noisily in the breeze. Looking across the top it was like a golden sea with channels running perpendicular to the track. He could make out a trail where she had run. He had the advantage but he somehow wanted to make her realise that he was a friend, not a foe.

Cade heard Hazard moving somewhere behind him, he knew he'd be moving tactically, with the local staff at the rear. He chose not to take any chances and as he was armed he too brought out his Glock, but not before sliding the MP5 behind his back.

He continued along the dusty farm track towards the barn. He had a superb view through the gaping hole in its side, into the cockpit of the Mercedes which had come to rest up against the back wall. The rear passenger door was open allowing him even greater visual superiority.

He approached, ever ready with the Glock, pushing it out in front of him, commanding the ground and constantly looking for options.

The driver was inclined at a grotesque angle, his upper body still in situ from the crash; chest leant across the steering wheel, its airbag now deflated like a cheerless party balloon.

His head was jammed into the side pillar between the headrest and he was motionless.

The second armed unit had arrived and were now deploying, causing the section staff to back up to the comparative safety of their vehicle. They weren't displaying signs of cowardice, just common sense.

Hazard approached the vehicle, on the balls of his feet, he progressed beyond the rear of the car until he could look at the driver in the bent door mirror. Again, he was motionless.

Perversely he now had to consider first aid. He was after all an unknown quantity; possibly just a driver sent on an errand, it was only Cade's intuition that led them all to reconsider how they reacted to the situation.

With two staff from the Leicestershire Traffic Department watching over the top of their weapons Hazard opened the drivers' door.

The male was in no position to fight. He was in no position to do anything. Hazard felt for a pulse and finding no trace at his neck tried again on his right wrist.

He cautiously rolled his sleeve back revealing a blue tattoo and a lifeless vein.

"Control, Sierra Two Zero the driver is one oblique one over."

Hazard had just passed the message back to his control room that the driver was dead.

Cade heard the message and knew that it may be the motivation the female needed.

He called out to her in a strong voice, trying to project above the racket of the helicopter.

"You in the field, I am a police officer, I am armed but if you do as I say you will not be harmed. The driver is not going to cause you any problems; he is being dealt with by my team. I want you to stand up and show me that you have no weapons. Do this and I will help you."

She didn't reply.

In the corn she lay completely still, barely breathing, terrified, the months and years that had gone before her now swamping her, overwhelming her coping mechanisms and preventing her from responding.

Cade tried again.

"The man on the plane gave me your note. I am a friend. I want to help you. Stand up and walk towards me. Do it now."

He combined compassion with an instruction. It was often how situations such as this were dealt with; empathy and control.

The breeze continued to rustle the corn. To Cade's right Hotel Eight Eight's rotor's fanned the crop, bending it savagely and creating a vortex of dust and plant debris.

He fixed his eyes on the point where she had gone to ground. Slowly, hair first, he saw her rise from the corn, tentatively standing, her arms raised to the sky, still holding a square metallic object.

"Good, drop the item in your hand…good, now turn around and face the tree."

She did as instructed.

Cade walked through the field backed by one of the two ARV staff and got to within arm's length.

"Hello miss, I am not going to hurt you, put your hands on top of your head. Good. Now kneel down, slowly."

She did everything she was told to do.

The ARV officer stepped forward and placed one ring of his Speedcuffs onto her right wrist, drew the arm down behind her back, then holding the rigid bar between the two loops he placed the second onto her left wrist.

She was now in custody, safe and no longer a threat.

"Eight Eight, one suspect in custody, plenty of staff here, we are resuming back to base for fuel. Good work by the ground team. Eight Eight out."

With that the blue and yellow Eurocopter banked right quickly gaining height and headed north towards its Derbyshire base.

Cade nodded to the unknown officer "Thanks pal, nice work, we'd like to take her back to the airport, I think she may be an immigration issue, you can arrest on suspicion of that if it helps. I'll travel with you if that's OK."

It was. The officer got the arrest and with it a potentially lucrative escort back to Spain. Officers around the world, especially those that were based at international borders prayed for a decent run to a foreign clime, a place where they could travel to for free, spend a few nights as guests of the British government and claim allowances when they returned; if the escortee chose to accept their fate and behaved all the way home, then all the better.

He provided the female with the standard caution and ensured she understood. She stood rigid, facing the oak tree.

For Cade the story was about to unravel and he would have no idea how it would affect him.

"Miss, turn around please."

Nikolina Stefanescu did as she was told. She had spent years doing just that, but this time as she turned she looked into the eyes of a man she instinctively trusted. They were blue, bluer than any she had ever seen and underneath the commanding and somewhat grimy face there was a hint of warmth that she hadn't experienced for a long time either.

He spoke slowly, but not in a condescending way.

"I'm Sergeant Jack Cade, Airport Police. You are under arrest, under the Immigration Act. We are taking you back to the airport where I will need to talk to you about what has happened today. Do you understand?"

She nodded her understanding; her English was as good as most of the other languages she spoke fluently.

He looked at her, despite the equal amount of grime it was a disarmingly pretty face that he looked at.

"Do you have a name miss?"

She cleared her throat and spoke, "I am Nikolina Stefanescu, tortured wife of Alex Stefanescu and mother of Elena. I have been held against my will for fourteen years by the man your authorities wish to capture. I am Bulgarian and wish to claim asylum from my government who wish to kill me. The fat man over there by the police officer, he was on the plane, he promised he would help me. He said he was an agent of the British government."

Her voice faltered; tiredness and defeat were now playing a part.

She stammered and spoke again "I have many things to share, things that will help you. They are on the drive." She nodded down to the ground where an aluminium-bodies Western Digital computer hard drive lay among the corn.

Cade stepped forward and cautiously picked it up and placed it into an exhibit bag that another officer handed to him, he sealed it and placed it in his pocket.

"I think we've heard enough Miss Stefanescu. Let's get you back to the station and get you booked in, from there we'll grab a drink and a meal and see what is so important that you would want to claim asylum from. OK?"

She nodded repeatedly, thankful at last that she was dealing with someone that she could trust. She cried for the first time in ten years.

She was led to a vehicle by the arresting officer as Cade walked towards Pullen. As he approached him he placed his hand out in a gesture of gratitude.

Pullen took it eagerly, his adrenalin levels starting to subside but still evident in the handshake.

"Jack, mate, it's been a blast. You've made an old DJ very happy; you'll need a statement no doubt?"

"Oh of course Geoff, but surely you'll wait to get back to Thames House before you knock that out. Stick it in the internal mail."

"What?" Pullen had no idea what Cade was referring to.

"It's the home address of M.I.5 Geoff, where all good British agents are based."

Pullen could only smile. He'd been rumbled. It had been an intense experience and he'd witnessed some of the best operators in action. He would dine out on it for months but he'd change the names to protect the innocent, he promised.

Besides, the pleasant Sergeant Hazard had offered to fire a round through each of his hands if he didn't. It seemed a reasonable deal and one he was more than prepared to accept, given that they were the tools of his trade.

Having accepted defeat the profusely sweating DJ wondered into the corn field and vomited.

As he wondered back to his beloved and somewhat overheated car, wiping the remnants of a partly-digested airline meal from his chin, Pullen called across to Cade, "So Jack, I'll bin those traffic tickets then?"

Cade ignored him and got into the back of the Leicestershire patrol car and wrapped the seatbelt around the Bulgarian.

As his face passed hers she exhaled and whispered, "Thank you."

Chapter Twenty One

They had been talking non-stop when Cade announced that they should take a break.

"Nikolina we have been talking for over two hours now, how about I get us some tea, or would you prefer coffee? I'm guessing you must be hungry too?"

She smiled a cautious smile and replied "Yes, please, coffee and whatever you have to eat. Thank you, you are a good man."

"I am, I am that. Listen, it's been a long day, do you need some sleep?"

She didn't. She was desperate to pass on everything she knew about the group known as Primul Val.

He knew that sooner or later he would have to hand her over to the Border Agency who would most likely refuse her entry to the United Kingdom and put her on the first available flight back to Spain.

The custody clock was ticking and for now he held her under the Police and Criminal Evidence Act on suspicion of allowing herself to be carried in what they believed to be a stolen vehicle. It was nonsense and the Custody Sergeant knew it but it allowed Cade to gain as much information from her as possible.

He discussed this with her as she sat in the sterile white-painted room that was sparsely furnished with two plastic chairs and a simple table, bolted to the ground to prevent it from becoming a weapon.

He had returned with coffee, for both of them as he needed a caffeine fix too and a couple of sandwiches from the nearby café. His ace card was a large carton of fries from McDonald's.

"Here, eat and relax. I am only here to help you. I have spoken to Immigration; they have allowed me to keep you in my custody until you are able to finish your story."

He took a bite of his sandwich which despite being two days old tasked like nectar from the gods. He looked at her, she was consuming hers as if she were a street urchin; the long stringy fries were also disappearing at a rate of knots.

She looked up, aware that he was watching her.

"What, why you look at me so…closely?"

He had been caught off guard.

"Sorry Miss Petrov I must apologise. You are the first Bulgarian female I have ever met, I was marvelling at your hair and your eyes."

She raised her eyebrows, almost playfully, "So, you find me attractive, no?"

He knew he had headed down a dangerous path so quickly slammed into reverse, but his damage limitation response failed.

"No not at all. I…"

"So, you don't find me attractive?" She pouted, pulling a face that only an eight week old Border Collie pup could better. He was putty in her hands and for the first time in many months she was enjoying flirting with a man.

"Yes, of course I do, you are a very attractive woman, but I…"

"I understand Sergeant Cade, you would love to take me out for dinner but you are bound by rules, yes? I know I used to work for government too. Don't you hate rules? Anyway, this is the most romantic meal I have had for years, so thank you, shining white knight."

He took a moment to take stock of the situation. A valuable lesson had been learned; never interview a female on your own. Fortunately he was on a break from the interview and the tape deck was firmly switched off. Quite how he would explain away the time between the tapes was another issue altogether but in reality this was never heading towards a court hearing.

He began his recovery phase which started by switching the tape deck back on. He quickly ran through the process again, as he put it, 'for the benefit of the tape' and then continued.

"OK Miss Petrov, just to recap the key points of our earlier interview. You are a Bulgarian national. You informed me that you worked for the government in a role which looked at statistics. After a while working with the unit they deployed you to Romania to gather information on a man you know to be called Alexander Stefanescu?"

He paused, allowing her to interject, she didn't so he continued.

"He attacked you, drugged you and had enforced sex with you. He also murdered another female and pushed her into a frozen lake. You saw him and his associates do this. He continued to imprison you and abuse you but rather than escape you chose to stay with him, hoping that you could gather enough information to have him arrested, or, possibly take an opportunity to kill him? And this was your objective. An objective tasked by the government of your country. Am I correct so far?"

She nodded.

"You are nodding, so I will take that as a yes. This series of events took place over a long period of time until eventually you both travelled to Spain, where you allege that Mr Stefanescu took part in a business transaction with another Romanian male, and that this was connected to high value cars, drugs and prostitution? Correct?"

Again, she simply nodded.

"I need you to confirm on the tape that this is true Miss Petrov."

"Everything you have repeated back to me is true Mr Cade, except I wasn't working for Bureau of Statistics, I was Intelligence Officer; this is why I stayed in Romania and Spain, so that I could get the information I needed. I knew the Directorate would end up killing my father if I didn't assist them. I believe they did in the end, during the winter...my poor father..."

She broke down and sobbed. Many months of abuse were now washing over her, exiting her body in tremors which were evident as painful gasps, open displays of tears and moments of silence, before she started uncontrollably crying once more.

Cade leant forward and switched off the tape deck.

After ten minutes and another drink she was able to continue. Cade began to wonder if it was an act, after all he was dealing with a professional, or, was she in fact a genuine case that warranted asylum and a place of safety?

"Mr Cade, I also knew that the Directorate would kill me once I returned. My father confirmed this. They were as dangerous as Alex in the end. I had no-one to trust, until..."

"Until?"

"Until you came along. Please help me." She gave him another desperate, pleading look.

He returned her once more to the story that she had allowed to unfold. He knew that Terry Barker was listening intently in another room and also realised that he needed to cover off a number of 'points to prove' if he was to have the slightest chance of charging her and removing her from the country. However, the more he spoke to her the more he realised that he believed her.

"Do you wish to exercise your rights to a solicitor?"

"No."

"Are you happy to continue with this interview?"

"Yes."

After nearly three hours of questioning and counter-questioning he had had enough. He had asked her initial questions then ran through the recall phase, each time her answers matched. Then he drilled down, seeking anomalies in areas of the interview, but each time she responded perfectly.

He knew she could have spent months rehearsing, being schooled by the authorities, but for what gain? It was clear, to Cade at least that she had sufficient evidence to support an asylum claim and whilst a few of his colleagues had run with the "Hell hath no fury" line he wasn't convinced.

Yes she had plenty of reasons to report to him to the Spanish authorities, and she had, but no-one had listened. They seemed willing to allow an enormous amount of luxury vehicles to disappear from their border without so much as a single question being asked.

She tried to report cases of domestic violence but each time she retracted, more from fear than lack of evidence. Each occurrence drove her further away from him and closer to the point where she had rammed that surgical steel needle into his thigh.

She had remained focused on the mission to the bitter end.

Cade presented the hard drive to her.

"Miss Petrov I am showing you police exhibit JC1 with label attached and signed by me. This relates to a Western Digital computer hard drive which you had in your hand when you were arrested earlier today. Can you tell me why you were carrying this?"

She cleared her throat and spoke, "It has photographs of my daughter and father on it, they are precious to me, which is why I carried it."

He looked at the drive then directly at her.

"Is there anything else on this drive that I should know about?"

She shook her and head and said "No, nothing."

He paused, trying to delve into his reservoir of interview skills. As he did so she leant across the table, took a piece of paper and motioned for a pen. She put her right index finger up to her lips.

He nodded, not quite sure what was happening but feeling that the key to the whole investigation was about to emerge.

He continued to tread water stating that he was reading from his notes, so in future should a solicitor be listening they couldn't accuse him of anything untoward – the worst case for an interviewing officer was an allegation that a client had provided evidence under duress.

She slid the note back towards him. It read:

'Jack – the hard drive contains data about Stefanescu, about me and about my negotiations with foreign embassy staff here in Europe. There are videos of me and other men, mainly African men. There are images of travel documents from Britain, Canada, the USA, birth certificates and diplomatic passports. I CANNOT talk about this on the tape. Please. Switch it off. Or I must stop speaking to you.'

He took a deep inward breath and announced that he had no further questions; he ran through the procedures with the tapes and asked if she had anything to add or clarify. She hadn't so he terminated the interview. He sealed the last of the four tapes and placed them with the hard drive.

He took the items back to the Custody area and put them in a holding cage, grabbed some more coffee and a packet of biscuits and walked back towards the interview room.

Barker joined him in the corridor.

"Jack. What was going on in there? I've heard enough to put her back on the plane but my boss may disagree and allow her to claim. Do you believe her, you were with her, how did she seem to you?"

"Scared Terry. Capable, trained, intelligent, but scared. Look mate, I know we don't know each other but I need you to support me on this – there's something special about this woman."

"You sure it's not just her looks and feminine guile?"

He laughed, placed his hands onto his shoulders and said "Terry, you know you may be right, perhaps I do fancy her. Either that or I'm the first bloke she's trusted in a long time. Or, she's playing me like a Kingfish."

"A what?" replied Barker, a keen angler.

"A Kingfish, they have them in Australian and New Zealand waters. Think Mackerel on steroids. I hope to head there one day and have a go. I hear it's a fabulous place."

He'd thrown Barker off the scent for long enough.

"OK Jack, this is your first big test. Give it a go, let her claim but for Christ's sake make sure you cross the T's and be careful. Agreed?"

"Agreed, and Terry, thank you."

He re-entered the room and placed the coffee in front of her.

"Right, it's your lucky day Miss. You get coffee, my undivided attention and a packet of custard creams."

"They sound revolting."

"So does Goulash!"

"That's Hungarian."

"Same thing…" he was playing her now.

"No! Mr Cade it is not." She pushed the biscuits back across the table.

"OK, OK I'm sorry but I doubt you know much about my country to be fair."

To prove a point she recited every English king and queen since 1600, added a few Prime Ministers and named twelve counties. It was certainly more than he could have done. Like most Brits he struggled to differentiate between Bucharest and Budapest.

"I am sorry too Sergeant, I am tired. But I need to tell you about the drive."

"You do. And let me tell you that I am putting my neck on the line here."

She frowned.

"I'm taking a chance for you. So please respect that and help me to help you."

"I will. I promise. Just don't send me back there. He is a dangerous man, I am safer here, not safe, they can still get at me, but safer."

She started to outline the contents of the drive.

"A few years ago Alex – or as he likes to be called The Jackdaw set up a team of criminals. They were either murderers or drug makers but they all had one thing in common, they loved money. The fall of Communism Eastern Europe saw a lot of people trying to use their skills to make more money. Many people were still poor. Some were even starving. I was a lucky one because my father worked for the government."

He nodded encouragingly.

"Well Alex's team grew, he added some technical people, some were good with computers, others with documents and others with money – they knew how to get through bank security systems and where to clean money."

"Clean? You mean launder?"

"Yes, launder. He hid about three million Euro in a hole under the floor of the main bar, he was the only one who knew it was there. The problem was that the authorities were looking for Alex and his men all the time, he had so much money but couldn't use it, so he hid behind businesses such as his night clubs and rarely left them. He was safe inside, his men watched over him, protecting him, day and night. Any officials who got too close were warned off or better still paid off – I believe that some were killed."

Cade continued to make the right sounds and gestures.

"He knew he had to leave Romania if he ever wanted to live a life of luxury so we travelled to Spain where he met up with an old friend. He was the one I told you about; Alex slit his throat, he made it look so easy. We stayed in Spain, he was able to live like a king, he provided me with money and jewellery and a nice car, but kept beating me and making me watch him sleep with other women. He would give me to his friends too."

Cade understood what she meant but avoided the comment "Why didn't you leave?"

"The simplest question Mr Cade, but the hardest answer."

"OK, sorry, I guess I will never understand your position?"

She replied with a faraway look "No, I guess you won't. Anyway he carried on stealing and exporting the cars to Eastern Europe, many of them were packed with drugs, in the door panels, in the seats and even in the fuel tanks. He got pretty girls with drug habits to drive them across the border. The guards were hopeless, looking at the girls instead of the cars. Soon he was very rich and Interpol started to hunt for him, but he laughed in their faces."

"Why" asked Cade, leaning towards her and now genuinely interested in what he was hearing.

"Because he had worked out a way of getting support from government officials and I…was the key. I was on, how you say this, the roller coaster?"

Cade nodded "Go on…"

"I couldn't get off Jack. I knew that one day soon I would have the chance to take everything from him and kill him. So I went along with everything he asked for. I left Spain and travelled to Belgium, Brussels to be exact."

Cade was writing notes as best he could.

"Alex made sure I had loads of money, a fast car, beautiful dresses, jewellery and invites to parties at the embassies. It was like James Bond but without 007."

They both laughed but the subject matter was getting more serious by the second.

"I started with a few Consuls, one from Italy, the other from Germany. I got to know them."

"What do you mean?"

"I slept with them Jack. They are busy men whose wives are often not with them. They love time with a pretty, mysterious foreign girl, especially one who speaks their language and asks for nothing in return."

"OK, but what *did* you want?"

"I wanted their knowledge Jack. I wanted them to introduce me to ambassadors from smaller countries, mainly Africa and South America. Before I know it I am having dinner with Ambassadors and Consuls from Benin, Burkina Faso, Guinea, Liberia, Senegal and Sierra Leone. I didn't even know these were countries until then!"

"You slept with all of them?" Cade asked somewhat bemused.

"No silly, I made them think I would. Yes I slept with the Italian Consul because he was cute; he was warm and loving and never hurt me, not like Alex."

He sensed that the story could change tack so quickly encouraged her.

"Go on, tell me more."

"I flirted with them, got to visit their embassies, let them drive my car – a Maserati Spyder. They were like small boys. I knew how to press their buttons. At one point I was seeing eight different government officials. All I wanted was their diplomatic passports, some other identity documents and some evidence to blackmail them with. Whilst I did this Primul Val were stepping up to the next stage of their plan."

"Primul?"

"Primul Val – The First Wave – it's what Alex called his gang. They all had a small tattoo of a wave on their right wrist. All blue, except his, his was black. Mine was blue, look."

She showed him hers. A partially-scarred, small homemade tattoo was evident on the inside of her wrist.

"Did you do that?"

She shook her head solemnly. "The scar yes, the tattoo, no. I woke up one day with it. I don't want to talk about it now. He forced that poor girl under the ice…"

"OK, sorry. OK? I won't ask again but I need to know how many people have this mark, where will I locate them?"

"How many? I don't know Jack, fifty, perhaps a hundred. Where? Romania, Bulgaria, Germany, Italy, Switzerland, America, who knows? So do you think you will go and arrest them all? You are foolish if you think this."

"No Nikolina I don't think that at all. What I think is that I need as much evidence from you as I can get, this will at least help me to influence my bosses and then we can start hunting for them."

"The hunter, hunted. I like that, but make sure you have the right weapons, these are very…" She paused, searching for the right word.

"Devious?"

"Yes, devious, very devious indeed. They are ruthless, greedy, dangerous men."

Cade knew that he needed more so he steered the conversation back towards the hard drive.

"You mentioned that there were videos on the hard drive? Tell me about them."

She smiled "Mr Cade do I have to? At the time it was right but now I feel bad."

"Why?"

"They are videos of me having sex with men. I felt in control but sometimes I felt scared. I did it for my country but in the end even my country fucked me."

Cade tried not to laugh – he wasn't sure if it was meant to be humourous, but the look on her face said anything but.

"I understand Miss Petrov, I do, really. OK, I will skip through those images when I view the drive later – OK?"

"Thank you, you are gentleman. If it helps, the best one is with the Ambassador to Benin. I bit him very hard."

It was a light moment which Cade allowed to develop. She started to laugh, almost hysterically; it was another outlet, a way of exorcising a few more demons.

"My God Sergeant Jack, what did I get involved in?" It was a rhetorical question.

He nodded sympathetically. "OK, tell me more about the documents. What is the connection with these?"

"The documents, now this is interesting. You should make notes or it will get too confusion."

"Confusing?"

"Yes exactly. I spent a long time in Brussels. I got to know the United Nations building very well, plus all of the embassies and consuls. I started by pretending to need assistance to enter the countries. I said I was a journalist, wanting to write for *Time* magazine. They believed me. It must be my looks."

She flicked her hair back and smiled. It helped to reinforce her beliefs.

"Anyway before long I had enough business cards to start a small folder, twelve countries in Africa, a few from the Middle East and six in South America. I wrote to each, creating a sense of urgency about my need to write about their countries and before long I was able to form a relationship with quite a few of the men."

Cade made rough notes; so far he hadn't heard anything out of the ordinary.

"After the first month my diary was almost full. I had to be very careful not to be seen by the other men I was dating, my skills helped me. I changed my car three times. At one time I had a Mercedes SLR, it was very fast, the Consul of Guinea, he asked to drive it. I let him. It was fun, until he crashed it. He didn't tell me that he couldn't drive!"

"He crashed an SLR? What did you do?"

"We left it in the street, I rang Alex and he sent another."

Cade shook his head. They were treating one of the best cars of all time as a toy – it was at least three times his annual salary. He hated The Jackdaw more and more by the second.

"Over dinner one evening Jean-Marie, the consul, gave me three blank diplomatic passports. He said they were a gift, an apology for smashing up my car. I said I couldn't take them but he insisted. I took them of course and that was the start of stage two of Alex's plans, for they would allow free travel throughout that region within the ECOWAS."

Cade was writing furiously, trying to anticipate what was next but he was way off the mark when it came.

"The eco-what?"

"Economic Community of West African States of course! It is a community in that part of the world that allows free travel for holders of those documents – and to have a diplomatic passport is even better. Some of these countries are centres for fraud; watch, in the future some will even become famous for it."

"OK, I understand. Carry on, please."

"People think you get false passports to travel, yes? Of course, but Alex knew that if you had a diplomatic passport it gave you more, the chance to travel without the authorities interfering, to open up frontiers and most important for Alex, to open up bank accounts around the world, especially in offshore tax havens."

"But what if these people are detected? Surely…"

Petrov held up her hand "No, surely not Jack, you see this is why the plan was so good. As you know diplomatic documents provide a privilege, immunity from prosecution, lawsuits, detention, even search at your border here."

"The Vienna Convention." It was a statement by Cade rather than a question.

"Yes, The Vienna Convention, created to allow the free passage of recognised diplomats. There are even cases of people obtaining fake diplomatic status by using a genuine diplomatic travel document, just like those given to me in Brussels that evening."

Cade, still new to border policing but learning fast was nodding encouragingly, reinforcing each nod with a sound and almost beckoning for more with his spare hand.

Petrov now knew that he was interested. At last someone who was prepared to listen. She thought out aloud, "Lift your head up from whatever dark deed you are doing Stefanescu. This man is coming to hunt you."

Cade missed the sentence but was ready for the one that followed.

"You see Jack, what Alex learned – he's a fast learner – was that if he found the right people he could get more passports, and more passports means more fake diplomats and more diplomats means more money. Simple."

Cade screwed his eyes up, trying to concentrate. It had been one hell of a long bloody day.

"Nikolina, take a break. I'll be back." And with that he left the room and walked into the adjoining observation area where Barker was waiting – albeit now waiting to head home.

"Terry, try and explain what the hell she is on about before my head bursts. I think I understand but I need to hear it in layman's terms please."

"Right, where shall I begin? It strikes me that she's talking about fake diplomats rather than false diplomatic passports. Now, if that's the case it's an international problem and I'll outline the key reasons why."

"Please do" asked Cade as he selfishly consumed the last of the custard creams.

"OK, your Miss Nikolina. She convinces the lesser known countries – or rather their representatives that she needs their help, in order that her agent can help the prospective country. So far? Good then I shall continue. The prospective passport holder contacts a pre-selected, preferably poor state and offers assistance. In simple terms Jack this means money, and often, to help out with what on the face of it are genuine, or as is often the case, less honest government programmes. Now this is where your charming redhead comes into the game."

"Do go on," Cade offered, tired but genuinely interested.

"During 'negotiations' she will convince her new-found friend that monetary aid might be forthcoming a little quicker and with fewer questions asked if the agent was issued with a diplomatic passport. During pillow talk she'll be explaining that a DP would allow the sponsor to travel and negotiate freely and as a result everyone will benefit."

"And that's it? You get a hot Bulgarian to sleep her way around the UN in exchange for some dodgy passports and the man at the top becomes wealthier than half of Monaco? I'm missing something."

"Indeed you are dear boy. The passports are genuine but the diplomats are not. The issuing authority turns a blind eye to this practice as they think they are likely to benefit. It could be personally or in some cases nationally. An example would be a small power station complex that was offered by two American businessmen recently. They convinced the government of a Pacific Island nation that they could build them a great little power plant, incidentally one which was funded by the Chinese. All they needed was two shiny new DP's and before you knew it the island would be literally buzzing."

"And?"

"And of course it didn't happen. The two managed to launder money through the island and got away before the good folk of

Paradise Lost realised that they had also emptied half of their Treasury."

"So these folk literally take on the persona of diplomats? But surely a white man can't assume the role of an official from a predominantly black country?"

"Bang on. So what they do is choose carefully. Those countries that have a history of British, Spanish or French colonisation often provide greater opportunities. Before you can say bonjour, plain old John Brown can be anything from an Ambassador to a Minister, a Minister-Counselor, a Counselor, First Secretary, Second Secretary, Third Secretary, Attaché, and Assistant Attaché."

"As she said, simple."

"Absolutely. All the while there are gullible nations there will be vultures waiting to pounce. Now, hang onto your hat because the best bit is yet to come."

"I'm hanging Terrence."

"You've heard of diplomatic bags? Well they don't just have to be old-fashioned satchels with a few secret envelopes in. Oh no, they can be anything up to and including a container. Now can you see how having a DP might be beneficial? Once your lovely little flower in that interview room got the DP then she just had to ensure that the new holder got a Diplomatic ID card too and they would be up, up and away!"

"You say a container? Surely Customs would search them now and then, even randomly?"

Barker laughed before adding "Jack, they are exempt from being opened or searched and as such criminal organisations can work across borders without fear of their ill-gotten gains being seized as proceeds of crime. And of course when the going gets tough…"

"Don't tell me, the tough get going?"

"No, not all JC the shiny new diplomat claims diplomatic immunity – even if he's fake. There are examples of it happening across Europe. Only recently a police officer in Brussels stopped someone with a false diplomatic ID card, the officer was so unsure what to do, he let him go. Even though the diplomat was drunk and had just crashed a car."

The story she had told Cade earlier about the Mercedes now had even more credibility.

"It's almost the perfect crime Jack and if your girl in there knows half of what I think she does then we had better hang onto her a while longer. You bed her down for the night; I'll go and process the claim papers."

Chapter Twenty Two

Cade had finally got home, hit the pillow and didn't remember a thing until his alarm dragged him kicking and screaming into the shower. As he had stood and shaved he looked at himself in the mirror and spoke.

"What a long day Jack, old son, but boy, what a day? I reckon I could get to enjoy this border stuff!"

And with that he rinsed the last of the shaving gel from his face and drew a detailed female shape in the condensation. As he showered the form disappeared, but the memories of the previous day didn't. She had captured his mind, if not yet his heart.

He had arrived at the airport, parked up and walked into the station to find Steve Hazard recounting the story to the nightshift who were having an end of shift chat with the early shift over a cup of tea.

"Morning Double O – you joining us?" asked an ebullient Hazard.

"Don't mind if I do."

Hazard introduced Cade to the night shift who seemed like a tight bunch, run by a youthful-looking Sergeant called Marty Halford.

Halford spoke for the section, "Steve tells me you did a cracking job yesterday Jack, good to have you on board. We don't often have pursuits, guns and helicopters so let's hope this is the start of some action."

"Thanks Marty, to be honest I thought it was like that every day. Hot Bulgarians, car chases, stolen goods, Interpol…"

"Too right mate – anyway your girlfriend has been asking for you. She's over in the Detention Centre. Best get your hair done and saunter over there!"

He finished his tea and walked through the terminal, catching a glimpse of himself in the window of the WH Smith's store; inadvertently he brushed his hair back and then started smiling.

"Easy tiger, she'd have you for breakfast!" It was Terry Barker.

"Morning Terry, thanks for yesterday, I really appreciated the support and your knowledge."

"My pleasure entirely, I'll tell you what, it's rare to come up against a story as good as hers. Looks as though she's going to be landed anyway – for now at least. Yarl's Wood Immigration Centre has been damaged by fire so there may not be enough room for her. She'll have to head there until we hear differently."

"I know it well. Got a bit of a bad reputation at the moment?"

"You could say that. Some reckon it's why the inmates tried to burn it down."

Cade nodded and walked off to find his prisoner.

"Good morning Nikolina. Long day yesterday, you ready for something to eat?"

She had her head down in her lap, her chin resting on the backs of her hands.

"I am, yes. I did not sleep. I kept having a dream that you shot me in that cornfield. I was scared, but not as scared as I was in Spain. Hey, even if you had shot me I wouldn't have been as scared." She smiled a weary smile and ran her fingers through her matted hair.

"Would you like a shower?" He asked innocently.

"Won't your bosses be angry if they find us?" She replied, less naively.

It raised a smile and another warning flag.

"I'll get one of the staff to take you whilst I get some breakfast organised. We really need to finish our talk from last night."

Fifteen minutes later he re-joined her in a day room at the airport. She was wearing fresh clothes and looked a thousand percent better. Whilst she wore no make-up she still looked attractive – actually, more so.

Cade provided her with toast, some cereals and a cup of coffee.

She devoured it, drained the coffee mug and looked up.

"OK, let's go. What else do you want to know?"

"Is that all it takes for you to spill state secrets? I'll have to remember that for next time." Cade offered this as an ice-breaker but soon found himself embroiled in a mind game once more.

"State secrets? You think I give up my countries secrets for a piece of cold toast and a colder shower?"

She threw the dish at the wall, it clattered to the floor and spun on its base, slowly coming to a halt. The room was now silent.

He looked at her and asked "Finished?"

She pursed her lips and replied "Yes, sorry, not necessary, you have been kind to me. I am still tired. Look, I tell you everything you want to know about Alex and his team but do not ask me about my country. OK?"

"OK. I am also sorry. Now, give me an example of how Alex used one of the passports and ID's that you obtained."

"Easy. He got one for Equatorial Guinea. It is the only African country which officially uses Spanish as their first language. He speaks Spanish, and to some people, looks Spanish. In 1995 an American company discovered oil and it became quite wealthy. Sadly the money didn't get to the poorer people, some of who didn't even have good drinking water. Jack, twenty percent of children die before they get to five…"

"Go on Nikolina please."

"Well, he found out that with a passport he could operate as an Attaché. He promised the government that he could get them some investors from America to help them build a new hospital and sort out their water problems. The President agreed as he thought it would help his popularity. Alex was given twenty thousand Euro to travel to America and complete the negotiations."

"So, what happened?"

"We went to Vanuatu instead. It is in the Pacific. We lived there for a few weeks; he used the passport to convince people that we were there to offer investment opportunities…"

"Don't tell me, they were fooled too?"

"Yes Jack, they were. We lived like a king and queen, the best restaurants, a beautiful villa near the Emtem Lagoon. In the day he did business meetings while I lay by the pool and at night we met up with more business people. I had never seen so much money Jack, and money can buy anything, even I was for sale."

"So what do you think he was doing whilst you lounged by the pool in your bathing suit?"

"Bikini."

"Whatever. What do you think he was up to?"

"He met with men, I think some were gang people from Australia, some were from China – Triad I think, he had the tattoo anyway. And even a man from Tahiti – he was there to launder money but pretended to be selling black pearls."

"OK, the Chinese, tell me more about them."

"What do you want to know? They were well dressed, all had English names but spoke Mandarin to each other, some had triangle tattoos, most were strong-looking but all had money. They talked to Alex about moving counterfeit clothing through Romania into mainland Europe. There was nothing he wasn't willing to get involved in Jack. The Australian men wanted him to arrange for females to move drug stuff from Europe into Australia."

"Stuff?" enquired Cade.

"Yes, stuff to make drugs with."

"Pre-cursors? Pseudo ephedrine? Contac?"

"Yes, pseudo. They wanted to make a lot of money with drugs but didn't want their men to get involved. Alex told them that for thirty percent he could arrange pretty girls to move the stuff from Europe straight into the main Australian cities. They also asked him to send pre-cursors from Holland by using the mail system. Hundreds of boxes were sent one month, hoping that some would get through."

Whilst he had formed the opinion that there was nothing that Stefanescu wouldn't get involved in he asked out of idle curiosity.

"Tell me Nikolina, is there anything he wouldn't do?"

"Children."

Her response was quick, decisive.

"What do you mean children?"

"He wouldn't harm children or make them do things. He loves children. We have a daughter; he would protect her with his life. He would kill me first."

"Where is your daughter?"

"Safe."

"Good, but I asked where she is."

"And I told you, safe." It was clear this was one area that was off limits so he decided not to push further but added "OK, but if she needs help and you can get a message to her tell her I'm always willing to offer aid. OK?"

"OK, thank you."

"Right, tell me more about the passports. Could I get one if I wanted to?"

"If you offered to sleep with me, then yes."

Cade offered a puzzled look in response. As attractive as he found her he wasn't sure where this was heading. The thought of having this girl in the station shower passed through his mind but he physically shook his head to rid the image. But I kept playing back.

"Concentrate Jack" he said out aloud.

"I am sorry, were you talking to me? She replied, bemused.

"Sorry, I was talking out aloud. Now, where were we? Oh yes I was asking you to sleep with me so that I could get a false passport."

"No, I was asking you to sleep with me silly. It is the other way around. You are the diplomat – you don't need the passport, I do. Look, shall we just do it here, right now on the table?" She pushed it, indicating that it would hold their weight.

"My God you are insatiable, I'd lose my job."

"Of course, but imagine the fun. And anyway, at least now I know you would consider it." She threw her head back and laughed.

Cade just sat and shook his head. He'd been played like the legendary Kingfish: Hook, Line and sinker.

He recovered quickly but was now partly stirred, partly curious and ever so slightly unsure where to turn next. It was time for the ace to appear from his sleeve.

"So you are an internationally-trained government employee who has slept her way around Europe and is willing to trade secrets for asylum – for safety. What would it take for you to work for me?"

He was pushing the boundaries and didn't even know if he could, or should, but he pushed anyway. The UK government was starting to take an interest in Eastern Europe and how a small but effective percentage of its people were impacting on their financial end state.

She was now the one with a bemused look.

"You think I am slut but you want me to be a spy for Britain? I am good enough for that then?"

"No, Britain does not have spies. I want you become my human source. You will have to go to an Immigration Centre for now but I will try and get you out, try and get you a temporary visa until the government can decide what to do with you. But you have my word you will be safe. Do we have a deal?"

"What about my daughter?"

"Yes, her too, but only if we can. Look I give you my word that I will watch over her the best I can and if she ever gets in trouble you can send her to me, wherever I am. But in order to do that…"

It was all a little too eager on his part and he felt deep down inside that whilst what he was doing was morally right he was likely to get his arse severely kicked by someone further up the food chain.

"Mr Cade, in order to do that I have to betray her whereabouts, and, trust you as I do…"

"It's OK. The offer remains."

There was a light knock on the door. Cade turned and saw Barker looking through the plexiglass window tapping at his Seiko.

"It's time Jack."

He turned to Nikolina and said "You have to go now. But I will come and see you as soon as I can. Then we will start to plan your new life. Trust me?" It was a statement rather than a question but she answered anyway.

"Like I trusted my own father." She held out her hand, he took it and shook it warmly.

Cade turned and began to walk out of the room. She had a look on her face, as if there was more that she wanted to tell him. In for a penny.

"Miss, is there anything else?"

"Why do you ask?"

"I'm not sure, call it male intuition."

"Then your instinct treats you well. Yes, there is something else. But I need to keep it…safe, for now. I have something. Next time we meet, I'll tell you."

It was a test. He knew it, she knew it.

"Then so be it. Until next time Nikolina, and be assured, there will be a next time. Look after yourself."

He exited the room and allowed his Immigration colleagues to take over.

"Precious cargo, OK?"

Barker nodded as he was joined by two Border Agency staff. They took her and a Nigerian female to a nearby prison van, loaded them into it as Cade stood and watched it head off towards Yarl's Wood.

He knew it was an unpleasant place but he also knew she was a very resilient woman.

She'd be fine.

Chapter Twenty Three

The next day Cade was called into Eddie Curtain's office.

"You wanted to see me sir?" he enquired, hovering just outside the door, hand above head height, leaning against the woodwork.

Curtain was on the phone but covered the mouthpiece long enough to offer an instruction.

"Come in Jack and shut the door."

He did and sat in the chair that the charismatic senior officer pointed to.

"Right Mary love I must go, one of the lads has just arrived and I'm about to use bad language, certainly not for a lady to hear so I'll see you tonight; don't forget to get the chicken out of the freezer."

Cade was ready for a royal dressing down.

"Fuck me Jack, you've been here a few days and already you've had air support involved, guns, bloody dead people on Leicestershire's patch, pursuits involving members of the public, a crash, some horny Hungarian trying it on with you and to cap it all I've got a bill for nine hundred bastard quid for a replacement hay barn. What are your plans for the rest of the bloody week?"

"Boss…"

Curtain raised his hand.

"Don't say a word, I haven't finished. I've had the friggin' Immigration Minister on the phone twenty-four-bastard-seven, bendin' me ear, I've had Stu Green from Leicestershire bendin' the other bastard for shootin' up half 'is county…Christ Jack what next? Tom said you were good but I didn't expect Miami pissin' Vice!"

Cade started to speak "To be fair boss…"

Curtain threw another hand up in protest.

"To be fair my arsehole, Sergeant! You've broken just about every bloody rule we've got, and some. You've broken rules that not even I broke back in the seventies. The Daily Mail's been on the blower asking why a ginger DJ was heading up the fastest pursuit the M1 has seen since the Kray Twin's headed north. The Home Office wants to know why there's a dead Romanian lying in a Merc under two ton of friggin' straw and to add the bloody cherry on top of me bastard birthday cake *Woman's Day* want an interview with your mysterious ginger Hungarian hooker. Christ!"

Curtain rubbed his hair vigorously as if he were trying to rid his mind of the dramas of the last few hours.

"Sir…"

"*What?*"

"She's Bulgarian. She's a redhead. She's not a hooker and the dead man was most likely transporting her to a certain death. She's tied up with a significant Eastern European crime group called Primul Val, they are at the forefront of diplomatic-based fraud, right across Europe, high value vehicle and drug trafficking and I think they could be the leaders in our emerging financial crime issues in the UK. Her 'boyfriend' is rapidly rising up the Interpol ranks and she was working for the Bulgarian government. And there is something else. Something she is yet to tell me. Something major."

He paused to let his words sink in.

Silence.

"Tell me you didn't have it off with her?"

"What?"

"You heard. The lads reckon you had it off with her in the interview room."

"With Terry Barker watching? Boss, it was my wife that was into that, not me. Look, I'll leave it to someone else to deal with. I needed a few days, possibly weeks but I reckon this could be the airport's greatest moment. I know you want to kick my arse and I'd gladly let you do it, but I think this is the real deal. But I respect your decision."

"Bollocks Jack you've put me in one hell of a situation. Listen son, I can see the potential here but I'm going to have to talk to the Home Office about this. This is not a case of blurred lines it's a fucked up mess and frankly I'm not sure that having anything further to do with it is wise. But for some reason I trust your instinct. Leave it with me? I'll cash in a few favours with Frankie Waterman and John Hewett."

"Sir?"

"Yes old pals of mine, we went to Bramshill on a conference together once. Frank's doing great things in the Met – organised crime or something, will never happen in our neck of the woods. Young Hewett's a real flying star: sophisticated, good-looking, athletic bastard, looks about twelve and he wears a Rolex Submariner, loves Aston

Martin's and all that James Bond shit. Ladies love him. I can't stand the man!"

"How can he help?"

"How? Easy sunshine, he's on secondment to the Home Office or the Foreign Office, some bloody office, somewhere, you know the type? All exotic tea trays, filo-bloody-faxes and desk tidies made out of the vulcanised foreskin of a South Sea Island pearl diver. Anyway he's got the ear of the Immigration Minister who just happens to think he's good-looking too, fortunately for John she's a female."

"And that's a positive?"

"Course it is. You've not seen Hewett yet. Right piss off and go and write this pack of horse dung up into something resembling evidence. Go on, get out."

Cade knew when to quit and left swiftly. He smiled on the way out of the office causing Curtain to throw one more rebuke his way.

"Oy cocky bastard! Stop smiling, I saw you ears moving!"

"Sir?"

"And another thing, you did well. Welcome on board. Oh and Jack."

"Sir?"

"I'll have that coffee now thanks."

Cade provided his boss with a well-made cup of coffee.

"There you go boss. Oh by the way, Bond swears by his Omega Seamaster. He's too classy to wear a Rolex."

"Sling your hook gobshite. I wear a Rolex."

"Really sir, I hadn't noticed."

Cade went to find a quiet place to write up his extensive notes on the preceding days' events. Leicestershire had taken the fatal crash file and an Inspector had reviewed the pursuit, finding no issues, other than the fact that a civilian was driving, who by chance only had a Learner's licence. That aside Leicestershire's Chief Constable had agreed to overlook a few of the finer points in favour of the rewards that the intelligence source could bring to the nation. Calling it a case of sweeping it under the carpet for the greater good of the nation.

Cade spent the rest of the day mapping out the events, obtaining statements from Hazard and his team and even managed to phone his new-found DJ companion.

Cade was greeted with an answerphone message.

"Yo, yo, yo this is DJ Pullen Power, leave your number bitch and the DJPP will be right back at you. Respect."

The phone beeped allowing Cade to leave a slowly-delivered droll message.

"Geoffrey, it's your friend from the police. It's Zero Nine Twenty. Can you ring me sometime soon please? Ask for me by name, oh and Geoff I think it's about time you got a new message, you live in Derbyshire not Harlem. Goodbye."

A young Constable put his head around the door.

"Boss, the boss wants to see you again. Sorry."

"Cheers, the name's Jack by the way, tell him I'm on my way would you?"

Cade hit ctrl, alt and delete, locked his computer and walked back along the corridor, knocked politely and entered Curtain's office to find Terry Barker sat next to the curved beech wood desk.

"Sit down Jack." Curtain was brief so Cade expected another dressing down.

Barker spoke first.

"Jack, someone stabbed your girl late last night at Yarl's Wood. West African girl – Guinea, Liberia, somewhere in that region anyway."

"Shit. She OK?" asked Cade, genuinely concerned.

"Lucky girl Jack, it appears she may well have had the training you alluded to in your briefing.

Cade looked puzzled and said "I'm not with you Terry."

Curtain was taking it all in, pen poised on his notepad but writing nothing down.

Barker continued "The African girl used a makeshift shank to stab her in the left shoulder. The wound is superficial but she has some cuts to her left hand too."

Cade nodded, feeling as if he had somehow betrayed her.

"I said I would look after her boss."

"I know Jack but it's not our job to mother these people, they are refugees for a reason you know, they are survivors, wait till you hear the next bit."

Barker cleared his throat and carried on. "Jack, the African girl is in hospital, your little Bulgarian honey kicked seven bells out of her and was about to shove the blade down her throat when the guards got to the cell."

"Christ almighty, will she survive? If she doesn't this is exactly what I didn't want."

"She'll survive; battered and bruised but she'll survive. She has a laryngeal fracture from being straight-armed across the throat. The guards entered the cell and found Petrov standing to attention, her palms out in front of her, almost waiting to be arrested. The difference was that her injuries were worse than her attacker's – at least visually. So when she explained in English what the girl had done the guards were quick to believe her side of the story."

"That's good. What this does though is add fuel to the fire boss. This is not a random act of violence, this was orchestrated and we need to get her out of there today. Sooner..."

"Calm down lad, as I said earlier we need to make sure you're not too close to this. We have made a request via Johnnie Hewett – the debonair bastard has come good too. Let's not ask how but she's got a spot in a stand-alone female unit at Dover. Once she's patched up she'll head there. The Home Office wants you to travel there too. Clearly your reputation precedes you Sonny Jim. Chances like this don't come along very often, best advice I can give you is ride the wave whilst you can, it could change your life. Grab what you need and get there as soon as you can. Stop overnight. If you get stuck for a bed a mate of mine, ex-job, runs a B and B in town, called The Armada, stay there until she arrives. I want you fresh for this. As you say, this could put us firmly on the map."

"Sir, thank you, I've got a good feeling about this..."

Curtain interrupted "I'm pleased to hear it Sergeant, just make sure it's not in your groin will you?"

Cade shook his head vigorously and smiled an enforced smile before departing for his office.

Barker made his excuses and was about to leave when Curtain stopped him.

"Terry, Jack has stumbled across something here you know, the Home Office have got his initial report, that's why he's heading to Kent. They genuinely think he's found a very big piece of the jigsaw and it's a jigsaw that has been costing the UK millions. It's not without risk but they are willing for Jack to handle her as a Covert Human Intelligence Source due to the fact that it falls under the interests of the economic well-being of the United Kingdom."

"My, that is pretty weighty stuff Eddie. Isn't there a risk of a male working with a female?"

"Abso-bloody-lutely" replied Curtain using another of his famous tmesis quotes. "But somehow they see it as a risk worth taking."

Two days later Petrov was deemed to be fit enough to transfer. She left the daunting Yarl's Wood for the equally intimidating but historically more impressive Dover Immigration Centre.

The secure vehicle drove from London and onto the M20 motorway where it cruised for about an hour, passing the impressive Eurotunnel operation before steadily climbing up and onto the top of the iconic White Cliffs of Dover.

The driver and his passenger saw the impressive vista open out before them, the Eastern Docks in the distance, sitting below another impressive cliff face, the crowning glory of which was Dover Castle, arguably one of the most impressive Norman fortresses in the world.

The ancient town was now littered with tourist shops which were fortunately supported by numerous historical strongholds, legacies of its roles in countless wars and none was more impressive than the castle. However as the crew reached a small roundabout they obeyed the road sign and indicated left and once more climbed a steep hill up to a place known as The Citadel.

At the summit they turned left and entered Dover Immigration Centre which had opened that year but had formerly been a youth prison and an adult facility too, prior to that it was owned by the British Army. Surrounded by an impressive moat it was an ideal location on which to establish a penal institution.

As the crew approached the main gate they looked to their left and could see the coast of France, clear enough to touch, but twenty one miles away at its shortest point. Countless people crossed it daily and as many ships cruised up and down the Straits – the busiest in the world.

Four hundred feet below in the relative calm of Shakespeare Beach, a fifty year old female cross channel swimmer began her own personal challenge. Alone, cold and intimidated by what lay ahead, frightened but at the same time excited she set off on her solitary journey.

In the back of the vehicle Nikolina Petrov was experiencing the same emotions. Wearing a large field dressing over a half inch wound which had been cleaned and Steri-Stripped, she winced as the guards helped her out of the white anonymous Iveco van and onto her feet. She offered a bandaged hand as a gesture to one of the guards who awkwardly shook it.

She wasn't secured, despite her previous involvement in a violent attack. She had friends, clearly.

An hour later the swimmer looked over her shoulder, the coast of England was becoming smaller with each stroke. She began to wonder what lay beneath her as well as ahead, shivered involuntarily but dug deep and carried on rhythmically pounding through the swell.

She crested each wave but was caught broadside by the seventh. It took her breath away and a moment of brief panic set in. Her support crew on board the pilot boat *Optimist* offered her immediate encouragement until she was back in control and once more able to plough through the water. The battle was obviously physical and very much psychological; seventeen hours, thirteen minutes and exactly fifty seconds later she would eventually win the war with nature, dragging her exhausted body onto the French shore.

At the same time Nikolina Petrov stood in her room, a cell by any other name, albeit it had a small television and a smaller window onto the outside world. She could see land in the distance and assumed it was France.

In the water a small white and blue boat made its way steadily south east. She wondered who was on board and where they were heading and wished for the first time in months that she was back in her beloved Motherland.

She eventually walked away from the window and lay on her firm but surprisingly comfortable bed, rested her head on the less comfortable pillow and drifted off to sleep.

She woke the next morning, groggy after a restless and noisy night. She could hear women shouting to one another until the early hours; some of the languages she understood, French, Spanish and even some basic Arabic. The theme was always the same: How to get back into Britain.

She washed and then ate the supplied breakfast.

A female guard knocked on the door and opened the viewing window. She could see that Petrov was sat on her bed and didn't constitute a threat. She entered the room leaving her colleague standing just outside the door, ready to respond if the need arose.

Petrov looked up at the overly-blonde guard and spoke.

"You can tell your friend that she won't be needed. I'm not here to harm anyone. I have been put here for my own safety. One day someone will come for me and I will leave, until then I can assure you I will never cause you any trouble."

"After reading the report about what you did to Miss Akinyemi I'm glad to hear it Miss Petrov. Actually I'm here to offer you your rights. Do you wish to contact your government, you know, let them know you are safe? I can supply you with a mobile telephone – you can keep it whilst you are here."

"Thank you Officer Taylor but my government are the reason I am here, so no thanks. I would like access to a computer. Is that possible?"

"It is, but not in your room. Anyway, how do you know my name?" The officer enquired, not feeling threatened, just curious.

"Easy. On the wall of the main office there was a list of staff names, one was Julia Taylor. You are wearing a necklace with a J on it. I added up the rest." She smiled. It was a warm and friendly smile but the guard now felt that she was dealing with someone different, capable and possibly trained to a higher standard than her own.

As she left she told her colleague to be aware and to exercise caution around the new Bulgarian girl.

"I hear she gave some Liberian bird a real hammering at Yarl's. The daft cow stabbed her with a wooden shank and thought she had the upper hand until Charlie's Angel in there took her apart. She's clever that one, something tells me she's not going to be here long but let's watch her like a hawk."

Cade was a few miles away from the centre and saw the same impressive view as he crested the white cliffs. He couldn't see France as clearly as it was shrouded in cloud.

The locals had a saying. If you could see France it was going to rain, if you couldn't, it already was. Cade should know, he was one, once. It had been a long time but it felt like home.

He reached the roundabout and accelerated the Ford Focus up Military Hill until he reached the visitors car park. He got out and using the driver's window as a mirror straightened his tie before walking the short distance to the main reception where he identified himself to a bleach-blonde guard.

"Morning boss, I'm Julia, I'm in charge of Hythe Wing. How can I help you today?"

"Morning Julia, you can help me by allowing me to speak to Nikolina Petrov."

He said nothing else which allowed the staff to look at each other in an inquisitive way.

"Sergeant Cade, what is so interesting about this woman? She gets stabbed, beats some African girl half to death and gets moved here. Now you show up and I'm getting the feeling that you are not a conventional copper, so…."

"So what? All you need to know is that she's most likely to be coming with me. Whilst I talk to her can you ensure that all of her possessions are organised and ready to go please? Now, if you don't mind can you take me to her, or bring her to me so I can talk?"

"I can but I think you have absolutely no chance of taking her with you. She's being held under the Imm…"

Cade interrupted her: brusque, but not rude. He closed his eyes, twice – it was a way of gaining time and it often threw people, mainly females, off the scent long enough for him to gain the upper hand.

"I am most aware of what Act she is being held under thank you Julia. Just get her for me will you?"

"I will, but not before I have spoken to the Unit Manager." Taylor was a little more defiant now and was enjoying the sparring.

Cade let her walk just far enough away to make her return journey more humiliating.

"Officer Taylor."

She turned on her heels, ready this time.

"This letter is from Jeff Rooker. You might have heard of him? Feel free to read it whilst one of your colleagues collects Miss Petrov."

Cade wasn't one to name-drop but having a letter signed by the Immigration Minister himself somehow added weight to his demands and ensured that the battle of wills was well and truly ended.

"Indeed Mr Cade. Apologies, I will fetch her myself. Tina, can you lend a hand please in case our little Bulgarian friend decides to take us on too?"

Cade smiled nicely and sat in the reception area, accepting a cup of tea from a less hostile member of staff and flicking inattentively through a well-worn copy of *National Geographic*.

An overly-long fifteen minutes later Petrov entered a side room and almost ran to Cade. If nothing else it added to the mystery.

Cade held her at arm's length – it was a deliberate move on his part; partly to retain an air of professionalism but also for his own personal wellbeing. He caught the guards exchanging knowing looks but at that moment had more concern for his prisoner.

"You look good Miss Petrov."

Cade offered the line somewhat unconvincingly.

"And so do you Sergeant Cade. I knew you would come to get me out of here. It is what kept me alive. Tell me, the girl who attacked me, is she OK? I had to do it Jack"

Cade smiled "Typical, assassin with a conscience; always make sure that your victims are looked after. Come on, I've got a warm car outside and a safe place to take you to. I'll grab your stuff, you sign for it."

She did as instructed, thanked the staff and walked with Cade, through the security screening area and out into the fresh air.

Cade plipped the remote and opened the doors on the Focus. He put Petrov's case into the boot and opened the passenger door; ever the gent.

He knew the staff were watching on the camera and for the hell of it wanted to give her a playful tap on the backside but thought better of it. Instead he chose to look up and give a quick American-style salute before getting in and turning the ignition on.

The Bulgarian spoke first.

"Jack, I don't know what to say, other than thank you. I know you believe in me. I know we can help each other, I know…"

"I know, you know. Look for now just trust me OK? From here we head to London. I'm not sure why but my bosses believe in you too and I've been seconded to a unit with the Metropolitan Police; between us we want to see if we can use your information to get on top of a growing crime problem."

"On top of? Like a man on top of a woman?" she asked playfully.

"Yes, if you like." He replied distantly whilst concentrating on merging into traffic along Snargate Street. Ten minutes later the Focus was up on top of the white cliffs once more and heading along the A2 towards Canterbury and London.

Cade has chosen a different route back, partly out of paranoia and mainly because he fancied a change of scenery.

By the time they had passed Canterbury, its exquisite cathedral nestling in the vale to his right, Petrov was fast asleep.

Cade took his eye off the road for a second to look at her.

"Christ, you are even attractive when you are asleep girl."

He found Radio 2 on the hi-fi and pressed on towards the capital.

Twenty minutes later the Focus crossed the broad expanse of the River Medway and climbed a steady hill before descending onto one of the busiest interchanges in the country where the M2 and M20 motorways merged.

Cade swiftly negotiated the roundabout and avoided the rush to get towards the Dartford Tunnel and Thames Crossing, choosing instead to continue along Watling Street, one of many old Roman roads heading to London.

She was awake now and chatting.

"You should have woken me. I wanted to see the history. I love history Jack."

She stretched out in the seat tightening her already-snug jeans, pushed her arms above her head and yawned. In doing so she snapped one of the paper stitches from her shoulder. It acted as a reminder that this was not a holiday.

Cade spotted the blood stain and offered to stop.

"No we must carry on. I will be OK. But Jack I do have one question."

"Fire away but if it's top secret I will have to kill you." The veiled humour was lost on his guest so he had to explain which took up another five minutes. Eventually he was able to answer her question.

"We are heading to the spiritual home of the Metropolitan Police at Scotland Yard. I have an appointment with a man called Jason who is going to help me, help you actually. Between us we are going to put together a plan to hunt down your illustrious Jackdaw and have him stuffed."

Once again Cade's use of English threw an otherwise linguistically-gifted Petrov. Another explanation followed which saw the duo miss the grassy expanse of Blackheath altogether.

She pointed at a sign and in her broadest Bulgarian said "Green Which – the home of the time, no?"

Once more she made him laugh out loud as he tried to explain the complexities of a complicated language to a woman who knew five fluently.

"Erm, no it's pronounced Grenitch – but yes, you could say it is the home of time. It has a fascinating maritime history too."

He was about to offer an insight into the traditions of the British navy when they entered the Old Kent Road.

"Monopoly!" shouted an excited almost schoolgirl-like Petrov.

"Yes, but you cannot collect your two hundred pounds as I used my Get out of Jail free card on you earlier!" Cade thought it was a perfectly-delivered game-based comment but she just shrugged and carried on looking out of the window.

He realised just how much history there was in London and having her on board simply added to the occasion. He was growing to enjoy her company. As he negotiated Westminster Bridge he found himself wishing it was a holiday and that they could get to know each other better.

It was becoming like a tour of London's most iconic landmarks as they drifted slowly by the Palace of Westminster.

"Big Ben!" she exclaimed.

He just nodded and tried to point out a few other highlights. Choosing this way to get to the Yard had been a success. She was relaxed now, singing to a familiar track on the radio by the *Eagles* and pointing at building after building.

They were both distracted further when Cade pointed out Westminster Abbey on their left.

"That is a very famous building, many kings and queens have been buried there, famous people too, it's where Diana and Charles got…"

Cade had relaxed and taken his eye off the ball for a split second.

His day was about to change.

Chapter Twenty Four

At the junction of Broad Sanctuary and Great Smith Street a white car screeched to a halt in front of them causing Cade to instinctively ram his left foot onto the brake pedal – the force of using the left foot brought the car to an abrupt halt.

Behind him a white van stopped instantly, its tyres protesting on the road surface.

To the uninitiated Cade had just avoided a crash with another tourist and the van had almost become an unwitting casualty. Cade knew different and placed the Focus in first ready to ram the white car which had now transformed from a bright white blur into a Vauxhall Vectra.

He looked straight at the driver, a swarthy black haired individual with hateful eyes and a stereotypical sneer. The passenger could easily have been his fraternal twin. Unable to take his eyes off them he ignored the number plate and cursed himself for his lack of street skills.

He glanced in the driver's door mirror and found himself looking at another set of malevolent eyes. The driver was wearing a simple white T shirt which did little to disguise his physique.

This was no accident. Cade knew it and now so did Petrov.

"Jack, go, go, go…drive. Get out of here!" She yelled, thumping the dashboard as if to offer extra momentum.

He had less than a metre to negotiate the front of the Vectra. The Focus obeyed his instructions as its tyres chirped and announced to the myriad pedestrians that yet another road rage incident has just occurred on London's busy streets.

He accelerated along Abbey Orchard Street before turning across the face of traffic on Victoria Street. The ever-alert bus driver on the 211 to Hammersmith managed to bring his vehicle to a halt and offered a solitary finger in protest. Seconds later the passengers had dusted themselves down, begun to ignore one another again and life in the metropolis continued.

Cade was hyper-alert now, looking ahead he saw the van once more. It was being driven at such a pace that he knew that it wasn't just another vehicle. It and its cargo were there for a reason and his best guess was that the reason was a red-headed Eastern European female.

In his rear view mirror he saw the Vectra trying to get beyond the bus, however its driver had now had enough excitement for one day and simply used its impressive, bright red bulk to keep the car at bay.

Without indicating Cade screeched into Dean Farrar Street, changed into third and hammered the car the short distance to the rear gates of Scotland Yard.

He had his hand firmly on the horn now and was waving his warrant card at the civilian gate guard who approached him cautiously, one hand on his radio microphone the other fumbling for his Browning Hi-Power but finding only a belt. His former role as a military police officer had caused the muscle memory reaction, either way he could smell trouble at fifty paces and this car spelled trouble with a capital F.

Cade, sensing that he was probably about to be shot yelled to the guard that he needed to see Jason Roberts and that the vehicles that were pursuing him needed to be stopped by a local police unit.

An armed unit had now arrived and having challenged Cade and his passenger were firmly in control. He obeyed their every instruction and prompted a confident but wary Petrov to do the same.

"Do as they say and you will be fine."

He then looked up at the Armed Response Officer who was staring back over the sights of his MP5.

"Guys we are not a threat, I need to see Jason Roberts. Tell him Jack Cade is here. Please."

As he waited for their response he looked carefully around, the two vehicles had gone, blending back into the busy traffic flow and disappearing.

If they had belonged to The Jackdaw then they had achieved their goal: Cause chaos, upset the enemy and make a point. A point delivered in broad daylight in front of a few hundred sightseers. They were bold and therefore dangerous.

Petrov hissed at Cade "Those men Jack, they were here to kill me. You too. They will not be scared of you. You said I would be safe. You promised."

He had. It was a lesson that he needed to learn from. Either that or pay the ultimate price. As a shaft of sunlight shone into his face he found himself reverting back to the preceding week. What he had got himself involved in here?

His daydream was interrupted by a booming local accent.

"Cade? Is that you? Christ boy they said you would make an impression but this is taking the piss old son. OK boys lower your weapons, I know how poor at shooting you both are and I really value my arse."

The voice belonged to Detective Sergeant Jason Roberts.

Roberts swaggered over to the car, ducked under the security barrier and stood up, swept his blond hair back out his eyes and recovered his Jaffa orange tie back into place. Cade noticed that the knot was at least as big as a man's fist. In fact a few members of Roberts' team were watching and they too had the same style of clothing. It was obviously a London Thing.

"Cade?" asked Roberts.

"I sincerely hope so or you have just risked having your arse blown off," replied a now-relaxing Cade.

"Nice one. Nice one indeed, a northerner with a sense of humour. Who'd have thought it?" They shook hands briskly.

"Actually Jason I was born in Royal Tunbridge Wells."

"Were you now, were you indeed? Now, forgetting all that, who do you support?"

Petrov just stared, open-mouthed, taking in the situation and slowly recovering from the earlier incident.

"Leeds United" replied Cade.

"Leeds Bloody-United. Dirty bastards Leeds. Do me a favour, you really expect to get help here? This is Chelsea territory my son."

He closed in to whisper to Cade.

"Although between you and me I support Celtic as I'm part Scottish, I'm more Jockney than Cockney, but for Christ's sake don't tell this lot or they'll have my balls for a wallet."

He turned to Petrov smiling.

"Kazvam se Jason my love, dobri doshli v London."

He had even impressed himself with his rudimentary Bulgarian which he had been learning for at least an hour.

She smiled which lit up the courtyard more than the mid-morning sun.

"Your Bulgarian is excellent Mr Roberts. You must have travelled there many times? Blagodarya vi, che mi pozvolikhte da posetite dnes. Ochakvam s netŭrpenie da vi pomaga."

She had thanked him for allowing her to visit and hoped that they could help each other.

Roberts took the least line of resistance and replied as only a true Englishman could.

"Lovely jubbly my dear. Right, who's for a Rosie Lee?"

Cade turned to Petrov.

"It's English for a cup of tea."

She replied "I thought that was a cup of tea?"

"It is, look, it's...complicated. People from London use two or three words to describe one, it's called Cockney and even I don't understand it."

Cade asked if he could park up the car as the 'Yard' once more returned to normal. He was directed to a visitor's bay in a far corner. He parked up and joined Roberts who was now teaching Petrov some classic Cockney rhyming slang. It was his way of calming her down after her recent exploits.

"Right my love, straight up the apples for you and we'll get the heavy metal on and get that Rosie underway."

She giggled and replied "Are you riding a giraffe with me Mr Roberts?"

It was clear that she too was having difficulty with a new language. But as with everything, she tried.

She walked up the stairs on her own as Roberts and Cade talked.

"Jack, what happened back there? We picked you up on camera as you came down Broad Sanctuary. We were about to deploy a team when you nearly came through the gate. Your motor pinged on the ANPR. Who are these people?"

"I'm still learning Jason" replied Cade "I'm pretty glad you had the number plate recognition software loaded with my registration though. Another five minutes away from here and I think the situation would have been a little different."

"You think? Things are rapidly changing Jack; we were talking to one of our units in the next Borough yesterday. They found the body of a young male in a factory doorway. Possible Eastern European. His throat had been cut, brutal stuff, it's been put down as a robbery but I'm not sure. If you fancy it later we can house your bird and go and take a butcher's at his body?"

"Jason, I can think of nothing finer to do. For the record she's not my 'bird'. I've been assigned to get her here and look after her whilst we work on Operation Breaker. I'm hoping you've got somewhere safe to house her?"

"Naturally my son. She can stay with one of our team. I tell you what I don't know how you keep your 'ands off her, she's a right belter. Stunning little body and those eyes...and that hair! And that arse? Jesus."

"Alright mate, calm down. Right, let's get this tea drunk and we can go and have a look at this body you are so desperate for me to see."

"Sorted my son!" Roberts vigorously clicked his thumb and ring finger together; he'd seen the local black guys do it and had spent weeks perfecting the action.

"Right come on let's get on with it. By the way, are you staying locally or do you need a room?"

"I was hoping to stay with her actually. I swore I wouldn't let her out of my sight."

"I bet you did you old dog" mocked Roberts, punching Cade on the arm.

Cade finished his overly-milky tea and went to talk to Petrov who was sat next to a female officer.

Roberts joined them.

"Good to see you getting along ladies. Jack this is Cynthia Bell one of our Analysts. Cracking girl, she's a real whizz with facial recognition stuff. She's going to spend a few hours running Miss Petrov through our directory of faces, see if she recognises any of them. You OK with that?"

Cade was more than happy. She was safe and she was in her element. For now, somehow she had forgotten her injuries and the recent event. Cade was looking at the screen when he heard a strident commotion.

Roberts' incessant cell phone rang again. This time it was the mortuary explaining that due to a small fire the body couldn't be viewed until the morning. Roberts was about to communicate the message to Cade when they became aware of a commotion nearby.

"I don't give a rat's arse if you are a Chief Inspector, touch me again and I'll throw you through the fucking window. What is it with you CID boys? You think everything is at your beck and call don't you? Well touch my backside again and you'll wake up with your balls in your mouth."

The female pushed the overweight and grey-suited male backwards with a flattened palm and stormed into the canteen where she noisily selected a mug and started angrily making herself a strong 'builders' tea.

The anonymous Chief Inspector made good his escape, fearing for his thirty year marriage and his twenty year pension and hoped that the little lady would simply forget all about it.

A few of the younger Detectives on the Major Crime Unit were laughing now causing the female to enter the main office once more. She selected the youngest, a prematurely bald officer only three years out of training school. Grabbing his face in her right hand she squeezed his cheeks until he felt like his back teeth were about to explode.

"Find it funny do you kid? I've had more arrests than you've had wet dreams darling and trust me if you laugh at me again I'll ram my fist so far up your arse you'll think you are the unpaid partner in a ventriloquist act. Do I make myself clear?"

He nodded, desperately trying to shake her hand from his ruddy cheeks.

She looked around, scanning the room, checking for anyone else that found it humorous that a boss had just indecently assaulted her. Seeing that no-one was brave enough to take her on she strutted back towards her desk.

As she approached her place in the office she brushed by Cade and Roberts.

Roberts cleared his throat, clearly aware of the potential of saying something wrong to an already volatile individual. He almost looked scared of her.

Cade put her at thirty, possibly younger. She had very short chestnut coloured hair which was supplemented by a very subtle hint of burgundy.

Her eyebrows were preened but not overly so, they arched gracefully, framing her eyes which were quite spectacular, brighter than anything he had ever seen, slate grey and blue in colour they were the window to her very soul and Cade formed the opinion that it was possibly a damaged spirit that lay deep within.

Her nose was small and ever-so-slightly bent, the legacy of a fight with a drunk at Shepherds Bush, the beat where she had carried out her formative years as a police woman.

She had quickly become one of the boys; with an ear for good intelligence and a flair for getting in the face of criminals she had swiftly earned a reputation as a gritty and brave fighter – the many faded commendations that now sat in a dilapidated cardboard box in her loft bore testament to this.

She had an almost imperceptible scar on her face running from her left eye down to her jaw line. It was too soon to ask but Cade made a mental note, when things had improved, to ask how it had got there.

Her lips were pursed and slightly twisted to the left as if she was chewing the inside of her own cheek. She was.

She had a good figure, possibly not as trim as she was when she left training school but she still looked fit enough to be eye-catching. Her breasts were almost perfectly shaped, large but not overpoweringly so.

Her upper body was very much in proportion with her lower half and she held herself impeccably upright, an almost perfect posture, the upshot of a broken back sustained in a hideous car crash a few years prior.

Her hands were more delicate than he had expected, almost those of a piano player, the skin was soft-looking and the nails immaculately manicured. She wore no rings and her recent suntan supported the fact that she was most likely to be unmarried.

A small and much-loved Casio G Shock watch sat on her left wrist, another legacy from the past.

Cade wasn't sure why but he found her deeply attractive. She wasn't pretty in the classic way, the way in which most men found women pretty, but she had a certain allure, a draw, as a spring tide draws the countless grains of sand away from a beach she began to rein him in and he simply didn't understand why.

She certainly wasn't his type, but then his type had ended up naked in a swimming pool with Grant Bastard Cooke and his band of merry swingers.

It was an odd feeling. Nikolina *was* attractive, very pretty in fact and the subject of many male fantasies. In truth he had been the envy of the station when he had arrested her only days before, but this girl was unusual, powerful almost, yet somehow needing a caring shoulder to lean on.

Jesus, as if he didn't have enough to contend with.

He blinked his eyes and brought himself back to earth. Whatever her appeal was he was unlikely to get within an inch of her anyway, given her alleged dislike of the male species. Perhaps she was disinterested in males too?

Roberts broke the silence.

"Jack my old son, this is Carrie O'Shea. Carrie is ex-job, long story and all that, anyway, these days she's far brighter, one of my best Analysts in fact. She can do things with an Excel spreadsheet that would make a quadriplegic come in his pants."

Cade shook his head. Jesus where did Roberts get them from?

Petrov simply smiled and carried on pointing at the computer screen.

Cade held out his hand and introduced himself to O'Shea.

"Carrie, I'm Jack, nice to meet you." His hand hovered awkwardly in the air for a few moments until he tried again.

"I'm Jack Cade, from East Midlands Airport, I hear you can do great things with software, I'd like to get to know a lot more about you. I think we can work well together; we may have a common bond. Would that be possible Carrie?"

She drank from an unforeseen Postman Pat mug, swallowed the hot tea and looked up.

What she saw was not what she expected. He had been described as a Sergeant so she surmised that he would be a Detective. But he wasn't, the business card that he had slid onto her desk just said Sergeant – Intelligence Manager.

His voice gave her cause to think that he was older, possibly in his fifties, but again, she was wrong. His rank and his role assured her that he would be as arrogant as all of the other bastards in her office but when she fixed her eyes onto his she knew that for the first time since her early teenage years she had found someone whom she could trust.

She connected with him there, and then.

His eyes were intensely blue, but warm; again it was completely contradictory to her foolish assumptions. His hand was equally warm, smooth but not soft, he wasn't afraid of hard work but he looked after himself.

Try as she might she found herself humming the baseline to the Paul Carrack song for the rest of the morning, and dwelling on one line.

'Tell me, how does it feel, behind those eyes of blue?'

Most of the team considered her a lesbian or at best bi-curious.

So what if she'd had 'that moment' with her brother's girlfriend all those summers ago? She was the victim after all, although she had learned a lot more about herself on that remote river bank than at any time since. It was a passing if intimate phase and yes, if she was honest she had enjoyed it, she certainly hadn't found a man since who could make her feel quite so aroused.

In truth she was blatantly heterosexual, always immaculately dressed and always, always compulsive about things that she did.

If she put fuel in her car the numbers always had to total an amount plus sixty nine. She wasn't sure when it had started or why but she liked to hear the attendant mention the figure when she finally got to pay. It amused and aroused her.

If she ironed her clothes the creases had to be 'just so', anything else would not do; the legacy of spending time at Hendon Police College and the consequence of having a famous father in the job.

If her hair didn't sit 'just right' she would wash it again until it did.

If she was ever lucky enough to have sex it would have to run in a pattern culminating in a certain position. If her partner was unwilling to let her take control – and most were – then she would literally disengage and never see him again.

It happened with Clive Wood, a middle-aged Detective who had been on the team for over ten years. One Christmas the inevitable had happened, she had drunk far too much at the office Christmas party and in truth Wood knew this.

He'd taken advantage of her; in fact he had made a bet with some of his peers that he would do just that. However as she had sobered up she took the reins once more, athletically and breathlessly undressing him.

It had been, up unto a point, a night to remember for the heavily married but rather overweight and desperately hirsute Welshman.

Outside The Yard the city was still heading hurriedly towards the festivities as he noisily turned her over face-down onto his cluttered desk.

He then opened the blinds so that they could both see out onto the street before he continued his vain attempts at seduction.

Her partially-naked body was easily the more attractive of the two; the myriad sodium street lights provided them both with a sultry orange tan, however despite her desirable figure and the erotic situation he failed in his quest to seduce her, alcohol doing its part in preventing him from keeping up his side of the bargain.

She soon resisted, dragging him onto the office floor and rapidly moved herself into her favourite position. Unexpectedly he didn't like it. In fact he protested so much that she simply climbed off him, pulled her knickers back on, dressed, switched on the office lights and dumped his garments in the lift.

She took the stairs as it gave her more time to enjoy the fact that he would have been naked and scrambling for cover whilst his sweaty clothes were bound for the main reception.

She reached the ground floor, waited for the lift to announce its arrival, propped open the door, said goodbye to the night security team, left the building and began the walk home.

She caught a glimpse of herself in a brightly-lit shop window; the tears of anger had reddened her eyes causing the pupils to subtly change colour from grey to green. It only ever happened when she was angry and occasionally when she was aroused. The latter had not happened for a very long time.

Wood made it to the floor below, running for his life to avoid the close-circuit television. He entered the changing room and found some old uniform items in his locker.

Pulling them on and struggling to do up the buttons he found himself thinking that he didn't know what was worse: being found late at night naked in Scotland Yard or being found in the Kingdom of the Detective – whilst wearing Plod's uniform?

From that moment Wood detested her and took every opportunity to perpetuate the myth that she was an ice-cold lesbian.

"She'd have to be to turn down Clive "Ivor" Wood" he had said to anyone prepared to listen.

A few days later between Christmas and New Year's Eve the unusually quiet office was home to Wood and O'Shea; everyone else had taken time off with their families.

After three long hours Wood had managed to avoid her gaze – and she, his. However she had spent a few satisfying minutes in the stationery cupboard selecting some new highlighter pens and a Staedtler 6H pencil – the hardest graphite compound on the market. It was the one with the red and black barrel; very traditional, O'Shea was also a strict traditionalist at heart and this design reminded her of her happier school days.

She took just one of the writing instruments, even though she had the opportunity to take the whole box, then after locking the cupboard she walked inaudibly back to her desk. Just as she had sat down he made the mistake of looking at her.

In her anger she snapped the new bonded lead on the desktop, then slowly, efficiently placed it into the aperture of her motorised sharpener until it appeared once more, pointed, unsullied and resembling a factory-fresh model.

She stood, adjusted her neat pleated skirt and straightened her blouse so it was 'just so' and walked directly towards Wood's desk.

He looked again. Here she came. For all intents and purposes she resembled a school teacher from the early Fifties; altogether very prim and quite proper.

Conversely, underneath her rather staid clothes lay a pair of very ornate blue silk knickers and an equally lacy bra that made the very most of her figure. She considered it essential to look her best in any situation and besides her mother always told her to wear clean underwear in case she got run over by a bus. It always made her smile, but she did as she was told, if only to arouse the Doctor who subsequently undressed her.

Stereotypically he pretended to pick up the phone and make a call but O'Shea was a few steps ahead of him. Seeing his left hand sat on the desk she took the chance to ram the sharpened point of her favourite pencil directly into the web between his thumb and his forefinger causing the lead to once more disintegrate.

She then twisted the point slowly, purposely; a chess player would have likened the move to that of the great Russian Master Vasily Smyslov – who deliberately twisted the end of a chess piece in order to gain a psychological advantage over his opponent.

His scream could be heard throughout the floor but they were alone. There were no witnesses and whilst the damage was intensely painful she knew he wouldn't need an ambulance and furthermore she also knew he didn't have the courage to make a complaint.

It was what she considered to be an 'understanding', a way of forever righting a wrong. And for now at least they were equal.

She smiled as she ground the lead into his thumb and spoke quietly into his left ear.

"You wanted something, you got it. I wanted something in return, now I've got it. In Latin it is called quid pro quo but you being Welsh I doubt you'd understand boyo."

She kissed him sardonically on the forehead as she twisted the weapon out of his hand and slowly wiped the blood onto his faded shirt sleeve. She then walked back to her desk and re-sharpened the pencil to remove any trace of blood and skin.

Any sense of revenge on Wood's part was forever absent; he simply didn't have the courage to take her on. However, it affected her greatly.

For a very short time she had found herself back in that cold, desolate and falsely-seasonal office, she felt as if she were gripping the barrel of her favourite pencil, ready to strike once more, but then looked up and realised that she was still holding Cade's hand. The glance had become a stare and it was now uncomfortable, she let go and spoke.

"Sergeant Cade. I'm sure you can find plenty of people in here that can help. I'm rather busy. It's been lovely."

With that she looked back down at her paperwork and acted out some note taking.

Cade wasn't buying into her sarcasm-laden act – Roberts had convinced him that she was the Analyst he needed – being ex-job gave her the edge and truth be told he quite liked her 'attitude'.

Sensing the importance the Home Office had put upon his project and the need to set some boundaries he replied.

"Correction Miss O'Shea. You *were* busy. Now, you are *much* busier. I'll see you in the morning at eight thirty. There's a café across the road. I'll buy you breakfast. We have a lot to talk about." Cade started to walk away.

She stood, causing a few in the office to sit up and pay attention.

Clive Wood nudged his partner and whilst involuntarily rubbing the circular, dark red scar on his left hand said in a thick accent "Oh, here we go again, hide the stationery, I don't think much to his chances boyo. If she grabs her pencil make a run for the fire escape!"

O'Shea stood with her manicured hands on her hips, ignored the Welshman and offered a belligerent challenge.

"What if I don't make it Sergeant?"

Cade smiled, continued walking without turning around and said, "You will."

Chapter Twenty Five

It was early morning and Cade was at the office before Roberts. He was a creature of habit and took the unoccupied twenty minutes to talk to a few of the team who seemed to warm to him and his passion for Eastern Europe.

"The fing is boss, we ain't seen none of that there Euro stuff around 'ere yet. This is Met ground, our manor. Do you really reckon it'll kick off here, right in the 'eart o' London? I mean, really? It all sounds a bit pony to me."

Cade's father had spent years in the Prison Service, rising slowly through the ranks and eventually gaining a reputation as a hard but fair bastard. He spent a lot of time with prisoners, both black and white and when he wasn't talking in a pseudo-Caribbean accent it was faux Cockney. As a result there was a rarely a normal sentence in the Cade household and as a consequence he could talk rhyming slang with the best of them.

"You think I'm 'aving a giraffe? Fillin' you with a load of old pony? Trust me on this one. Yer plates are on the end of your Scotches for a reason old son, perhaps you should use 'em to get out there and find out what's going on under your bugle!"

The office went quiet for a moment as one or two of the staff tried to translate what he had just said.

Roberts chose that moment to spring into the office.

"Morning all! Kettle on? Lovely – mine's the usual black, no sugar and bring me a chocolate Digestive. I see Sergeant Cade is learning the lingo. For those of you that require a little of the old local translation he was saying get out on your bloody feet and find out what's going on under your noses! Well go on then piss off the lot of you!"

He turned to Cade.

"Bloody 'ell, the Met's not what it was Jackie lad – half of 'em aren't even from London anymore. It comes to something when a bleedin' Northerner knows more than half of my team."

"I thought you said you were a Jockney?" Cade countered.

"Yes, I did. I did, didn't I? Anyway, that'll be our little secret unless you want my size ten up your Arris!"

Cade knew exactly what he meant and as he whistled *O Flower of Scotland* he looked at Roberts, pointed to the door with his thumb and said "We ready Jason? Let's go and look at this body shall we?"

They travelled off the area to the public morgue at Camden. Whilst the Met could and would go anywhere in the Capital they were fiercely protective of their own Boroughs. Given Cade's current mandate Roberts knew he could go wherever he wanted.

"As you can see Jack, a typical street robbery victim for this part of the world, he's got reasonable dress sense, nice shoes, swarthy, probably Albanian, most likely he's done the dirty on his dealer or stepped onto someone's manor without knowing."

Cade took a while to scan the naked body which now lay on the clinical stainless steel bench. The male that lay before him was now just a shell of a former life with pallid skin and dark, heavily pooled blood in his back and hips and was at best probably in his early twenties. Even in death he appeared to have a scornful look upon his lifeless face.

Cade looked up at Benjamin Mortimer, the local Mortuary Technician. He smiled at the irony of his surname and then asked a question.

"Do you mind?"

Mortimer replied casually as he munched on a sandwich "No, of course, be my guest. He's been dead for about twelve hours by the way – you can see the liver mortis clearly just here."

He moved the body reverently but scientifically explained his every movement, clearly passionate about his job.

"I believe this young man was moved after his initial death but you'll need your experts to confirm this for you. He was found face down but the pooling is in his back. Fascinating isn't it? But I guess you two gents know all of this?"

He carried on moving the body with one hand whilst he consumed the food with the other.

"Livor mortis starts approximately twenty minutes to three hours after death and is congealed in the capillaries in around four to five hours. You can appreciate how those little rascally myosin heads continue binding with the active sites of actin proteins and how the muscle is unable to relax until further enzyme activity…"

Roberts held up his hand.

"Chief, that's all well and good my old China but what killed him?"

Mortimer laughed out aloud and pointed to his neck.

"Well I'm not prepared to stake what's left of my tattered career on this Detective Sergeant but at a guess I'd say the three inch hole on this side of his neck!"

"Cheers. Nice one. Eloquently put Doc thanks" replied a slightly awkward Roberts.

"Oh I'm no Doctor Mr Roberts, just the man who gives the dearly departed a loving home for a short while."

He looked at Cade who was now busy examining the body.

"A man after my own heart, bloody brilliant the human body isn't it? What have you spotted?"

Cade nodded to the right wrist he was holding in his latex-covered hand and said "This. Look Jason, you'll be seeing a few more of these soon."

Roberts got closer and saw a small blue tattoo. He looked back up at Cade and spoke.

"And?"

"And it's the mark of Primul Val."

"Who's that? Some bird that works down at the all-night supermarket?"

"No sadly not, it's not short for Valerie, it's Romanian and it means The First Wave. This young man is not Albanian, he's Romanian and that worries me."

"Hey mate, one less criminal as far as I'm concerned" replied an indolent Roberts.

"I understand Jason, but why this concerns me is that he's either been killed by the opposition – of which we know nothing about – in fact we didn't even think there was one – or, perhaps more interestingly, he's been killed by his own. Now that is attention-grabbing."

The light went on in Roberts' head. "I get it old son, I get it."

Cade snapped a few images of the deceased's face and the tattoo, which stood out defiantly, a deep blue on the ashen skin.

Both men thanked Mortimer, asked him to secure the body and left the chilled room, taking a lung-full of fresh air as they re-entered the world of the living.

"Never get that bloody smell out of your nostrils can you Jack?"

"No. But I bet you remember your first as much as I do?"

"I do mate – prostitute. I was searching the body for marks of violence, drug marks, weapons you know the sort of stuff. Anyway as I lifted her dress up I found she had a nine inch penis. As you say, you never forget your first!"

Cade tried desperately not to laugh, he was a guest after all but it was apparent that Roberts had a lively sense of humour. They would get along very well indeed.

"I remember mine as if it were yesterday Jason. I was very young in service and ended up going down to the local morgue with an older Constable. He said he had a great way of me embedding with the team. So, being new and keen to impress I said yes."

"Go on mate, I'm all ears" replied Roberts who felt he had heard them all but was conscious of being a good host.

"Well the older bobby got me to lie on a steel body tray and covered me with a light blue hospital sheet. As he was sliding me back into the fridge he gave me my briefing. He said 'you lay there for about five minutes and then one of the other new lads will come in to inspect you. He'll open the drawer and as he moves your sheet you can sit up and make a ghost noise – it'll be absolutely hilarious'.

"Christ I bet the poor bugger nearly shat 'imself?"

"No, he didn't. You see I lay there in that dark chilled locker for about seven minutes, I know because I counted every bloody second. The place was dead quiet, still, eerie. Anyway all of a sudden from the tray above me a cold clammy hand landed on my face and an unseen voice said 'fucking cold in here isn't it kid?' – Apparently the gathered masses of Four Section found it hysterically funny when my head struck the tray above me. In my abject panic attack I'd hit it so hard I ended up in accident and emergency. Happy days indeed! Bastards."

"Christ what a laugh. I wish we could still do such things. The job has changed me old mucker, the job has changed."

"You're right, and on that rather depressing note I have a breakfast date with your somewhat feisty analyst," said Cade as Roberts turned the key on the Mondeo and headed back to base.

They were sat in rush hour traffic so Roberts decided to brief Cade on O'Shea.

"There's more to her than meets the eye Jackie lad. She was a great street cop who sadly met her demise in unfortunate circumstances. Nasty job-related crash nearly killed her too. The twat that was driving should have known better, reckoned he was the next Nigel Mansell but he came unstuck when he put the car into a bend that he simply didn't have the skill to negotiate. Any road the job closed ranks on her, poor bugger. She got a pension and a small pay out but justice was never seen to be done."

"Not good. I know how the job can close ranks – it's brilliant when the chips are down but it can be a brotherhood when it wants to be."

Cade thought for a while about the events of his own demise – or at least the end of his marriage and how the job, or at least some of its key members had seen to that. Then, equally, he thought of Tom Jackson and how he had saved him, if nothing else, from a prison sentence.

Roberts' cell phone rang and broke the temporary silence.

"Yep, why not, we are in the area, might be connected."

Cade looked at his new partner inquisitively.

"Might be something or nothing Jack; a local branch of Barclays Bank has reported a problem with one of their ATM's. We have started to see a few of these jobs and we've had some source info suggesting it's Romanians doing it. Someone is tampering with the outsides, putting something onto the machine perhaps. Could be connected to your team? We aren't seeing a lot of issues with bank machines at the moment. Fancy a run down there?"

"Yep, sounds good. At this stage I have no idea what the group are capable of Jason. It seems that they are the full spectrum…lower-level bank machine jobs, online fraud right up to inter-governmental document scams and lines of credit enough to make a Rothschild look like a pauper. Should we pass a message to O'Shea given that we'll be late?"

"Jack, you are a Sergeant, she's an Analyst. Lovely girl and all that but she can wait. "

"Fair enough. You were the one who said she had a temper."

They drove to Artillery Row, a few minutes from the Yard. Roberts pulled up outside, placed a card in the window of the Mondeo and they walked into the branch. It was eight thirty.

A disinterested bank employee showed them the targeted machine. She pointed it out and stood gazing down the street already longing for home time picking a piece of skin off her thumb that had been annoying her for days.

Roberts looked at her and said "Black please my love, no sugar and my good friend Sergeant Cade will have a Rosie Lee, no sugar."

The brunette tutted, turned and walked inside; whether she would return with the ordered beverage was completely unknown.

"Doesn't look like much Jack, typical amateur effort once more. We've had a lot of these scratch marks but never anything tangible. I despise amateurs mate, give me a real crook anytime."

Cade looked up and down the street, to the floor and then upwards to the roof, constantly scanning for the unseen. He paused then took a deep breath and spoke.

"Jason, I suspect that you have one or more real crooks working right under your nose. We are ten minutes away from Scotland Yard and someone has been stealing money in broad daylight, or they will be soon."

Roberts scratched his head.

"I'm not with you mate, the bank said that no money is missing and they've had no complaints from customers. End of."

Cade smiled and continued "No Jase, start of. Start of."

Roberts was now intrigued but getting frustrated, the thought of someone criminally 'taking the piss' on his parish was not appreciated.

"Go on…enlighten me do," said a defeated Roberts.

Cade rubbed his hands together, pursed his lips and began.

"It's like this my friend; this ATM is a busy one, but mainly during the day, so as such it's vulnerable. The scratch marks are indicators of attack, by that I mean that someone has placed a device in or on this machine, most likely at night; they leave it there the next day and then come back the following night."

"A device, what like a bomb?"

"No, thank God. I think it's something like a grabber, a simple piece of kit often referred to as a Lebanese Loop. It grabs the card as it is dropped into the dispenser. The customer doesn't get their cash, hears the card being retained and then enters the branch to complain. Then the offenders return, place a slim metal plate into the slot and recover the card, the device and the cash. Sometimes it's a ten, perhaps a twenty, if the offender strikes gold it's a fifty, either way it's free and as the victim is unlikely to be charged they often don't report it, either because they can't be bothered or can't because the branch is closed."

"But it's hardly Ronnie Biggs territory is it Jack, I mean a twenty at best, a day. Do me a favour you'd make more money robbing someone or busking!"

Cade licked his right index finger and held it up to the breeze.

"You are right, but the wind is changing. The Met, along with most forces, are concentrating on robbery, mainly the theft of cell phones, but cash too; am I right?"

"On the nose mate. But still, twenty quid, is it really worth it?"

"Think broader Sergeant, start multiplying things a bit. Let's count how many bank ATM's there are within a square mile of the Yard."

"Jack I haven't got a bloody clue and I doubt you have either."

"Actually Jason it's fifty. Another fifty in Belgravia and another in Pimlico, shall I continue?"

Roberts got the point.

"I get the point Jack and I guess we aren't exactly looking at an area where the occupants would miss twenty sov's are we?"

"Indeed. The biggest pain in the arse is the loss of the bank card. But imagine it though Jason, fifty machines here, fifty there – you'd only have to be lucky five times a day in each area. We have to be lucky all the time. At worst our offender is earning two hundred pounds a day. Moving around in that patch, changing people, changing cars, it all means they are unlikely to get spotted. Multiply that across London and…"

"Shit on a stick!"

"I couldn't have put it better myself Jason. But as they say, 'wait, there's more'."

"Do go on my friend," Roberts offered in an encouraging tone.

"I think they are retaining the card for the short win. It's been bugging me all week how the offenders can benefit from this – as you rightly say nicking a twenty pound note is hardly worth it but what if the offenders are working in larger groups, not just men, but women and children too?"

"Christ mate, I like it, keep going."

"What if the women are looking over the shoulder of the victim when they enter the PIN number?"

Roberts paused, thought about asking a great question but just as he did in his schooldays he paused too long and regretted it when Cade continued surmising out aloud.

"They then wait for the victim to leave, recover the card with the PIN number and head to another bank and withdraw the daily allowance. Now…"

Roberts was quicker this time "Now start multiplying that by fifty banks a day Jacko! Fuck me that's a whole lot of money and hardly any risk!"

Cade could see his new partner was now one hundred percent engaged.

"Jason, we should start recording each crime and plot it on a map, looking at trends, hotspots, crime corridors, cross-checking CCTV recordings in the areas, but first we need to get the banks on board, get them to actually admit the money is going. Let's talk to Interpol too, see if they can offer any thoughts on what is happening across Europe, perhaps even further afield."

Although he may as well have been talking Klingon, Cade was right; the banks were already subjected to huge public scrutiny and great disdain. Whilst their CEO's lived like oligarch's the average customer found themselves paying inordinately large rates and charges that they simply had no control over. For the banks to admit they were failing in what appeared to be an area of simple security would have added to their woes.

To the public this was going to be seen as a victimless crime and therefore uninteresting. Somehow they needed to make it attractive; to the banks, the customers and above all an over-burdened police executive.

DS Jason Roberts turned to Cade.

"Jack, do you think our boy at Camden morgue might have made a mistake, possibly let the cat out of the bag and that is why he was killed – rather than being killed by the opposition. If so that does indeed make your team ruthless."

Cade sighed heavily before replying.

"Jason, to a point I'm guessing as much as you are, but having spent a few deeply intense days with Petrov I reckon they are capable of anything. She reckons he beat her repeatedly, sometimes during sex, other times just for fun. He drowned a girl by pushing her into a frozen lake simply because she came second in a fight with Petrov. He made Petrov watch it all. He's a psychopath by all accounts – but a clever one."

Roberts was shaking his head in disgust but now doing what he did best – thinking on his feet.

"Right, sorted Guv! We take it to the banks, possibly even get the media involved, but above all we need to know that people are reporting this, encourage them however we can, then we plot up like you say, start thinking about surveillance, cross-match the top five locations for each area and then we sit on them. I like it." He clicked his fingers together vigorously.

"Good plan, but keep the media out of it for now; the last thing we want is to alert them and give other thieves the heads up. Do you think your bosses will be on board with it, given the other current activities?"

"Absolutely mate. Just let the Crafty Jockney brief them. I'll elaborate slightly, might need your help with this one, but we can make it sound international, all sexy and Bond-like."

Cade nodded "Agreed but let's keep Double Oh Seven out of this shall we? All he would do is carve up half of the City of London, shoot a dozen bad guys and lure Nikolina onto a super yacht where they would make endless love as they sailed off on autopilot into the sunset."

"Jealous?"

Cade replied in a faux Connery-esque voice "Absholutely. Which reminds me, I need to talk to Nikolina today, she might be able to fill in some of the blanks; perhaps we could get O'Shea involved in this?"

He quickly dropped the Scottish accent "Christ, O'Shea, look at the time. Let's get back or she'll never forgive me!"

Chapter Twenty Six

They got back to the office. Roberts went to the early briefing and decided to use the opportunity to engage his team – he'd engage the bosses later, but this was a fresh approach to a new and insidious problem and he knew that with a hint of luck and Cade on his side he had a real chance to put his name firmly on the map and finally make the transition to Detective Inspector.

Cade walked calmly over to Petrov who was already assisting her new-found colleague, discreetly making suggestions on how best to track down a group she knew more about than anyone in the building.

"Good morning, how did you sleep?"

"I slept well Jack Cade, did you miss me?"

"I did Nikolina, I did. How is the shoulder?"

"Good. Better each day. I feel safe now. It helps. I am enjoying being here in the famous Scotland Yard. Who would have thought it, a communist spy in the Lion's Den?"

"Indeed Miss Petrov, best you don't broadcast that from the rooftops though," Cade replied.

She looked puzzled, "I will not be on the rooftops, this is dangerous? No?"

He smiled, another translation error to correct, but it made her the attractive person she was. He decided to let her carry on with her work.

"I'm going to start work with Miss O'Shea Nikolina. You have my number. Ring me if you need anything. And do as they say. I know you are trained to look after yourself but you *never* leave here on your own. Do I make myself clear?"

He did. She liked him even more when he was forthright and dominant.

Roberts joined him and made an announcement asking his team to join him in the Briefing Room.

"Right everyone gather in. Quickly please. Sergeant Cade is going to brief you on what we discovered yesterday. Jack, if you would be so kind?"

"Thank you Jason. OK team I know you are all busy so I'll keep this as brief as I can, but it's important that you all get on board with this. I've spent a very long week in the company of Miss Nikolina Petrov, the young lady sat outside with your Crime Analyst. What she told me during a series of interviews was enough to engage the Home Office and change my career almost overnight. The group she associated with, all the while working undercover for her own government, are street-smart, clever, cunning, computer savvy and bloody ruthless. If you remember nothing else from this briefing, remember that."

He took a moment, checking that all were listening.

"Right, what we are starting to see here in London is a trend. Forget all you know about bank fraud; the days of the chemically washed cheque and the crusty old forger are long gone. This is new, hot off the press and so simple it's ludicrous. But, and it's a big but, this will spread like wildfire across Europe and I suspect the world. Mark my words on this."

People were nodding now, a few even made notes in the back of their pocket books.

"What DS Roberts and I saw yesterday was a device called a 'Lebanese Loop'. In essence it's a metal strip or piece of plastic that is inserted into the ATM's card aperture. They are so easy to construct and equally inexpensive that offenders can leave them in-situ and walk away if they are disturbed."

He drew an example on the nearby white board.

"Look out for these things during Stop and Search procedures please, especially near to ATM machines. OK, imagine our victim walking down Grosvenor Place this morning, he or she was followed by another prospective customer, probably well dressed and apparently 'normal'. This person could have been male or female. The person stands behind them in the queue and discreetly observes the victim inputting their PIN number and making a fund request. Once complete the ATM tries to eject the card but this lip prevents the card from being ejected. The machine senses that the card has not been ejected, and retains the card."

Some of Roberts' staff were now shaking their heads in disbelief at how such a simple system could be utilised almost under their noses.

"The cash drawer does not open; the money is retained by the machine. In most cases the victim's account is not affected. The victim thinks that he or she has been the subject of a genuine bank problem and goes into the branch. Meanwhile Johnny Thief makes off with their card and whatever cash has been dispensed. They then continue to use the card until it is officially reported stolen. My guess is that at the moment we are seeing at the very least a fifty to seventy five percent success rate. I'll leave you to work out why this is suddenly more lucrative and less hazardous than stealing mobile phones. Right any questions?"

He looked around the room and noticed that O'Shea had already left.

His briefing had been thorough and passionate. He fielded a couple of simple questions then walked out of the room and walked a few paces to O'Shea's desk. He decided to be direct with her as it had quickly transpired that any other approach was liable to leave him open to an onslaught.

She looked good this morning, slightly prim, very preened, he thought internally that she was 'like an attractive owl', wise beyond her years but with an undisclosed secret. It made him smile for in reality it was a ridiculous analogy. The warning signs were clear to him: he found her attractive.

He stood at her desk; he was wearing a light grey suit, pale blue shirt and a darker blue tie, classy but understated. His shoes, as ever, were immaculate; the leather uppers glistened as layer upon layer of Parade Gloss created a shine that was worthy of any military establishment.

His horological addition was a silver Seiko Kinetic Direct Drive divers watch. He favoured its looks and the weight suited his wrist, and as a bonus it kept excellent time.

He slid the blue shirt cuff back to reveal the time and pointlessly pressed the crown.

"Miss O'Shea, I feel I am a little late for breakfast, my sincere apologies, something came up, however as the Italians will tell you we are not yet too late for cappuccino. Would you care to join me?"

She placed her favourite pencil into the sharpener and with equal futility sharpened it. It was a similar gesture, designed to give her a moment to compose her response.

"Well Sergeant Cade, I'm neither Italian nor a coffee drinker so your apology is not accepted."

"Is that roight, well in dat case it's a good job we share some Oirish ancestry Miss O'Shea. Perhaps your ladyship would allow me to buy her a cup of English tea instead?"

What she wanted was to tell him to go forth but for the first time since Harry Hodgson had asked her out in the sixth form she felt truly attracted to a male; giggly, almost schoolgirl-silly. And she hated him for it. Her pencil whirred in the housing as she battled with her internal dialogue.

'Damn you Jack Cade with your perfectly-fitting bloody suit, your perfect shiny bloody shoes and those damned eyes. My God I could drown in those damned things.'

She appeared to glaze over so he clicked his fingers. The rapid compression and decompression of air as his finger and thumb rubbed together was enough to bring her back to reality.

"Miss O'Shea – if you are not careful you'll wear that pencil away. Your chariot awaits." He pointed to the lift.

"I'd rather take the stairs."

"Then the stairs it is, after you." He gallantly held the door open, allowed her to walk through then got into the lift.

When she joined him in the public foyer she seemed somewhat displeased.

"Are you an arsehole all the time Mr Cade?"

"Yes, well, most of it anyway Carrie. Look I'm sorry but you challenged me and I won't back down. It's childish I know but honestly I think you are as bad. So, what say we wipe the slate clean and start again, after all I value my thumb and I hear you are a mean shot with the old pencil?"

It was a gamble but it paid off. She laughed out aloud. The reaction even made the Concierge look up, he knew it was O'Shea but he had truly never known anyone that was able to break the sea ice that surrounded her. He nodded to Cade and winked. Cade reciprocated and allowed her through the main doors.

They sat down in the nearby café. Cade ordered a cappuccino, O'Shea an Earl Grey tea.

"Grab some food, please, my treat."

Cade ordered Eggs Benedict, his new partner ordered a three egg omelette, extra bacon and another tea.

"Hungry girl, I like it. Must be the Emerald Isle coming out?"

"Mr Cade, it's got sweet Fanny Adams to do with me being Irish and everything to do with me being hungry, on account of you making me wait and besides, you are paying."

"Touché O'Shea."

"Fuck off Cade."

"That's more like it. Now we can start again. I'm Jack, my dad is Mr Cade. I'm in my later twenties, been in the job for a while and recently after dumping my sex-obsessed swinging wife ended up at East Midlands Airport on secondment, which in truth was an old bosses favour to get me away from an irritating prat of an Inspector. The role was to pick up the incoming intelligence and establish a new unit there. The theory being that like most provincial airports it was vulnerable…"

She was nodding now, apparently interested. Even if she wasn't she knew how to play the game.

"...I'd only been there five minutes when Petrov's aircraft arrived; she got kidnapped by an as yet unidentified Eastern European male, we ended up in a pursuit across half of north Leicestershire with me behind her in a battered Vauxhall Astra at the hands of a sweaty DJ, and to add to the growing paperwork she nearly got shot in the equation. I ended up interviewing her for hours. She was heading for London, she thought it was to start a new life but in fact she was heading for a shallow grave in Epping Forest."

O'Shea almost wanted to make notes, she was captivated.

Their food arrived along with the extra tea. She pointed to the teapot.

"Help yourself."

It was an opening and one he could build on.

"Thank you, I will. As I was saying Petrov came into my life when I least expected it and before you could say, "Get in my office Cade" I had a telephone directory down my trousers and a worried look upon my face. Needless to say I had a great boss – it helps. He saw the potential of what she held close to her chest and the rest as they say is history."

"Have you had a good look at that chest Jack?" She was almost playing with him here.

"No, not yet and I doubt I will either Carrie." First name terms now.

"Tell me you are not interested and I'll pay for breakfast, you're a northern Sergeant so I know how poor you are."

"How kind, actually, yes she's a pretty girl but no, I'm not attracted to her, I never mix business with pleasure. It's like scotch and orange, it just doesn't work. Oh and Carrie..."

"Yes?"

"I'm richer in many ways than just money, I have a lot of friends and I'd like to think that now includes you."

Direct, to the point, flirtatious almost. She was almost hooked.

"Pity you're not rich Sergeant Cade or I'd think about taking you off the market myself."

"Who said I wasn't?"

Hook, line, sinker.

"Well, are you?"

"I am. Hang around long enough and you'll find out why. One day I will be even more desirable. An old lady told me once that I would find my fortune in a mystical place. She was a medium, although to be honest I'd put her on the large side."

"The eternally-intriguing Jack Cade, where will it ever end I wonder?" She looked over the top of her teacup and held his gaze for about five seconds.

"As I mentioned, hang around long enough and you may find out."

Her eyes lit up, dopamine excited the neuro triggers in her pupils causing them to dilate and then she inhaled almost imperceptibly. Her brain was being flooded with norepinephrine as her hands unintentionally moistened. As strong as she was normally she suddenly found herself completely out of control.

Cade felt it too.

"Right, talk to me about Eastern Europe, what do you know, what you don't know, your theories, hypotheses, I want them all. It strikes me that the Met is ignoring the growing threat on their doorstep and trust me, from what Nikolina tells me it's only just beginning. The sooner we formulate a plan, engage the banks and engage the bosses, and then lastly the government we can start. And if we don't start soon it will become cancerous and then, I suspect, too late."

"I'm all yours Jack. Do with me as you wish. If it's analytical brilliance you are looking for you've found it. I'll get back and start plotting the known occurrences on an i2 chart; from there we can add any CCTV imagery and perhaps throw our net wider; someone needs to talk to Interpol. Any news on that body at Camden?"

"All good ideas; no, no news at all, he's just another random victim. The big difference is he has the tattoo."

"Tattoo?" she asked inquisitively.

"The First Wave – it's the unit I'm hunting." He checked himself, "I should say *we* are hunting. Set up by a Romanian national who has experienced the power, prestige and financial allure of leadership within a criminally minded group. He's learned how to steal high-value cars and ship them across the borders of Europe and interestingly how to manipulate the diplomatic world in order to launder money."

"Don't tell me, that's where your perfectly-formed hot little redhead comes into it?"

"Find her attractive do you?"

She bristled. What had he heard? That bastard Wood had been talking again.

"No Sergeant Cade I do not." The wall had been rebuilt.

He made a mental note to watch himself in future and apologised.

Breaking down her own instigated wall she offered an olive branch of her own.

"Look, I'm sorry. Do you fancy going out for dinner tonight, nothing flash, tapas, local place; cheap and nasty like me?"

"And the Rioja?"

Chapter Twenty Six

"Even nastier!"

"I prefer Crianza but the Rioja is fine; young and fruity. It's a date, but don't tell Wood, we don't want him all jealous now do we?"

She found herself wondering quite how he knew so much about her already.

"Who is your source? Roberts?"

"Yes. Does that bother you?"

"Not really, I'm the talk of the office; the Welsh bastard deserved everything he got, he took advantage of me. It will never happen again."

"I'm glad to hear it Carrie. It's a man's world in there, we both know that, but I'd like to think I'm a little different to the pack. Tell me about your accident?"

"There's nothing to tell. A total prick of a male chauvinist who wouldn't back down, we crashed, I got injured." She favoured her left side, trying to subtly shield it.

"Don't cover yourself up. It's character-ful. Look…"

He rolled his left sleeve up to reveal a substantial scar on his forearm, which ran from his wrist to his elbow.

"Me too. I'm proud of it. Mako shark got me in the Indian Ocean."

"My God. Incredible. You are a lucky man."

"I am. Trust me the only shark that's ever attacked me wore a wedding ring like mine. Actually I ran through a plate glass window as a kid, tore the bloody thing to pieces; nearly killed me. My dear old mum wrapped some fresh nappies around it and stemmed the bleeding. We drove across the Kent countryside in an old Ford Escort, right through the biggest thunderstorm I'd ever seen. I got a pound for every stitch."

"Bastard! At least now I know why you are rich."

"You do, but let's keep it as our secret. I'll get dinner tonight and I'm not taking no for an answer."

"It's a date. I need to ensure that Petrov is housed and secure then we can relax. Your team are doing a fine job; forgive me if I appear a little…paranoid?"

"It's quite refreshing actually Jack. No-one seems to care anymore; I can tell you care deeply for her." She was being genuine, but fishing nonetheless.

"I do, but not in the way you are insinuating Carrie. I was treated terribly by my former wife and to be honest I doubt I will find another female that I trust for a very long time. But in you I see someone who I can work with, and frankly, that's a start." He chinked his teacup against hers.

They finished lunch and headed back to the office.

As they negotiated the stairs Roberts came bounding down towards them.

"Jack, Carrie, car park now, we've got a break!"

"A break – you mean a burglary?" Where Cade came from it meant just that.

"Negative, a break in the case my dear chap." He smoked an imaginary pipe emulating the great Sherlock Holmes.

The three got into Roberts' Mondeo. Before Cade could be a gentleman and offer O'Shea the front seat the car was on the move. Cade jumped in and clicked the safety belt into place.

"Why the hurry mate?" Cade asked, reasonably.

"Branch of the Royal Bank of Scotland on Grosvenor Place has been done; I reckon it's our team. I want to get there sharpish in case they are still in the area."

"OK, I get it, is Petrov OK Jason? I need to know, she's my responsibility."

"She's fine Jack, relax. This is the Met my son! Clive is keeping her very close at hand today. He'll pump her for everything she's got."

Cade looked in the passenger mirror and saw O'Shea discreetly shake her head from side to side. O'Shea stabbed him with a pencil when he misbehaved, Petrov would disfigure him and ensure he never manhandled a woman again. O'Shea had heard a few stories of her empty hand fighting techniques from Cade and quietly hoped Wood might let his wandering digits explore. Just a pity she wasn't there to watch events unfold when the inevitable happened.

Roberts skilfully whipped through the late lunchtime traffic and pulled up onto the pavement, dropped the sun visor down displaying the Met Police logo, locked the car, straightened his lime green tie and walked into the branch.

Cade waited outside the stone building, which was originally called Iron Trades House, now just another commercial building, one of many nestled around the far more impressive Buckingham Palace. Like so many in the area it was steeped in history. Built in the nineteen thirties it had just been completely modernised, everything about it was fresh and clean.

O'Shea joined him and observed quietly.

Roberts was like the proverbial bull in the oft-associated china shop. He'd been talking to the staff at the counter for a few minutes when he realised his team members were outside.

When he joined them he found Cade photographing the ATM machine and pointing out almost imperceptible marks on the outer surface of the till. Roberts watched, always willing to learn but feeling slightly out of his depth.

Cade unfolded a Swiss Army knife and gently lifted a piece of glue off the facia. He held it up and rubbed it between his thumb and forefinger.

"The whole building has recently undergone a makeover Jason. It's as clean as it was the day it was built. I'm sure you would agree this will work in our favour."

He continued to rub the fresh adhesive in his hands until it dried and dropped onto the pavement. He then brushed his hands together to remove the last of the residue.

"It's peel-able, probably easily obtained from a DIY store. This is one of the m.o's that Petrov had told me about."

Roberts moved closer, he'd remembered what Cade had showed him at the previous branch.

"But I thought you said the devices they used are internal Jack? Grabbers you called them?"

"I did Jason and they are, but this one…is different. This represents a whole new era of bank-related offending. Can we get Scenes of Crime here sharpish?"

Roberts nodded before Cade continued.

"I'd like a set of photographs and a fingerprint job putting in too. I'd like every possible second of local CCTV securing, and can we close this machine to the public until that happens? Tell the manager why it's so important, he may be the first of a kind in the UK; something to put in the bank industry newsletter."

Roberts took the job on, phoned for a Scenes of Crime Officer to attend as a matter of priority, grabbed some incident tape from the boot and with O'Shea gathered a few road cones from a nearby workman and created a 'no-go' area. Satisfied the machine was now off limits he rang one of his team.

"That's right, SOCO, straight away. I want every bank that has an ATM within a square mile of this place to be visited. I do not want to drop the ball on this one sunshine."

Cade walked up the street, looking up, down and sideways as he always did at a crime scene. Seeing only a few remote cameras and the daily rush of vehicles he returned to O'Shea who was studying the ATM.

"Is it really that simple Jack? Really that lucrative?"

He smiled. "I've been studying this for a few years now, it started as a bit of job-related hobby but since Petrov arrived I've read up on nothing else. I found a court case stemming back to 1996."

Cade recounted how Andrew Stone, a computer security employee from Hampshire was convicted of stealing around seven hundred and fifty thousand pounds from ATM's.

"He did it by filming his victims from across the street – using high powered video cameras. He made sure he obtained the card and PIN numbers, and importantly the expiry dates. Then later he would return home and use blank cards and an embossing machine to produce cloned bank cards; quite brilliant, you have to admire his skill at a time when cyber-attacks on banks were almost unheard of."

O'Shea could never see herself admiring any criminal but she nodded anyway.

"The really clever bit Carrie was how he realised that if he produced multiple cloned cards he could also beat the daily limit set by the banks. The man was an emerging genius really. At his peak he could withdraw nearly ten thousand a day, and life was very rosy, until he got caught of course. He got sentenced, but as with all financial crime it rarely matches the monetary gain and I suspect he's back out on the streets now."

Roberts had finished organising one half of his team.

"I'm putting some resources into this Jack. I don't know why, but something tells me you are onto something. This could be the next big thing. We just need to get one step ahead of them."

"Catching them would be a good start Detective Sergeant. I think we are miles behind. Somehow we have to try and out-think them, and these people are cunning, very clever and I suspect already moving into the next phase."

He clicked his fingers again causing both O'Shea and Roberts to snap out of their thoughts.

"Got it! The adhesive is a remnant of a device that they have used. Secure the branch CCTV and let's get someone…Carrie, you…get in there and start reviewing the footage between…" He stopped and calculated a period when he would commit the same crime.

"Between?" said O'Shea eager but slightly impatient.

"Sorry, between 21:00 and 04:00 – I know it's a long time period but I doubt many genuine customers would have used the machine – in fact go one step further, see if the bank can confirm how many transactions there were and focus on those. The offenders may have used the machine conventionally first then added the device."

Roberts was rubbing his chin vigorously and stroking the label on his tie with the other hand. He had the mannerisms of an ex-smoker, almost desperate for something to occupy his restless hands.

"Jack for Christ's sake, talk to me about the device. What are we talking about here, something that traps notes, an advanced version of the grabber…the Lesbian Loop thing?"

"Lebanese? No, I suspect not. I'll lay what's left of my tattered reputation on this being an electronic device. It needs to be a three-stage process. I lay awake for hours last night…"

"Thinking about hot steamy water trickling down Petrov's pert breasts?"

This earned him a powerful slap from O'Shea who drove the back of her hand across Roberts' triceps causing him to yelp. Cade would later describe the sound as being exactly like that of a chastised infant canine.

"No Jason. No I did not, romantic though you make it sound. No, I found myself thinking about how I would rip off the general public on one hand and government departments on the other. If one system worked I'd be well off, if both were successful I'd be very wealthy indeed, and as we keep saying these are clever people. On this hand I've got bank machine fraud and on this passport fraud."

"So?"

"So what I came up with was a package that you attach *to* the existing bank machine, the customer places their card into the housing and the magnetic data is copied onto a small hard drive."

Cade had hardly finished when a disbelieving Roberts countered his idea.

"It's the work of Professor Hawking himself mate – can't be done."

"A tenner says it can," replied a confident Cade, his fist planted on his throat as if using an electronic voice box. "All we need is a few bits of readily available equipment and a willing partner in a plastics factory."

Cade, O'Shea and Roberts returned to the Yard; en route Cade outlined what was needed and how relatively simple, yet exquisitely brilliant the system was. As with all of his brightest ideas he hadn't got a clue where to start when it came to building it. He'd need an expert for that. And he knew where to find one.

Chapter Twenty Seven

Roberts was devouring a pie that he had located somewhere between the car park and the office. He turned the last part around, examined it slowly then spat the remnants into a nearby bin.

"Do you know what boys and girls? I'm vegetarian from this day onwards. I swear I've just eaten an ear. It's not happening. Carrot and parsley pie it is for me from now on."

He walked nauseously towards the bathroom.

Cade and O'Shea sat at her desk and were quickly joined by Petrov. She was remarkably upbeat and appeared to have completely lost her sense of fear; a fear that had previously consumed her and that had risen up during the preceding days. Cade looked at her and found himself wondering where she gathered her physical and mental strength from.

"So, how are Batman and Robin?" asked Petrov, causing O'Shea's feathers to ruffle slightly but enough to make her respond in a semi-caustic tone.

"I'm neither The Caped Crusader nor his slightly less impressive sidekick Nikolina, in fact, I'm nobody's sidekick. Jack and I have been busy sweeping up the remnants of your groups' offending."

It was the first time he'd observed it but there in front of him was a combination of professional and personal jealousy. He wasn't quite sure how the situation had arisen but he knew that it needed attending to: in one corner he had the girl every man in the office couldn't avoid taking sideways glances at and in the other a woman he found profoundly and almost strangely attractive. Somehow he had to keep them separate – and yet his priority had to be Petrov; his force and the Home Office had decreed it.

"Nikolina, let's go for coffee, we need to talk."

318

They walked across the road from the bland yet famous landmark that had become the flagship of the Metropolitan Police. As they crossed the road Cade scanned the street and the skyline as if Petrov were his Principle. She was. Something caused him a deep-seated sense of concern. The activities with the van and car earlier in the week had almost been forgotten but they had planted a seed that was germinating deep inside Cade's subconscious.

Whilst the 'Wave' were industrious in their preparations to bleed London banks of every penny they were also likely to have long memories when it came to betrayal – and Petrov had not only betrayed the group and its figurehead, worse still she had betrayed her lover. He doubted they had finished with her yet and here he was having coffee with her in an insecure location; unarmed, unsupported and unaware.

"Now, my wonderful Bulgarian friend I need your help." He blew across the top of his coffee, cooling it slightly.

"Fire away Jack. I am all yours," she replied, her tongue darting around the rim of the latte glass.

"Thank you. Can you remember Alex ever talking about a device that would take money from a bank machine?"

"You mean like PE-4?"

He laughed and continued "No, not quite, I don't anticipate his team blowing bank machines up just yet. It was reported once in Italy last year. The bank experts believe that someone tried to detonate a device inside an ATM but I don't think even Alex's web spreads that far. I don't know whether he has the skill?"

"Money talks Jack. He can hire anyone and there are a lot of ex-military people in Eastern Europe needing work."

"Agreed, but it's too risky, why detonate a bomb and risk taking out the branch and everyone near it when you can use more subtle systems?"

"You mean like oxyacetylene?"

Cade's face morphed from blank, non-descript to pure curiosity and he found himself thinking that this girl was a modern-day miracle: attractive, educated, trained and knowledgeable. Her instinct and operational skills belied her age.

"Oxy? Why? You are way ahead of me, Please explain?"

"I am always ahead of you Jack that is why you always chase me, no?"

There he was again, caught in the headlights.

"Look, Alex once talked; he always talked after we made love – that was when I got the best information from him. I would go to the bathroom once he was asleep and send my text messages. One time he talked about using oxyacetylene to blow up a bank machine. I think he meant what you call an ATM. I didn't know why he told me these things, but he did. So I listened."

Cade nodded vigorously, Roberts would kill for this type of information. He considered ringing him and asking him to join them but he didn't want to risk a change in dynamics. Roberts would question her on crime for ten minutes then spend the next hour trying to get into her knickers. Cade would flirt with her if he had to; tough job, but someone had to do it.

"He said that his team hadn't worked out how to do it but they knew it could be done, he said that he wanted Primul Val to be the first. He always wanted them to be the first. He was always planning to be Europe's most wanted man."

Cade tried to ignore the last part of the sentence, but hindsight would teach him that to do so was a mistake.

"OK, so it didn't work, how do you know?"

"Because he took me to a place once, somewhere out in the Spanish countryside, we were high up in the hills on a rough track overlooking a place called Camino. They tried to make it work on an old safe. There was an explosion. One of his men was very badly hurt. He was burning Jack, like meat on a barbeque, they just left him there. I can still smell him…"

She stared through Cade, clearly reminiscing about the incident.

"We were about to drive away when he made one of his junior men go back and finish him off. He hit him with the cylinder until he didn't get up. They pushed the safe and the man down a ravine into some undergrowth. He is probably still there. Then, we just drove off and went for dinner Jack. He even gloated that he liked his steak medium rare. The waitress didn't know what he meant, but everyone else that sat with him, pampered to his ego, they knew. How could he be so cruel?"

Cade found himself wondering how such a beautiful woman could have remained with such a heartless creature. Despite his hesitation he knew all too well that women were strangely attracted to powerful, aggressive and dominant men. His ex-wife was. But Petrov had an agenda. She was collecting for her government and she was a woman scorned.

"Thank you Nikolina. Please, if you can, tell me about the bank machines. I think Alex has worked out a way to steal money from them. I think he might use a device that he puts onto the existing machine. Am I right?"

She paused, sipped some more of her coffee then responded in a cooler tone.

"Jack, if I help you, you will make sure I am safe here in England? I need to know, please. I pretend that I am not scared, but I am. I have the scars, I have the dreams. I have my daughter, I…"

He held out his hand and took hers. It was most likely a breach of something, somewhere, some local bloody Standing Order about a 'distance policy'. Christ it hadn't stopped that bastard Cooke so why should it stop him? He held her firmer and looked at her, willing her to look up.

"Nikolina, you have my word. Tomorrow we will start work with the Home Office – they are the people who have made sure that I work with you and they are also the people who can provide you with asylum from…from wherever it is you think you cannot go back to."

She smiled a weary smile.

"Jack, I can't go back to Spain, Romania or Bulgaria. There are people in all of those places that either want to abuse me, kill me or imprison me. If you cannot help me, you must help my daughter. Me? I am better off dead."

"I promise to help."

"You promise Jack?"

"I do Niko I do." He had shortened her name; it was a mistake, as much as the empty promise was. He knew there was no way he could protect them both.

"Right, tonight I have to go to a meeting with Carrie. Jason has told me that you will be guarded by Detective Wood. He is a good man, ex-Army and he knows London better than almost anyone on the team. You will go to the safe house and he will remain with you until I return. OK?"

"OK. You have good meeting with Miss O'Shea but watch out for her Jack, she looks at you in a special way."

He laughed it off, somewhat uncomfortably then announced that they needed to get back to the office.

As they exited the café a dispatch rider hissed by on a mountain bike causing Cade to tense up and grab Petrov, pulling her close to him. She seemed oblivious to the risk, or, he was becoming paranoid.

He looked at her. Those incredible eyes looked back.

"You can let go now Sergeant. I will be fine."

He let her go, happy that the rider was just that. They walked across the road and back into the police headquarters. Each time he closed the door behind him he released a quiet sigh. He'd only been in the city for such a short time but already mistrusted almost everyone, hardly a healthy start to the relationship.

They got back into the unit and as they walked past a whiteboard Petrov stopped.

"Jack, I never showed you how."

He turned, a little unsure about what she was talking about but as always gave her his undivided attention.

"The bank machine silly!"

He playfully slapped his own forehead.

"Of course, the bank machine…go on, draw it."

Seeing them stood at the whiteboard Roberts bounded out of his office and joined in the conversation. Standing alongside Cade he commented in a stage whisper.

"Alright my son, thanks for the invite for coffee you old dog. Now what's all this malarkey?"

"Remember you, Carrie and I were talking about the potential device earlier? Well Nikolina is going to show us what Alexandru created. I think this might be the break you crave Jason."

As they spoke the Bulgarian had already started her diagram. She briefed the growing team expertly, talking them through each stage and pausing for questions which never arose.

"OK, this is the plastic housing. Alex had a man in Malaga who worked for a company called SuperNova – they made plastic injection mouldings, he paid him twice his monthly wage to make a…a…house for the machine…"

"A housing?" offered Roberts attentively.

"Yes, a housing Jason. He paid him well and also reminded him that if he betrayed him he would take his children and harm them in the most creative way possible. The housing looked just like the one on the bank machine." She pointed to it with the blue marker pen.

"Just here is where it fitted to the existing machine; just here the bank card goes into the slot and behind here…"

Cade spoke up "Goes a card reader?"

"Bingo Jack you win the prize!"

She seemed fired up with the enthusiasm in the room until the ever-conceited Wood chipped in, his accent thicker than ever.

"OK, I gets all that little lady but how do they know what the PIN number is eh? It strikes me that they ain't so clever after all." He looked around haughtily, hoping to gain some points among his junior colleagues.

One theatrically coughed the word 'wanker' earning himself a rebuke from Roberts, who in truth was frustrated that as the boss he could no longer join in with the banter. He agreed with the heckler. The sooner he could get rid of Wood the better. Such a pity he was a good investigator.

She continued, expertly brushing his cynicism to one side like an unwanted and annoying Horse Fly.

"Should you pay attention Detective you will note that there is a card reader behind the housing. It gathers information from the magnetic strip on the bank card; the card is also read by the bank computer. The bank provides the amount of money selected by the customer and the machine returns the card...."

It was Wood who interrupted once more.

"See, like I say, absolutely bloody useless. I could knock up a better machine in my shed."

Roberts ventured forward and offered his support.

"Clive, I'm sure there's a lot you could knock up in that shed of yours but let's concentrate on listening to Miss Petrov shall we? We my fine friends are on the verge of becoming the first force in Britain to get one step ahead of a team that is taking the piss out of us and the bank industry. Someone put the kettle on and get me a custard cream, McVitie's, none of that cheap crap."

Cade smiled, he liked the way Roberts worked. He was young in service but old fashioned in values. He aspired to greater things and it was clear that at the heart of his enthusiasm was the desire to slip some Inspector's pips onto his shoulder.

Cade knew that the Latin motto almost hidden within the shining silver insignia meant 'three joined in one' – he thought it fitting as he was now working with Roberts and O'Shea.

Petrov finished her briefing, "Thank you Sergeant. The card is returned, the customer is unaware that their data has been captured by the reader and most important of all, before you say anything else Mr Wood is this."

She drew a red circle on the diagram.

"This is the other part of the machine, situated higher, above the number pad. It is a cell phone with a small camera. When the card is inserted it films the PIN number being entered by the customer. Later on, when the streets are quieter one of the team returns and removes the device. The team have the bank data and PIN number and now, well now, they have fun. They go onto the internet and buy things. Watches, electronics, currency, hotels, flights and of course they withdraw cash. Alex told me that they could even think about selling the bank information to other thieves."

The room was quiet.

It was Cade that broke the silence.

"OK folks, there you have it. All we need to do now is work out an offending pattern. We know they have most likely hit this area, where are they liable to go next? Where would you offend and why? It's obvious we need to role this out to the frontline Jason; we need the boys and girls to be our eyes and ears. Thank you Miss Petrov, most helpful."

She smiled; he returned the smile and left her to mop up the meeting, fending off a few late questions from the younger suited and booted Detectives who in truth were struggling to make them up, but the longer they kept her there the greater the chance of a flash of cleavage or an opening for a date: Moths to her flame.

The day was ending, a couple of CID staff were staying in the office to clear up some paperwork whilst two others were out and about, hoping to be the first to catch an offender 'bang at it'.

Roberts had gone home early. For him early was five o'clock, regardless of what time he started. Outside, the Great Commute had begun as people from all walks of life jostled like ants to get from A to B.

O'Shea was working later than most, her desk lamp blazing, her mind racing. She looked down the office. Had he remembered?

Cade was briefing Wood about his role. On no terms was he to allow her out of the apartment. If they needed to leave – if her safety was compromised – then he was to call it in first, then move.

With a larger-than-usual list of Witness Protection cases the local specialist teams were unable to assist so Roberts' crew were running a roster for the time that Petrov was with them. None of them were armed, if they needed additional or specialist support they had to get on the radio and make those requests.

Cade knew it was far from ideal but he had to work with what he had and according to Roberts, despite his arrogance, Wood was the primary option. And he'd be just fine alone.

"It's the big city Jack, help is seconds away here, it's not like Hicksville where you lot come from!" Roberts had announced as he left.

With everyone briefed they commenced the initial phase of the nightly operation. Petrov followed Wood to the car park with Cade in tow. Gary West, the driver for the evening was two steps ahead.

An older grey Volvo estate was the vehicle of choice: strong, dependable and relatively bland. Petrov turned to Cade and gave her million-dollar smile, tucked her head down and got in the back of the car. She was joined by Wood who had his work-related and personal kit in a black bag. West looked across at Cade.

"Ready boss?"

"Ready Gary thanks. See you in the morning Nikolina. Ring me if you need anything. Sleep well, you've earned it. Tomorrow we will start work on stage two – the hunt for The Wave. There is more that you need to tell me, you just need to tell me. OK?"

Chapter Twenty Seven

He pushed the Volvo door closed with a resonant thud.

They left the car park, turned onto Victoria Street and quickly blended with the rush hour traffic.

West scanned constantly. Wood did the same; professional to the core he appeared to have lost his arrogant edge. Fifteen minutes later and only a few miles away they pulled into an underground car park, waited for the all clear from the equally anonymous silver Ford Fiesta that had been following them and decamped from the Volvo.

They moved quickly and deliberately from the car to the lift and from there to the apartment. They had done this every night since Cade had arrived. He had conducted the same run himself but now after a repeated string of successful runs he felt easier.

The team entered the apartment, disarmed the alarm, drew the curtains and turned on some lights. They were in.

West called into the control room announcing that Operation Breaker was complete, shook hands with Wood, waited for him to secure the door and left, retracing his steps to ensure that he hadn't been followed.

Satisfied that all was normal he called Wood and gave him the good news. They were in, they could relax. Wood threw the Sky remote to Petrov.

"Help yourself, I'm a Discovery man myself but you're the guest."

"I am fine thank you. I will read."

She hadn't seen this side of Wood in the week that she had been at Scotland Yard, it was evident that he was a team player and perhaps he had just been showing off in front of his junior colleagues? Either way, she felt relatively at ease.

"Right miss, you know the drill, you take the main room and lock the door and I'll be in the lounge. If anything happens, anything out of the ordinary, you stay put. Do not under any circumstances leave that room. I will knock twice and twice again on the door when it is safe. Understood?"

She nodded. These people were trying their best but their training lacked the raw brutality of hers. She could disarm this Wood character in a second. But he needed to feel that he was in charge.

"Yes officer, I understand, thank you. Shall we eat?"

Wood walked to the kitchen, opened the freezer and removed two ready-meals.

Petrov gently eased past him and took the containers.

"Please officer, allow me, go and sit down, I can do this."

Who was he to argue?

Twenty minutes later Wood had untied and lovingly removed his leather shoes. They were handcrafted by Church's of Northampton.

His Consul's from the Classic Collection were one of his only vices. He considered them an investment. One day he would tell his wife.

Leather uppers, leather soles, polished to within an inch of their lives. They were a trademark of his. His physique was another, or rather it was until he had let himself go a little, a hint of excess here, a lack of exercise there.

He checked the door, looked out of the curtains, down onto the street below and satisfied that all was as normal as London could be he sank himself into the black leather armchair and flicked through a few channels on the television.

Petrov had eaten and made her excuses and headed to bed. She had endured a long day.

"Bless her. She wants to try working for a living." Wood said to no-one in particular.

He would remain in situ until relieved by a team mate at 06:00 hours. For him the morning couldn't come soon enough. Such a pity he couldn't spend it with the rather appealing Bulgarian.

"Now that is pure sex. God I wouldn't mind half an hour with her." Again to no-one special; his dulcet Welsh tones singing out the sentence.

He knew he needed to remain alert but if anyone wanted to get through that bloody door then God help them. Besides they would need at least the equivalent of the police 'Big Red Key' and he would ensure that any greeting was very personal.

"Yep they'd need an Enforcer," he said out aloud as he navigated through the sports and then the films, "or a small explosive charge of some description: Bang!"

He laughed and in time with the 'Bang!' pulled the alloy ring on a can of orange Fanta causing its gaseous vapour to explode out of the small pear-shaped aperture.

"A whole night away from normal work, a can of Fanta and a chicken tandoori, that plus eight hours at time and a half, away from my nagging wife, what more could a man ask for?"

He was, he decided, living the dream.

He finished his meal and looked at the main door once more. Whoever might have the foolish idea of entering without an invitation would also be advised to prepare for an unfriendly welcome.

Wood had been a renegade in his early youth and subsequently spent his formative years in the Parachute Regiment after his parents threatened to abandon him. Joining as a boy soldier at Catterick, North Yorkshire he had learned to fight, like so many young men, via the non-genteel art of milling.

Milling saw two combatants, possibly friends, drawn into a gladiatorial circle. They wore standard Physical Education clothing; dark shorts and a white vest and boxing gloves. That was where the finesse ended.

Some partook by ducking and diving, avoiding a blow at all costs, waiting for the chance to strike but losing valuable points in the process. Others entered the ring, looking at friend or foe and swung every punch as if it were their last. It was described as 'controlled physical aggression' and Wood excelled at it.

On his upper right arm he wore a faded and somewhat larger than originally-inked tattoo, it said *Utrinque paratus.*

For the uninitiated it meant *Ready for anything* and was the time honoured regimental motto of his beloved airborne unit.

Less than an hour later the combination of the carbonated drink and the spice of the curry started to play havoc with Wood's acid reflux, so as was his nightly custom he opened the fridge and hunted for milk. The large appliance illuminated the room, casting a beam of yellowy light towards Petrov's bedroom.

Wood was stood looking at the door; doing what many men would do in his (polished leather) shoes and wondering what Petrov looked like in bed.

He couldn't help it. His wife, God love her, was once eight stone and had been his childhood sweetheart – now she was twice that weight and twice as hairy as he was. She once looked like a film star, he told people, but now the star was faded and Mrs Sheila Wood was an ever-expanding shadow of her former self.

She had long and straggly armpit hair that Wood had given up complaining about. It had been many years since his lips had trodden a path from her delicate wrists, upwards and along her arm, pausing to kiss the smooth erogenous depression that led to her breasts.

If they ever had sex it was swift and uninteresting, and Wood often found himself thinking of his favourite actress when the 'moment' arose.

Little did he know that Sheila was also thinking the same; different actor, same thoughts.

And right now the beautiful Bulgarian was laid in that king sized bed, all Egyptian cotton and scatter cushions, wearing a businessman's shirt no doubt, and her skin smooth from the recently applied passion fruit body lotion.

"Oh God she'd smell good enough to ruddy eat," he sighed and tried to console himself by surfing through the channels again but to no avail. Every station featured beautiful people, doing beautiful things.

The more he tried to put her out of his mind the more she drew him nearer.

"Stop it man, she's half your age and most likely half your weight, and bugger it probably a quarter as hairy. I bet she's as bald as a Coot down stairs…"

His conversation was somewhat louder than he had realised and quite bizarre given he had no audience. Except that he did.

Although she made no sound he became aware that she was stood at the doorway to the bedroom. Fortune had shone on the boy from the valleys, she was indeed wearing an over-sized mans' shirt, her hair darker than he remembered, damp no doubt from a recent solitary shower.

All that was missing, in Wood's mind, was a pair of high-heeled shoes and a come-to-bed smile.

Sadly she had neither and her look gave out altogether different signals.

"I couldn't sleep. I could hear you talking; I thought there was someone here."

"I thought we agreed miss, you stay in your room at all times. If anything should happen to you my boss would have my guts for garters."

"I don't understand?"

"It doesn't matter – I'd be in trouble."

"I understand that. I wouldn't want to get you into trouble Detective."

Was this a hint, a subtle signal that she found him interesting, possibly even attractive? In his day, ten, possibly fifteen years earlier she would have done, so why not now?

His mind was racing. He was alone with a stunning girl in a swanky London flat, what would his mates in Swansea make of all of this?

He stood up and placed the empty can on the kitchen worktop.

"I think we've got some brandy in the cupboard somewhere, would you like one?"

Petrov sensed another sea change in Wood and it made her feel uneasy. Surely he shouldn't be drinking on duty? The English police were famed for their integrity and rules.

She declined.

"Fair enough, have it your way miss."

"You don't have to call me miss, Detective Wood."

"And you don't have to call me Detective – it's Clive."

"OK, Clive, anyway we have long days ahead. Would you please post this letter for me?" She handed him a handwritten white envelope

– it needed a stamp and was addressed in blue biro to somewhere unpronounceable in Bulgaria. There was no return address.

"Sorry, it needs a stamp. I will pay you. I am going back to bed; it must be time for you to go to bed too?"

This was the second signal and perhaps his last: Now or never Clive.

He walked towards her accompanied by his finest seductive face.

"When I'm on nights Miss Petrov, I never sleep, I stay rigidly awake. I can go all night." He winked but his signals were lost, desperately.

He was at the door now, he could smell the passion fruit – was there a hint of mango in there too? Either way it was gorgeous. Do it Clive.

He stepped forward and placed his arms around her waist, his powerful muscles pulling her towards him. The instant it happened he knew it was wrong, knew his marriage, his career and everything that accompanied it were doomed, but he wanted her and nothing else mattered.

She was struggling now, both physically and mentally. Why was her protector doing this? What would Jack say? Was this expected of her? Should she say yes?

No, this was not right, not right at all. She should fight.

He was strong but she would use his own strength against him.

"Let go of me Clive. This is not right; you are here to protect me!"

He didn't respond. It was too late; he'd overstepped the mark and was now verging on animal, his deep-seated sense of arousal and power had overtaken years of exemplary service and wiped away decades of rational training. The least that could happen was that he found a few moments of pleasure.

He had her in a bear hug, vice-like and impossible to escape from, it was everything but romantic. If she could release her arms she had a chance.

He picked her up and shuffled her backwards towards the bed, his intentions were now clear. For Nikolina this situation was wholly déjà vu and she was back, tied to a bed in a Romanian apartment at the mercy of Alex and his guests for the night.

Not this time, not again.

She exhaled and managed to gain a few centimetres of space allowing her some liberty. She drove her hands upwards pushing his arms outwards before striking him quickly across the temples. It was a temporary distraction but all she needed.

He stepped sideways to avoid the blow that never followed, then started talking, all too quickly.

"Miss, I'm sorry, this shouldn't have happened, please go to your room."

She was now on the offensive, equally animal and highly driven; she needed to show that she wasn't a plaything for men to enjoy when and wherever they chose.

She stepped sideways too, but opposite to the direction chosen by Wood, creating an arc for a straight-arm strike across his face. All the years of experience and training, those heady days in the milling circle at Catterick, all were useless. The blow struck him just underneath the nose, her radius bone slamming into his filtrum and causing hideous pain across the top of his teeth.

The blow was so fast, so unexpected that he had been caught completely unaware. His nose was pouring with blood as he staggered backwards, falling to the kitchen floor. He was, for now, unconscious.

She considered a follow-up strike, a kick or worse, but she could clearly see he was unlikely to pose a threat in the few harried minutes it took her to compose her thoughts, gather her immediate belongings and leave the apartment.

She dressed hastily, checked to see if he was still breathing and then left, closing the door quietly behind her. Quite where she would go she hadn't considered. She would rather take her chances in a foreign city than in a flat with a goal-driven man.

Her mind was now a miasma, a whirlpool of emotive reasoning, of interrogatives and anger, but mostly disappointment. The very people that had promised to care for her had turned against her.

She pulled her phone from her pocket and started to dial Cade but stopped. There was his car, the Mondeo, moving quietly down the street towards her. He had been in the neighbourhood all the time. He was the back-up. She sighed in relief, pleased to see the man she saw as her saviour.

The Mondeo headlights were on full beam, dazzling her and causing her to place her hands across her face, but instinctively she walked towards the light. She knew that Wood would be awake soon so she needed to explain her side of the story to Cade – in the hope that he would believe her and not one of his own team.

Within a few paces of the car she heard a familiar accent, it was Wood. He was running at full pace up the street, phone in one hand ASP baton in the other. She heard the metal partitions slide against each other as Wood engaged the weapon.

Two paces.

He was gaining ground. When would Cade leave the car? What was he playing at? Was he afraid of Wood too?

One pace.

Decision made.

She had reached the Mondeo passenger door. As she entered the unlit cabin a hand appeared and grabbed her wrist. She didn't resist, she was safe, tumbling into the car and slamming the door behind her as Cade accelerated away: first gear, rev limiter reached, second, third, fourth and into the heart of London.

The last event had taken sixty seconds and in that minute she had realised that she had walked into the hands of something far worse than Wood could ever have been capable of.

Five streets behind them Wood was down on one knee piling air into his lungs, reloading his ASP and desperately trying to prioritise.

The girl. The car. The males. The gun.

He wiped his nose which was bleeding profusely again, the result of his sprint down the stairs from the apartment and out onto the street. How the hell would he explain this to Cade, to Roberts – to his wife!

"Get a grip man, make a bloody decision. For once in your wretched bloody life do the right thing."

He pulled the job phone from his pocket and hit speed dial 1.

With no response he tried again and then once more. Each call terminated in Cade's answerphone.

He tried Roberts' cell – again he found himself talking to an answer machine.

He leant back against a low wall finally able to breathe freely, dialled another number into the phone and quietly, despite not being a religious man, prayed that someone would answer.

Chapter Twenty Eight

Back at the unit O'Shea was clearing the backlog of emails and data. She had been diligently entering names, vehicles and locations into an i2 chart – a visual display of every piece of intelligence that they had gathered, from open or more secure sources. It was looking good.

"Looks great Carrie, top job, now, how about that meal?"

She was startled and chastised herself for not hearing him enter the office but she was quietly delighted. He *had* remembered.

"Oh, yes, OK, why not?" she replied nonchalantly, "I'll get my jacket; it looks cooler out there tonight."

"Shall we walk?" Cade needed a break from the relentless London traffic. The Mondeo was parked opposite the Yard, it could remain there for a few hours at least, no one, not even the most diligent Parking Warden would dare to ticket it.

O'Shea walked to the coat stand suppressing a huge smile.

They exited the building and in a few minutes were on Broadway. Their conversation was quickly work-centric but eventually Cade asked about O'Shea. What lay behind that apparently frosty exterior?

For the first time in eons, actually for the first time ever she relaxed and found herself talking about family, most of whom had drifted to the four corners of the world. Her father was 'ex-job' and had drifted to his own corner of the world, but in reality was only miles away as the crow flew. She seemed guarded on the subject so he made a diplomatic withdrawal.

It was her turn.

He waxed lyrical about his childhood and skilfully managed to avoid his formative years, swiftly arriving at his entry into the world of policing. She found herself placing pieces of the jigsaw, a piece here, another one turned and turned again until it dropped quietly into place.

She knew he had skeletons and the subject of his recently estranged wife was as raw and tender as her own paternal relationship.

She felt that some of his jigsaw pieces needed to forever remain face down.

They called a truce without saying another word.

"Here we go, as I mentioned, it's cheap – for London – but plentiful. You will not leave here hungry."

Her internal dialogue spoke differently.

"I hope you leave here hungry for me Jack Cade."

They found their table, surrounded by others and yet due to the bustling, noisy crowd they were also relatively isolated. It suited them both; they would have to flag any work-related conversations. They agreed immediately, chinking their Rioja-filled glasses together and ordered the eight-course meal for two.

Cade checked his phone, nothing. Good. Roberts had total faith in his team and he knew them better than Cade, better than anyone. He'd turn it to silent, if it was important they'd get hold of him.

"You know Carrie, we didn't get off on the right footing and for that I apologise. I had had one hell of a few weeks leading up to my secondment to the airport – all of which, let me say, seems eons away. I feel we turned a corner today."

She sipped her wine allowing its slightly bitter taste to explode on the tip of her tongue before responding.

"Jack, I can be a real cow when I want to be. Men treat me like dirt and therefore I reciprocate. But I believe in equality, I mainly hate all men. The boss? He's different, a real softy underneath all of his bright ties and blarney. He looks after me, so I'm loyal to him. Don't get me wrong, he's the last person in the office I'd sleep with!"

Cade smirked, "I thought that would have been Clive Wood?"

God what was he thinking? He slid his hands under the table subconsciously as she picked up her three-pronged fork and examined it playfully.

"Relax Jack, a bit late there, remember I already did, and what a mistake that was. He's fat and hairy and above all, Welsh. I've no doubt his on-off wife loves him, she's Welsh too so they probably make complete sense to one another during their passionate displays of frantic lovemaking, but I will never be visiting that particular entertainment hotspot again. I broke my favourite pencil that night."

He paused, still a little unsure whether he was reading her correctly, but took the chance.

"I heard you almost broke the lead in his pencil too…"

She burst out laughing, bringing the pulsating place to a brief standstill. Normal service was soon resumed but O'Shea was still giggling a minute later. She was more attractive when she smiled; it was as if he had released her true persona.

"You are a funny man Jack. I like you. It's been good working with you this week, I've learned a lot. You are a great teacher; I hope I'm a worthy pupil?"

It had been an incredibly short but conversely a rather long week and he felt slightly vulnerable, the location, the vibrancy, the wine all helped to relax him but he was aware of letting his guard down too far, too quickly. He became conscious that he was daydreaming.

Here he was in court; three-piece suit and a pocket watch, meticulously recounting evidence to the masses. He could smell the wooden-panelled courtroom, the hint of much-worn leather, powder from the iconic wigs created a haze in a shaft of sunlight that cut through the elevated and grimy window – all the better to keep prying eyes away. He turned to his side to see O'Shea, the Defence Counsel, dressed and ready for business.

Well-polished black shoes, a smart black skirt, slightly too short, a white, crisp blouse sitting perfectly in place, its familiar detail, pleated, hanging, just so. Her black silk damask robe shimmered in the solitary ray of sunlight. She wore black, overly-large glasses and had the customary short hairpiece in place. She was far from friendly, but deeply eye-catching, sassy and darkly sexy.

She was leaning forward at her desk, her chin resting on her hands, attentive and wise beyond her years.

"Your witness Mr Cade."

"Christ sorry, where was I?"

Cade had re-entered the conversation, feeling as if he'd been absent for hours.

"You OK Jack?" she asked

"Yes, was just… thinking something through. This food is outstanding."

He leant over and topped up her glass and did the same to his.

With the meal finished Cade made good on his promise and picked up the bill. She was right, for London, it was great value. He tore the receipt into six pieces and dropped it in the nearby waste bin.

They walked outside, O'Shea slipping her jacket on and involuntarily shivering.

Cade noticed, "Do you want mine too? It's cooler than of late."

The perfect gent.

"Ah, the perfect gentleman, no I'm fine, a brisk walk will warm me up. I'm only ten minutes from here. I have a flat on Old Queen Street, just up the road from the Chilean Embassy. I'm a lucky girl; they are hellishly expensive these days. My landlord took a shine to me years ago and never asked for anything in return."

She stopped, half in a channel of light, half in a shadow and turned to Cade.

"Look, I know it might be a little clichéd but would you like a coffee?"

It was. He would. But should he?

"Yes that sounds lovely, why not?"

Premature? Over-eager? He had nothing to prove and no-one to report to. He was now his own agent and a free one at that.

They arrived at a narrow one-way street deep in the City of Westminster. The last building, a refurbished Georgian four storey combination of commercial offices and a few flats was where O'Shea lived. It was a street where wealthy, influential and occasionally famous people resided. Its black-brick Georgian facades were much sought-after and properties were starting to attract eye-watering price tags.

She flashed a plastic card across the door entry system and entered the stairwell. Cade noticed three wire cages against the wall, traps for incoming mail. He assumed hers was the empty one, heaven forbid it would be in disarray. He smiled at the notion of her letters landing in the bottom of the cage in an aligned form.

The door closed quietly behind them as they climbed the stairs to the very top. She opened her own front door and invited Cade into a surprisingly spacious apartment. He looked out of the front window; the city was coming to life now. She was within striking distance of some of the most iconic landmarks in the world and he found himself nodding approvingly.

"This is great Carrie. What's the rear view like?"

"Better since I lost a bit of weight to be honest Jack," she replied without hesitation, stirring two cups of French roasted coffee and carrying them both towards where Cade was stood.

"I meant…"

"I know what you meant, I was being facetious. Come on, I'll show you."

She walked through the flat and climbed another small set of stairs until they arrived in her bedroom. She opened the large Georgian window.

"OK, over there is St James's Park – lovely in the summer, to the left is Clarence House and further left is where my friend Elizabeth lives."

"Elizabeth?"

"Christ Jack, you must be tired, HRH…who were you thinking about?"

He wiped his eyes and grimaced.

"Oh *that* Elizabeth! How is she these days?"

"She's fine, sends her love. Come on the coffee's getting cold."

They sat for twenty minutes, chatting about this and that and that and this, dancing around, avoiding the blatant chemistry that was filling the room with alarming signals and heightened sexual adrenalin.

With the coffee finished she offered him an encore from her impressive drinks cabinet.

"You are the guest, after you."

"On a school night, is that wise?"

"Go on, I dare you, live a little."

"If I were a mercenary man I'd have a measure of that Balvenie twenty one year old port wood – that's an expensive bottle."

"It's a classic, a famous reviewer described it as something akin to gently touching the inside lip of someone you love or lust with your tongue, he said it was warming and sensual. Does that appeal to your senses?"

She was flirting outrageously with him.

"It does, but should I swallow my pride and accept your hospitality?"

She poured a healthy amount into a glass, simple with clean-cut lines and a heavy base. He tipped it gently into his mouth and let the liquid flavours erupt onto his taste buds.

He looked up and said "that is superb, you know your malts, shame they are getting so pricey these days," leaning his glass forward and allowing her to refill it.

"You only live once Jack, there's that quote, something about risking going too far…"

Her sentence petered out; she placed her cup on the floor and gazed at Cade.

"Jack, I think I want to have sex with you right now."

He was shocked; yes he had been a little flirtatious, maybe too much but her forthright nature took him by surprise. They'd only known each other for a matter of days. So when she said she wanted 'coffee' she really meant it.

"Carrie, I, er…I…"

"It's OK Jack, I understand, why would you when you can click your fingers and end up in the sack with Miss Bulgaria? I get it, I really do."

She looked horrified, embarrassed and humiliated. The evening was in dire danger of collapsing, folding in on itself like an earthquake-struck historic building.

She went to stand but Cade was swift. He stood first and placed both hands on her shoulders and then lowered himself down so that their eyes were level.

"Now, just a moment, this is not what you think. I am not rejecting you. I'm actually a little out of practice here and for the record Miss Bulgaria as you call her has provided me with a text book opportunity to experience her Eastern European wiles at very close quarters, however, I have no desire to take up her offer. I am here to protect her, not abuse her trust. I am thinking about her this evening, but in a purely professional, utterly platonic way, OK?"

She didn't know whether to laugh or cry. Once again this bloody man had stopped her in her tracks. She leant forward and kissed him gently on the forehead, he smelled quite incredible, an intoxicating scent of vanilla, mandarin and tonka bean – he must have applied it hours ago and yet it still lingered; she found it added an instant suggestion of eroticism and arousal and she wanted more.

He took another mouthful of the Balvenie and placed the glass on a nearby Beechwood table.

She lingered and kissed him again, this time would be different; he would taste of dried fruits, of honey and spice. He raised his head and met her lips full on; both of them held their eyes open, gazing directly into each other's pupils.

He noticed for the first time that the whites of her eyes were reddening and in turn altering her slate grey pupils to green. She was crying, almost imperceptibly, but crying.

His heart rate increased and matched hers. For a short moment he remembered Elizabeth Delaney and their clandestine moonlit union. It seemed like so many months had passed and yet unbelievably it was only a few short weeks before. God he was becoming as bad as Penelope in his sexual conquests – the fanatical whore.

He whispered "what's good for the goose…"

She didn't hear him. For the first time in many years she was in close proximity to a man she found attractive, who she felt able to share her most intimate secrets and critically, whom she trusted.

Cade was breathing shallowly, there was something intensely different about this girl; part of him knew he should pull away, leave the flat and try to recover some semblance of professionalism, but a much bigger part resisted, wanted to put a metaphorical finger up to the world, the job and everything that surrounded it and wanted to live the moment for all it was worth.

He kissed the tears away and held her close to him.

With her head on his chest she undid his shirt, tempting though it was to rip the buttons apart she resisted, she could feel that the moment was sitting on a knife-edge; a hint of imbalance either way could change things permanently.

She also resisted taking the lead – after all it had led to Wood's disagreement with a stationery object.

Despite the rush of thoughts ricocheting around her head she knew she had to ease back, allow him to take control. If he didn't object she would do things her way, but for now it was wonderful just as it was.

He reciprocated, gently unbuttoning her blouse until it gaped open. He stood, causing her to follow his lead.

He slipped the blouse over her shoulders and allowed it to fall to the ground. Instinctively she bent down to pick it up, fold it and place it on the arm of the sofa.

He put his foot onto it and held it firmly in place.

"Leave it. You can iron it tomorrow."

His dominant nature excited her – so much so that she did as she was told and left her still-pristine shirt where it had landed.

Cade knew it was likely to drive her crazy – he'd seen her desk; disciplined, manically ordered, if she wasn't a Virgo, she acted like one. Her home was no different.

He smiled and kissed her again. She swallowed audibly, bit his tongue gently and removed his shirt.

His hand ran expertly across her back, locating the fastener to her pretty and undoubtedly expensive white bra and gently released its grip. His left hand ran up and under the lace, tracing the line of her right breast until the surface changed to his touch. She gasped and took a deep breath.

Why was this man so gentle?

His fingers traced circular lines around her nipple, over and over until her breathing became unrestrained. She was close.

She pushed him backwards "No Jack."

He stood his ground "Carrie if you want me to stop then I will."

"Oh God no, please don't stop, the other one is feeling…lonely, you must be even-handed sire."

It was a ridiculous medieval spur of the moment thing that she would later find amusing, when her mind would inevitably return to the events of the night before.

She blew air through her lips, exhaling, trying to regain control but was failing and if she were honest she loved the feeling of helplessness.

It was all he needed. His fingers walked across her cleavage and stopped on her opposing breast, she was so obviously aroused. He gently stroked her, quickening in time with her breathing until once more she implored him to stop.

Regaining her normal breathing she eased herself onto her knees. Looking up at him she said "Just not yet Jack? Please, I am so aroused but I don't want this to end. It's been a long time since I…"

He placed his palm across her lips applying sufficient pressure that meant she could either pull away or linger; she chose to stay. He held his palm in place and raised his other hand, putting his index finger to his own lips, instructing her to stop talking. She was breathing through her nose now, purposely, and perceptibly.

She felt in control but stimulated like never before.

He raised his thumb and forefinger, leaving the three other fingers across her lips and gently squeezed her nostrils shut.

Now her eyes gave a different message. They widened markedly displaying a hint of fear but an over-riding signal of pure pleasure. As if to endorse that she approved, she nodded.

'Leave it there Jack Cade, I love every moment of this game.'

She tried to raise her hands to undo his belt but he dropped onto his knees and pushed her back against the arm of the sofa. She placed her own hands behind her back. She was raising the ante but overtly becoming more submissive.

'You are in charge Sergeant Cade. You are in charge.'

He leant forward and whispered into her ear "Only those who will risk going too far can possibly find out how far one can go."

She was verging on panic - but intensely willing - he unexpectedly allowed her some respite by removing his hand allowing her to consume the air around her and recover.

"Christ Jack!"

"Sorry, I thought you wanted me to…"

"Stop! Stop it man. That was incredible, please…do it again, but this time for longer. No, wait!"

He was confused but intrigued, what had she in mind?

"Those words you whispered, are they yours?"

With his head tilted slightly and laughing at the ludicrous topic of interruption he replied "I wish. You were hunting for them earlier. They belong to T.S Elliot. They are from a collection called *Transit of Venus*; when you get a moment, research the man behind the publication."

He got comfortable and then continued. "He was called Harry Crosby, a bon vivant and heir to an American fortune. He lived a decadent, hedonistic and open life; I think you, him and his wife would have got along just fine. But enough of that…"

"Oh would I Mr Cade? You think you know all about me do y…"

He placed his hand back across her face, ending the bizarrely analytical conversation and commenced the powerful act of dominance once more, instantly stopping her in her tracks and sending oxygenated blood to her most intimate regions.

With his spare hand he emptied the whisky glass, holding the warming liquid against his lips.

He lifted her onto her toes, discarded her bra and ran his lips against her neck, focusing gently on her larynx. She writhed, feigned resistance and offered moans of encouragement. She was naked from the waist up, so was he.

He removed his hand allowing her to breathe again and kissed her once more, this time easing small amounts of the Balvenie into her willing mouth. It tasted sublime; sweet, warm and wild.

A small amount ran over her chin and onto her neck.

She tipped her head backwards, revealing her throat.

He followed the rivulet of liquid as it traced a meandering line towards her cleavage, licking it away with a deliberate stroke of his tongue.

His hand traced downwards, across her right breast, along the contours of her ribs and lower across her soft stomach until he reached the luxuriously lacy top of her matching white and obviously expensive knickers. They were a revelation and certainly not what he expected to find.

His fingertips slipped underneath the material, causing her to take a sharp intake of breath. He could feel her immaculate silkiness beneath his exploring fingers and began to circle his index and second finger, just as he had done earlier, rhythmically and in time with her panting breaths, lower with each cycle.

Her luxurious underwear was now slipping onto the floor. She kicked it away with her foot taking care to ensure they landed in an obvious place, so she could retrieve them later.

Annoyingly Cade could hear a sound, more evident by the second, louder and louder, a deep constant rumble.

He ignored it. O'Shea tried her hardest to disregard it too.

After twenty seconds it became an irritant. O'Shea apologised, her frustration evident and fished around in the cushion of her sofa to find Cade's work phone – her intention being to turn it off. Whoever it was could wait. Fortuitously she glanced at the screen, it displayed three missed calls.

The black pixelated letters on the Nokia 3410 were clear on the green screen.

One call was anonymous, a landline. The other, a cell phone number stood out on the display with a time and date. Whilst no different to any other missed call, this one, even the screen, looked different, more alarming. More demanding. The call was from Wood.

Chapter Twenty Nine

Petrov was disorientated, her natural compass had failed, the result of being in an unfamiliar place and under extreme stress. The clear plastic carrier bag that had been rammed over her head had only sought to exacerbate the situation.

At the point of sheer terror one of her captors had removed it, tempting though it was to watch her panic through the translucent material he was under strict instructions to ensure she lived.

She had been transferred from the Mondeo into an anonymous van, one of many hundreds that would visit the city that day. She tried to imagine where they were heading, to listen for tell-tale sounds that might later benefit her, but she heard only silence. It was late and they were most likely in an area of London that would not attract visitors.

As she lay in the foetal position in the back of van she heard distinctive Romanian accents. One, a male was talking to another, also a male, they boasted about what they would do with her if Alex had given them carte blanche. However they all knew better than to tamper with their beloved leaders' girl.

Her only chance of salvation lay in convincing her captors to let her go, or possibly to contact Alex and provide a plausible story – she was consumed with fear but trying to think on her feet.

Her training should be kicking in by now; she had disarmed Wood – more's the pity – so she could do it again. She knew there were three of them, all male, all she needed was a chance. However with her hands bound behind her back and her feet shackled by plastic one-use cable ties she felt powerless.

Rewinding the evening's events she realised that Wood was just a fool, an overweight man who thought he had a chance. Hindsight taught her that she would rather have gone the distance with him than find herself at the behest of this group of foul-smelling individuals.

She was still fully clothed, all previous such events at the hands of Alex or one of his many associates had commenced and ended with her being naked. This felt different.

Her mouth was bound with duct tape but she could see each of her custodians. For evidence gathering this was a positive, for the longevity of her life not so. She knew that their intention was to harm her, abuse her and then most likely kill her.

A phone rang in the twilight. A guard answered it and then placed it against Nikolina's ear.

The voice began in a rasping tone, measured, but menacing in a familiar way.

"Well, well my lovely we finally get to talk again. How are you my dear Nikolina? Of course, you cannot reply. Won't Mr Cade be upset, he and his little team of heroes? So, tell me Niko, should I spare you or leave it up to the imagination of my fine men to decide how to deal with you?

She tried to say the words but it was futile.

The featureless voice spoke again, quietly, assured.

"You had everything Nikolina, everything. I always said I would hunt you down like a dog if you betrayed me, and now you have. At least I have our little girl to care for, such a pity she will never see her mother again. I cannot ever trust you now and you know what trust means to me? Of course you do. Oh well, bye-bye, I would like to say I will see you in heaven but it appears I will not be going there. The Devil has a plan and a place in one of his blackest corners, just for me."

He laughed his familiar crow-like laugh.

"At least you will look good for the cameras my pretty. Farewell."

He paused before disconnecting the phone.

She was panicking now for she knew her end was in sight; unlike so many previous complex situations she was simply unable to escape from this one. The circumstances, the tape across her mouth, and the desperate sense of fate started to create a feeling of complete anxiety and foreboding. She was too afraid to cry.

She had no idea of time or place when the van eventually came to a stop. The two males in the rear of the Transit placed her on her back. The driver joined them and sat on her feet immobilising her. He produced a pair of scissors, her eyes expanded and she formed a muffled scream.

The male cut through her clothing with the aplomb of a master tailor, making cuts here and there until they were able to remove her clothes.

One hissed at her, "Tempting though it is my beautiful thing I have my orders and a few minutes with you is not worth the pain and suffering he will cause me."

As part of a pre-ordained plan they picked her up and laid her onto an A-shaped wooden frame, fastening her arms and legs into position with cable ties. Finally her neck was also tied to the wooden template. At the top of the A was an aperture through which they had tied a length of rope.

Outside the van a few cars headed home alongside the embankment to the River Thames. Soon it would be quiet and they could carry out the next phase unhindered. An hour slowly evaporated, they'd coolly eaten some cheese and consumed a bottle of cheap wine between them. One of them, the youngest couldn't take his eyes off her; she was beautiful, their wretched plan seemed a waste, but who was he to argue if he wanted a life of opulence?

The Driver was different; he'd removed her clothing with skill but without a hint of empathy. He had dark, almost black, raven-like hair and black soulless eyes that matched his mood. He lit up a cigarette, took one deep drag and flicked it, almost whole into the side of the road. The red embers fought to stay alive but quickly extinguished and soon were as cold as the Victorian gutter that they ended their life in.

It was time.

He checked the environs for passers-by and seeing that the street was deserted he tapped on the back door and climbed back in, making his comrades ready for the last phase of their lucrative mission.

The Driver removed a red plastic petrol can, opened the vessel and made a small hole in the duct tape that laced across Petrov's mouth. Playfully he pretended to tip fuel into her mouth but in reality the fuel was intended for another act. Despite his bravado he'd made a mistake, a teaspoon of the fuel had entered her mouth and she began to choke.

They quickly raised the frame so that she could recover and in doing so offered her a last chance of salvation. Perhaps it wasn't her time after all?

The Driver leant forward and spoke, flicking spittle into her face as he emphasised his ill-educated and nicotine-stale words.

"Worry not. You will not die by burning to death my lovely. No, Alex has another plan for you. The petrol is to burn the van later. After all, we don't want to be caught now, do we?"

Two of the men laughed, the youngest was becoming more ill at ease by the second.

Summoning up what strength she had she blew the foul-tasting fuel out of the tape and straight into his face, it stung wildly as it entered his eyes and ran down his face. Ordinarily this would be punishment enough but in her circumstances she needed fortune to shine on her.

It would. Ever the compulsive smoker he had removed the last one from its packet and had chosen that time to ignite it. The vapour erupted and swiftly engulfed his head and face. Searing hot flames tore into his skin and hair, which in the confined space of the van began to overpower the other occupants. Unlike her his screams were not muted, but with limited or no foot traffic his cries for help were likely to go unheard.

His colleagues smothered his face with an old sheet and sat him against the metal wall of the van. The damage was done. His eye would never recover and he would bear the scars until he died.

Growling with rage he instructed his associates to carry on with their role. They opened the door and carried her onto the tree-lined street. The Driver followed, hissing instructions, constantly scanning for road users, favouring the damage to his face and wanting her last moments to be as painful.

He tied the rope to the wrought iron fencing and then ordered that she be lowered over the side and down to the mudflats that lay beneath her. The younger male climbed over the fence and down a ladder that had been bolted to the algae-covered river wall many years earlier. Despite the constant attention of the elements it had withstood the test of time.

They had rehearsed this repeatedly – albeit on dry land. The plan was coming together precisely, albeit they had missed a serviceable set of steps about fifty paces to their left.

The youngest male was now on the shoreline, stepping carefully in the faded light, avoiding the mud and debris that littered the riverbank; scaffold poles, weather-beaten timber, man-made detritus and various other non-descript hazards.

He was joined by the second male, a forgettable man in his forties with a wispy black moustache, the type that indicated that its owner was unsure whether to sport it, or not.

The frame was pushed down into the mud at their chosen location, an old outlet from a nearby water system, beautifully made during Victorian times and directly in line with the iconic Battersea Power Station. The rope was removed and thrown into the river soon drifting out of sight and adding to the debris field.

Petrov pleaded with the male, her eyes full of expression of fading hope and longing, longing to be anywhere other than here. She had realised where her fate now lie.

Her body was strapped to the rudimentary frame. The lower part of which was buried into the glutinous mud ensuring that her feet and shins were trapped.

But for the fact that she was naked, and petrified, she could in lesser circumstances have been one of the many people who foraged among the foreshore for long-lost treasures; just another ignored resident of an anonymous city.

In Romanian across her forehead in black permanent marker it had been written:

Tradator.

Traitor.

Running from right to left over the top of her thighs were four letters:

"WH" and "RE".

Alex had been most explicit about this. He wanted Nikolina's svelte body to provide the most intimate of missing letters. It was a final gesture of hatred for his most costly whore.

The hours had passed quickly. It was nearly four in the morning.

In a quiet corner of the city, off Ebury Bridge Road the van had soon become engulfed in flames, erasing all trace of both it and any evidence it contained.

A week later the police would identify the vehicle, stolen a month before from a hapless courier driver and now another undetected crime in a city where such events were not the exception.

Having removed every conceivable hint of their existence the occupants planned to disappear into the underbelly of a metropolis that was starting to waken, to open one semi-interested eye on a misty, late-summer morning.

Nikolina Petrov stood rigid among the frigid waters of the capitals' artery. In an hour and forty minutes it would be high tide and she would disappear beneath the water. If she was lucky, someone, somewhere may see her and set her free, but the calculations were not in her favour.

The construction workers at the adjacent power station did not board their barges until six; by then unless providence had played her part Petrov's pretty head would be submerged.

The speed and power of Old Father Thames increased her anxiety ten-fold. She prayed for an early dawn, of deliverance, but the waters kept coming, rising up her body, slowly, purposefully enveloping her.

The smell of the river was overpowering; the mud, water, fuel and remnants of its historic past all combined to create an unmistakeable odour. Were she to live she would recall it, were she to live, she would recall it fondly.

The river water started to enter the opening in the silvery tape. Her tongue pushed against it in a futile gesture but she was tiring.

All her knowledge, her training, wasted.

Her exquisite body was now almost beaten, the tide tugging at her breasts and rocking her body gently from side to side. She was beyond cold, slipping rapidly into a hypothermic state and now her tears flowed, adding their own genetic footprint into one of the greatest waterways on the globe.

She forced her tongue against the gap and upwards to avoid the water that was now trickling from her nose and into her throat. Her hair was taking on a life of its own, swaying in the water, almost ethereal; it retained its defiant red colouring but was becoming darker by the second.

Her eyes, once sparkling and welcoming, the window on a positive future, now lost all sense of hope. The water lapped onto them, more aggressively now, high tide had arrived with a vengeance.

Across the river she could make out the blurred outlines of workers arriving for another shift, she could see them; they were oblivious to her presence, laughing and joking about the events of the night before.

Her hearing was the last sense to cave in. Somewhere a siren announced the arrival of organised chaos, a loan gull flitted across the surface of the river, calling out to an unseen mate and a dredger chugged tirelessly from her right, heading downstream to Dartford.

On a nearby road bridge a solitary red London bus chugged its way anonymously south, heading home to a local equally anonymous depot.

She wished she had taken the time to tell him everything. Seconds from the end of her short life she started to count off the things she still needed to do, checked the ones that she had and lamented the ones she had not. Now, as her life ebbed she considered the one person left in the world that she trusted. She bore him no malice, for unlike the others he had been as loyal to his word as he could have been.

'Find her. Protect her. Please.'

She closed her eyes and said a quiet prayer. She could see her mother and father, her relatives and the few friends she had nurtured and knew that she would be with them soon. She considered her short and interesting life and finally consented to the river consuming her.

As the stale water filled her lungs she breathed her last and thought of Cade, hoping that he would remain true to his word, shielding her beautiful daughter from harm.

Her spirit flowed downstream, captured temporarily by swirling eddies before being released to drift once more, hidden by the mist and carried on the current.

Chapter Thirty

As Petrov had fought her tumultuous battle with her unknown foes Cade and O'Shea's evening had ended in absolute frustration. The temptation to ignore Wood was paramount and it was a thought shared by Jack and his newfound and unexpected liaison.

"Seriously Clive this had better be important?" said Cade with an air of annoyance. "Carrie, I'm sorry but I have to."

"I know Jack. It's fine, really, there'll be another time, perhaps?" Her comment was more of an optimistic question than a statement.

He leant forward and kissed her whilst dialling his answerphone messages, slipping his arms into his shirt.

"There will be. I promise."

He deleted the first, it was from Penelope, enquiring about some banal problem that he wasn't interested in nor cared about. The second was from Wood, the third from Roberts.

The messages started to scroll with Wood first.

"Boss, it's Clive…" he was out of breath and sounded full of dread.

Cade switched the phone onto speaker mode and beckoned for O'Shea to listen – all the while re-dressing herself with as much dignity as she could muster.

"Boss…I'm sorry, I made a mistake. I shouldn't have done it. I don't know what came over me…"

"Get to it man," said O'Shea unsympathetically. "I bet he's made a pass at her Jack, I can almost guarantee it. I told the boss not to trust him. Didn't I?"

Wood continued, fighting for breath.

"She's gone Jack. I was so bloody stupid, I tried it on with her and she broke my bloody nose. Look, I deserved it right? I did, I know I did. Fuck it Jack she ran off, so I chased her. I drew my baton and bloody chased her for about half a mile. I was trying to call you."

The first missed call.

"I rang again; I was within seconds of grabbing her. She was getting into your car. I knew I'd be knee-deep in shit so I backed off and let her go. It wasn't until the Mondeo drove past me that I saw that she had been captured. It was your car Jack, the section Mondeo, but you weren't in it. Some bastard had a Glock to her head."

The second missed call.

"I've rung Jason. He's travelling to the flat with some back up. Jack I'm so very sorry, I've fucked up royally so I have. MP are aware and units in Chelsea, Kensington, Westminster, they all know. I'll resign in the morning, but until then give me chance to hunt these bastards down?"

The message ended.

His phone rang again.

"Jack, Jason, been busy mate? I gather Clive has rung you, given you the SP and all that? Instead of enjoying a nice vegetarian Ruby with Mrs Roberts I find myself tearing the city apart looking for your fuckin' bird, might be nice if you answer your bloody phone once in a while."

Cade paused theatrically. "Finished?"

"I 'ave mate. Not called for."

"No, Jason, it wasn't. Need I remind you it was your bloody staff that were allegedly looking after her?"

"Touché. Right let's call a truce and crack on. I've got all ports alerts in on the Mondeo. We've got India 99 up and MP has put out a message to all section and Trojan staff too. I want the latter given that Clive reckoned they were armed. I've put in a call for CO19 to join the hunt. All adjoining forces are aware and we've put an ANPR alert on the motor. I want these bastards nailed son. Nailed, to a fuckin' great cross outside West-fucking-minster…"

"I know, fucking Abbey. I get it. We'll find her Jason. Where do we start?"

"Needle: Metropolitan haystack."

The fact that Roberts had called in the aces was an indicator of his concern about the situation, and his career. The Trojan's, or Armed Response Vehicles were never more than eight minutes away from any armed incident in London, CO19 on the other hand were a specialist unit, called out when the ante was well and truly upped.

"Start point? At the beginning I guess me old China. I've got a team going to the area around the flat – we'll start our search there, given that she could be miles away by now, the worst we can do is try and see if they've been a little slapdash in their planning. Agreed?"

"Agreed." Cade had little choice, he knew his counterpart was right, but he felt impotent.

"Any theories Jack? I mean, do you think that she's been forcibly taken or is this a set-up?"

"Plenty, but the obvious one is they knew she was likely to talk and they wanted her in their hands rather than ours. Call me cynical but I doubt there will be any ransom demands and no, to answer your question I don't think this is a bluff."

"Oh come on mate, there's always hope and you are the current expert on all this Euro-stuff remember. Let's not give in just yet. This isn't a problem, it's a challenge."

"Fuck off Jason."

"Fair point. I'll ring you in thirty."

Cade stretched his aching neck, allowing his head to fall backwards.

He stared at the wall for a moment before erupting.

"Christ Carrie, what sort of a shower of shit do you work for? Eh? Tell me? It's like Cirque de fucking soleil but without the acrobats. Keep Detective Wood away from me or seriously I will put him in hospital. That poor woman has risked everything, for what? To be let down by another group of people who just want to exploit her...."

"Jack..."

"Back off Carrie...I mean it, leave me alone for a minute." His jaw muscles were clenched, his teeth ground together to the point where he wanted to crush them.

O'Shea knew that what she was seeing was a mixture of anger and raw emotions, strangely she gained an enormous sense of compassion for Cade, watching his overt sense of helplessness, his obvious anxiety at having let Petrov down. His anger and emotions were palpable. For the first time she saw how incredibly blue his eyes really were, the emotions heightening the irises to an almost unnatural level.

She walked away, leaving him to his thoughts. Nothing else would have sufficed.

Ten minutes later she returned. She was angry too. Her agenda was biased towards her own feelings – she truly regretted missing the opportunity to sleep with this highly attractive man.

"Jack, listen to me then tell me to back off, but please listen?"

He nodded.

"I have nothing to offer other than my analytical skills, but I can sift the wheat from the chaff better than anyone in this city. I don't have your street skills anymore but I see patterns in raw data that most couldn't see if they stared at it for a year. I could earn a fortune in the banking industry, but I stay because I hate criminals too. Please, Jack, let me help?"

Her tone was measured, calm and reassuring, it was exactly what he needed and somehow she even made the phrase 'data' sound sexy. He smiled, rubbed his face, exhaled and apologised.

"Bang out of order Carrie. No excuses. I guess we both want the same?"

"Absolutely Jack, in every possible way."

"Carrie, at any other time…"

"Jack. No excuses right? Good."

He was right of course; his priorities had altered in the last hour, however much they were both frustrated the next few hours were critical. They owed Petrov a debt of gratitude – Cade knew that she had offered up her soul and a raft of information that the British police may have unsuccessfully sought for years. She held the key but now Cade had no idea which lock it would fit. And somehow he knew there was more to this beautiful girl – and a lot more information, some of which she had promised to tell him, when the time was right.

"Come on, we need to get out on the streets. Roberts rates you higher than any analysts he's ever had – you should be honoured. Let's get that analytical mind of yours operating before we end up personally and professionally distracted!"

"That was kind of my plan. She'll show up Jack. It's London, people still talk, despite what you read in the papers. We'll have her back within twenty-four hours. If not I have a few ideas. I'm not alone; we have the might of the Metropolitan Police behind us. But yes, for now let's go and see what havoc we can wreak on this amazing city."

She turned towards the door, stopped, thought about re-arranging her sofa cushions, saw Cade's eyes following her every move, smiled and headed for the stairs.

She paused. Sensing he might have overstepped the mark he leaned towards her. She put her arms around him and they hugged for about a minute. Short enough to feel a sense of warmth, long enough to show compassion. He'd never embraced a comparative stranger for quite so long, quite so intensely. They both exhaled slowly.

He held her at a distance and smiled, "Thanks Carrie, I've known you five minutes and yet I feel a sense of connection I never had with my wife – or any other woman for that matter. If I never tell you again I think you are a very special person."

"Thanks Jack, that's what they all say. A shame, I'm fed up with being either everyone's entertainment or just 'special'. I was hoping that I might have found someone I could finally fall for. It's not just about sex you know…"

"Carrie, you don't need to justify your obvious and insatiable lust, it's OK."

"Sod off Cade."

"Sod off Sergeant Cade."

He slapped her forcefully across her backside causing her to shriek.

"You'll wait, my little obsessive, compulsive lovely."

She kissed him vigorously, pocketed her cell phone and put her jacket on.

"I'm ready Ca…Sergeant Cade, let's go and kick some serious backside."

O'Shea was correct. The might of the biggest metropolitan force in Britain was starting to swing into action. A juggernaut, it would slowly get up to speed, calling on various individuals and departments, the emphasis and importance slowly gaining impetus as each link in the chain of command was reached. It might take an hour for the ripples to come to a halt, for command and control to take over but at least Cade was content that something was being instigated, no doubt by an equally manic Roberts.

Armed with this knowledge Cade and O'Shea set out to carry out their own search for Petrov – a foreigner in a foreign land.

It was late, the temperature had dropped and a hint of mist was rolling in from the Thames. The streets resembled a scene from a Dickensian horror film, the sodium lighting doing its best to add to the unnatural atmosphere.

Out of the darkness an iconic shape appeared, first, a pair of yellowy headlamps, long past their sell by date but doing their utmost to illuminate a path for their driver, they belonged to the familiar large-grilled façade of a Post Office red AEC Routemaster double decker bus.

The Routemaster was one of those globally recognised icons, as familiar as cheese on toast and as dependable as a comfortable pair of tartan slippers.

Cade stepped out into the street and held up his warrant card.

"Jack, what the hell are you doing?" asked a still excitable O'Shea.

"I'm availing myself of the benefits of a warrant card; free travel. Come on, let's talk to the driver, he'll know these streets better than most."

"But why don't we wait for a job car? It would be quicker, surely?"

"Surely it would, but even plain ones stand out like Bulldog's testicles. So, when in London…"

The Routemaster driver saw Cade appear through the enveloping mist, pumped his right foot on the brakes, temporarily closed his eyes and hoping for the best came to an abrupt halt. Empty but for its driver it was one of the last of a line of dependable, driver/conductor vehicles still in service in the city.

At the wheel was an Afro Caribbean man in his late fifties called George Douglas.

Douglas was heading to his professional home. The last of the line, he and his beloved steed had seen every type of human behaviour, upbeat and equally, negative. Douglas even had a name for his bus; Dolly.

He often joked that he and Dolly were like an old married couple, they spent countless hours together, but hardly ever talked - the only difference being that when they did she always won the arguments.

He sat on a seat long past its best; worn, gnarled brown leather cosseted him, but every crease had a tale to tell. The steering wheel was enormous when compared to its modern counterpart. To his right a pair of simple switches, one for the headlights the other for the wipers.

To his left the model number was inscribed simply on the wall of the vehicle and a green sign informed the driver that the poorly fitted sliding window was his emergency exit. Douglas opened it in the summer when the temperature in the cab became unbearable. With only one non-fault crash in his driving history he had never needed it for anything else.

Douglas and his partner had covered almost half a million miles with only a break for six days when he had lost his real-life childhood sweetheart Cynthia; she had been so brave, succumbing after a silent, valiant and belligerent battle against stomach cancer.

Douglas wasn't always a slightly bowed man; he had once been a part of the Jamaican youth athletics squad, long before the nation would stun the world with its repeated list of champions. His thick wiry hair wasn't always tinged with silver either, but his chestnut eyes had always been passion-filled and when he and Cynthia danced to Otis she loved nothing more than to look into them, losing herself, and for a short while her problems too.

During the seventies and eighties Douglas had sported one of the best moustaches the fleet had ever seen. The morning after he lost the love of his life he shaved it off, hair by hair, allowing each one to slip quietly away into the plumbing of his Victorian terraced home south of the river.

Those that knew Douglas said he changed from that day on.

He switched routes, moving north of the Thames but had negotiated that his old colleagues looked after Dolly at Camberwell. His Regional Manager, a man who unlike many of his peers recognised that loyalty was a two-way street had allowed it to happen. It was one of the reasons his crews were the most engaged.

Douglas had certainly seen it all and now on his penultimate drive to his favoured garage he found himself confronted by yet another fool, except this one was waving something at him. He shoved his spectacles up onto the bridge of his nose, focused and then rammed his foot into the worn carpet, hoping Dolly would do as she was told.

He slid the drivers' window back with his right hand and started to tell the white man exactly what he thought of him.

"What in God's heaven do you tink you are doing bwoi? 'Ave you got a death wish or sometin'? Why I should come out there and kick your backside from 'ere to Camberwell…"

Douglas continued to focus, he knew in reality he had needed new glasses for a few months, but like Dolly they had been faithful servants. He'd make do, for one more day.

What he saw through the frosted lenses was a police warrant card inscribed with the name Jack Cade.

He shook his head from side to side before sucking air in through his teeth.

"Well there's a surprise, a po-lice officer. If you ask me your lot are either cynical, paranoid or racists…"

Cade paused and replied with a gritty façade, "Sorry, I don't believe a word of that, either that or I'm hearing voices, or perhaps, is it because you are black?"

Douglas looked at him with an equally stony face then burst out laughing.

"Boy you are sometin' else, some-tin else. Girl, you should keep your hand on this one, he's a keeper. Now, if you don't mind I've got a bus to deliver safely back home…"

Cade smiled, knowing his approach had not been without risk.

He held out his hand "Jack Cade, temporarily assigned to the local police – and this wonderful lady is called Carrie, she drew the short straw. Look my friend, I wouldn't normally ask, but we've had a very serious incident tonight, one of our team has been kidnapped. I don't make a habit of forcibly stopping wonderful old girls like this but I need your help."

Cade stroked the cooling front wing of the Routemaster causing Douglas to instantly mellow.

The wonderfully soulful eyes that looked back at Cade had lost their bitterness; Douglas leant out of the window slightly and returned the handshake. His skin was burred but warm.

"OK Sergeant – this may be the most reckless thing I have done, but what do you need?"

Cade swiftly explained – what he needed was to drift through the streets unseen and Dolly was the perfect Trojan horse.

"Come to the front of the bus once you board, if you need me shout through the window to the left of the cab, I'll hear you, but I must warn you if tings get hairy this old girl will respond. I held the lap record at Chiswick Driver Training Centre, man I could put these beauties sideways!"

"Will do. Tell me, isn't there another way to communicate? Do you have a cell phone I can give you a bell on?"

"Mister the only bell on dis bus is the one you press to get my attention. My Conductor Eddie normally does that but I dropped him off earlier – he had a hot date. One ring for stop the bus, two for it's OK to go and three rings to cancel the two rings. Easy right? By the way…"

"Yes."

"You might want to try it on top, you get a better view."

O'Shea bit her lower lip in an attempt not to smile before following the instructions to board the bus via the iconic rear door.

Cade and O'Shea stood in the aisle on the iconic vehicle waiting for their new team member to get going. She started giggling, an act that rarely visited her.

"I think you need to ring the bell Jack…"

He leant up and hit the button twice.

Douglas started his companion and hearing its durable Leyland engine rumbling into life looked in his right hand mirror and merged back onto the road. He had rediscovered his youthful exuberance once more. His eyes shone. Where was Cynthia when he needed her?

As the Routemaster took them along the quiet street Cade turned to O'Shea.

"Come on you, upstairs."

O'Shea was genuinely surprised and feigned a servant/Lord of the manor role-play.

"Ooh sire, I never thought…"

"Daft bugger, we'll see more from up there. Go on, after you."

O'Shea navigated the curved staircase aware that Cade was immediately behind her. He knew that she knew that he was staring at her backside. It was a great view after all, but now was not the time, nor the place. They made it to the front of the top deck and started to scan left and right.

"Shit this is one hell of a big city Carrie!"

"It is, but you know, if it was me I'd either be on a ferry to Calais by now or I would look to lay low nearby, why risk being stopped by a random patrol vehicle?"

Douglas duly stopped at traffic lights and controlled junctions, moving off effortlessly with such a light payload. He looked in his periscope mirror and could see his passengers. They were an attractive couple and like many on board Dolly were probably finding the temptation to engage in a clandestine sexual act almost unbearable. Alone and later at night many couples did.

He laughed when he recalled a young couple doing just that. It was in the early eighties, slightly intoxicated, she was the driving force, pulling her summer dress over her head and revealing a young tanned body, a pair of matching white knickers and a smile. Her lover was a year younger and almost unable to restrain himself. He certainly couldn't believe his luck.

From the moment the Conductor had rang the bell they had begun. Her underwear was nestled on her shoes and her outstretched hands were up against the front window, her conquest industriously entering her, his right foot on the seat next to him providing extra leverage, looking over his shoulder, the fear of being caught adding to the excitement. He wouldn't last long.

What they hadn't accounted for was a certain Jamaican called George Douglas. In his prime and desperate to get home to see his own beloved girl he had voyeuristically watched the whole act through the periscope.

Upstairs his only passengers were enjoying a different pastime.

Downstairs, neatly isolated from the outside world George Douglas whistled through his front teeth, he was impressed with the boy's stamina, a man after his own heart.

Why had he never had Cynthia on board a bus? What a wasted opportunity. He made a mental note for the next time he met up with his sweetheart. In the meantime he was content with driving back to the depot whilst watching the overhead activities.

At the moment of no return he had rung the bell shouting 'All aboard'.

He chortled to himself aware of what he had just done.

The females' hands slid down the window, she was gasping for breath, trying unsuccessfully to be quiet, her face ending up on the periscope lens, panting, hot and all sense of worry momentarily abandoned.

The girl smiled. It was almost as if she had known.

Quite how Douglas had not crashed was beyond him. He got home that night and made love to Cynthia like never before.

Some thirty years later Cade stood in the same spot, watching, scanning, looking for a hint of something, a speck of evidential support, knowing deep inside that his plan was probably as flawed as Roberts'. This was a pro-active, well-trained team that would be long gone.

Wood had a lot to answer for but that could wait. Right now all emphasis was on finding Nikolina.

He remained deep in thought. Myriad questions raced through his mind, he swiftly dealt with those obvious to anyone in the law enforcement profession but dwelled on a few that haunted him.

'Would they ever find her?' 'Had he offered her the right amount of protection?' 'How would he maintain his promise to bring her daughter to safety?'

The last haunted him more than any other.

His eyes started to lose focus, the more he concentrated the more he drifted, and a series of watermarks on the glass screen soon became all he could see. Eventually he drilled down even deeper until he could make out the Kitemark on the safety glass.

It was O'Shea that brought him back around with a gentle but deliberate question.

"Do you think we'll find her Jack?"

"I don't know. I don't know why I'm on this bus either to be honest and I certainly don't know why I let your so-called team guard her. I could throttle Roberts too given half a chance. My force and yours – they put me in a position of trust Carrie, a bloody Sergeant caring for a top-flight gangster's girlfriend. What *were* we thinking?"

He looked, for the second time that day, visibly furious, but also fearful of what he might discover.

She held onto the polished chrome seat handles, placing her hands where the ghosts of millions of others had done before her – all those hands leaving countless fingerprints and greasy, dirty marks. If only they could see her now. For the first time in years she simply didn't care.

She moved towards him, in the nearest sparkling handle a distorted image developed. She stopped and deliberately put her arms around his middle. He initially resisted but tiredness took over. He leant back into her supportive body and sighed. She kissed him on the nape of his neck. It felt good. He continued to watch every side street but slowly she won him round. It may have been a long time since she had done this with anyone but Cade found himself thinking that she was very much an experienced participant. He also knew that he was deeply attracted to her.

She was highly aroused and just like her white-clad eighties predecessor she wanted her man. The thrill of the situation engorged her body and emotions with chemicals, causing an imbalance that she futilely resisted.

An image flashed uncomfortably across her mind. She was horrified that her knickers lay abandoned on her lounge floor – what if a burglar were to enter her flat, what would he think?

Douglas looked up through the prism.

"Oh bwoi here we go again Dolly, what is it with dese endless displays o' lovemaking? It's a good ting you and me are retiring soon girl!" he laughed out aloud, clapped his hands together and carried on driving.

Roberts rang Cade's cell phone again.

"Come on Cade, answer the poxy thing. I have news you northern bastard."

He heard Cade's answer phone message.

"Jack, pick up mate. I've got an update. We may have had a sighting of the Mondeo - Battersea area. Local Section lads have also found a Transit. Fire brigade attended to it a while ago, completely gutted, down some shitty back street. Pretty sure it's a stolen motor. Checking CCTV, it's them mate. They switched her from the Mondeo. Sorry, no sign of the girl. Where are you? Ring me mate, I know you are up to your nuts with O'Shea but get back to me ASAP. Out."

Douglas eased Dolly onto the Chelsea Road Bridge and began to cross over the Thames heading south. He merged onto Nine Elms lane and ran alongside the old power station at Battersea, these days more synonymous with Pink Floyd than producing power. It was always his favoured route at this hour. The four miles made all the more pleasant with a floodlit view of the Thames which always looked at its best at high tide.

As they passed a non-descript service road a Ford Mondeo joined the road in front of them from their right. Without headlights the only thing that allowed Douglas's fading eyesight to see the car were the myriad streetlights. He cursed and pressed the miniscule horn.

The Mondeo had exited so rapidly that it began to fishtail, its tyres scrabbling for traction, the noise of which caused Cade to turn around sharply. He pushed O'Shea to one side, terminating her advances as quickly as they had begun.

"Carrie, ring Roberts. No, ring the control room. Then Roberts. Ring. Ring!"

He pressed the bell repeatedly and ran downstairs to the lower tier.

Ahead, the Mondeo balked in slower traffic, where the occupants were heading was anyone's guess, but now, for a short while at least they were the hunters, hunted.

Cade rubbed his eyes. "Now what?"

He yelled through the window as arranged. Pointing ahead whilst trying to dial a number on his phone.

"George – that's the car, follow it!"

"I'm one step ahead of you bwoi. One step ahead." Douglas yelled back.

He accelerated but the old girl seemed asthmatic, almost ready to retire.

"One more day. Come on girl!"

Chapter Thirty One

Douglas rammed the bus into a lower gear, accelerating as hard as he could, offering a balance of urgency and sympathy. He tapped the wheel and shouted "Come on Dolly, now is the time!"

O'Shea was busy talking to the Control Room, passing information on their location and trying to abbreviate an unnecessarily long story.

Cade's phone rang.

"Yes!"

"Jack, it's me we've had a possible sighting of the Mondeo near Woolwich, I'm deploying staff there now my son. We'll have that bastard in custody before you…"

"Jason stand your team down. We are behind the bloody thing…stand by…"

He paused, shouting through to Douglas.

"George where the bloody hell are we?"

Douglas was otherwise engaged, fully committed to the chase.

Cade hammered on the window again.

"Douglas bloody answer me – where are we?"

Cade could hear Roberts shouting into the phone but he needed the information and for now Roberts could wait.

He could just make out what the Jamaican was saying.

"We are on Nine Elms Way…no wait one…now on Wandsworth Road. I can see the sign. Wandsworth Road Jason heading…north east."

Roberts was now relaying the information to the Control Room but also desperate to fill in some gaps.

"Jack what the sweet Jesus is going on my son? How the hell did you pick it up?"

"Call it luck, call it female intuition."

"Classic! You had a sex change in the last half hour?"

"Twat. I mean O'Shea. She's my lucky talisman Jason. We are on a London bus, don't ask me the number, it's red if that helps? It's the one that's trying to keep up with our bandit car."

"Do they know you are behind them?"

"Not sure, unless they happen to notice a twelve ton bus being driven by a manic Jamaican. For now I think we've got the element of surprise."

"Top man. I'll get our Air Support up – can you see the girl?"

A cold wave washed over him. Until that moment Cade hadn't given a second thought to whether Petrov was in the car – either alive or dead.

"Not sure Jason. Note sure. Sorry. OK stand by, we are slowing for the lights, if he goes through then they know we are onto to them…it's a stop, stop, stop. Where are your boys?"

Cade was trying to remain calm, he thought about decamping and running to the car but he knew that they needed Dolly to remain in her Trojan Horse status. And unlike him his opponents had at least one weapon.

"Kennington Lane heading…Fuck it Jas' I don't know which way we are heading but they are starting to increase speed. George has just shouted Elephant and Castle."

"I've got you son, I've got you. Air Support are going to be overhead in five, area cars inbound, I reckon they are heading south, my guess is Old Kent Road, Black Heath and onto the A2 – nice and quiet, foot down, through Dover and across Europe before you can say you've met the Met."

Cade's mind shot back to the journey he had taken with Petrov. It seemed like years before and yet could be counted in hours. They had travelled from Dover along the same well-trodden route on their first journey into London. It had been Petrov's first visit to the iconic city and unbeknown to her the start of her demise.

They had followed him.

"Jason, hard right, hard right onto…Walworth Road. I think they know something is wrong."

"Bollocks Jack, they won't expect a frigging bus to be pursuing them, keep going, and get your man to force them off the road if you have to."

"Deliberately crash Dolly, you don't know the driver very well."

"Dolly? What the…?"

"Forget it, it's too long a story. Any more news on our potential kidnappers?"

"None pal, look it's likely that they are part of the group that Petrov was ID'ing. Makes sense yeah? So let's catch the bastards then we can start to put the pieces into the jigsaw. Smart money says she knows a shed load of info, her beloved boyfriend knows that and well, the rest as they say is history."

"Agreed. Jason there was something she wasn't telling us and this is already going to take some serious writing up."

Roberts sighed. It was the best possible answer. Paperwork would be the death of him.

"Heygate Street, we've got some traffic which is helping. Where the living bloody daylights are your men?"

"Nine Nine is overhead, he's got obs on you Jack. Your man can back off now. Let's do this by the book yeah?"

Cade knew the protocols backwards, chapter and verse. All police officers did. The 'Red Mist' was notorious for getting in the way during a pursuit. Adrenalin and the overwhelming desire to get the bad guy had been the undoing of many an experienced officer. Sadly for Cade, George Douglas hadn't read the book.

"Jason. Find the girl. Find Nikolina. Please."

Cade pressed the red button on his phone terminating the call but Roberts had already gone.

Overhead an Aerospatiale AS355N registration G-SEPA and one of a number of helicopters utilised by the Metropolitan Police, announced its arrival on scene. As its rotors cut through the air, its crewman used succinct communications to relay information and a visual update to the control room Inspector, who used the Computer Aided Dispatch system, hence why he was better known the CAD Commander.

"MPS from India Nine Nine, target vehicle is on Walworth Road heading east, stand by, stand by, deviation onto Heygate Street, Heygate Street."

These were the icy, professional tones of the third crewman, the Mission Commander who relayed his information expertly, calmly notifying both the CAD room and those units listening on the ground.

In front of the Mission Commander and alongside the civilian pilot sat the Observer, checking his on-board digital maps and communicating with the pilot and alternating between maps, on board electronic systems and the ever-changing London skyline.

"Vehicle is continuing east, normal road speeds, our bus has departed the pursuit and is heading along Walworth Road. If units can deploy to the…"

Both crewmen exchanged a few ideas before the commander continued.

"…junction of East Street and Old Kent Road and another unit onto Thurlow Street and Albany Road. Over."

Cade was still alone. O'Shea had chosen the upper deck as a safe haven rather than risk the stairs. Dolly was creaking and swaying but somehow allowing herself to stay in the race. Despite what the eye in the sky had broadcast she was far from done.

Cade shouted to his new teammate.

"George we've lost them, we need to turn left."

"No way!" bellowed Douglas, "We go down here, then we turn left, you just watch me bwoi, this old girl is not done yet."

Cade rubbed his face, concentrating on his chin.

"This is going to end in tears, I have a feeling in my water."

His phone rang.

"Cade, Roberts. Nine Nine is in control now, units deploying, we've got them my son. I'm en route with Dave, they are somewhere near the Walworth Road nick. Heaven only knows where you and the rest of the Double Decker's have gone!"

"Roberts."

"Yes I know. I'll go fuck myself."

"Good man. Hey Jason."

"Go ahead."

"This is just the start you know. We are going to need some serious help. This isn't just a random couple of crimes, it's an angry boil that hides a deeper festering infection."

"And I know just the dynamic duo to lance it. Out"

Roberts was temporarily gone, it was a good job as Cade's cell phone battery was diminishing, along with his tolerance, by the minute.

He turned to see O'Shea haphazardly navigating the staircase.

He banged on the window, "George, pull over as soon as you can, we've got to think this through."

Douglas was unhappy, he wanted to show those foreign bastards a few lessons in respect. But he knew Cade meant what he said so reluctantly he eased Dolly to the side of the road and applied the brakes.

"Rodney Road, speed approximately seven zero, no opposing traffic, approaching Flint Street, right hand deviation. He won't make it at this speed MPS. Brake lights, brake lights, hard left onto...Catesby Street. Narrowly missed a red Renault. Can see driver and front seat passenger. Possibly one, maybe two rear seat passengers."

India Nine Nine's crew continued to relay the critical information.

A local unit joined the commentary.

"MP from November 4 we are on Old Kent Road turning onto Massinger Street. Where do you want us? Over."

"November 4 hold at your present location, target vehicle is currently on Catesby towards Congreve Street over."

"Yes-yes."

"India Nine Nine vehicle is now Congreve heading south east towards East Street. Rear passenger has thrown something from the vehicle. Received?"

"MP received – all units stand by. Any unit that can check Congreve and East Street for property please?"

The chess pieces were being skilfully manoeuvred.

"November 2 onto Old Kent Road and stand by near the Thomas A Becket pub – thank you. November 4 back onto Old Kent Road please. Units are to deploy Stinger if possible. Trojan en route, ETA four minutes. All units to be aware that occupants may be in possession of a firearm."

The last sentence sent a chill down the spine of Police Constable Darren Simms, with only three years in the job he'd pretty much seen it all and knew the local beat like the back of his hand. The only thing he hadn't experienced was an up close and personal familiarisation with a pistol.

Other local units were now joining the incident. Local panda cars were zigzagging across south London vying for position should the Mondeo lose control. Officers on board these smaller vehicles knew they were no match for the more powerful, faster area cars but they could run as fast as any of their colleagues in a foot chase. And listening to the commentary this would be a very rewarding arrest with limited paperwork.

For PC Daz Simms it could be the kick-start his career needed.

"November 51 MP – I'm on Portland Street heading north."

"51 received."

"Nine Nine to that unit, stand by. Target vehicle is going to pass you any moment now – from your right heading west. MP is this vehicle stolen?"

"Nine Nine from MP, yes, yes. Confirm vehicle is one of ours."

The operator hated admitting that her staff were chasing one of their own.

"November 51 air priority!" It was PC Simms, using the call familiar to police officers across the globe.

"Ford Mondeo failing to stop, at least three up, towards the one way street, he's got opposing traffic MP, still failing to stop."

His sentence was delivered in a few seconds.

Simms was trying his utmost to remain calm; he could taste the excitement as his adrenal glands released their potent chemicals.

"51 from MP you are to continue your commentary, however should the situation become dangerous for you or any other road users you are to abort, received?"

Simms was thrashing the Ford Focus' five speed gearbox, second to third and back again, the noise of the 1.8 engine jostling with the sirens for primacy, sirens which ricocheted off the mixture of residential housing and run-down commercial buildings.

He heard the operator but ignored her. This was his first full-bore pursuit and these people were not going to get away.

"Nine Nine - 51 has no opposing traffic, it is safe to continue."

The two vehicles hurtled along King and Queen Street, with three or possibly four people on board the Mondeo was slower and now Simms had gained ground.

"Alpha 55 can I come in please?"

"Alpha 55 go ahead."

"We have recovered a small bag of clothes from outside 48 East Street. Believe it to be the object seen being thrown from the Mondeo."

"Received."

A continuing list of abbreviated and acronym-laden comments made its way onto the event log.

"MP from 51 speed six zero, road conditions are good, no opposing traffic, safe to continue, one vehicle ahead. Target vehicle is braking, now wrong side of the road, speed seven zero."

The latter part of the commentary aroused the CAD Inspector who slid his microphone into place and prepared to abort the pursuit.

Simms desperately wished for more power and a decent hands-free system.

"Braking, braking, vehicle is turning left, left, left…into…"

Nine Nine's observer completed the sentence.

"…MP he's into the Poets flat's – left at Shelley, it's a dead end, preparing to bail out. Can you get units to this location please?"

The force, like many others up and down Britain had become used to this type of activity, drivers, often only in their teens would try to escape in an area in which they had first-hand knowledge, better to elude the 'Five-O' with their cumbersome body armour and equipment, whilst they sprinted away into the night in their tracksuits and Nike's.

But this vehicle was different.

"Into the car park MP, he's doing a 180 and we are back out onto King, turning left."

Simms had been in the pursuit for five minutes and was already mentally exhausted.

His eyes saw only what they needed to, allowing him to stay in the chase, whilst his brain processed every piece of information before him, even hazards that didn't eventuate flashed through his unconscious mind. His hands and feet were working in perfect synergy as he balanced risk with excitement.

"Left onto Browning MP, speed five zero."

India Nine Nine's observer announced that the junction was clear as they hovered at a thousand feet, their thirty million candlepower Night Sun searchlight illuminating the road and surrounding areas.

Without warning the Mondeo braked fiercely. A small set of white lights illuminated as the car then accelerated in reverse, its front tyres competing for traction.

Despite the assistance of the vehicles' anti-lock braking system Simms had no option but to run into the back of the bandit car, the impact was severe enough to deploy Simms' airbag.

Both vehicles came to a halt. Curtains at a nearby block of flats started to twitch as the local neighbourhood came to life, awakened by the activity outside their anonymous, mundane dwellings.

Simms unbuckled his seat belt and attempted to waft away the clouds of black powder from the airbag detonation, all the while providing a brief but breathless sitrep.

"51 RTA outside Barrett House. Stand by for an update. Can I have some back up to this location please?"

The operator spun around in her chair. "Hear that boss? Local unit has crashed."

Every unit within five miles was descending upon his location. Eager for the chase and better still the arrest, officers were hammering their own patrol cars along side streets, adding to the excitement, furthering the knowledge that something interesting was happening in south London. The problem was it was happening all the time.

The CAD Inspector knew that his hardest job now was to maintain control – the last thing he wanted was a shooting on his shift, the second was one of his own getting hurt. For some, the political correctness had become so commonplace that the former was more concerning than the latter.

Simms stopped. He recalled the last words of the operator, 'be advised that occupants may be in possession of a firearm.'

Something deeply intuitive made him stay in the vehicle, which whilst battered and bruised was still just about driveable. Seatbelt off, he watched and waited as India Nine Nine hovered obediently overhead, a hawk watching its prey.

The murky street was intensely illuminated by the Night Sun system, mocking the one remaining headlight on Simms' vehicle.

Instinctively he placed the Focus into reverse and started to back away from the target car. His front air dam clattered onto the road, leaving similar damage on the Mondeo's rear end. A fine mist emitted from Simms' car, the result of a punctured high-pressure hose hidden somewhere deep in the engine bay.

"MP from India Nine Nine the target vehicle has deliberately rammed 51. 51 appears OK; he's in his vehicle. Occupants of the Mondeo are also remaining in theirs. Seems to be some form of stand-off. Another unit to each end of Browning please."

Overhead the AS355 realigned itself, better to illuminate the entire street. The commander could see a larger vehicle approaching at speed along Browning. The white BMW 5 series was an icon in the city. A star on its roof was all the aircrew needed to see.

On board were three officers and a mobile arsenal – enough to deal with most immediate action scenarios. Conventionally the units would work in pairs but their counterpart was twenty miles away, supporting a cross border operation on a motorway heading south into the adjoining county of Kent.

The Driver concentrated on the rapidly unravelling scene before him. His passenger, or as he was referred to, the Navigator, dealt with the radio, and in the rear the third man, the Observer acted as a liaison between the unit and other specialist staff. All were armed with Glock 17 semi-automatic pistols; the Navigator and Observer were readying their Heckler & Koch MP5 sub-machine guns.

Dressed in dark blue with matching body armour, carrying ballistic equipment including shields and helmets, the trio could strike swiftly and take control of most situations in a coordinated and highly-trained approach.

The Navigator made contact with his CAD operator.

"MP from MP 413, on scene Browning – air priority please."

As his sentence finished two of the Mondeo's occupants exited their vehicle.

The driver, a young male in his early twenties, but no more, looked startled, lost, and arguably more scared than he had ever been. He was holding a dark object in his right hand. Dressed in ill-fitting jeans and a cheap, fraudulent T-shirt he looked like a boy thrust into a man's world.

His front seat passenger was entirely different. His frayed looks belied his relatively young age.

Simms stared at him through the windscreen of his patrol car, his mind alive with electric stimuli, desperate to absorb every last detail. As hard as he tried to focus on the developing scene his eyes kept focussing on the heating element in the Ford's windscreen, its zigzagging wires mapping out across the glass shield.

Simms blinked and blinked once more.

The passenger looked as angry as the recent wounds on his face, which bore the hallmarks of deep-seated burns, burns which openly wept as the male glared at his opponent through coal-black eyes.

Sensing an opportunity to take control Simms opened the driver's door and began to exit, as he stood, struggling against the weight of his stab-proof vest he heard a challenge.

He was in the way; an unnecessary and deadly obstruction.

"Armed Police! Get onto the floor *now*! Do as I say and you will not be harmed. Do it. Now!"

The voice's owner was confidently, quietly and efficiently weighing up the evidence before him, figuring out in milliseconds how to contend with at least two potentially armed criminals and an unarmed young officer with adrenalin still coursing through his veins.

Frankly he hoped the kid would hit the ground too. A 'blue on blue' was categorically all he needed to make a bad week worse.

He raised the barrel of his matte-black phosphated-bodied MP5 from the low-ready position in a single arcing motion; staring at the driver tactically over the top of his weapon, his leather-clad right index finger moving decisively from the safe position to the firing position, easing pressure onto the trigger: ready.

He knew his colleague had the passenger painted with his own site. But there was still the rear passenger to contend with.

The Observer was ready to move in with his Glock and assist with any arrests.

Tried and tested, they had done it all a thousand times.

And then the moment changed, in half a heartbeat the situation erupted. The driver began to yell something, his voice was heavily accented, the Observer had heard it before and he was convinced it was Russian, but why here, in London?

The young male started to shout to Simms, his nearest opposition, but he was shouting for clemency not control.

"The girl! The girl! I know where she is! Help me!"

He brought his right hand up in line with his shoulder. To an onlooker, trained or otherwise it appeared threatening. But Simms had heard the call for help.

He rotated his upper body to look at his colleague and in a critical, intense and focused moment he sub-consciously saw the first round leave the weapon. On board India Nine Nine the Observer saw it via his high-powered lens, a brief escape of smoke from the barrel was all the experienced crewman needed to see.

What he had observed were the expanding propellant gases escaping, exerting rearward pressure on the weapons' mechanism, allowing the round to leave the weapon and in turn facilitating the whole process, which repeated in the time it took to blink.

The sub-sonic 9mm Parabellum round had past Simms before he had chance to register its presence. It covered the forty metres in an instant, striking the driver in the chest. With a muzzle velocity of over a thousand feet per second the round appeared to hit its target almost before it had been registered as a distinctive crack in the evening air.

The operator squeezed the trigger again.

The second round deployed, leaving a gaseous miasma in its wake, wafting into the marksman's face, teasing his nostrils with its acrid chemical stench.

The round struck the young male in the collarbone, shattering it. His fall from grace was as far removed from a Hollywood film set as it could be. He simply dropped to the ground, and in doing so released his grip on the phone he had been holding, which clattered onto the pavement.

He was dead before he was able to have another conscious thought.

He would never have the opportunity to purge his soul, to steer the hunters to their prey – the girl was so pretty, she shouldn't have been left there, like that. Alone.

The officer implemented years of training; scanning over the top of his weapon, left and right, finger outside the trigger guard, watching the target intensely in case he returned fire. He knew his team needed to neutralise any further threats, to take control, but not at any cost.

Simms could see the rear seat passenger clambering from the back and into the driver's seat. He knew that they were going to try to escape. He shouted back to his colleagues, desperately trying to communicate what he was observing.

He took the opportunity to seize the moment, leaving the relative safety of his car, he ran towards the deceased male, quite why, the subsequent enquiry would reveal, he wasn't entirely sure.

He had covered a few paces towards the Mondeo when he saw the passenger raise a pistol in his direction. He heard his colleagues challenge again. His conscious mind was spinning out of control, fight or flight were his only options, like a batsman caught between the wickets at the nearby Oval he was marooned.

The endless hum of the helicopters' engine added to the disarray, it was the most surreal moment in his short life and shorter career.

The passenger levelled the weapon across the Ford's rooftop and squeezed the lightweight trigger. The first 9mm round missed Simms completely and embedded in a nearby wall, the second left the short barrel of the iconic Austrian weapon before the passenger had felt the trigger reset.

The mechanism was silky-smooth, almost imperceptible as it fed another round from the fifteen remaining, allowing the whole process to repeat itself, hurling a third projectile on its way towards a terror-struck Simms.

Simms' body reacted to the second and third bullet as each hit him in the side of his chest; whilst his vest was not ballistic it was able to suppress the raw energy of the round and most likely saved his life.

What the vest failed to do was reduce the energy to a point where it wouldn't cause a few of his ribs to implode; the intercostal cartilages giving way and allowing at least one of the ribs to puncture his lung.

He tried to leap spectacularly over a low boundary wall but the effect of being shot at such close range forced him unceremoniously onto the pavement, his pale face skimming across the concrete, before he lay motionless, in intense pain, quietly praying for leniency.

The passenger then turned towards the ARV crew and fired indiscriminately. At such close range it was chaos.

Nine Nine took over the commentary attempting to broadcast a live TV feed back to the CAD room. The pixelated, distorted images were all Inspector John Daniel needed to see. It was his worst nightmare. How the hell he would explain this unravelling skirmish on the streets of London to an already over-stressed Deputy Commissioner was the least of his problems.

One thing was for sure, despite his incredible experience and blemish-free career his days as a CAD manager were most likely over. Hopefully he would be offered a role that suited him and appeased his ever-loving wife. It was time to move on.

He took his glasses off, laid them on the desk, rubbed his eyes, put them back on and re-engaged with the situation. His skill lay in his ability to organise disparate groups of people in tactical situations.

"Nine Nine keep the feed coming please. Trojan sitrep ASAP."

He turned to one of his more experienced Desk Sergeants and shouted, "Has anyone spoken to Roberts? His crew started this mess. Get him on the bloody phone sharpish!"

The ARV navigator fired three rounds. The first struck the rear hatchback window frame and ricocheted at a sixty-degree angle into the night sky. The second struck the Glock causing its plastic components to shatter in the passengers' hand, breaking a finger and tearing skin from another.

The third round sliced through the targets neck, avoiding the left external carotid artery but damaging the sternocleidomastoid muscle.

Bleeding profusely the passenger ducked into the Mondeo as the third member of the team gunned its throttle and accelerated along Browning Street.

Nine Nine's pilot instinctively followed, leaving the ARV crew to regroup. A local unit moved forward upon their instructions and tended to Simms who was still down but not out.

The Observer keyed the microphone, "MP we are back on board and will continue the pursuit. All area cars are to maintain cordon and control only. Do not approach this vehicle."

"MP received" the operator repeated the instructions from the ARV crew as his colleague organised an ambulance to the scene. Satisfied this was done he shouted across to Daniel.

"Boss, Deputy is on the blower, wants an update shall I put him through?"

"Oh please do Derek, please do."

The Trojan team were racing along Browning hoping to pick up the damaged and highly sought-after Mondeo. With air support it was just a matter of time before they located it.

"India Nine Nine we have a temporary loss. Vehicle is somewhere in the vicinity. Stand by."

Unbeknown to both crews the new driver on board the Mondeo had turned right into Colworth Grove, a dead end street about half a mile from them. With his lights off and bringing the car to an abrupt halt using the handbrake he had become all but invisible.

Nine Nine swept along the road and banked, turning sharply to repeat a run across the top of the local residential area, half of which was coming to terms with a fatal police shooting on its doorstep.

The ARV slowed, its driver, used to playing cat and mouse had decided that it must be somewhere nearby. The area car at the larger junction of Browning and Walworth Road had not observed anything other than a taxi, and even that had been stopped and searched.

Now all they had to do was triangulate the area, close it down and wait.

The crew on board the AS355 saw another vehicle travelling along Walworth and turning slowly onto Browning. It had a triangle on its roof. A dog patrol had arrived.

Both units exchanged quick-fire information on their back-to-back radios as they wound their windows down, listening to India Nine Nine as she gained height and created a larger search area, infrared camera ready for any foot chase.

Cade had been joined by O'Shea.

"You OK?"

"Yes fine. You left me, but there was no way I was negotiating those bloody stairs at that speed. I sat tight and prayed that our man George wouldn't flip the old girl over!"

Cade looked at her, deliberately but not so intently that she found it disturbing.

"You and I make a great team kid," he said in a Bogart-esque voice, "Of all the buses in all the world..."

They stood quietly now, outside the bright red transport symbol, for the first time in what seemed like hours. Unusually the air was still, the traffic was light and all that could be heard were Nine Nine's rotor blades as it maintained a search pattern over Camberwell; the sentinel quietly watching over its most coveted possessions.

"Jack."

"Yes."

"Where is she?"

Cade paused, trying to play down his inbuilt fear before replying through pursed lips "I have absolutely no idea Carrie, none at all. We have let her down."

O'Shea wasn't sure whether to offer a hand of friendship, to stroke Cade's arm, embrace him or just leave him to this thoughts. After a few well-chosen words she chose the latter.

"Jack, I need to help here. I'm experienced beyond your wildest dreams and I need to use that knowledge. Frankly if I don't I'll go bloody mad. At least let me offer some thoughts on where I think this might head, you never know I might..."

Cade held his hand up, as if to quieten her.

"Go ahead" said Cade as he saw Roberts' details on his phone, "I've got a few minutes of battery time left so make it snappy mate."

"Jack, one dead in the Mondeo, one of our local lads is down but OK, the passenger and an accomplice have escaped but we've got enough staff to sink a battleship. They are somewhere near Browning Road. We've got every man and his dog searching now. Are you OK? Where are you?"

"We are and we are also somewhere near Browning Road. Any news on Petrov?"

"None. Jack, these bastards shoot first so for Christ sake be careful, no more heroics tonight, yeah?"

"Yep. 10-4. Jason, tell your boys to keep at least one of them alive. It's all we have. Stay in touch. Out."

Chapter Thirty Two

The air was suspiciously still. Police staff were used to the dead of night. When everyone else was sound asleep, they would walk, run and pursue criminal elements, often leaving a residential street completely unaware of their presence, slumbering and oblivious.

Cade recalled with some lasting amazement the time he had run through a couples' bedroom in the darkest hours, en route to the back door, in pursuit of a burglar. The couple never stirred, despite the frantic foot chase.

But this evening was still young and fortunately the foot and vehicle traffic was lighter than most staff could recall.

It lent itself perfectly to a chase between a canine and a human.

In a side street the Mondeo sat, it's remaining occupants still trying to cope with the situation, frantically trying to work out an escape plan, the passenger diligently wrapping his jacket over his shoulder, trying to stem the flow of vivid red, oxygenated blood.

He knew he had three options: escape, die trying or surrender. Where he came from the police would make him pay for the near-death of one of their own. But this was England; perhaps they would be more charitable?

He chose escape.

He turned to his counterpart and smiled. Despite the smile intending to settle their nerves it looked manic, his grey face, his anthracite eyes and the metallic tang of blood in the cockpit of the vehicle all helped to add emphasis to the futility of their situation.

"My brother, we achieved our aim. The Boss will be happy, whatever happens to us he will take care of our families. Start the car, let us go home to Craiova and drink some Tuica."

The dog handler was tracking something in the shadows; quietly as possible he crossed from one street to another by negotiating a number of small rear gardens until he came to a wall, about six foot and certainly well within his grasp. He jumped up and looked over into the street.

He looked down, straight into the cabin of the stolen Mondeo.

He lowered himself back down. Think man, think.

Like his father, Constable Andy Pickers was a career dogman. His father was famous, infamous some said, and Andy had lived under the shadow of an all-spanning series of legendary stories for twenty years. Now it was his turn.

His radio was silent but he could hear something behind him. His shadow-black German Shepherd Sultan started to growl; a torch light illuminated both the dog and the handler as a well-meaning neighbour challenged them.

"'Ere you, beat it before I call the fackin' police. You listening?"

It was at that moment that the Good Samaritan saw the handler and his distinctive uniform. The officer had his index finger pressed firmly to his lips and with his spare hand held out in a classic 'stop' he hissed back, "I am the bloody police, now piss off before you get shot. Go!"

Nine Nine's own light cut a swathe through the area bringing life to every gloomy corner.

As he returned to the wall the handler heard the engine start. He lifted himself up and onto his forearms as the car sped up the street in order to turn around.

"Seven Seven MP. Target vehicle is on Colworth!"

He grabbed his dog and practically threw him over the wall. Pickers followed, his black Magnum tactical boots landing simultaneously onto the footpath. They had done it a hundred times; in thirty seconds they were both on the street. Quite what he was going to do had yet to be processed in his cyclonic mind.

"Nine Nine we have visual with Seven Seven over."

"Trojan, we are on Browning, permission to go for a hard stop or TPAC?"

Tactical Pursuit and Containment was never meant for this type of scenario but given the severity of the situation and the risk of the vehicle getting back out onto the streets of London most thought it the wise thing to do.

Except John Daniel.

"Negative Trojan. Deploy Stinger. Do not engage in TPAC. Received?"

Daniel had just spent the last five minutes being lectured by an incredibly fractious Deputy Commissioner and despite his basic police instinct to stop the targets at any cost he knew he already had a fatal police shooting to deal with.

"Fuck political correctness!" Daniel said to no one in particular as he threw a stapler across the room.

The driver turned the car around in three movements and hammered it back along the short street. The passenger was bleeding more profusely, but having chosen escape he now no longer cared about the here and now, he just wanted to savour the distinctive aftertaste of his favourite plum liquor upon his parched lips, even if it was to be his last act.

He looked down the street and saw the handler and a large, impressive black dog. He was a good looking dog indeed, too good to kill, but the officer was an inconvenience.

He lowered the window and awkwardly placed the Glock onto the doorframe. The pain was excruciating and affected his aim, but he needed to give the enemy something to concentrate on.

The dog handler was running towards them, appearing from behind the safety of a parked car and into their path. His dog was alongside him, straining on a long search lead and homing in on its target.

What kind of police did they have in this country? Were they really so keen to die, just to prove a point?

He fired the first round, which missed hopelessly. The second struck a black wrought iron gate and disappeared into the night.

He fired again and again, indiscriminate and desperate, his every attempt missed its target. By the time they had reached the junction he had fired seven rounds.

Spraying his CS gas into the vehicle was in hindsight not an ideal solution to the problem but it was the only tactical option that he had, other than throwing *Sultan* into the cockpit, and he loved that dog more than his wife, so option one it was to be.

The dog handler would buy a lottery ticket the following day and a year later, when most had forgotten about it, he and his partner would collect a gallantry medal for their actions.

The effects of the CS were instantaneous, even Pickers got a face full of the noxious spray, its crystalline properties causing a forceful and uncontrollable shutting of the eyes and a profuse discharge from the nose. The passenger, already in agony, started to scream; he rubbed at his eyes, which were already raw. When would this day end?

The driver lowered his window; it was a sensible but futile attempt to ventilate the cabin. In seconds his olfactory system was working overtime as he tried to clear the irritant from his eyes, nose and throat. He spat foaming mouthfuls of saliva into the street, rubbed at his eyes and tried desperately to control the car.

They reached the junction, without waiting to see if their way was clear he turned wildly right and into the larger road.

The Trojan team – together with their back up, were ready.

The slithering bed of spikes flew across the carriageway as the operator deployed the device from the relative safety of an armour-plated vehicle.

"Stinger deployed!"

The remaining crews tracked the Mondeo with their weapons but it failed to stop. Its front left tyre was already starting to break apart, the result of the savagely-sharp hollow metal tubes ripping into their vulcanised flesh.

Seconds away Cade was talking to Douglas when his phone rang for the last time. The battery icon was blinking furiously.

"Cade. Speak, I've got less than a minute of power left."

"Cade, Roberts, target is on the move. He's heading your way. Keep your heads down or the Deputy Commissioner will have my balls in a baguette. Out."

Cade grimaced at his colleagues' culinary description before shouting, "Come on Dolly let's go. George head south let's see if we can at least watch the circus."

He boarded the bus with O'Shea, who ran up the aisle to the window, replacing Cade as a new set of operational eyes. Quite what she was going to do hadn't really passed through her mind. The closest she had come to getting any recent operational experience had been with a certain Welsh detective and she fought a daily battle to erase that particular night from her memory.

Douglas was back on board giving the aging vehicle everything it had. She protested at every gear change but Douglas had already decided that he wanted his beloved Dolly to go down in history as one of London Transport's finest.

Cade stayed at the rear door, choosing to hang onto the safety bar, ready to deploy, if the chance arose. He stared at the passing buildings which blurred into a continuous line. His attention shifted. His frontal lobe was focused upon the immediate situation, whilst his temporal lobe jousted for position, playing havoc with his emotions. Neurons communicated effectively with other neurons, electrical and chemical stimuli played their critical part in the process too. But none of it made any sense.

He was transfixed on the passing street scenes, subconsciously mouthing the words "Where are you?"

Douglas had reached fifty miles an hour, only six below her mechanically restricted top speed, as a passenger waved manically from a bus shelter in a vain attempt to stop and board. Seeing Cade clinging feverishly to the doorway, the would-be passenger decided that discretion was the better part of valour and chose to walk the two miles to work.

Back on board O'Shea saw it first. She turned and yelled down the aisle.

"Jack, it's there, coming towards us!"

He leant outside the bodywork, the flexors pumping in his forearms as he struggled to maintain his grip. She was right, the Mondeo was travelling towards them, fifty, sixty, seventy, he couldn't tell but he knew it was travelling way over the speed limit and its path was erratic. Its front tyres were torn to shreds.

Behind it was a growing convoy of white vehicles, blue lights recoiling off nearby walls as a cacophony of sound filled the air.

The situation was surreal and contrary to modern myth, nothing slowed down, in fact every movement was enhanced, quickened and more intense.

Daniel was deploying his troops across the region. India Nine Nine was relaying every last second of footage and updating the movements of each and every vehicle on the ground. The Trojan team had the lead and were providing the ground commentary.

From the north another three units were approaching, coming up fast behind the solitary double decker bus but still some distance away. Local units, both uniformed and plain clothed were turning out of nearby stations.

Inside the Mondeo the young Romanian male fought valiantly with the controls, with one hand he changed gear and then wiped his eyes, with the other he battled with the steering wheel. Unable to see clearly, the passenger groped around in his pockets to find his phone. His eye was hideous, permanently damaged, and to exacerbate the situation he could bleed to death. His arrogance would help him survive though; it had since he was a young boy, growing up without a father.

Enough of that, he needed to tell his boss the good news.

The girl was gone; there would be no more trouble from her, the traitorous whore.

Douglas turned to O'Shea and yelled over the dying Leyland engine – his vain attempt at a Star Trek quote dissipated into the night air.

"I canna give her any more Captain!" His laughter boomed around the confines of his cab.

O'Shea was simply too scared to laugh. Here she was, in the care of a man who to the outside world had nothing to live for, who seemed hell-bent on joining his long-departed wife and trapped in an aging, overtly red relic of London's transport system.

Some thirty feet away she saw a man who had entered her life in what seemed like days ago, but it could have been hours, years or simply moments. However long it had been she craved his company and yet she couldn't let go of a simple piece of stainless steel in order to navigate the short distance to him. She resembled a distraught passenger on a pleasure boat unwittingly trapped in a swell; all at sea, lost and out of control.

Cade was futilely yelling words of encouragement and command to his new-found partner but she couldn't hear a syllable. Surrounded by a night sky alive with the sounds and sights of a full-born police pursuit he found himself laughing. Adrenaline did that to you, often at the most inopportune moments.

Blue lights danced off of nearby architecture, sirens rebounded back and forth, a discord held captive by long-forgotten, sterile and forlorn buildings.

Douglas broke the habit of a lifetime and grabbed one side of the overly-large steering wheel with both hands. Not since his frenetic days on the training circuit had he thrown his 'old girl' around with so much gusto. He too was fuelled by his adrenal gland and had never experienced the dangers of Red Mist – the point where the sub-conscious makes the call to overstep the mark.

As the Mondeo bore down on them he weaved, jousting with the opponent, matching its every attempt to evade them and a cortege of desperate, disparate pursuers.

Daniel could only watch from behind his detached screen as the procession galloped towards a climax. The imagery that beamed real-time from his air unit was crystal clear. He and everyone around him could see, witness and almost taste the drama unfolding. He controlled all of his ground units but was unable to regulate the one which had played such a significant part and on which were two of his colleagues: out of touch and in harm's way.

"For Christ's sake get that bloody bus out of the way! Do I need to remind people we have a foreign force officer on there, let alone two bloody civvies?"

"Trying sir, no comms. She's on her own."

"India Nine Nine we will use the Sonix to tannoy the bus."

It was a grand gesture but one which Daniel knew was too late.

"Yes, yes, Nine Nine do it. Now."

Tyres of all dimensions and quality roared their disapproval on the carriageways. Heartbeats raised. Brows furrowed.

Douglas's eyes widened. The whites of which were now brighter than the moon, his teeth a splendid accompaniment. This was it. No criminal was going to make a fool out of George Douglas and least of all the second love of his life.

The Mondeo, now travelling at eighty was completely out of control, the driver now a passenger. He fought against an overwhelming demonstration of pure physics and lost. He tried to close his eyes but saw the bus lurching into his path.

The Routemaster started to lean, its comparatively thin tyres simply giving up, releasing their tenacious grip and leaving the road surface. In seconds the twin-decked vehicle had exceeded its tipping point and began its unceremonious fall from grace.

The front offside bodywork was the first to make contact with the tarmac, its lightweight alloy body searing against the surface, causing a shower of minor sparks and a hideous scraping noise.

In the CAD room voices stopped, throats became parched, hands ran through hair.

Douglas knew this was the end, he let go of the wheel and looked towards the evening sky. He thought of his girl and closed his eyes – he was already with her, whispering her name when the two vehicles collided.

O'Shea started to fall, her grasp on the cold metalwork now as tenacious as a first-day mother at the gates of school. Her tumble through the void was far from graceful, life for her did not slow down it simply carried on at its normal frenetic pace. She hit the row of seats diagonally behind her and felt the life rush from her body as her diaphragm released a blast of warm air from her lungs.

Fortune favoured her as her now limp frame wrapped around the legs of a much-used seat, her head jarred into the foot well and her lower body became trapped in the industrial metal ware. As unladylike as it appeared it would save her life.

Unable to scream she waited for the inevitable, but it never arrived. Instead she clutched onto life, heard the collision and felt herself being consumed by twisted metal, exploding glass and a cocktail of debris; decades of dust, dirt and the stench of heated lubricants surrounded her.

She closed her eyes and prayed for clemency.

However she saw not her life flashing before her but Cade.

Looking along the aisle she could see through the rear window, out onto the street, nausea almost overcame her as she tried to focus on him.

Cade's body had exited the bus. Unable to sustain his own grasp on the vehicle he had chosen to release his vice-like grip on the gnarled leather safety strap. Waiting until the vehicle was on its side he simply let go.

A casual observer would refer to it as assisted suicide, a stuntman, a moment of genius. To Cade it was a semi-conscious decision based upon his early teenage years and of repeated falls from an ancient motorbike. His grandfather had taught him well.

"Relax Jack, let go, try not to anticipate the conclusion, for the end will be what it will be."

The words had remained in his mind, sealed in a faded cerebral envelope and unopened, unused until now.

He slipped quietly, almost gracefully from the rear open door, landed on the road surface with a disagreeable thump, exhaled and contrary to everything his mind was instructing him to do, he relaxed and let go.

Now spinning along the tarmac surface he became aware of the pain in his back and legs and eased the pressure by raising them both, lifting his head and placing the central point of contact onto his belt, its leather shredding in seconds but providing temporary respite.

Cade came to a halt, took a moment to gather this thoughts, ran through a mental checklist to ensure his body was functioning, fought off some initial nausea and then exhaled. The delivery van that nearly hit him brought Jack Cade swiftly to his senses.

The driver took a moment before exiting the van and yelling at the prone figure on the floor.

"Are you fuckin' mad chief? 'Ave you seriously got a death wish or what?" As he spoke he jabbed his index finger against his temple.

Cade sucked the available air into his lungs, slowly exhaled and then spoke.

"Son, you have no bloody idea. Two minutes ago I was a passenger on that bus…"

He nodded up the street.

The driver, previously distracted by Cade's motionless figure had completely missed the chaos only a few hundred metres up the road.

He pointed out the crash site to the prone officer, somewhat pointlessly Cade thought.

"Are you shittin' me? Whoa! Look at that, would you look at that?"

"Christ, you've got a knack of asking multiple questions haven't you? Has anyone told you that?"

The irony was lost on Jerry Batchelor, career van driver and Chelsea football fan.

"Give me a hand mate, I need to get to the bus." Cade was forthright, leaving Batchelor with no room for negotiation, but he tried nonetheless.

"I'm no doctor chief but I reckon you should stay on the deck until someone checks you out. Besides, there's enough Old Bill there to sink a battleship…leave them to do their thing, they hate us mere mortals interfering. Trust me on this?"

He pushed his hand into Cade's making him wince as the skin flapped on the heel of his palm.

"Jerry Batchelor."

"Jack Cade, Sergeant Jack Cade actually, nice to meet you mere mortal."

Batchelor smiled a toothless smile.

"I guess there's no point in ordering you around anymore then – Sarge!"

The front of the Mondeo had struck the bus's cockpit, demolishing the aged glass, ripping it from its rubber surround, the dense shattered screen hitting Douglas in the chest.

The Ford, its airbags already deployed, was nothing more than a high speed, relentless sarcophagus. Its own bodywork disappearing into a maelstrom of dust and metallic debris. The driver was killed instantly – the post mortem almost running out of injuries that probably attributed to his demise. Douglas would last only a moment longer.

The brutal crash had torn the Mondeo's safety cell in two, the driver, what remained of him, would later remain in-situ as the emergency services contemplated how to remove him.

Lethal shards of metal had penetrated his body, slicing through his precious skin, separating tendons, ligaments and bone.

The explosive collision was heard from the helicopter, which appeared, along with every other emergency vehicle to stop, to suspend in time and wait for the inevitable screams.

Silence.

"Nine Nine crash, crash, crash. We need fuel, repeat we need fuel. We have to RTB."

Daniel looked at his team. Initially trying to separate the words crash from refuel – in a moment of sheer desperation at the notion of also losing his air support unit on what would transpire to be the most taxing night of his career, he exhaled and started to speak.

"Just perfect. OK, show Nine Nine returning to base but let's get them back in the air ASAP."

On the darkened, hackneyed city street the two vehicles had now become one. Whilst the majority of the bus was intact, to the casual observer the Mondeo was all but gone. What remained was an unblemished passenger seat and the sole living occupant. The male appeared to be seriously, alarmingly injured but these were existing injuries, wounds from a previous encounter, disfiguring damage from his meeting with a stunning, frightened whore.

The bus had come to a halt, shielding the scene from onlookers, both on the ground and in the air.

No-one present expected the passenger door of the Mondeo to open, but it did and in a hundredth of a second the passenger was gone, providence on his side, running into a nearby partly-derelict building, carrying his firearm and praying that the chemicals coursing through his body would help him to escape.

The reality was that the act had not been seen at all. In that moment, that precise moment the aircrew were scanning back along the street, preparing to depart the scene, Cade was explaining himself to a commuter and O'Shea was otherwise engaged.

The passenger had no need to run as fast as he did, his heart now pushing blood through the entry wound in his neck.

Frantically trying to slow down his breathing the passenger began his escape.

He ran along Larcom Street, staying on the right hand side to avoid any obvious shadows cast from the regularly-placed street lamps. Past once-grand three-story homes he jogged now, desperate to maintain his strength until he reached the familiar outline of a church.

He pushed against the black wrought iron gate but it was locked – a sign of the times. St. Johns Walworth church in the Diocese of Southwark, once a haven for any man who sought peace and sanctuary was now a fortress.

Was he not worthy of salvation?

He looked back along the street, waiting to see his pursuers, but he was alone. The helicopter had gone.

To his right he could make out an alleyway so he continued to walk as quickly as he could, fumbling for his phone and forcing himself to calm down. He was losing blood but the wound appeared to be more superficial than he had feared.

He could do this. He stopped in the alleyway and leaned against the red-brick wall. Now shielded from view under a Lime tree he waited, recovered and made a phone call. He whispered into the mouthpiece. The sound of a friendly voice calmed him a little. He was almost home.

Thirteen minutes later a dark red Vauxhall entered the street, turned around and parked. The driver flashed the hazard lamps once and waited. The passenger shuffled towards the car, opened the rear door and laid down on the back seat.

Without looking at the single occupant he mumbled into the well-worn caramel-coloured upholstery.

Artur Gheorghiu was safe.

"Drive…"

ARV officers approached the crash scene, cautiously stepping forwards, weapons at the high ready, coordinated, composed and practiced. The first area car from the north came across Cade cautiously walking in the road. A newspaper delivery van had narrowly avoided him and was rendering what first aid the driver knew to a patient that neither wanted nor needed help.

The ARV officers cleared the Mondeo, finding only one desperately mutilated occupant. Other team members searched the iconic red bus, now laying on its side, a stranded whale on a metropolitan beach.

One member lay down, pushing his weapon through what was left of a window, his high-powered Surefire torch illuminating the cabin. His colleague called out the grim message that the bus driver was almost certainly deceased. He called for paramedics to be on standby nonetheless; hearing how the vehicle had played its own part in the chase he considered it the honourable thing to do.

Once the rest of the vehicle was clear he would call the medics to the scene. It was risk management, but he'd seen enough bodies in his fourteen years to know who he could and couldn't save.

He continued to slide cautiously into the cabin of the bus, his weapon leading but still under his control. To his right he heard a noise.

Safety off.

And again. There it was.

He arced the weapon around, the Aimpoint laser sight now ominously illuminating potential targets.

Daniel watched, whilst his fingers weren't crossed he wished he had a rabbit's foot to stroke. He caught a glimpse of himself in the computer screen. He'd aged at least five years.

At the edge of the street another ARV operator stood, leaning into his weapon, looking over the sights, ready. He'd been joined by a red-eyed Andrew Pickers and his faithful friend who was laid on the pavement anticipating his next command. To him, it was just a game, to his potential victim, the imperfect ending to an awful day – a visitation from the Land Shark.

Once more, as he crawled into the bus he heard the noise, but this time it was a lower, visceral noise, helpless as opposed to a threat. Even more reason for the seasoned copper to proceed with caution.

The officer edged his right index finger onto the trigger. The weapon was so accurate that he would only need one shot at this range. As he methodically traced around the cabin he suddenly stopped. There, in his sights and looking like the grey remainder of Daniels' fortunate omnivore was a female face. Ashen, scared and silent.

"Miss, can you show me your hands? Do as I say and you will not be harmed…"

The face cracked a half smile.

"Do you not think I would have shot you by now mate? I'm on your side, from the Yard. I'm with DS Roberts and Jack Cade…" she started to weaken.

"Jason Roberts?"

"No, Julia, who the fuck do you think I meant?" She was stronger again.

"Then you are indeed one of us. I joined with Ginger Roberts. Does he still lob biscuits around at briefings?"

"He does, now, as much as it's nice to lay here and discuss your career and my boss's tendency to maim people with a bloody ginger nut do you think you can arrange for the Fire Brigade to send some beefy men to rescue me?"

"I can miss, I can. Are you alone?"

"I am. The other passenger got off without paying, he's laid on the road, about two hundred metres behind us. Will you find out if he's OK? Please?"

The officer shuffled forward, nodded, smiled and extended a black gloved hand. O'Shea reached out and grabbed the offered fingers, squeezing them gently. He leaned back against the framework of the ancient carriage causing the metalwork to creak.

"MP from Trojan. One passenger on board the bus is safe. The other is with our team further up the street. Sit rep on him ASAP please. Driver of the bus is beyond help. Passenger of the Mondeo likewise. Can you get the Major Incident Team en route? We need to close the road sharpish and get the Duty Inspector down here too, it's a bit of a mess. Over."

Police the world over so enjoyed diminishing the true pandemonium of a crash scene. It was far from a bit of a mess. It was a lot, of a bloody great amount of chaos brought together in a twist and turn of metal, wood and bone.

Cade would be terribly bruised and flinch at the merest pressure on his skin, silk would be bearable, cotton, not. It would take a few days to subside, but he too had survived.

A patrol crew pulled up alongside him, the brake discs on the Ford ticking as they cooled. The passenger, who was deftly balancing a cell phone between his cheek and his left shoulder spoke first.

"Greetings. Would you be Sergeant Cade?"

Cade nodded.

"Jason Roberts sends his best, do you want a lift?"

"Thanks boys, is O'Shea alright, what about the bus driver? Nikolina?"

"Stand by Skipper, one question at a time." The Met officer used the standard local colloquialism for a Sergeant as he tried to offer a calming voice. Whoever this bloke was he was clearly suffering from a higher level of stress, poor bastard.

"Sorry skip, the bus driver didn't make it, nor the driver of the Mondeo. Good news though, your girl is fine. She's being looked after by a firefighter."

"Which one?"

"I'm guessing the one with the obscenely-sculpted muscles, the girls always go for the good looking ones don't they skip?"

"I meant which girl...which girl?" Humourless.

"Sorry boss, I meant the girl on the bus. I didn't realise there was two of 'em."

Cade felt disloyal to O'Shea, she was important, he even found himself thinking about her in his quieter moments, but operationally and morally his mind was only on Petrov.

Cade lifted himself carefully out of the back of the patrol car, as he did so he acknowledged the update, failing to correct the officer about his apparent ownership of Carrie O'Shea. He visibly winced as he walked slowly towards the bus, finding himself a little peeved that a man ten years his younger and twice as broad was rescuing the trapped maiden whilst his yellow-clad colleagues, all equally good looking were alongside him, ready to lend a gallant hand.

"Bloody firemen..."

In the CAD room at the heart of the Metropolitan Police Service the broadcasted scene provided a watchful Daniel with a moment of insight and solace.

"I'd like to work with that lad one day. Balls of steel."

No one heard what he said, but it mattered not.

He was busy scratching his chin, wiping his eyes and generally wondering when he could go home. This night would be the end of him.

Tea? Yes that's what he wanted right now, and to fall into the arms of his childhood sweetheart. But they would both have to wait.

George Douglas, God rest his cheery Caribbean soul, was gone. Cade was accounted for. O'Shea too. The driver of the Mondeo was dead. All staff were accounted for, including Simms who was being transported to Kings College Hospital. Any other battlefield scrapes were hardly likely to be reported. There were no civilian casualties outside of the immediate pursuit.

But for the rat-like gnawing sensation in Daniel's fraught mind, it could, allowing for the minor drawback of two criminal fatalities be considered a successful operation.

However a deep-seated 'something' was troubling him.

He focussed on his own reflection once more, realisation hit him square in the face. The same cerebral notion pummelled Cade, and O'Shea was but a moment behind them both. They all knew that Petrov was gone.

Daniel cradled his head in his hands, stared at the ceiling then ran his palms precisely over the contours of his face before finally opening his eyes and speaking.

"Where-is-the-bloody-passenger?"

Chapter Thirty Three

The majority of the team had been stood down, sent home to rest.

Those that could sleep did so.

The search had continued throughout the nightshift. Teams deployed far and wide, starting with the kidnap point at the safe house, recovering every piece of potential evidence: locking down the scene, security CCTV footage, pending the discovery of a body, somewhere, some time.

They slowly fanned out from the anonymous address, beat officers asking open questions of residents and business owners all to no avail. Detectives covered the same ground, asking what they considered to be more robust questions, those that had human sources used them, again, despite a willingness to help none were able to offer the nugget of gold that was needed to allow the investigation to move forwards.

Another team traced CCTV imagery, trying to establish the intended route of the Mondeo, looking for ideas, traces of hope, elements of guilt. Nothing. They hadn't even changed the number plates.

The fact that the car belonged to the police hampered any start point. Everyone knew where it *should* have been and that was parked, secure outside the Met's iconic flagship. Almost everyone south of the river knew where it ended up, buried, in the front of a bus.

Another unit, consisting mainly of civilian analysts were dredging through old intelligence noting's for the area around the safe house, in relation to the pursuit and the subsequent ending.

Border agencies were tasked with examining the arrival of Eastern European nationals – those that had previously left a footprint, not the thousands who routinely and legitimately entered the country.

The tabloids were fended off. For now they would only hamper the investigation. They got the scraps they needed and went to press with the simple lead:

"Gunfight at the Old Kent Corral!"

It was a typically puerile headline, designed to attract the attention of myriad readers who routinely handed over a few coins in exchange for a few less facts and a blend of near-naked women.

Roberts, his team, Cade and O'Shea and a few senior staff members were still on duty. The long night had segued into an even longer day ahead. Jet-lagged, hungry and frustrated they all sat in a briefing room waiting.

Cade sat awkwardly, perched on the edge of his chair, on what he could best describe as an 'arse from hell' whilst O'Shea simply looked pale, most likely the result of shock. She moved cautiously, shielding her developing bruises. Roberts knew that they both needed more in-depth medical intervention but neither was willing to seek it. He chose not to push the matter.

Clive Wood had been stood down, pending the result of the initial inquiry. The team wouldn't blame him for Petrov's possible death, for her disappearance yes, but not for her demise.

The coffee arrived along with an assorted array of breakfast items, paid for by the local Commander Frank Waterman. He knew this was likely to be a long day and the old adage about armies and their stomachs never rang truer.

He had them placed them on the large briefing table, nodded to all present, lowered himself onto a high-backed office chair and spoke.

"Good morning all. First and foremost let's eat whilst we talk. Thank you to you all for whatever part you played in last night's events. I've heard some incredible feedback from the various commanders who were on duty, not least John Daniel in the CAD room. It's pleasing to hear this folks, across the board there were some gutsy decisions made last night. Constable Simms will live to fight another day although he may not be walking the beat for a while. Miss O'Shea, what can I say? You've got bigger balls than some of my male staff. Quite what you were doing on the bus in the first place is subject to heated debate on the top floor of the Yard."

He winked at her. Clearly there was some history between them.

"I was, attempting to analyse the situation boss, trying to give Sergeant Cade some guidance."

Waterman turned to this left and acknowledged Cade.

"Sergeant. How are you?"

Cade shuffled uneasily before replying.

"I'm fine sir, one hundred percent. Top work by your team, I'm indebted."

He smiled again.

"Bullshit Sergeant, this was a team effort with you leading the way from what I've heard from DS Roberts – and trust me, no-one bullshits better than Jason, he's a master, isn't that right Jason?"

Roberts could only nod his approval as he tore into a bacon sandwich, discarding his vegetarian regime for as long as it took to devour it.

"Team, let us not forget that what Jack has brought to our table is a smorgasbord of highly organised bloody chaos. But at least we are now aware of the chaos. Cyber-crime, financial crime, call it what you like, it's here to stay and it's happening, now, out there..."

He pointed broadly across the rooftops of a busying city.

"Jack, I've spoken to Eddie. He sends his best wishes and tells you to get what's left of your arse back up the East Midlands. I've got a contact of mine working on keeping you here. Question: Do you have anything pressing that you need to get back to?"

In the past Cade would have run through the things that were important to him, taking a while to mull it all over then replied, however it took him a millisecond to respond.

"No sir, I don't."

"Good because quite frankly I don't see anyone else with half the knowledge you have. By the way let me have your expense claim, it's causing Eddie's dyspepsia to re-surface."

"You know him sir?"

"I do, we went to Bramshill together."

He was referring to the internationally recognised police college in the heart of the Hampshire where the best of the breed were sent to train in commanding a modern police force.

"Christ, me Eddie and Hewie were legends."

"Hewie?"

"John Hewett. Swarthy, debonair bugger is Johnnie. Top man actually, he was there on some Foreign Office programme, likely to be something big one day, he'll certainly beat me and Eddie to the PM's cocktail invitation list. Got his fingers in a whole tray of luxury finger food has young Johnathan. Parents were big back in the day, worked for the Foreign Office, our little Johnnie lived in Hong Kong, Singapore, The Gambia, you name it, and he learned the languages too. Parents are of course long-retired, living out a life in France last I heard – rumour has it his folks fell out with the government over some trade deal with China. He's a clever bugger mind you. Loves the finer things in life. Young and gifted and honestly, not many people know much about him."

There was that name again.

He looked around, realising he'd digressed.

"Anyway, let's crack on. What do we know? What don't we know? And as they say these days, what do we know about what we don't know?"

He threw a whiteboard marker at Roberts.

"Jason, I know you are tired but the quicker we get what we know on that board the quicker you can all bugger off home to bed and dream about what we don't!"

The team muttered their exhausted approval, hoping that some of the fresher minds in the room could assist.

As with all whiteboard brainstorms it started with the event and then cascaded up, down and sideways, some relevant, some not, but all important. Knowledge gaps they were called.

Different colours denoted different lines of enquiry. Time lines were added, tasks too. Within fifteen minutes patterns were forming.

After forty minutes they had more than enough to continue. New team leaders who had arrived into work to hear of the scenes from the previous night were furiously making notes and working out how to deploy their staff. Further south other units of the Metropolitan Police had arrived for work and now found themselves in possession of a simple photograph. The image showed a starkly attractive girl who appeared to be attracting a lot of importance. There was clearly some prestige to be had for the unit or individual that found her.

Frank Waterman had seen enough. He knew the operation was in good hands. A DI and six staff had arrived to offer support – their speciality was simple, old fashioned detection. Nothing too flash but they would be deployed to turn over the stones. Uniform staff had the girl's picture. They knew there was a male person of interest too, although since his escape from the Mondeo God only knew where he was. Lastly, they knew not to talk to the media.

Waterman gazed around the briefing room and looked at the growing group.

"Last and by no means least, and I hate to say this, we cocked up. What's important to me is not how long we linger over this but how we recover – and right now…," he paused and looked at everyone in turn, "…what counts, what really counts is finding the bastards that pissed on my parade, and importantly, the bastards that took that young lady from under our nose. Let us not forget that they stole our own bloody car!"

Everyone present nodded.

"We owe it to her, we owe it to the…people that took her, to the people that shot at my staff…endangered lives on the streets of

London and above all we owe her family. Anyone who disagrees is free to leave. Anyone?" He scanned. "Good. Let's move on."

It was a statement laden with honesty and frustration. Here was a commander who actually cared about the reputation of the team, rather than his own.

Without another word he stood, causing the staff to rise also. He motioned them to sit, nodded his appreciation and left.

Cade warmed to him immediately.

He reached out and poured a couple of cups of intensely strong coffee, handed one to O'Shea, who he decided looked like death warmed up and another to Roberts who looked marginally better.

Roberts smiled at Cade, offered a mock chinking of his coffee cup and spoke.

"Bloody hell my son that was close last night, too close. My old girl would have killed me if she could 'ave seen me."

Cade glanced at O'Shea, whose mind was spinning furiously, trying to sift through the fog of the previous few days. She returned a thin smile, enough to let Cade know she was tuned into him but not enough to give anyone with a law enforcement background the slightest hint that there was more than chemistry between them.

Roberts had spotted it, subtle though it was.

Cade continued.

"Jason, I can honestly say that my stars did not predict what happened last night. The last time I travelled on a double decker bus I was six. I got such a bollocking off my grandmother for messing about on the stairs. Needless to say it didn't end in the death of two people and the loss of another under police protection...seriously mate what *was* Clive thinking of?"

The best that Roberts could do was say a wearisome "I don't know Jack. I've sent him home, stood him down, I'll deal with him tomorrow. If it's any consolation he really is a good bloke, a top detective, just lets his cock do the thinking at times. He's gutted, I've never known him to be so humble."

Roberts was as tired as the rest of the team and Cade knew it.

"End-of Jason. Sorry, we are all on our knees, let's wrap this up and leave the morning shift to chase up the loose ends. They've got enough inky equations on that whiteboard to arouse Einstein.

Roberts knew his northern counterpart was right but he also knew that his team had led to the incident unravelling – or at best, contributed heavily to it. His career options were most likely limited from now on. The least he could do was feel a few collars and lock up the bastards responsible.

Their minds and bodies were exhausted.

The door out onto the street, their chosen forms of transport and a home, wherever that might be were all beckoning.

"MP this is MP1 you receiving?"

"Good morning MP1 this is MP do go ahead."

Andy Scott, the middle-aged Constable in charge of police launch *Patrick Colquhoun* announced the vessels' intention of heading upstream from the Marine Unit's historical base at Wapping.

"MP, we've got a report from the skipper of the *Jack D* that he's seen something which he describes as odd opposite the power station. We know the crew well and trust their judgement so we are going to take a look. We are en route, ETA around twenty minutes. Can you see if a land unit can have a butchers too please, somewhere opposite the station, on Grosvenor Road?"

Despite his surname Scott was a pure-bred Londoner. His father had worked on the river and his father before him. They could trace their maritime heritage back to the late seventeen hundreds.

For Scott to be the skipper of the *Colquhoun* was a dream. She was a brand new boat, still undergoing trials for the police. Faster, larger and altogether easier to handle than her aged predecessor and she made work, which for Scott was a vocation, an absolute pleasure.

Day or night, good weather or inclement he would prefer to be nowhere else than on the Thames and on board what he considered his boat. She represented the latest in a line of similarly-named patrol boats, each one able to trace its lineage back to their namesake.

Colquhoun a local Magistrate had joined forces with former naval man John Harriot. The two were to become the founding fathers of river policing in London, at a time when the concept of the Metropolitan Police had yet to be conceived.

Colquhoun and Harriot had the experience and support of the East Indian Trading Company and the judiciary. They set about crafting a force who would make the treacherous river, its wharves and environs a safer place.

Primarily created to counter the vicious gangs that preyed on shipping during the late seventeen hundreds, their Marine Policing Unit would become the forefathers of modern policing in England.

Scott steered the boat into the channel, applied some power and started the short journey west. With the morning traffic at its worst it was likely the launch would get to get to the scene before any land-based unit. With the right conditions and cognisant of the rules of the river Scott fully intended to be the first on scene. He had a feeling about this one.

Clive Wood had purchased his home, which sat on the first floor of a renovated block of flats among equally modest and somewhat identical dwellings. It was tucked away behind a grand old pine tree on the upliftingly-named Sunny Gardens Road in the area of North London called Hendon.

He'd chosen the area after he had left the Regiment. Knowing he was going to be accepted into the police, and importantly knowing he would be training at the nearby Hendon police training centre, he had poured his recently and desperately unexpected, if not modest inheritance into property.

The flat belonged to his late aunt who adored him and as luck would have it had insisted that her nephew inherited the property – on the strict proviso he used what was left of the windfall to restore the home to its former glory.

He told his beloved Sheila that it was the smart thing to do, especially in that part of the city. When all the other Para's were remaining near Aldershot or heading north, he could, for once, see the writing on the wall. And the writing said 'Profit'.

Within two years he was proven right when a valuation showed a fifteen percent increase in the value of his modest two bedroomed flat. It made the wretched but free commute to the Yard worthwhile. With a discreet flash of his warrant card he'd board a bus or a train each morning having already forgotten about his wife and lose himself in the journey.

It was only about eight miles door to door but on some days it could take an hour.

He would arrive at work, engage in post-weekend banter with anyone who was prepared to join in. It normally revolved around Arsenal Football Club, or better still a Welsh victory – in any sport.

Having hung up his suit jacket he'd grab a cup of tea; three sugars and hardly any milk. The strong beverage would be lovingly consumed as he checked overnight occurrences and any mail that had arrived. As the senior Detective Constable he saw it as his duty. He was disciplined, if nothing else.

He was never, ever late.

Except today.

The *Patrick Colquhoun* arrived ahead of schedule, Scott called in their position and waited for a larger boat to head past them, downstream to the Thames Estuary. His was a well-known voice to the Port of London Authority operator, but he made sure the communication was brief and professional.

Travelling at a shade under ten knots he was pushing things – but he had a legitimate excuse, at least he would if something were to go wrong. He was responding to an emerging incident, a hazard to river safety and one which would soon be supported by a PLA patrol boat.

The PLA 'policed' the ninety five miles of the River Thames, from Teddington to the North Sea. One of the busiest rivers and waterways in the world it could claim many records, one of the more unusual being that PLA staff removed over four hundred tons of rubbish from the river each year.

The latter was at the forefront of Scott's mind as he cut through the water, a two-knot tide helping him along his journey. He recalled the skipper of the *Jack D* referring to an object in the water. Nothing more than that.

Man-made, most likely, but it wasn't there the day before and Terry Walker knew the river better than most.

He apologised to Scott at the beginning of their conversation – 'I 'ope I'm not wastin' your time officer?'

Scott and his crew slowed alongside Battersea Power Station, called in their intention to cross the river and began the gentle manoeuvre, as soon as the skipper eased the rudder to starboard he could feel the continuous wrench of the tide.

He knew the river well, he'd grown up among what many referred to as the liquid history of the Thames. However, more than anything else he offered his respects to the 'Old Man' every time he allowed him set foot upon the water. His team would never board their boat without the appropriate safety equipment or clothing. Today, pleasant though it was, would be no exception.

A veteran of the force who after many decades still considered himself to be only a river apprentice, he would dedicate hours to educating those that chose to use the river, boat owners and especially party-goers who would think nothing of leaping into the frigid, dark waters after a night of alcohol-fuelled merriment.

With the flow running at ten miles an hour, five times faster than most humans could swim, the vast majority were doomed from the moment they broke the surface; the fortunate ones were swiftly swept beneath the swirling maelstrom and held at the rivers' behest.

If their families were lucky the victim might surface within a few days, but invariably it would be weeks before the hapless soul rose to the surface, then, at best unrecognisable.

The team had finished their handover. What they had missed wouldn't matter now. There was more than enough to whet the appetite of any investigator: a group of apparently seasoned organised criminals insidiously fleecing the banking system of one of the largest cities on earth, numerous crime scenes, a pursuit, a firearms incident, culminating in the shooting of an officer, two fatalities at the hands of police staff and a significant crash, claiming the life of a stalwart of the London transport system. Yes, quite enough.

Roberts practically crawled to his car, a good boss he ensured his team left before he did and then called across to Cade and O'Shea who were walking to the main gate.

"You two love birds want a lift anywhere? You'll need a new car since you smashed my other one up!"

Cade dismissed him with a backward wave.

"No mate, we're fine, we are heading for coffee and then bed."

It was a momentary lapse.

"Nice. I promise not to tell a living soul."

Cade looked at O'Shea, biting his lip at the transgression.

"Sorry."

"I'm not. It's been a long night Jack, come on, let's do as you said, grab a coffee then head home to my place. That way only you, Jason and I will know the truth."

He was already walking in the general direction of the Chilean Embassy and Old Queen Street.

He was almost marching now, a second wind had kicked in.

"Come on O'Shea, let's get you back to your place and en route you can finish that sentence you never completed on the bus, the one about how you need to help me."

She raised her eyes skywards. He'd heard her. He'd remembered. He'd certainly do, even her mother would approve.

Clive Wood sealed the off-white, famous name, ninety gram, watermarked envelopes and placed one upon her pillow, ensuring that it sat 'just so', the other was addressed to Detective Sergeant Jason Roberts. He placed that on his bedside table, propped up against the faithful reading lamp.

Ten minutes later he had carefully knotted his favoured old regimental tie, using a single Windsor knot he had created a basic but classical accessory, stopping to slip the loop over his head and adjusting it, then he lovingly slipped on his gleaming leather shoes, the one's handcrafted by Church's of Northampton. The pair he had never told his wife about.

The main tie looked good. It's maroon background allowing the silvered wings to stand proud. Pure silk, hand-made, slip stitched and lined. As with his shoes it reeked of quality. It was new, he'd saved it for a special occasion.

The cufflinks followed, matching the tie, maroon with silver detail. His trousers were sharply pressed and his blazer, darkest blue with a silver winged badge on the left breast pocket. It completed the outfit.

He gazed at himself in the full length mirror. Staring into the eyes of the man before him, he nodded.

"You'll do boyo. You'll do."

Actually, the outfit was far from complete.

He unwrapped a worn maroon beret and a pair of white gloves from some old tissue paper and walked to his bedside, placed them reverently onto the end of the bed, fastidiously picking a piece of lint from the hat badge before dropping it onto the carpet.

He then returned to his wardrobe, paused as he looked at his number one dress uniform, ran his hand across the black tunic, its epaulette's piped in red, complimented with a solitary brass button.

The collars were completed with two silver winged emblems.

Five more brass buttons featured, one above and one below a pure-white dress belt which had a gleaming silver buckle. Again, that crest resplendent at the very centre.

On the right sleeve were three gold stripes. Medal ribbons sat perfectly in line on the left breast, immediately above the pocket. He removed two more regimental ties from the stainless steel bar that held them in place.

Wood walked quickly to the small staircase, its white oak wooden balustrade offering a view to the lounge below.

The first tie was the same as the new one he proudly wore, the second, dark green with silver wings and a discreet number III under the emblem - a legacy of his short but exciting secondment to 3 Parachute Regiment.

He slowly, deliberately knotted the two lengths of silk together so that they became one, then securely tied one end around the banister and the other around his neck.

He raised a cut-crystal glass of Laphroaig, for a brief moment savouring the burning liquid on his tongue. God it tasted good. He then said farewell to his home, counted his friends, whispered goodbye to his long-suffering wife, said sorry to no one in particular, climbed inelegantly over the banister and started to sing a song from his past.

It was to the familiar tune *Battle Hymn of the Republic* or as it was often mistakenly referred, *Glory, Glory, Halleluiah!*

He sang it with gusto, just as he had so many times before:

The day's he lived, loved and laughed, kept running through his mind,
He thought about the girl back home, the one he'd left behind,
He thought about the medics and wondered what they'd find,
And he ain't gonna jump no more!

Chapter Thirty Three

With the final word sung he stepped into the void for the last time.

Chapter Thirty Four

O'Shea was keeping pace with Cade as they reached Old Queen Street. In their haste they had forgotten to buy the coffee that they had promised themselves.

Cade was fuelled with adrenalin anyway, so would hardly sleep and O'Shea was counting on it.

She stopped in the street, which had come to life, suits of all types and sizes were wending their way from home to office and back; industrious, financially-motivated ants, grey and blue, some checked, some striped

She pitied them all.

"Jack, all I need to know is…"

He portrayed a hurt look and spoke, "Of course, yes, I will respect you in the morning Carrie."

It earned him an overly aggressive punch on the chest.

"Bastard, I meant all I needed to know was that I was adding value, doing my thing, proving my worth…"

"Go on."

"Look, I can't think of any more things to add…"

At risk of receiving another punishing blow he added "Neither can I but I just wanted to see you writhe."

O'Shea was smirking to herself. Her best relationship interactions often occurred when fuelled with adrenaline but with Cade she seemed to be able to relax, to live. As much as she wanted their relationship to blossom exponentially she was also painfully aware that Nikolina still being missing was testing his every waking moment, and many of his sleeping ones too.

She could physically feel the vein of excitement coursing through her, and yet she was a little troubled. She had promised herself many years before that there would be no more heartbreak. Contrary to the urban myth, and unlike some, she hadn't slept her way around the Metropolitan Police but had taken part in an occasional short term relationship, however each one had left her somewhat pessimistic that any man would ever tick enough boxes to satisfy her.

Since the escapade with Wood, the only vaguely physical interaction she had enjoyed was with an item she had ordered discreetly online – she referred to it in her own mind as her friend. Could Cade change all that?

It was all too soon perhaps? It was hardly a rebound for her as her last encounter had been with Wood, and this new man, who she initially thought of as arrogant had captured her heart without apparently trying. She had looked into his eyes just once and had instantaneously felt the butterflies flitting from place to place inside her stomach. Every time she closed her eyes and thought of him they reappeared and were a physical indicator of the impact he had made on her.

Conversely she worried, momentarily, that she knew actually knew very little about him though. Did it matter?"

Like a pair of college students they briefly chased one another around the upmarket properties, rousing interest from a few passers-by and a bike courier who swerved expertly to avoid them.

The rider gave them a look. Cade returned it with an added 'you haven't got a clue pal, not a clue.'

The rider received the subliminal message clearly and carried on with his day. Cade's had come to an end.

Scott slowed the patrol boat, turning it into the tidal flow. He knew all too well the dangers of grounding the vessel or striking something under the surface.

He updated both the police and port control rooms and then started to task his crew.

"Dave, let's get some eyes out on deck mate. Andy, grab a hook in case we need it. Chris, suit up, I need some capability if we need to get up close and personal."

They were all the same rank, but everyone on board knew who the Master of the vessel was. Scott's experience was legendary, way beyond policing circles.

"Easy now, easy. There, about twenty foot off the bank."

He pointed from the cabin as he held the boat against the outward flow.

"Dave, start grabbing some imagery just in case, I don't like this."

His colleague pulled a small waterproof Fuji digital camera from his pocket, turned it on and started taking shots of the general scene.

As they drifted nearer he could make out the top of a wooden frame. It was certainly man-made. It had rope at the apex, fastened rudimentarily but enough to prevent it from falling apart.

Dave Wilcox called back to his skipper.

"Looks like a wooden frame, it's stood up in the water, no real issue for us, the top is just under the surface, certainly not going to cause any…" Wilcox raised a hand, stopping himself talking.

"Dave? You alright. What have you seen?"

"Just stand by a minute Scottie."

He braced himself against the bow and took a series of pictures on the compact camera.

"Stop! We've got something here…I can't quite make it out, but let's see if we can recover it anyway…"

He stared into the bottle green river as Scott delicately controlled the *Colquhoun* in the shallow water. The Thames had a history of being a polluted waterway but as each year passed it became cleaner, even sustaining new marine life. It had issues with silt, just like any river and its colour could change in a heartbeat, sometimes due to the available light, sometimes the weather and always due to the presence of a boat.

The silt was churning beneath the rear of the *Colquhoun* as Scott balanced the need to manoeuvre with the constant tugging of the river. He managed to steer her into a position where he could call to Chris Lyons, an experienced crewman and diver.

"Drop the anchor here Chris."

Scott could now move the boat into a position that suited the operation, he was now in control, rather than Old Father Thames.

They were joined by a Port of London boat. A brief exchange between the two resulted in the PLA boat heading slightly upstream, where she would remain, offering a visible presence and in turn making the police operation safer.

The *Colquhoun* was a stable vessel, ideal for river work; safe, secure and well-equipped.

Constable Dave Wilcox leaned out from the stern, demanding his eyes to focus. He strained to see through the gloomy water, as they got closer to the wooden obstruction he saw it for the first time.

About a foot below the apex of the frame a dark mass of reddish-brown hair was drifting back and forth in the water. Wilcox traced a line from the frayed ends back to a face.

He leaned out further, peering through the water until it cleared momentarily, allowing him to look into a pair of lifeless, scared, green, opaline eyes.

He knew instinctively that he was looking at a face. He was adamant it belonged to a female, but who was she?

Whoever she was and however she had ended up here she had died a cruel and terrifying death. Somehow Wilcox knew that her demise had occurred on the spot where he now observed her; shackled to a basic wooden frame, naked, alone and with her mouth covered in grey tape, tape that was starting to peel as a result of being submerged.

He hoped she had died quickly.

Her wretched impassive face moved gently and rhythmically with the ebb and flow of the river. Her hair swung back through the water, covering her face and settling on her chest before floating ethereally downstream again.

He could now clearly see her upper torso. Her breasts were moving gently in the water but Wilcox found himself thinking that what lay before him was the least arousing image of his relatively chaotic career.

"Who are you my girl, who are you?" He almost shed a tear.

The face stared through the dark green water straight at him, causing Wilcox to shudder involuntarily. He had recovered a disproportionate number of bodies from the Thames but she would be different, unlike the others this one was clearly not the result of misadventure.

Chris Lyons was suiting up when Wilcox yelled back from the stern. "Body!"

O'Shea had got to the front door of the building first. She ran her plastic card across the reader, waited a second then opened the immaculate door. Cade looked left and right and entered the doorway, his attempt at appearing un-surreptitious failing entirely.

Neither knew what the time was as they were both now beyond exhaustion. The heavy Georgian door closed behind them, darkening the shared hallway.

Occasionally shy, often compulsive and always in control O'Shea stepped towards the jaded but somehow vibrant Cade, placed her hand behind his head and drew him towards her. The kiss was electric. He responded instantly, she could feel him.

Without waiting for an invitation he placed his hands expertly down the back of her trousers finding bare skin, he pulled her towards him.

She remembered where she had left her underwear, used and laying on the lounge floor. In the past she would have cursed, worried – worried that a burglar might see them and think less of her, but in the dusky hallway she cared not one iota.

She mirrored his every move but as she did so he let out an involuntary gasp; bare, abraded skin.

"God I'm sorry!"

"It's fine, really."

It wasn't. It hurt like hell but he wasn't going to accept that a severely grazed arse would get in the way of what they both wanted.

"We can do this…but what about your neighbours?"

"Jack? Here? *Now?*"

"Why not? I'm too bloody tired to get up those stairs!"

She bit the bottom of her lip. This wasn't quite how she envisaged things but she was hardly in the mood to stop.

Before she could allow another thought her blouse was half unbuttoned, half pulled over her head and now laying on the hallway floor. Cade pulled back slightly, admiring the view.

"This feels vaguely familiar," he said, nodding.

"And so does this." O'Shea replied, her hand firmly on Cade's zip. She was clawing at him now, passion overcoming her fear of being caught. His trousers were undone, she lowered herself onto her knees and skilfully released him from his underwear.

He ran his hands through her hair. It felt sticky, tired and not unlike his own. Somehow the fact that they were exhausted, both dirty and injured made the situation seem more animal, more desperate, more exciting.

Her dry lips made contact with him. He watched her run her tongue across them making the whole image even more stimulating. To hell with being caught. To hell with being professional. To hell with it.

She was carrying out the act with real vigour, enjoying every moment. Cade was leaning back against the solid wooden door now, pushing himself into her, stroking her hair, his thumbs massaging her neck.

He ran his hand down her back, undoing her bra. Although it was poorly lit he could clearly make out the shape of her breasts. They looked as good as they did the day before. He partly wished he could reach them.

This act was going to end soon, he knew it. He tried to take control. Despite not wanting to, he knew that if she continued that it would bring things to an end, for now. He was human after all and so very weary.

His breathing started to quicken, hers too. She looked up at him, her green-grey eyes looking directly into his. Another act to bring him ever closer to a climax.

"Jesus Christ! Please stop Carrie."

She quickened, he let her.

He heard a noise outside the door. Not now. No. Not *now*.

It was the postman, whistling the same non-descript tune that he did every morning. He rammed the various items of mail into the letterboxes, one by one until each occupant had received their bills, statements and junk mail.

The irony of the postman doing what he was doing wasn't lost on Cade who started to laugh. He loved the notion of his fellow man looking through the letterbox to see the normally prim and proper O'Shea, on her knees, doing what she was doing.

Her eyes widened as she looked at Cade.

Cade was busily biting the left side of his lip. He held his hand up – as if to say stop but O'Shea continued, shaking her head negatively for effect and making the whole thing even more arousing. The tail wagging the dog and very much in control.

Sensing that her very actions might curtail any subsequent activities she slowed, deliberately, occasionally she would stop and make direct eye contact with him. It was incredible. Penny was good at this but he would dearly love to tell her to her face, one day, that Carrie O'Shea was so, much, better.

"Carrie…I…"

He was lost for words, focussing his every attention on her, knowing equally that what he was doing was probably, deep-down in the annals of police regulations a sackable offence and that made it even more sensual.

He had finally met someone that he felt genuinely connected to – mentally as well as physically. With Penny it was physical, it was, he thought, what she did best, but ultimately he liked a woman to have an active mind too.

Petrov kept flashing through his own. Try though he might he couldn't erase the image of her beautiful face.

O'Shea was equally engaged, aroused more than at any time in her life and for once almost allowing the man to take charge.

His actions were quickening and she knew, she could hear that he was approaching the end. She had been ready for him for at least ten minutes – in fact she had been ready since the moment she had first looked at him.

She pulled away.

"Don't you stop Sergeant Cade…not until I say…"

Cades phone began to ring.

"No! Not again, for God's sake Jack ignore it. *Please.*"

He obeyed her wishes, whoever it was could leave a message. He hoped they didn't expect an answer any time soon.

As O'Shea continued to stimulate Cade to the point of frenzy a familiar voice began to talk on the phone speaker.

"Jack, if you are there, pick up mate, please? I need to talk to you…Jack? OK, I guess you are busy, but we just got busier. I'm on my way down to the river. You need to come right now."

O'Shea stopped instantly.

Cade looked at his new mistress, placed his hands by his sides, palms upright and shrugged his shoulders.

"Carrie, I promise this is not the end, I want you with a passion you can perhaps only begin to imagine. God knows why because you are a lousy lover, I mean, how many times have we started this now? In twenty four hours?"

Another punch, but this time followed by a kiss. She tasted of very sensual pastimes, of wickedness and abandoned lovemaking. Her tongue darted among his mouth, seeking out new places. Awaiting the signs of arousal she paused a second or two then gently licked his lips whilst playfully unbuttoning his shirt.

"Go on, ring him," she said pulling away once more, "I don't fancy you anyway Cade."

She was walking up the stairs to her flat, dressing slowly, provocatively, hoping that Cade would follow.

He was dressed, dishevelled, but dressed and his phone was already dialling.

"Roberts."

"Jason, Jack. What's so important, did we not have a long enough night?"

"Marine Unit have found her Jack. I'm sorry. Stand by I'll send you the grid ref but it's fair to say you won't miss us. O'Shea should know where to come. Meet me there and we'll re-group."

Cades phone buzzed in his pocket. 512907.9N 00839.8W

O'Shea was outside the front of the flat, flagging down a passing taxi.

"I need you to get us onto Grosvenor Road mate, quick as you can please, opposite the power station."

The driver acknowledged a weary-looking Cade, who was climbing into the back of the iconic London cab whilst reading his cell phone. Cade nodded back.

The driver responded. "There ain't much opposite the power station love. You sure that's where you want to go? Nothing ever 'appens there?"

O'Shea gave a pained smile. "It does today."

The driver let out a whistle as they approached the scene. It had only taken him nine minutes to travel the 1.8 miles and now he saw why the woman seemed to be in a hurry.

"You should have said my love, I would have driven faster. Which paper do you work for? Looks like a juicy story. What 'appened then? Someone die?"

She fished around in her pocket and produced her ID card.

"I'd rather admit to being a cop than to working for a tabloid. How much do I owe you?"

Her terse reply had driven home the message.

"Sorry my darlin'. I meant no offence. If someone 'as died then I apologise. Me brother-in-law is a copper at 'ammersmith. Do you know him? Robbie Greensmith? No? Fair enough. Have this one on me. I was going this way anyway."

O'Shea was already walking towards the scene.

A Mobile Incident Unit vehicle had been parked on Grosvenor, directly opposite the disused station that had become more famous since it had been shut down than during its fifty years of generating electricity. Although long-since closed the four unique chimneys stood guard over the river, watching and waiting for the future when people might one day see the sites' regeneration – it was once the largest brick-built building in Europe – and would one day transform and become home to a future, brighter business community

The Incident Unit was parked next to the same flight of steps that the group had overlooked. With the timeworn, black, ornate iron gateway now forced open, critical staff could access without impediment.

The offending group had fortune and the tidal system on their side, whereas the police team had discovered that Mother Nature was against them, all they could do was wait for the river to drain into the sea and slowly, mockingly reveal its prey.

Whilst every instinct encouraged the recovery of the lifeless body, the staff on board the *Colquhoun* and their colleagues on dry land knew they needed to photograph and document the entire scene first. From the edge of the road to the scene itself a SOCO team would map, photograph and capture evidence. A suitably-clothed search group carried out a microscopic examination of the location too.

Once the tide had reached its lowest point they would search the mud flats for more clues, albeit most would have been washed away, but with providence on the side of the investigators something may have been ensnared among the historic artefacts and more recent flotsam and jetsam.

There was nothing anyone could do to help her, the least they would do would be to treat her with dignity and catch the cold-hearted bastard that had done this to her. To a person they wrongly assumed her offender was a single individual.

Roberts was in full swing and had sought out the Shift Inspector, a man he had known of since the late nineties when he famously disgraced himself at Hendon Training School in a sordid escapade with a fellow female recruit who he would later describe to his adoring entourage as 'pretty but in an unconventional way'.

His recent rise through the ranks had surprised everyone, not least himself.

In minutes, and without a fight Roberts had convinced him that he needed primacy over the investigation.

The Inspector pointed down to the river. "She connected to that escapade last night, the one with the bus? What a bloody cock up that was. A wonder none of us were killed too, luckily it was only two of them Hungarians."

Cade had joined Roberts and wasn't in the best of moods. He was tired, hungry and limping.

"They were probably Romanian, not Hungarian. There's a difference you see." He said it aloud, hoping that as many of those present would hear, not least the Inspector.

"And the driver of the bus? He was a first generation Jamaican migrant called George Douglas. Incredible man he was too. As the Inspector says, lucky it was just him, could have been many more. Oh, and her..." he pointed down to the frigid grey body, "She's Bulgarian by the way..."

The Inspector didn't suffer fools gladly and was known for his outspoken nature, but he sensed he had overstepped the mark with the shuffling suited individual in front of him. Whilst he was unlikely to kowtow to him he thought it would look good to act contrite in front of the local staff.

He interjected quickly, a little too quickly for Cade's liking, cutting him off mid-sentence.

"We 'aven't met. I'm Inspector Dave Payne. And you are?"

Roberts introduced O'Shea and Cade to the ebullient and ever-sarcastic Essex-born boss. He had realised Cade was a little too 'sensitive' to enter into a full-blown professional conversation with Payne, a man he'd never met but had heard a lot about via the urban grapevine.

There were two Inspector Payne's in the force and both worked south of the river. One was known as Constant and the other, Nagging. This one was Constant.

"Right Sergeant I'll leave you to do your detective stuff and then when you are done no doubt my boys and girls will clear everything up once again and you can all Foxtrot Oscar back across the river. Typical Yard, all care and no responsibility. Who was this slag anyway? The boat crew say she's got something offensive written across her fanny, must 'ave pissed someone right off!"

He rapidly shoved what was left of a sandwich into his mouth, brushed the crumbs from his face and started to walk away.

Cade was leant against the wrought iron railings, reflux was building in his throat, venom pooling in his fists. He needed to focus on the operation down below him or he knew that Payne would most likely end up in the river as well.

O'Shea joined him and placed her hand on his shoulder. It was a calculated risk. He didn't resist.

"Ignore him Jack. He's a complete wanker. Terrible reputation, dressed for export by his last boss. I was at Hendon with him. He's clearly forgotten I ever existed. You know how it is with the arrogant ladder climbers? They forget their past and who they have trodden on."

He understood, but it didn't excuse him.

"You finished Inspector?" Cade had turned around and was looking Payne in the eye. He was trembling with nervous energy and exhaustion. "You said your bit? Made yourself look good in front of the troops? Cracked a few well-placed jokes? Thrown in a bit of black humour for good measure?"

He had got Payne's attention.

"Yes, fuckwit I am talking to you."

Pandora's Box had been opened, just enough to let a thin and dusty shaft of light into its darkest corners.

Roberts stepped between them holding up his hand in a gesture of peace.

"I'll deal with this Guv. Jack's had a long night, we all have. No offence."

Payne flicked the last corner of his sandwich over the railings and onto the embankment, a fortuitous gull catching it before it struck the water.

"Good. 'Cause if I wanted to, I could 'ave this northern colleague of yours put back on the first tram to Manchester. At a push I could write you up for turning up at work dressed as a bloody scarecrow. Look at you, what a bloody disgrace. Did you sleep in that suit?"

He was spitting his toxic words towards Cade, miniscule pieces of saliva, mixed with leftovers of his breakfast were landing on the pavement and glancing off of an already soiled shirt.

"Do I make myself clear...Sergeant?"

"Crystal...Inspector. No doubt when this is all written up you'll also want an apology out of the bus driver for causing chaos on your pristine roads, and the girl that is floating around in your cesspit of a fucking river? That's right, you seem to have forgotten her. That slag, as you so charmingly call her, that poor woman, strapped to that frame without an ounce of her dignity left, happens to be my friend..."

He paused, not for effect, but to let the welling nausea pass.

"She was also my informant...their informant," he gestured to Roberts and O'Shea. "And above all the best informant that your Commissioner has probably had since trams left the streets of London and headed to Nottingham – which, for the record is where I am seconded from, not bloody Manchester!"

Payne looked back towards Roberts and snorted his displeasure.

"I'll deal with this muppet later Roberts. Trust me I'm in no mood to do it now, some of us are busy. What's your commanders' name Cade, back up in whatever grimy northern mill town you hail from?"

Love – Fifteen.

Cade smiled. It was far from a friendly gesture.

"It's Curtain, as in pull yourself together man. Eddie Curtain, he's a Chief Superintendent. I can give you his number if you like. Ask for him by name, tell him Acting Inspector Jack Cade sent you. I'm sure he'd just love to hear your theory on northern policing."

Fifteen all.

Payne shrank a little, knowing he'd met his match. He could also tell that Cade was a moment away from boiling over. The last thing he wanted was another fight, with so many professional witnesses; the last had seen his promotion frozen for a few years, he was handier with his mouth than his fists and Cade had the look of somebody quietly capable, if not a little unhinged.

He gestured back to the river.

"She's all yours Cade. She's all yours."

Fifteen - Thirty.

Cade paused, allowing the defeated Payne to head towards his vehicle. As he removed his hat and started to enter the car, Cade called over to him.

"Oh Inspector, for the record, the girl in the river? The one who gave up her life to make yours a little safer? She's called Nikolina and she would have kicked your arse all over Battersea for calling her what you did."

Thirty – All.

"Oh and David, just one other thing."

Cade was beginning to enjoy himself at last.

"This stunning lady stood next to me is called Carrie O'Shea. She's the best Analyst this force will ever have. She used to be a police officer just like you and I. She should look familiar to you. I'd say she's unconventionally pretty, wouldn't you?"

Forty – Thirty.

It took Payne a second to compute Cade's words but as he did so he stared at O'Shea. God she had blossomed into a good-looking girl.

Game. Set. Match.

Cade became aware of a video link beaming a direct feed from the *Colquhoun* up to the Incident Unit team.

"Do you mind if we observe?" Roberts asked a boiler-suited Constable.

"Not at all skipper, the imagery is really clear, new kit this, helps us enormously, saves us having to get wet too."

As desperate as he was to be on the patrol boat Cade knew that the logistics of getting from the embankment and on board were likely to make any request problematic. The uplink helped, whether he should watch was another thing entirely.

The screen was not dissimilar to the size of a laptop computer, but far more substantial. The hand-held camera on the *Colquhoun* was transferring crystal-clear imagery not only to the shore team but also had the ability to beam up to an air unit or the CAD room.

The initial image was blurred as Dave Wilcox altered the lens, attempting to provide wider-angled footage. He manually twisted the focus ring on the camera which was fitted with a polarising filter. The filter did its job – a little too well – cutting through the light and allowing the team to see deeper into the water.

There she was.

Cade could just make out the female shape, within reason it could have been the body of any young woman, but he knew it was Petrov. He needed no further full-colour imagery to confirm it.

Over the next few hours the river would continue to drop. It had reduced in depth by half a metre whilst the team had been on site. Every ten minutes the waterway would reveal a little more of her.

Cade had seen enough and walked towards the Incident vehicle to see if they had some water. He needed to rinse his mouth which had filled with acid. He was hungry but could not eat. He took a mouthful of the bottled water and swilled it around his teeth. A voice carried across the short distance between where he stood and a patrol vehicle.

A member of Incident Unit was busily walking past Cade and in a stage whisper said "I see you've met 'Constant' boss. Ignore him. We all do."

Another voice joined the conversation, belonging to Dave Payne who was busy trying to look busy and engage with everyone he could.

"I'll deal with you another time Sergeant Cade. You'll keep, and I shall be ringing Curtis as soon as I stop holding this city together."

Cade emptied the water into the gutter before replying.

"It's Curtain, as in well-hung." Cade then spelled out the name, deliberately annunciating every letter, knowing that Payne would never hear every one, his door firmly slammed, shutting out the world and particularly the bolshie northerner.

Cade was angry with himself for allowing Payne to get the upper hand at a time when what really mattered, what actually meant more to him than winning any argument was the humane and dignified recovery of one of the bravest souls he had ever encountered.

He turned towards O'Shea who was tapping his arm.

"Jack, she's here."

The recovery team had fought against the constant downstream pull of the river and had managed to extricate Petrov from the wooden frame, taking exquisite care to photograph the tape bindings and the position of her body. Whilst the steep embankment wall offered shelter from prying eyes their operation was highly visible to anyone using the river – or worse still any photographers on the opposite bank.

She was carried to the highest accessible part of the muddy embankment and placed carefully into a body bag. The white bag, recently adopted by the police to aid with exhibit identification, had been used to carry the remains to a scoop stretcher and then up the flights of steps and onto the pavement.

The staff involved were exhausted, covered in foul-smelling mud and sweating profusely, despite the relatively cool air that surrounded them. The team withdrew leaving their most senior man to talk to Roberts and Cade.

Mick Parker, a veteran Constable and long-term member of the Dive Squad had simply lost count of how many similar recovery operations he had performed. He always said, to his closest friends, that every job was entirely similar and yet utterly unique. It made sense.

He didn't shake hands with either of the officers but spoke clearly and with empathy.

"Mick Parker. Sorry to have get you gents down here for this, I understand she was an ally of ours? I'd love to get the bastard that put her through this. Dark, unadulterated evil if you ask me. Which you didn't. Look lads, if you need to look at her we'll put a temporary shield up and you can do whatever you need to do. Be aware she's been in the water for a while, not as long as some I've seen, but long enough. Just be forewarned."

Parker called to his team to get the portable screens and soon only Cade, Roberts and Petrov were behind them.

"Carrie. You need to be here to." It was Cade.

Despite her background she had never seen anyone taken from the river before, but apprehensively stepped into the temporary morgue – a place of relative quiet considering the location – Londoner's busily going about their morning routines wholly unaware of the events unfolding on their doorstep.

Roberts nodded towards the bag and unzipped it.

Cade fought back tears of anger as Roberts grabbed for a tissue in his jacket pocket, anything to shield himself from the noxious smell that drifted up from the bag.

O'Shea felt herself becoming emotional too. She had seen bodies, of course she had, but this poor girl, once a potential contender for Cade's affections was now laying in a cold, damp bag on a colder anonymous street, in a city she had only known for a few dynamic, horrendous days.

Her once-lustrous hair was matted to her forehead and the left side of her temples and cheekbone. Her eyes, thankfully, were closed. A bright white band of skin, stretching from ear to ear, across her chin and finishing just under her nose bore testament to the presence of duct tape – now removed and secured as an exhibit.

Roberts had opened the bag to reveal only her face and neckline but Cade knew he had to see what they had done to her. He subtly nodded to Roberts who continued to open the J-shaped zipper, down and down until it could go no further. Cade squatted at her side and pulled back the thick plastic until he could see her white torso, the skin already bleached by the water. He opened the bag further, finally revealing the indelible marking on her hips and hairless pubic area.

WH RE.

Cade's fists balled, he wiped his mouth, involuntarily pushing back the urge to vomit. Now the tears flowed.

He could not stop picturing her last moments. It wasn't enough that she was alone and stripped of dignity, what really hurt Cade was how she finally died.

Her larynx would have gone into spasm, a vain attempt to avoid the water pouring into her lungs. The subsequent haemorrhaging would provide any Pathologist worth their reputation with further clues to how she had died.

Water, under pressure would have been forced into her lungs. The forensic examination would quickly establish the cause of death as drowning – in freshwater and with the obvious added malice of being forced onto the wooden frame and anchored in place, to drown, slowly, through a miniscule hole in a wafer-thin piece of tape.

Cade wished she had gone quicker.

Her organs would have cooled quickly, adding confusion when trying to establish the exact time of death. At least freshwater had less of a catastrophic effect on the body than salt. It would take time but they would eventually put a time on the death certificate.

Roberts gestured to O'Shea and they both made their silent exits leaving Cade kneeling by the side of the gleaming white bag. He had so much to say, and yet his words would not leave him, he could form them in his mind but his vocal chords were too constricted to utter a sound. He held his hand against her cheek, expecting her to speak once more, expecting those vibrant, excitable Eastern European tones to add urgency to her every word. Just once more.

She was so very cold.

He bent down, it was unconventional, improper - perhaps, but she had briefly captured his professional and personal heart, therefore at risk to his own health, to his reputation, he bent down and kissed her on the cheek. He needed to know she still had friends, albeit they had cruelly let her down.

As he began to pull away from her face he detected a faint aroma, it was subdued but it was a common smell, an everyday scent. He stayed in position for a few seconds, desperately trying to distinguish the odour from the more powerful and stomach-churning smell of the river and of death itself.

He gently prized her cyanosed lips apart and placed his nose next to her mouth.

He began to nod.

"Yes..."

He called his colleagues back behind the screen.

"Smell her. Go on. Please Jason."

Roberts joined Cade at Petrov's side, he was already dry retching but he could tell Cade would not take no for an answer.

"Mate I'm going to be sick, what are you trying to prove. Hasn't the poor girl been through enough without us squatting beside her and sniffing at her like some weird deviants?"

"You don't smell it do you? Carrie, come on, please, this is important, might be crucial..."

Gathering herself O'Shea also sat down on the frigid pavement and joined in the activity.

"Close your eyes, try to rule out your other senses...it will come to you, trust me."

Cade was one hundred percent convinced, he just needed the endorsement of his colleagues.

O'Shea slowly stood up and took a breath of what she considered to be cleaner air.

"It's petrol Jack. Were they going to burn her?"

"No, I don't think so. They would have done that. Why go to the trouble of doing what they did? I'm not sure what they were doing but it's there isn't it? Just a hint? It's in her mouth, for some reason they poured petrol into her mouth. The autopsy will confirm this but we need to start thinking about why they did this. Why would they be carrying fuel?"

Cades words drifted across the embankment as he searched his soul, trying to help the girl who had walked into his life some weeks before, a hundred miles to the north of where he now stood. Shivering in a breeze that blew off the Thames and clawed at his skin he wondered where this would end.

An undertaker was given permission to remove Petrov to the nearby Westminster mortuary. Cade had said goodbye and was now walking to Roberts' vehicle, as he dropped into the rear passenger seat, ever the gent, he caught O'Shea's distant smile as she sat in the front. It was a look of compassion and pity, but there was genuine warmth there too and he knew that he needed to exploit it before someone else took her away from him. He vowed it wouldn't happen again. Penny was firmly in his past, Carrie was possibly, hopefully, his future.

"OK team, let's head back to the Yard, get some refreshments and then we'll start the debrief all over again. I'm expecting the Spanish Inquisition over this lot so let's all get our stories exactly the same. Jack I can leave you a car, see you back there, you might want a minute?"

"No I'm fine mate, let's just go. We are only getting in the way now."

They had driven a mile when O'Shea said without warning "Petrol! Arson! They needed to burn something."

"Never?"

Roberts was a little too sarcastic and corrected himself swiftly.

"Jason, shut up man. They needed to remove as much evidence as they could, what better way to do that than to destroy it with fire? The petrol was used to torch the vehicle they were in, and my money is on a van. Get the CAD room to run a search on all vehicle arsons over the last twenty four hours. I would dump a vehicle on wasteland or in an industrial area - fewer capable guardians..."

"Capable?"

"Guardians. It's what Crime Scientists call those people whose presence prevents crime occurring."

"Right you are. I shall use it in my next briefing."

He handed her his phone. "Here, ring the CAD room and let's start work on that idea, it can be stewing whilst we head back to work."

He smiled "You're a genius girl, sometimes we need to think small rather than big. Why not torch the vehicle? Makes sense. But why tip fuel into her throat...Jack? What do you think?"

He looked in the rear view mirror. Cade was fast asleep. He left him to his dreams.

The team arrived at Scotland Yard within half an hour and were through the side staff door and racing up the many stairs to the unit, entering the main briefing room.

Roberts took control.

He gave those present a copy of the overnight log detailing exactly how Petrov had been located. Cade sat and tried to digest the detail, losing himself in the report. He felt nauseous once more; angry and responsible. He had made a promise to her, one which he meant, but was unable to keep.

He folded the report, scoring the fold with his thumb nail and re-joined the meeting when he heard Roberts speaking.

"Thank you team, grab a tea or coffee or whatever you want, grab a bacon sandwich too, I suspect the day is going to be long. We've got brass coming into the briefing room so let's look as lively as we can please. I know we are all knackered, me too, I hadn't even got home when my phone rang."

He looked around the room, counting the staff.

"Where's Clive?"

"You stood him down boss, remember?"

"Yes, of course, silly me, first round is on me in The Sanctuary after work – everyone is welcome and I mean everyone, we'll 'ave a right old London knees up..."

Roberts was trying to lighten the mood, parading at the front of the briefing room, in the style of a Dickensian character when the Assistant Commissioner arrived along with Commander Waterman, two Superintendents and another male wearing a dark grey suit, white shirt and navy tie. He had a good head of hair and was naturally tanned. In a completely heterosexual way Cade thought he was a handsome man. Of the four he also looked the most approachable.

"Sergeant Roberts I presume?"

The humourless voice belonged to Superintendent Phil Jenkinson, a product of the East End of London and an ex-Royal Engineer who had risen quickly through the ranks and had lost not only countless hours of sleep in his quest for early promotion, but almost every hair on his head too.

"Sir, yes I am Jason Roberts."

"Good, well stop fucking about and get the briefing underway. Some of us are busy trying to police this Godforsaken city. Where are we at with this bloody charade?"

Jenkinson glared at Roberts, drilling holes through him with his overly-bloodshot anthracite eyes.

"Sir, I just want to apologise, it's been a long night, the team are all…"

Jenkinson was about to tear Roberts apart once more when Waterman pushed his chair back and stood up, about to speak, his face darker than a thunderhead when the Assistant Commissioner cleared his throat.

"Thank you Frank, I'll sort this with your blessing?" He paused, allowing his own seniority to sink in.

Waterman nodded, aware of the political posturing and the danger of undermining a senior officer in front of junior staff, but found himself wondering where this opinionated bald barrow boy had come from. Jenkinson would have to wait for another day.

The Assistant Commissioner continued.

"Phillip, I'm sure Detective Sergeant Roberts meant well, he is after all only looking after his troops and that is commendable. Agreed? Good. Proceed please Sergeant and let's not mince our words here, I want honesty. If we cocked up then say so, if anyone deserves a medal, tell me. If we are looking at war on the streets of London and we've missed the clues, then again, hold no punches. Forget the media. They can get their snouts in the blood-soaked trough tomorrow. Right now all I care about is ensuring no-one else gets shot at or drowned in my city. Fair enough? Good, pass me a coffee would you?"

He gestured towards Cade who leaned to his left and grabbed a mug.

"Sugar?"

"No thank you, Mrs Johnson says I'm sweet enough."

It was clichéd but it broke the ice.

Johnson was a good operator, a team player and a natural leader. Cade handed him the coffee and at risk of rebuke in the pub later that day placed his hand out in the time-honoured fashion.

"Jack Cade sir. Seconded from the frozen north."

Malcolm Johnson scratched his exaggeratedly brown hair and smiled.

"Aha, yes, your reputation precedes you Sergeant Cade. I understand we have you to blame for bringing the circus to town?"

Cade thought for a second or two and replied, "Sir, with all due respect I only put up the tent, the tigers were already loose."

Johnson, who was chewing the end of his expensive bi-focals cracked a half smile and countered, coldly, continuing the analogy, "Do you take me for a clown Mr Cade?"

"No sir, only the Ring Master."

Roberts was looking for somewhere to bury his head. This was all he needed.

Jenkinson was visibly furious, his lips whitening over his teeth,

Johnson exhaled. "It has been a very long night Sergeant Cade so I shall forgive the 'with all due respect', as I think we all know what that means. However your circus analogy was brave, I'll give you that, especially in this exalted company. So, crack on, why don't you and give us the best show on earth right now?"

Cade looked at Roberts who was still licking his wounds. Roberts nodded, giving Cade the air time he needed.

Cade stood at the front of the room, it offered him a greater view, and standing opened up his lungs so he could deliver a polished and measured briefing.

He looked quickly towards O'Shea. She smiled a knowing smile. It gave Cade the impetus he needed.

"Sir. The situation is not good. We have three people dead on the streets, two of whom we believe to be members of a crime syndicate from Romania and the third an innocent civilian. Another occupant of the initial target vehicle is in hiding somewhere and…"

"For Christ sake Sergeant, we know all this, press on man, I've got a meeting in half an hour at the Home Office – facts!" Jenkinson clapped his hands together, patronisingly to emphasise the urgency.

Cade erased his internal monologue and ignored the interruption before continuing.

"…a police officer in hospital with injuries and this morning…"

Cade swallowed visibly and sighed before continuing.

"And this morning, the reported tragic death of Miss Nikolina Petrov a Bulgarian…"

Jenkinson stood and pointed at Cade before talking to Waterman.

"Commander, is this the best we've got? Seriously? A Sergeant from a foreign force standing here telling me a love story. I want a briefing that is true to the word; brief. I don't give a damn about any Eastern

Europeans, whether dead or alive, quite frankly they deserved what was coming to them from what I have read..."

This time it was Cade who interrupted without his usual caution.

"And what exactly have you *read* Superintendent?"

"I beg your pardon....Sergeant."

Cade was riled now. Roberts shook his head but O'Shea nodded, thinking almost out aloud, 'Go on Jack. Tell this arrogant bastard how it is. Go on, for me, if nothing else.'

"I said, what *exactly* have you read....Superintendent?" Cade was picking an obstinate piece of food from a back tooth, if nothing else displaying a total lack of respect for the senior man.

Jenkinson had disliked this man the moment he had introduced himself to the AC – how dare he. Bloody northerner.

"Well to be fair Sergeant, not a lot from your end of the woods. All I am hearing about is an amateur three ring circus since the moment this girl arrived into East Midlands Airport."

"And there was I thinking that the circus analogy was between me and the Assistant Commissioner..."

"Jack. Steady now...let's not let this descend into a bar fight." It was Waterman.

"Sir. I'll continue if I may? My point is that the group that calls itself The First Wave are most likely behind the biggest financial crime spree this city has ever seen, and in fact may ever see. We are only starting to scrape the surface. I was fortunate enough to meet Miss Petrov, who in turn became my source and steered me towards the group. She gave us information that enabled us to implement Operation Breaker and in doing so it cost her...her life."

He paused again, visibly upset at the loss of the operations' greatest asset and someone who Cade had grown to be very fond of in a short space of time. He admired her for far more than her good looks.

"If Miss Petrov hadn't have been so courageous this operation would not have continued. There is no doubt we would not have infiltrated until much later, then at worst it would have been lower level disruption, at best a few pieces of low-hanging fruit..."

Jenkinson was once more on the offensive. His peer had not said a word since they arrived, choosing instead to make notes. The ex-army officer was now bristling.

He was smiling a fabricated smile.

"Commissioner, if you expect me to sit here and be lectured by some northern monkey about how heartbroken he is about the loss of a Russian girl who died with the word whore written across her bikini line... then I'm sorry but you don't know me very well at all. For the record I don't give a fat rat's arse about this bunch of gypsies, I do care about my city and above all I care about my crime stats and…"

Cade walked towards the Superintendent, his knuckles whitening. His rigid index finger poked Jenkinson in the chest. "She was Bulgarian, and she wasn't a gypsy. And there's more to this than we know. This is just the start. You mark my words. She had information – seriously damming information but we never managed to extract it from her. She risked her life, left her child behind to face an uncertain future and ultimately gave up her life for a person she trusted, me."

He could feel bile rising and a solitary tear welling.

"And yes, she died for you, and me and everyone else in this room. Is that not enough, Superintendent?"

He slowly removed his finger and wrapped it back into his fist.

O'Shea stood to speak, holding her arm across in front of him.

"Boss, Carrie O'Shea, Strategic Analyst for Op Breaker. What Jack, Sergeant Cade is saying is one hundred percent accurate. Without Petrov's information and Jack's passion and knowledge this team would be ten steps ahead of us instead of two. That girl gave her life for something she believed in, she died in a frigid river, alone and terrified and the least you can do is hear us out. Please."

And having delivered a short but impassioned speech she sat down.

Cade was exhausted. His mind was like a centrifuge. He knew that O'Shea had probably just prevented him from leaving the field of play and having an early, lonely bath. He owed her and he would repay her when the moment arose.

The briefing continued for another ten minutes, covering what they knew and importantly what they needed help with. Roberts stood – his confidence recovered.

"Team, thank you. Gentlemen, any questions?"

Superintendent Barry Brown spoke for the first time, he had a broad Yorkshire accent. In his early sixties he was on an annual contract to the police, having officially retired some years before.

He looked around the room, turning his head silently, not unlike a Barn Owl, sat on an elevated roost and watching an oblivious mouse scurry across a hay-strewn floor.

"Detective Sergeant Roberts, Sergeant Cade, Miss O'Shea. Commander, Operation Breaker team. I for one am happy that you are doing what you are doing. I retire at the end of the month and frankly I haven't seen a more passionate and engaged bunch of people in thirty years. In fact I haven't seen people so excited since I worked on Operation Magician a few years ago."

Cade knew that he was referring to a massive operation that the Metropolitan Police Flying Squad had conducted to apprehend a well-organised team of jewellery thieves who had planned to target the iconic Millennium Dome and steal the flawless Millennium Star, at the time the single most valuable gem on earth, worth two hundred million pounds.

He continued, "So my point is folks, keep on doing what you are doing, you will get there and rid this city and the country of this insidious cancer that is spreading towards us from Eastern Europe. That way Mrs Brown and I can retire in peace."

He gathered together his paperwork, stood up and waited for the Assistant Commissioner to join him.

"Oh, and Sergeant Cade."

Cade waited, expecting another reprimand.

"Sir?"

"In my day I would have punched his lights out for calling me a northern monkey." He winked at Cade before walking towards the door.

Jenkinson was incensed, following Brown out of the door without a word to Roberts, shuffling, trying to keep pace with a swiftly exiting Assistant Commissioner who had shaken hands with Waterman and told him to put whatever resources he needed into Operation Breaker.

As the lift door closed he said "Crack on Frank, shout if you need anything and hang onto Cade with all your might, keep the secondment going for so long that they forget he's here. I like him, a lot. With respect indeed! Shame he and Phil didn't see eye to eye! I'll try not to let him interfere again, problem is the Commissioner thinks the sun shines out of his arse. Off his head more like. Leave it with you."

The door slid to and the digital readout tumbled as the lift headed down to the foyer.

Cade sat back at the briefing table, transfixed and beyond exhaustion, O'Shea sat next to him, quickly and discreetly rubbing his leg. Roberts was busy tasking his team. He needed to remain busy or he would fall asleep on the job. Like Cade and O'Shea he had noticed that the distinguished and suited male had remained behind. Quiet and unassuming, he stood looking out of the elevated and tinted window across at the vista before him until his eyes stopped on The Mall and finally, Buckingham Palace.

He waited for the energy of the room to cease and then spoke.

"I wonder if she's home?" He said to no one in particular.

Roberts was first to answer. "Sorry, who? You wonder *who* is home?"

The male smiled "Why the boss of course. I wonder how HRH would have dealt with Jenkinson? Off with his head!"

Roberts, ever the genial host was laughing, oblivious to who his guest was, he too was wearier than he could ever recall. The male slid a chair back and sat down, the four people looked at one another before O'Shea decided she needed to introduce herself.

"Carrie O'Shea, I'm..."

"A Senior Analyst. I know Carrie, I heard your impassioned speech remember? And you Jack are you going to shake my hand too?"

Cade exhaled, blowing air across his lips. "Of course, apologies, no excuse, I'm getting too old for all this. Jack Cade, northern monkey and Acting Inspector from..."

"Nottinghamshire. Yes Jack I know. I've done my homework, I've read your files, spoken to your force. Eddie sends his best, he asked that I came on board to try and round up the tigers..."

He beamed a huge smile before continuing, "Tigers indeed. Christ that was funny. I'm John Daniel. I doubt you'll recall but we spoke on air last night. At the time…" He glanced down at his Seiko, "I was the CAD Inspector. It was my last shift in there and thanks to you lot, one I'll never forget. I passed my promotion board a few weeks ago so I'm moving on, back into an ill-fitting suit to be a DCI but wanted to drop in and say hello en route home to bed. Ignore the critics, you did a damned good job, in exceptional and trying circumstances, all of you."

"Thank you sir. Appreciated. And sorry about the dreaded paperwork."

Daniel took a moment before finishing his carefully-considered sentence.

"And I'm sorry you lost the girl Jack."

Cade found himself drawn to Daniel, he had a personality that made him appealing to both men and women and above all he appeared to put his people first.

"Thanks for making the effort to drop in sir. With respect...you look as shagged out as we do. I know I appreciate your visit, and I'm sure these two southern shandy drinkers do too! So, where's the new office? What's the new role? What wearisome group of misfits have they sent you to manage?"

Daniel laughed openly as he extended the farewell handshake with Cade by placing his other hand on top. He released the grip and turned and was walking out of the briefing room towards the lift when he stopped and pointed along the hallway.

"Not far as it happens Jack. Just down there. Second door on the left, it'll always be open to you and your team of wearisome misfits."

"How can you be so sure?"

John Augustus Daniel, Detective Chief Inspector, Metropolitan Police smiled the smile of a confident man, after more years than he cared to remember he was now at the helm of a passionate and capable team once more, and he instinctively knew that no matter what kaleidoscope of chaos lay ahead of them he could rely on, fall back on and above all trust them implicitly.

They were a group of people who out of respect would have previously referred to him as the boss or sir, but after today it was more probable that they would simply, and respectfully call him the governor.

"How can I be so sure? Easiest question I've had to deal with in recent weeks Jack. As of a few hours ago I have the hugely unenviable task of taking this team, moulding it into one – *e pluribus unum* and all that - and that means being your new boss."

He took a second to gauge the favourable response in the room.

"Indeed. I suggest we all sleep on it. See you in the morning – bright but not too early. You get the coffee, I'll bring the cake. We have work to do Jack."

"We do sir. Out of many, one – and all that." He smiled, it was a welcoming smile.

"Then I take it that means you will consider transferring and staying down here in the city that never apparently sleeps?"

Cade took a moment to formulate a compelling reason why he shouldn't, looked at Roberts and lastly O'Shea then said "It looks that way sir, yes."

Six words, simple easy to say and life changing. He'd been through hell over the last few weeks, lost at least one good friend – possibly more – lost a wife, thank heaven for small mercies, caused no end of chaos and disorder and somehow convinced a police force with whom he had no physical or spiritual connection to offer him a role, a salary, somewhere to live and above all to take control of and guide a new team.

He'd also broken open a tomb, what it contained and how it would impact upon his life, and those he was now empowered with protecting he had not the slightest idea. Already considered a subject matter expert on Eastern Europe and in particular its criminal entities the truth was he knew only what he had experienced, no more. But the topic and its peoples intrigued him greatly and if this was to be the start of a dynamic, risk-laden period of his life, then fine, so be it, he was a willing student.

Nikolina Petrov had chosen to trust him, with the two most precious things in her short life. Her daughter's future and her own safety. He'd failed in the latter and it would hurt for a very long time. He'd meet the daughter one day, somewhere of that he was certain and if luck played her part he'd end up face to face with the bastard that self-appointedly called himself her father and also conceitedly, The Jackdaw. Regardless of the risk that this posed he was actually looking forward to it. This was not Hollywood, of that he was painfully aware and in the world of films and actors reality was often overlooked. He'd hurt this bastard if it broke every bone and strand and sinew in his own body.

Petrov intrigued Cade in the short time he had grown to know her. Her bravery was without question. Her quest would remain just that. Her goals unattained, washed away with her down the river, dilute and faded. She had one more untold thing to tell him. He owed her many things, if all he were able to achieve was the completion of her goal then he could rest, and sleep the sleep of kings. If not he knew he was destined to carry the cross and it was heavy, roughly hewn and cumbersome. They always were.

In a short time he thought he had learned who to trust – 'keep your friends close and your enemies closer still Jack', someone had said that to him recently – and equally he had learned who not to depend on.

This was a whole new way of life, a new city, a new job, new team, and new colleagues. A new place to live, to police, to take pride in. It had already adopted him; this smoky, intriguing and never-ending skyscape that he stared out and onto. Once he had mourned his old life he could begin to live again and that life was rapidly departing, slipping through his fingers – the past.

Three questions remained paramount in his mind and he needed to answer them before he could sleep:

Where would he find Alex Stefanescu?

What was the information his reluctant partner was so willing to trade – and how would he now find it?

Who could he trust?

Whilst he stood, distracted and gazing out over the City of London John Daniel had quietly stepped away.

In direct contradiction of his long-term promise Daniel had walked into his newly-acquired office and kicked the door shut behind him, closed the blinds, selected the comfier of the two office chairs and leaned back into the soft black leather, his feet up on the desk.

He closed his eyes and reflected upon what he had become, where he had got to and importantly, where he and his new team would head in the coming days and weeks. He wondered how he would make up to his long-suffering wife Lynne, missing their wedding anniversary for the first time – ever.

A single refracted shaft of morning sunlight fought to break through the cream-coloured, dog-eared vertical blinds, creating a chromatic haze on his flickering eyelashes. He let out an extended and satisfying sigh and then muttered the words once more, before drifting into a deep and desperately needed sleep.

"You and I Jack, we have work to do…"

Seventh

Acknowledgements

There are countless people I could thank – and hopefully some might even be classed as my satisfied readers – after all no author willingly spends years of their life writing something that they hope no one will enjoy.

Embarking on this journey a few years ago I knew the story I needed to tell – a story that to a great extent is almost entirely true. I can vividly recall the moment this trilogy germinated as an idea almost nine years ago, on a cold Wednesday at an international border in the Southern Hemisphere. A sobbing red head with lustrous curly hair and startling green eyes looked at me and said, "Where shall I begin sir?" I recommended the beginning – it seemed a mighty fine place to start.

As she told her tale a large part of me was of course the ever-professional police officer; gathering information, thinking about the next phase of a highly likely follow-up operation and offering a mixture of empathy and compassion. The other half of my eager mind was forming the story – *The Seventh Wave* – a tale of love, lust, pure unadulterated evil, of greed and hardworking, dedicated, underpaid and at times unappreciated police officers, trying to make a difference, wherever they may work.

But as is always the way with these end pieces there are a limited few who have gone that little bit further to help me. In some cases a lot further.

My wife Amanda who has to listen to my endless and ever-brilliant ideas, nodding wisely and praying for salvation. My wonderfully-supportive children who seem to have grown alarmingly quickly since I first came up with this idea and my parents, for having me and for supporting the idea that a humble police officer could also one day become a writer. To my English teacher Ken who insulted almost every piece of work I ever submitted – thank you for giving me the ambition to at least prove you wrong.

To Russell, for his logo ideas which will feature throughout the series.

To my dear friend Claire – for her tireless proof-reading and suggestions – some of which I even used. Claire offered a woman's perspective on some of the scenes, assuring me that these would make them more appealing to her fellow female.

Finally, to the men and women of the police force, in New Zealand and Hong Kong and Great Britain – the world is a safer place because of you. As clichéd as it may sound, I am proud to have served with you.

Seventh

About the author

Lewis Hastings is a pseudonym. He was born in 1963 (a by-product of the long, harsh winter of 1962) in Kent, the Garden of England.

By virtue of his father's role as a Prison Officer he became somewhat nomadic, moving from county to county during his formative years.

As quickly as he made friends they became a distant memory.

His school life was a heady cocktail of fun, misery and abject failure explaining why he decided not to pursue a university career. Thrust into the world of full time employment at seventeen and having taken the entry exam he turned down the chance of a career in the Royal Marines for the love of a good woman.

Regretting the decision not to wear the Green Beret he forged out a highly unsuccessful and miserable career in sales; a way to pay the bills and provide a home for his growing family.

In 1988 a cathartic event changed his approach to life and he spent two frustrating years trying to forge a new career as a Police Officer. By doing this he would in fact continue a family tradition stemming back to the early 1800's.

His career commenced with the Nottinghamshire Constabulary at a time of enormous change. He was soon posted to some of the most beautiful and equally dangerous locations in the county where he learned the noble art of policing including community, intelligence and vice work (the latter, whilst challenging, at least offered a secondary income).

In 2003, wearing a different uniform he found himself in New Zealand, soon realising that the age-old maxim about familiar excrement and days of the week still rang true.

This is his second book. When initially launched his first book, a warts and all autobiography, *Actually, The World Is Enough* sold one copy. He has since surged onto the world stage to critical acclaim, given at least twenty more away and may break into double figures any day.

Seventh is the first novel in the Jack Cade trilogy: *The Seventh Wave*. The sequel *Seven Degrees* will also be in print in 2017.

He is married with two children, a lake-loving Labrador and lives in a house.

CPSIA information can be obtained
at www.ICGtesting.com
Printed in the USA
BVHW04s1511300418
514842BV00001B/33/P